*In the Flicke*

# CARAF Books

Caribbean and African Literature
Translated from French

Carrol F. Coates, Editor

Clarisse Zimra, J. Michael Dash, John Conteh-Morgan,
and Elisabeth Mudimbe-Boyi, Advisory Editors

# In the Flicker of an Eyelid

Jacques Stephen Alexis

Translated and with an Afterword by
Carrol F. Coates and Edwidge Danticat

University of Virginia Press
*Charlottesville and London*

Publication of this translation was assisted by a grant
from the French Ministry of Culture, National
Center of the Book

Originally published in French as *L'espace d'un
cillement,* © Éditions Gallimard, 1959, new edition
© 1983

University of Virginia Press
Translation and afterword © 2002 by the Rector and
Visitors of the University of Virginia
Printed in the United States of America on
acid-free paper

*First published* 2002

1 3 5 7 9 8 6 4 2

Library of Congress Cataloging-in-Publication Data
Alexis, Jacques Stephen, 1922–1961.
 [Espace d'un cillement. English]
 In the flicker of an eyelid / Jacques Stephen Alexis ; translated and
with an afterword by Carrol F. Coates and Edwidge Danticat.
    p.    cm. — (Caribbean and African literature translated from
French)
Includes bibliographical references.
 ISBN 0-8139-2138-4 (cloth : alk. paper) — ISBN 0-8139-2139-2
(pbk. : alk. paper)
 I. Coates, Carrol F., 1930–    II. Danticat, Edwidge, 1969–    III. Title.
IV. Series.
 PQ3949.A34 E8413 2002
 843'.914—dc21

2002005246

# Contents

In the Flicker of an Eyelid                          1

First Mansion, *Sight*                               5

Second Mansion, *Smell*                             57

Third Mansion, *Hearing*                           105

Fourth Mansion, *Taste*                            143

Fifth Mansion, *Touch*                             173

Sixth Mansion, *The Sixth Sense*                   211

Coda                                               229


Glossary                                           237

"Letter to Jacques Soleil,"
by Florence Alexis                                 241

Afterword by Carrol F. Coates and
Edwidge Danticat                                   255

A Note on the Translation                          272

Acknowledgments                                    273

Bibliography                                       274

*In the Flicker of an Eyelid*

. . . You prostitutes, flaunting over the trottoirs or
  obscene in your rooms,
Who am I that I should call you more obscene
  than myself?
—Walt Whitman, "Autumn Rivulets"

# FIRST MANSION

*Sight*

To my hope I give my eyes,
those precious gems. . . .
—Guillaume Apollinaire, *Poèmes à Lou*

ine! Nine or ten? No, she must be mistaken. Saint-Anne's must have just struck ten o'clock. She didn't hear the clocks at the Saint-François Hospice or the Asile Français. With all the racket of firecrackers, nervous motors starting, squealing brakes, angry horns honking, tumultuous drums, all blending with the breathing of the sea—you can't tell what is what. All of a sudden, the festivities become unusually intense. The insanity of the marines living it up is contagious! The Rara drums must not be far away; no further than Bolosse anyway. What is it with everyone? On Palm Sunday! The drivers must be making tons of money—taxi drivers driving marines and truck drivers with their Rara celebrants. People keep dancing in the hall. The record player never stops. And this headache!

La Niña Estrellita looks at her genitalia with the lips pulled open—like a gaping wound, or more precisely, a raw, burning heel in a shoe that's too big. In a frenzy, he penetrates her, rooting like a pig in its own filth, mercilessly crushing the body passively abandoned to him. Ah! This headache pounding the back of the eyeballs! It's that beer. Pabst beer really doesn't agree with her. Ah! *Coño!* This is the fourteenth marine astride her since early morning! And there are more in line behind the door.

La Niña's lower belly is just a slippery patch of skin with no sensation—in spite of everything, it throbs mechanically and professionally beneath the paunch weighing down on it. This husky fellow's torso is crushing her ribs and his mop of unwashed red hair keeps sweeping over her face, the little whore staring bitterly at the ceiling has the look of a Madonna in ecstasy. She rolls slightly to one side.

*In the Flicker of an Eyelid*

A formidable charge of sulfur and potassium chlorate has just exploded close by, bringing a collective shout from the crowd. The boys take risks! Without discussing misfortune, the lesson from the last time didn't do the trick: one foot torn off! Intermittent whiffs of whiskey breath, crushed bedbugs, and cat piss are really disgusting! Every now and then the Yankee presses his fat knees down on his partner's kneecaps, making La Niña Estrellita's bones move around. She shoves the untiring horseman off with an abrupt movement. A car has just pulled into the courtyard. More marines arriving! Their nasal chatter and war cries of "*Whoopee!*" and "*Mierda!*" can be heard clear into the bedroom. This strange guy has come three times without even noticing that he is crucifying her. What a slob! His groans are squeaking like a Hawaiian guitar as he hums some monotonous song about a cowboy roaming the endless prairie in search of love.

And that music keeps on . . . !

> *Estoy equivocado,*
> *Equivocado está-á-á. . . .*
> (I'm wrong / It's wrong-g-g-)

Will they ever get enough? La Niña Estrellita suddenly and angrily digs her fingernails into the nape of this hairy hominid! Lost in his dream of paradise, he doesn't seem to notice. Astraddle his filly, he raises up abruptly and sprays his drunken juices, his hot, disgusting, sticky sperm into her. With a great, resounding cry, he lowers himself and prepares to begin again. He wants more!

"Oh, no! You great pig! Enough is enough! You're going to pay and get the hell out! Don't drop any more, you've come all over the place!"

Shoving him away, La Niña Estrellita sends him sprawling to the other side of the bed. She stretches vigorously and painfully, taking her time. Flabbergasted, the marine watches her, his eyes wide.

"*Huh? What's wrong?*"

"I told you, that's enough! You're too much! Four times! *En-*

*tiendes?* Understand? *Four times! No more! Finished.* Go show yourself somewhere else!"

"*What's wrong?*" he replies. "*I'll pay. OK?*"

"Oh no, my piggy! No! ¡No más! No more! Enough! Come on, split! *Get out!* Don't you understand? No idea? Well, you'll see!"

She sits up, ruffles her hair with a nervous hand, stiffening her fingers into a claw to scratch her entire scalp. Putting her feet on the floor, she gets up slowly and takes two or three steps. Her toe joints crack. She's dizzy. In front of the mirror hanging on the armoire, she glimpses her bruised, nude body. At this rate, how many more years can she last? How many seasons can her breasts stay in more or less the same shape? La Niña Estrellita! Phooey! As long as she can keep on! She twists the blue cascade of hair and throws it over her left shoulder. Her naked silhouette droops in the mirror. She has to lean against the wall.

The man has finally come back to earth. He gathers his senses slowly. He gets up, sticks a hand into his clothes, hanging over the chair, and holds a wad of *greenbacks* out to her. He smiles sheepishly. He is generous, and that stops any possible argument. La Niña Estrellita walks over, grabs the money, hunches up against the marine, rubs her hips against him for a second, caresses his hairy torso with her nipples and plops three or four little kisses on his mouth.

"Hmmm . . . hmmm . . . hmmm! Thanks, sweetie!"

She has to watch her reputation! La Niña Estrellita pushes him away again—gently but firmly.

"There, my little pigeon! You're a darling! But I'm bushed, understand? *Tired out!* Come on, go! Be nice like all the American sailors when they want to. Get the hell out!"

She smiles again, puts his marine cap on his head, knots his black tie around his neck, and leaves him standing there as she heads toward the corner wash basin to put away her money.

What a profession! A bell rings. The high mass has just ended. She dampens a washcloth and wipes between her legs, over the pubic area and crotch. That feels good! She has to lean against the screen again. Her head is really spinning. She needs a little fresh air. Grabbing a crimson satin robe hanging on the screen, she flips it over her and, with her hand on her forehead, moves slowly toward the door, leaving the room to her client, who's still dressing. There it is! Her depression is coming back! She's falling into that gaping black hole where she has been floundering for about a week. Sometimes, you just want to swallow some iodine and end it all! She goes back over to the nightstand, feels around in the drawer, grabs a bottle of Maxiton, and swallows two tablets that she washes down with what's left of a glass of water. *¡Mierda!* That knotted, burning sensation in the middle of her chest! Without even looking at the marine, she heads for the door and pushes it open. In order to get out, she has to push back and even shove her way past four or five blond guys who are trying to paw her.

"Hands off, *gringos!*"

Like a sleepwalker, she crosses the big room as a bunch of clients, sitting at tables nursing glasses of rum and soda, rum and Coke, or beer, yell after her:

"La Niña!"

"La Niña Estrellita!"

They can go fuck themselves! Let them yell "La Niña Estrellita" until she's gone! What then? If her fellow workers want to keep on, no problem! La Niña looks quickly toward the bar. The boss, Mario, shakes his head disapprovingly from behind the counter. The record player is blaring a bolero of passion, despair, and golden sun:

> *¡No quiero verte llorando!*
> *¡No quiero verte sufrir!*
> *Porque te adoro tanto,*
> *Al verte llorando*
> *Me siento morir-r-r!* *

---

*I don't want to see you crying!
I don't want to see you suffering!
Because I adore you so much,
When I see you crying,
I feel myself dying!

*Sight*

La Niña Estrellita pulls her shoulders back, letting her tired breasts stick out and be tickled by the satin of her robe. She arches her waist, makes her hips sway, and walks down the entrance steps of the terrace without answering the bordello clients, who are still calling. Ah! They must have stopped watching her. She lets herself go, wallowing like a schooner in distress. She's really built, the slut!

It's nice and sunny, a sun of pure gold, an orange sun the likes of which you find only in the Caribbean during the month of March. The sea swells rhythmically with a great sigh of relief.

"Ah! Ah! Ah!"

That feels good. Your lungs seem to fill with each swell of the great blue sea! A series of firecrackers explodes, one after the other. Oh! Those kids! In the distance, a drum hiccoughs to the epileptic rhythm of the *rabòday*. Sounds of racing motors, squealing brakes, angry honking, and the nasal twang of English are transported by the trade winds. La Niña Estrellita wanders aimlessly through the courtyard, stroking tufts of the century plant and the coleus along the central walk as she passes. The high heels of her slippers catch and wobble on the irregular stones of the walk, causing the sudden swaying of her body, sinuously wrapped in her tightened robe. The headache is going away, but the Maxiton has not yet taken effect. The depression is there, like the puncture of a sharp claw in the hollow of her stomach, between her two weakened and aching breasts. Ah! It must not even be eleven o'clock. What a season! One more warship and she will have to be hospitalized!

La Niña Estrellita swings the gate wide open, stands with her back against one of the palm trees that mark the entrance to the Sensation Bar. She rests her head against the trunk and, through her half-closed eyelids, begins contemplating the green fronds, the sun-charred street through which passersby, excited kids, and occasional cars come and go.

"¡Qué calor! ¡Dios! God, it's hot!"

For a moment, the street becomes calm again—there are fewer people going by, but exploding firecrackers and other crazy sounds come through more clearly from the avenue. A

candy vendor comes up with his box of sweets hung against his
hip with a brown leather strap across his torso. He is going to
take his spot at the corner of the avenue.

"Antoine! ¡*Ven acá!* Come here and give me some mints—I'll
pay you later."

Antoine, a young fellow of ivory black complexion with lively
eyes, comes over and opens his candy box with a side glance at
the opening of her robe over the two tired breasts, two honey-
colored breasts with creased, deep-violet nipples.

"Aren't you going to the Rara celebration, Antoine?"

Antoine shows his blinding white teeth. His dark, shining face
takes on a happy glow—he's an adolescent who has grown up
too fast and has been marked by life.

"Well! You know. . . . There's a little group around Fourth
Avenue in Bolosse, but they're not too hot! A bunch of kids.
This afternoon I'll take the bus to Léogane. At the Ça-Ira cross-
roads, I can do some good business and exercise my hips a bit!"

Antoine is nice, but what a parrot. La Niña's mind is blank.
She made a mistake in provoking this outburst.

"Are the marines still coming ashore, Antoine?"

"I think most of them are ashore. There may still be a few
small groups leaving the ship, but most of them have landed.
They're everywhere! Most of them have found a place to settle
in for a bit. We'll be alright for one or two hours, and then
they'll change nightclubs. Traffic has slowed down a little—
haven't you noticed?"

"Thanks, Antoine. Thanks, you can go on."

Leaning against the palm tree, La Niña Estrellita contentedly
swallows her saliva, freshened and cooled by the strong mint
candy. It's a bit like a little cold snake that she can feel slither-
ing down to the level of her false ribs and, as a result, more or
less relieving the angor that was cramping the hollow of her
stomach. Those firecrackers! Her mind is still blank, and nervous little fibrillations run through her body. She is only slowly
coming to life, and the street show is more bearable than the atmosphere in the bordello bar or the stuffiness of her room. The
heat! With her back against the smooth trunk, La Niña Estrel-

lita looks on. A group of little girls is crossing the street with palm branches in their hands. They are returning from high mass.

"*¡Chiquita!* Little girl! Give me your palm branch!"

One of the girls turns her hazel eyes, sparkling in the sunlight, and looks with great interest at the "lady" leaning against the tree. Most of the girls are frightened by the woman's suggestive, bright negligee as well as by the barroom where the marines are shoving each other around, across the courtyard. But after a moment of hesitation, the hazel-eyed girl walks right up to the "lady." The lady smiles at her. Embarrassed, the girl hunches a shoulder but holds out the palm leaves anyway. La Niña Estrellita slips one of the long, arched palm ribbons from the bouquet—a yellow ribbon streaked with green. Without feeling self-conscious, she smiles at the little girl again—quite openly—and holds the mints out to her, seeming to offer the entire roll. They exchange a friendly glance. Dark pansies with shining stamens, the child's eyes unabashedly, and even with a glimmer of impertinence, focus for an instant on the bitter, faded flowers coveted by the exhausted little whore. For the duration of a suggestive glance, La Niña Estrellita's eyes come to life once more. The little girl goes away. La Niña Estrellita watches her for an instant and then lets her head fall back against the palm tree. If she had dared, she would have kissed this little girl. Oh, well!

Slowly, La Niña smooths the palm leaf between her fingers. Without looking, she begins to fold it. Bit by bit, the ribbon becomes a little yellow and green cross, skillfully formed and knotted. La Niña pulls out a pin, pulls the corners of the skirt that is open over her legs, and attaches the little cross inside the robe over her left breast. The leafy little cross makes a fresh design on her crushed and burning breast.

"*¡Qué calor! ¡Dios!*"

The persistent firecrackers make her jump every time. Things are really not going well today.

La Niña has noticed a man in blue overalls. He's coming toward her. He is walking hesitantly, but as he notices the red shape leaning against the tree, his head draws back a bit. He slows down and walks past, keeping his eyes on her. Through her half-closed eyelids, La Niña glimpses a stocky silhouette with a rhythmic gait. The man's shoulders are slightly rounded. On the back of his neck, a small golden chain is shining just below the mop of black hair with its slightly auburn sheen. As he walks, his neck moves perpendicularly, back and forward. La Niña opens her eyes. The man's gone, already out of sight. But . . . He's retracing his steps. La Niña closes her eyes. He walks past her again. Then she opens her eyelids and looks at the bobbing neck. A bit farther on, he stops and pretends to tie a shoelace. His shirt is immaculately white. The straps of the blue overalls cross on the wings of his broad back, with its powerful latissimus dorsi muscles. The man comes back. This time, he looks directly at her without blinking. He walks in front of her and comes back four or five times. La Niña keeps her eyes half-closed, but she's watching him, too. . . . He has crossed the street. He is standing on the sidewalk across the street, nearly opposite La Niña, without taking his eyes off her. She closes the lower corners of her robe, which has gaped open and is showing her legs again. She presses the free corner of the robe between her calf and the palm tree. Then she opens her eyes and looks straight at him.

The man is wearing heavy cloth shoes. They are neat and have been coated with white, but a small brown spot can be seen on the outside of the left shoe. A corn on the little toe must have rubbed the cloth, eventually making a hole and showing the little circle of brown skin, a warm, earthen sienna spot. He is not wearing socks. The skin of his instep is a bit burned. His legs are strong, very strong, a bit bowed, with powerful muscles, and his lower calf is visible below his trousers. These are the legs of a worker. Not just any worker—the legs of a dock worker, a sugarcane cutter, or a road worker . . . but that can't be true since his overalls, relatively new and freshly washed, have visible spots of heavy oil. So, he's a mechanic, but not just any mechanic. A mechanic who must do heavy work, who walks a lot. The man is going back and forth, as if he were waiting for somebody; he hurls a pebble for no reason and begins pacing again, but without taking his eyes off La Niña. Ah! That curiously swinging, elastic walk! The way he sets each foot on the ground gives the impression of a dance step. A contraction runs through La Niña's body, a palpable physical reaction, as if her flesh were rebelling against the man's glances. La Niña, whose trade is to capture men's attention!

Her depression is what's causing that. That sensation of a void in her head is creeping over her torso, her stomach, and even her legs! A kind of hollow rubber doll, that's what she is! The Maxiton really isn't working today. The boss is probably going to think she's ill tempered. No matter! Mario can yell, but he won't throw La Niña Estrellita out just like that! Not yet, at least! She will go to consult Doctor Chalbert tomorrow; her medicine isn't working any more. It's not strong enough. *¡Mierda!* Now she's trembling! Her heart is racing. There's this sensation that she has taste buds throughout the inside of her body—with her chest, her torso, her stomach, she is tasting the bitter liquid that keeps flowing from an inexhaustible faucet! Why is she alive? For what joy, what minute of relative satisfaction, if not a moment of peace? No, she is living for nothing! Or rather, it's for a kind of persistent and even excessive nausea—some smirking despair, deadening fatigue, drunken sprees, deeply blunted sensations, and bliss that becomes more blurry every day! Tomorrow, she'll go to see Doctor Chalbert, but she won't tell him, "Kill me!"

Instead, she'll say: "Help me live! Let it last! Longer!"

"*¡Mierda!*"

So what does this man want of her after all? He's crazy. Nobody looks at La Niña Estrellita for more than an instant! Nobody undresses her with his eyes: they usually grab her with their paws! La Niña always offers herself; men can turn her over, take her however they want, maul her, lick her, drink her as much as they want, according to their own vices. As long as they pay up! La Niña Estrellita never feels very deeply what is being done to her—they can do whatever they want. And she doesn't give a damn! She treasures life—sure! She just has to repeat to herself:

"I'm still alive because I feel myself—because I feel myself bitter, biting, despairing, shaken with cold and burning sensations, and little moments of bliss!"

Indignant, La Niña Estrellita deliberately lets her robe fall open. Look, since you want to eyeball me. Her legs and her lower hips show beneath the ferocious sun—dark honey among the foliage of the century plants and the coleus. "¡*Mierda!*"

This man's legs are funny. Maybe she has seen legs like that somewhere? God! She has clasped so many legs, caressed so many thighs in her life! This man must be a lecher. Really powerful thighs. His trousers are a paler blue at the knees. His thighs rise straight, massive, like military columns—directly to the hips! His short, stocky thighs frame the bulge of his crotch. He carries it to the right. He stands first on one leg, then on the other, making one hip rise as the other falls. At that level, the classic cleavage of his buttocks is visible below the bone. This man is really strong. Why is he looking at her that way? The firecrackers keep going off. La Niña straightens up. Finally, she can't take it! Won't she ever have a place to go for a second without somebody looking at her—can't she be alone and say:

"Niña Estrellita, here you are—the sun and the light spread over you like friends who don't paw you. For a little while, you've got the right to be a little girl surrounded with sunlight, the purring of the sea, and the waving foliage!"

She is about to call him over to salt and pepper him, insult him in terms so spicy that he'll have to wonder whether that mouth is human or really a sewer outlet! Exactly! He wants to get to know La Niña Estrellita? Well, he'll learn! He'll give up being a voyeur! The voyeurs don't pay; they sneak on the bus! She's got to let him have it. She's going to. . . . But, suddenly, here comes a taxi around the corner; it's full of well-sauced marines. La Niña's depression disappears in an instant. This man is going to see her in the hands of those drunk marines! They're all going to paw her, to go after her mouth, and the golden weight of her breasts. Her depression has disappeared, leaving shame in its place. No, this man mustn't see that!

She flees. She runs around the walk and heads straight for the

*Sight*

"pond," that little raised swimming pool surrounded by a wooden fence. She races up the steps, opens and closes the gate behind her. The water is bluish over the cinder block bottom. Two or three years ago, after being up for four nights, Fejita from the Bataklan took a swim in the pool one morning, and they found her dead. A stroke, they said. La Niña Estrellita drops her robe and slips into the water. She floats freely with her face out of the water.

"*¡O mi cielito del Cáribe! ¡O Virgen del Pilar, aquí está tu Niña Estrellita!* Oh, my little Caribbean sky! Oh, Virgin of the Pillar, here is your Niña Estrellita!"

The Caribbean sky is blue—without a wrinkle or crack. The sun is of spun gold—an orange hue during this month of March, as only such Caribbean months can paint the sun orange. The water is cool; her bitterness subsides. Her awakened pubis and irritated clitoris are less painful. Doctor Chalbert's medicine has taken effect. La Niña relaxes, and she gives the shadow of a smile to the serene, radiant Caribbean sky.

"*¡O mi Virgen del Pilar! ¡Te agradesco!* I thank you, Virgin of the Pillar!"

Finally her spell has passed. Mario must be having a fit in the bar. Mario's not a bad fellow; sure, he yells, but he does what he has to. He's not the worst "hotel" boss she's known. He earns his living the best way he knows. If there were no Niña Estrellita, there would be no Mario! The customers must be calling for La Niña, their Niña. La Niña, after all, isn't just anybody. She has a place! There are quite a few "joyless" whores dreaming of becoming a Niña Estrellita! Not easy! Her pals are jealous, but her stocking is filling up little by little. Ten more years and . . . She should go back to the bar and dance with the customers. She will put on the new record that is so beautiful: "Desesperación." The water feels good. A sense of peace comes from above and penetrates her.

"*¡O mi Virgen del Pilar!*"

La Niña Estrellita makes the sign of the cross. She is floating calmly in the bluish water. The firecrackers are popping farther and farther away. There's a new to-do: motors starting, brakes squealing, horns barking, all at an accelerated pace—the *rabò-day* resounds on the drums in the distance. The sea is breathing calmly. The sky. . . . The water feels good. A broad smile shines across La Niña Estrellita's face—like two faded flowers, her eyes smoothed out on the dark-honey oval of her face, a face like that of the kindly, long-suffering Madonnas in the old colonial churches from the time of the conquistadores.

"¡*Desesperación!*"

La Niña Estrellita is singing. . . .

After hesitating for a long time, the man has gone into the Sensation Bar. He glances searchingly toward the veined foliage where the silhouette, tightly wrapped in crimson satin, disappeared a short time earlier. Not seeing her, he heads awkwardly toward the bar. He climbs the steps, stops briefly in the little gallery where the customers are sitting at tables, and then heads toward the zinc bar with a tense but decisive step.

"Rum and Coke!" he orders.

Sitting on a high stool, the man tries to prop his legs against the counter, which drops almost vertically to the floor, without a footrest. With his nose in the glass, he watches the little bubbles rising in the reddish brown drink. He takes little sips, lapping a little piece of ice with a quick movement of his tongue. As soon as he swallows a mouthful, he leaves the bit of ice on the tip of his tongue, letting the combining sensation of the solid-liquid shock spread through his body.

Ah! He has experienced a lot in his life! He has gone through days alone with his rhythmic, supple, elastic walk. That's his temperament. His gestures are not self-conscious, but rather, rhythmic. As his body moves, an arm or a leg, his head bends toward his destiny or his luck, turning left or right, his hand comes up or moves away, and his foot rises or lowers, beating time. Each movement is flowing, made without abruptness, and nobody would say that any aspect of a given gesture has not been anticipated. Elastic, feline—that's it: an animal leaping into space into order to keep his balance, certain of his landing. Most days are uneventful. How many out of the ordinary days could he find in his life? Not many, in fact, although he has always lived adventurously, passionately. But he has always known, has always held a profound conviction that some day a turn would come unexpectedly, some little chance, that might be objectively foreseen, the snap of a finger that would suddenly speed up his life.

And yet he has meandered around this southern Caribbean Mediterranean! In Cuba—Oriente and Havana; in Mexico—Veracruz; San Pedro in the Dominican Republic; La Guajira in Venezuela; Guatemala City, Panama, Port-au-Prince today; and maybe Tegucigalpa or Maracaibo tomorrow. You're walking down a street, you turn left without really knowing why, you turn right, you take off again straight ahead. The avenue suddenly rises as if toward the sky; the boulevard slopes down. In fact, why is that boulevard sloping down? He follows it. Why is he going down? Some girl? Bah! Just keep going. Go to work. Or to a strike. Why are we striking, fellows? Fights. It has been rough. Were you hurt? We run off with the cops on our tails. One city, then another. Keep going. A street. A dead end. Go back. Go around in circles, plowing the streets like a pleasure yacht. Here's a good wind. Wander on. . . .

"Yeah, I'll take that street, and I won't tack left at the first street, but right at the third."

There you are in jail! Then, freedom! Here's a street, almost an alley. The left foot steps in front of the right, almost with a dancing step, both light and heavy because of the slightly bowed legs.

"Well! You here, *hombre?* What a life, huh? Do you remember? Do you recall? So, what's become of you? Let's drink to that? OK?"

*¡Un fuerte abrazo!* A great hug! You hug the old chum, pulling him to your chest, whether he's a Honduran or a Haitian. So long!

"*¡Vaya con Dios!* God be with you!"

The toes land, and the heel barely touches the ground. El Caucho. They're right to call him "El Caucho," the Rubber Man. He likes to be called El Caucho.

"I'm usually called El Caucho, fellows, but you can call me by my real name if you want to."

They always call him El Caucho. So long, fellows. It's been rough, but sometimes we had a good time anyway, right? That's life. We'll meet again, you can be sure of that. The ship's whistle is screaming. The wind strikes you right in the face on the poop deck of a sailing vessel. A wave of the hand. The train whistles. The transporter makes curious jerks. A large city tumbles right down the mountains into the sea—that's the way it is. Dwarf palms, giant coconut trees, and poincianas that wave their red flares. A mall separates the long avenue in two parts. You keep walking. Your step lengthens deliberately. It's hot, but you're at ease. The March breeze is nice, the trade wind from the sea is a delight with its salt and iodine. You're lulled with the delight of being alive, joyful, at peace, with a personal little adventure asleep in your heart. You'll take that street. You take it. You keep walking. The samba of life. Your heels barely touch the ground. You're walking aimlessly when your head suddenly tells you to stop. You see a woman in a robe of crimson satin leaning against a tree—a woman with flowing curves, two lively feet, and in particular two eyes! Two eyes almost closed. Two eyes with lashes branching out. You can't leave! That's the Caribbean!

The foot in the red, high-heeled slipper has a curious arch. You'd almost think it was deformed. The foot seems to be fragile, but when it shivers, you can see its hidden strength and the great tenderness it conceals. Somebody who might have cherished the entire world without being loved by the slightest blade of grass! Somebody who, in an instant of distress, would have no confidence in herself, but who would remain unbeatable—who would fight without surrender: a little topsail that might rip with a stiff wind while continuing to hold on furiously and desperately in a wild storm. No mistake—that foot cannot fool you, despite its indeterminate, gemlike color of burnt honey, accentuated by the crimson robe. Legs, thighs, hips that hide like tall quivering birds beneath the skirt, while still creating the impression of a great wing, or better still, a great flame in the wind.

## Sight

The belly is less defined—vibrating as if to hide a secret. A protruding curve of the torso, nervous respiration with arms raised above the head, abandoned like useless objects, hollow armpits, slightly fuzzy. He barely saw her hands. Her tortured neck displayed great endurance, but nothing was as expressive as the withdrawn feet and the closed eyes. Her entire being, temperament, heart, and feelings, her entire personality, have taken refuge in those feet and in the eyes that he has seen only closed.

His chums know that they can count on El Caucho in a fight, for a helping hand, to assist them in approaching a *muchacha,* for a slap on the back or an arm around the shoulder when needed. His chums say:

"We ought to go see the boss, but we may get fired. . . ."

That shouldn't stop us! Without hesitation, without saying anything to anybody, El Caucho will go tell the old monkey:

"Boss, the workers want this. . . ."

And the boss listens to El Caucho, even when he's asking for a raise.

"Some fellow!" say the guys. "There's no union, but El Caucho is a kind of union himself!"

"And when are you going to decide on a union? You've got to organize one, see!"

El Caucho always has business to take care of. As soon as two fellows start sparring, he gets into it. With his crazy tendency to play Solomon, it's not unusual for him to catch a fist in the face. Is there someone who hasn't played straight with the workers on his team? El Caucho steps in right away. He simply says:

"Let it go! Why get all upset? I'll talk to the guy! Hey! Big fellow!"

You've got to admit that El Caucho's makeshift solutions don't always work out. Even if they bring about a peaceful outcome, it's not enough to change a guy's behavior. Never mind! El Caucho just starts over at the next opportunity. Incorrigible. He says:

"*¡Hombre!* He's not any different from the rest of us! Every man is looking for the same thing in life! Give him a chance!"

Some guy comes to work with a funny look on his face. He

picks a quarrel with everybody—he's aggressive, wild. The reaction is immediate, naturally, since a worker can't let people
walk all over him at work. El Caucho shows up in those cases:

"Gotta find out what's wrong with him. . . . Just wait. I'll go
see."

When the workers see El Caucho coming over with his elastic gait, a slight smile comes across everybody's lips.

"Hey! Here's El Caucho! What a guy! What's got into him?
Did he eat some explosive peppers?"

One day, Almanor jokingly told El Caucho:

"Hey! El Caucho! You think you're God Almighty sometimes, right?"

El Caucho didn't answer, but he was upset. No, he doesn't
take himself for the good Lord nor for anything else, but he has
suffered so much in his life! Suffered so much that he isn't afraid
of suffering or of anything else. He has suffered so much that he
sniffs out the guys who are suffering, feels their suffering, and
loves them as is, no matter what they are. And that hasn't got
anything to do with ideology. Of course, he has political principles he holds to. He has always been a born fighter, militant
unionist, "tough" guy, and sometimes he seems to be an insen-
sitive person, pitiless when necessary with wild troopers who
don't play fair; other times, he looks like an idiot because he just
lets himself go along. But why is he like all that? Why does he
get mixed up every time in strikes and political activities to the
point of being the tough guy, the headstrong fellow wherever he
goes? He's always being followed, hunted! Certainly not because
of his brains and all he has learned in books, but because of his
heart—that's for sure! He is El Caucho. El Caucho can't do any
differently than he does. El Caucho strides the way he does because he can't walk any other way, because he can't stop himself from empathizing with every living being. Action, reflection,
study, books, have improved his gift for participation: they have
made him more rational, more determined, but they did not
make him. Sure, his natural inclination directs him toward every
living being—little plants, herbs, ants, baobabs, elephants,
caimans, men—it has progressively grown into a love of hu-

manity, love of progress, and love of justice, but this deliberate, after-the-fact humanism has always remained essentially the wild fruit of his spontaneous attraction for each living entity, whatever it might be. He has been tough and pitiless in fights— you do what you have to because workers' demands are not for choirboys—but each time he has decided to be tough, he has suffered terribly because of it. When you love intensely, you can't keep from suffering. No, he doesn't think he's the Good Lord, but he is El Caucho. It's his nature as a born man of action, it's his home field, his Caribbean, his milieu, his climate, his village, his childhood, his mother—it's life after all that made him blossom that way. Bah! He's no luckier than anyone else because of it. Something smacks him in the face every time. He has no house, no family, no real friends, and he is always forced to get the hell out of any place where he has begun to take root and become attached. Because he is El Caucho, he will always be that way. He suffers daily because of it, but he is glad, proud, happy.

What has struck him about this girl is her feet and her eyes. She's really shapely, beautiful, *preciosa,* but that's not why he stopped. El Caucho can never keep right on going when something catches his attention, no matter what the result may be— he stays to see what will happen. He can't do otherwise. Those eyes! How can a human being have eyes like that? And he just saw them closed. What a curve in her eyelids! A sinuous line, a kind of big question mark lying on its belly.

"I can't take it any more," says that little fringe of eyelashes, "but I'll continue on my little journey all the way to the burnt-honey temple. In spite of everything. . . ."

A continual flutter enlivens the little comb of curved lashes:

"We are fluttering to keep from looking at life. I want to, I don't want to. . . . I don't know. . . ."

Naturally bluish—a blue of boredom, blue of revolt, blue of lassitude, blue of resignation, the iris of every blue in the world—the edge of the eyelid says:

"*I am in the blue!* I've got the blues."

As for the eyeball, it seems to move ceaselessly beneath the eyelid, an eyelid that is not honey-colored but chiaroscuro, the shadow of gold, sunny night. . . . The eyebrow is a straight line. She must not pluck her lashes. The brow is disconcertingly clean, a military column—rushing on unbroken, in one breath, to disappear gradually in a kind of crow's-foot. With her crow's-foot, this woman can't be a birdbrain or have the fickle heart of a dragonfly. No doubt—she's a real woman, or at least somebody who has all that's needed to be a real woman. When she parted her eyelids, her eyes became two roses, two real roses, a bit worn, a bit faded, but vibrant, absolutely round roses with few petals, a black heart, thick, emanating from amid the crown of radiating lashes, a capital "O" beneath the endless, horizontal line of the eyebrow. That was at the moment he crossed the street. El Caucho himself couldn't stand or look straight at the roses of those eyes. He beat a retreat!

From the opposite sidewalk, the details have softened, but the impression has persisted. That form is really the stem created to bear roses. A supple eglantine that bends and then straightens up in the stiff evening wind or the tornado of frantic nights in the brothels—a frail plant, stubborn, desperate, that clings to the desolate, rocky ground and survives during arid seasons in the bordello. How do these roses remain roses? She left because the "company" car, the taxi loaded with marines was coming down the street. That's for sure. She fled. She didn't want him to see her in the hands of those men. Why not? By running away, she was admitting some complicity, a link with him. That's unusual! As for him, he stopped and couldn't pull himself away from the spot. She remained there, not moving, letting herself be observed, without trying to attract him, and then ran away at the instant when her professional duties were going to cast her like a puppet into the lecherous hands of the crazed marines.

El Caucho searches his memory in vain—he can find nothing that would remind him of anything like this. He has had lots of passing adventures in his life—you've got to be honest. One woman caught his attention with her laughter, another with her youth, still another by her bed skills, but laughter, freshness, skill all lost their attraction for him very quickly, and each time, he has let the line stretch out until it broke. So it's not the recollection of one or another female that the red figure leaning against the palm has evoked. His mother? His sisters? Of course not! Where does this resonance come from—his character, his memory, clairvoyance, second sight, or imagination? Why did those feet, little live animals with an existence nearly separate from the rest of the body, produce a vibration in his head, a shock, a recoil? Why do the roses of her eyes have that vibrancy, such a constraining, irrepressible, magnetic presence? It's as if, at some earlier time, he had had a dream, quickly forgotten, and this reality suddenly revived the old dream, gave substance to a vague image, lost and then lost again, an image that had never materialized despite the retinal persistence. Those feet are two living animals—the roses of her eyes are two flower sorceresses. She ran away so that he—El Caucho—wouldn't see her in the role, the lascivious activity of a *manolita* caught in the fiery pit. So she assumed that complicity. She said yes. What question was the "yes" answering?

El Caucho wedges his feet between the bars of the stool, leans against the bar, wiggles his behind to get more comfortable, and bends his back in order to get rid of the vague tension of his spine, right between the shoulder blades. He puts his elbows on the zinc counter.

"Rum and Coke!"

With his nose in the glass, he watches the little bubbles dancing in the reddish brown liquid. He takes little sips, lapping a piece of ice each time.

"*¡Qué calor, este domingo! ¡Dios!* God, it's hot this Sunday!"

The bar erupts in an explosion of yells:

"La Niña!"

"La Niña Estrellita!"

Clusters of firecrackers resound in the still air, the sounds of traffic on the avenue become more intense, and the drum beat fades for a moment in the distance. La Niña has just made her entrance. They call to her from table to table as she comes through the gallery. El Caucho cannot see her from the bar. She doesn't turn around. She is probably saying something to the men calling her. In fact, they quiet down. A flash of lightning crosses the large mirror that covers the wall of the bar. El Caucho sees the comet that flashes through the hall where two or three couples are dancing. Mario, the patron, raises his head, and addressing El Caucho, he bursts out laughing:

"La Niña Estrellita! What a woman! She drives them all crazy!"

El Caucho nods in friendly agreement. He quickly fits into the mood of any company. He seems to be smiling at the patron from behind his shining mustache. Hunching his shoulders, he bends over his glass again.

Less than three minutes later, the confident clacking of heels, a resounding, almost triumphant step is heard. El Caucho stares at the mirror. She comes in.

"Ah! La Niña! La Niña Estrellita!"

She really does drive them crazy! She would have them walking on their knees. Smiling, she stops, casts a glance in the direction of the bar, and sees the man watching her. Her smile immediately freezes. She is wearing the same high-heeled slippers with black, tight slacks molding her shape. A sparkling, cream-colored scarf, floating over her hip like snowflakes, highlights her waist. Beneath her simple blouse, a short-sleeved, blood-red jersey, she is naked; she's not even wearing a brassiere. Through the mesh of loose, diamond-shaped knit designs, you can clearly see the flesh and the golden fruit of her breast. A real little buccaneer! Once more, El Caucho sees her charcoal brows, her sparkling eyes, the childish nose, her whimsical mouth, the shape of her face—that indescribable oval—an ellipse, but an ellipse that's constantly contradicting itself, that's disconcerting with a whole series of conflicting curves trying to take over and dominate. La Niña's uneasiness has taken off in a second, like a black bird.

"La Niña!"

She blossoms, joins legs and feet, undulates her hips, slightly flexes her knees, first to the right, then to the left; she jumps in place, throwing her joined heels to the rear, a sort of stallion's kick. A long cry of enthusiasm rings out through the hall:

"La Niña! La Niña Estrellita!"

A man darts toward her with his polo shirt flaring out around his lazy, well-nourished figure. This is Félicien, a regular. Nobody is quite sure what business he is in, but he pretentiously tries to look like the perfect Havana *guajiro*. He's a *palgo*.

> *Soy como soy . . .*
> *Y no como tú quieras.*
> (I'm the way I am / And not as you would like.)

The rhumba whinnies, farts, and wavers. La Niña dances with abandon; she is at once arched, suggestive, sinuous, first offering herself and then withdrawing her body, a wave of carnal, happy, ethereal, tormented, mercurial, sculptural lines—an elastic, orgiastic figure of the bubbly, Venusian Caribbean.

❊

❊   ❊

From her place at the end of the gallery, La Niña Estrellita is observing the hand of the man leaning with his elbows on the bar. That hand rises and descends rhythmically with the *guarracha*. Without letting on, La Niña does not take her eyes off him. That paw gives an impression of being a great rain crab coming out of his hole into the falling rain, almost jumping, happy. The palm must be calloused, rough, joyful, and fraternal. But if it swoops down on someone, it won't be a *kakakòk*. She's angry with herself; it's clear that she shouldn't pay much attention to some fellow who might have dared provoke her. Any man she belongs to has to be calm, a good guy. The little finger of his left hand seems stiffened, not following the others that are keeping time. His fingers are thick: a team of hefty rugby players—comic and brutal! It must be fun to dance with a man who has a hand like that. The suppleness of his wrist isn't that of a tailor, a virtuoso, or an acrobat, but it certainly seems

*In the Flicker of an Eyelid*

to have an innate sense of rhythm, time, movement, an authentic elasticity—sensual, feline—that still has an element of good humor and fantasy. When he dances, he won't look for pleasure first—his choreographic sense will be realized by a hint or a suggestion of a step rather than prosaic completion—all of that enhanced at times by some mischievous childishness mixed with grace and harmony. Even with a massive-looking hand like that, this man must have incredible delicacy, he must be a born and tireless improviser. He probably doesn't lead his partner, but gently guides her in the dance step that he has had the lightning intuition to suggest, and he leads her irresistibly, magically, without the partner having the time to pull away or the possibility of escaping because he cradles her, swings her, dips her—making her savor all the little emotions from the physical joy of joined bodies. He undoubtedly participates fully in the movement—not just his legs, but his back, torso, shoulders, arms. . . . As he dances, he must look for the most secret surfaces of the body, taking possession with a pressured touch that is at once imperative, light, supple, surreptitious—nesting, nestling, nuzzling in tenderness with dreamy, cuddly dexterity, taking hold of you, surprising you constantly, suggesting pleasure, eliciting delight in order to wrest it away with cruelty and malice at the moment where you'd like to fade into eternity. It has been a long time since she has thought of such things. She, the very person whose senses have been nearly dead for such a long time! Hey, La Niña, what's happening to you? What's taking hold of you? Why are you recalling those lulling reveries that you've avoided or forgotten for such a long time? What's going on in those buried depths of your memory? Why isn't this bird like all the others?

"Ha, ha! And after all that, you haven't slept with her?"

La Niña bursts out laughing raucously, sways her waist like the back of a swan, winks with complicity, taps her glass to make the condensation run down, and upends it. Outside, the firecrackers keep popping noisily. Traffic has slowed a bit, diminished in intensity.

"Not possible! She was a virgin? You'd better believe she

pulled the wool over your eyes. I know the trick! Me too—with a little alum and a lot of patience, I can reconstruct an evening's hymen for a ninny like you!"

La Niña throws her head back and laughs. She reveals her clear gums, and the little star framed between her upper incisors sparkles with fire. She raises her arms above her head in order to display her armpits and the velvet fur. At the same time, with a little coarse laugh, she distractedly slaps a hand that is sliding along her thigh.

"Don't touch!"

Immediately, she pulls up the zipper that revealed a patch of her hip. The man is still there. He is probably watching her. That is . . . Yes, she has to take a turn around the tables—right?—has to give a bit of La Niña Estrellita to everyone. No! Not now! This is no time for foolishness! La Niña takes one drink after another. She wants to be woozy, barely conscious—without delay! No, from the bar, he probably can't see her. Maybe he can manage to see her hand once in a while. La Niña bends her waist, projects her breasts, offering herself to all the lusting eyes. If only they knew that she doesn't feel a thing when she makes love! She exchanges banter, throws back quips, and sparkles with witticisms and off-color responses. She squints her eyes, casts glances at the men, and remains inaccessible. Disappointing.

She gets up and goes over to a table where the marines are sitting. She sits down on one man's lap, takes a cigarette out of his pack, gets a light, and right on the mouth, she kisses the young fellow who offered his lighter:

"Thanks, doll!"

The doll is a marine with patches of stubble who must have just escaped from high school. It's really impossible to be seen from the bar. She throws out two or three *jokes,* the only jokes she knows in English. No! She won't make love now!

"*No, I said! Not now! Oh! You or someone else, what difference? I can't take the entire U.S. Navy into my bed at the same time! And I need to relax. Sorry, honey! Give me a drink, sugarcane!*"

She drinks quickly, gets up, and lands at another table. The Haitian regulars are sitting there.

"La Niña! Sit with us? What are you drinking?"

"A glass of kerosene with a slice of lemon, ducky! Say! Don't you know what La Niña drinks any more?"

She sits down, crosses and uncrosses her legs, pretending to be at ease. She remains calmly seated with her back to the bar. She can be seen from there, in fact. She lowers her voice and plays at being fatigued. She turns and pushes away the hands playing with her nipples, fends off the palms caressing her belly, and slaps the fingers pinching her buttocks.

"Hands off! I'm tired, I tell you! If I listen to you, I'll die this season! If you don't behave, I'm getting out of here!"

No, from the bar, she probably can't be heard. Why does this man keep watching her so intently in the mirror? What does he want? God, how inviting! And yet, he can't be a timid fellow; certainly not. That look is not an invitation, in any case, but rather it's a kind of sign of complicity, of solidarity, even of intimacy.

"Phooey! You men are always bragging and then, in bed, after a few pretty awkward strokes, it's all over! All tuckered out! By the way, don't you think this beer has a funny taste? Could Mario be giving us watered beer now? What if he heard me? Yours is alright? I'll take it—order another one!"

And La Niña pours the contents of her glass on the leaves that reach the railing of the gallery.

Yes, she's getting high. Slowly, but it's coming. She drinks. She changes tables and goes to sit in the middle of a group of marines, some young fellows. They're delighted to see the star of the club at their table. The entire American navy knows that La Niña has been the most sensational whore of La Frontière for several seasons—she outclasses all the other *manolitas* of this red-light district, and it seems that she'll still hold on for a good while. La Niña doesn't want to make love now—the word is going from mouth to mouth. La Niña is tired. The marines let their attitude reflect that of other customers. These fellows don't touch La Niña; they just look at her the way they contemplate

Lily Marlene or Mae West on the screen. With excited eyes, they speak or jabber a few words in Spanish or Kreyòl. When the marines aren't too drunk, they're not bad fellows, at least the younger ones. La Niña crosses her legs and plays the tired vamp. From where she is, she must be perfectly visible from the bar. And if she put her hand on her shoulder like this, the man certainly ought to see her clearly. La Niña keeps her back to the bar and remains quiet. She is content to make faces, raise her eyebrows or roll her eyes, blinking and showing her pearly teeth. What's wrong with her? Why is her heart beating so fast? Why is she putting her hand on her shoulder? So the man will notice her? Why does her hand, and her entire posture, take on this naive, childish, timid, virginal look that she has managed to maintain after so much experience? She doesn't know! Why all these questions? Everything is simple. She's like that because she's La Niña. That's why people began calling her *la niña*, the urchin, the kid, the little girl who sparkles, *que echa chispas*, who throws off sparks. She is changeable, bright, dark, joyful, tormented—an enchantress like the stars. But why exactly has she remained a *niña*, Niña Estrellita for better or worse, in spite of alcohol, evenings, nightmares, sleepless nights, her horizontal submission and the succession of guys—in despair of her life, turning one trick after another, all the emptiness—and yet, still pure? Damn! La Niña is smiling, but her back is tingling, and she stretches her hand above her shoulder, offering it openly, just as a nice little girl offers her doll. She presents it nicely before the glances of that man she would not approach for anything. That's it, La Niña! That gesture is the true La Niña!

El Caucho is on his tenth rum and Coke. El Caucho drinks when he wants to. Then for a while, he doesn't drink. When he is not drinking, there's no particular reason—simply because he doesn't have the urge. At times, somebody offers him a drink, and he refuses it because it's not what he wants; no matter what anybody does at those times, he won't drink. At other times, he will get dead drunk just because he feels like it. In fact, that only happens occasionally. One day is no worse than the next for El Caucho; so it's a whim when he starts bending his elbow or ties one on. When he is really "plastered," El Caucho looks grim, but he isn't really nasty. But at those times, you don't want to pester him. If somebody bothers him more than once, El Caucho will say:

"Stop!"

The fifth time, he will say:

"Get away from me!"

The tenth time, he simply glances at the obstreperous fellow with his threatening look. After that, nobody can answer for what he might do. At times, nothing happens; in other circumstances, onlookers may come close to witnessing a really bloody scene where the tease gets ground into hamburger meat. El Caucho is never sorry for anything he does, drunk or not, even when he is sober again. Besides, as "plastered" as he might be, he always knows exactly what he's saying and doing. At those times, all his actions are always incredibly deliberate—speaking, looking, urinating, except for bending his elbow. That he does in an instant. You might say that El Caucho knows how to drink, loves to drink, although he rarely does it. It's frightening what El Caucho can take in once he starts. In certain situations, at the baptism of a friend's child, for example, El Caucho accepts only a half-glass. On other occasions, at a wedding for instance, he may have seven drinks and stop. At times, at a wake, after work, or at a first communion, he might have thirteen and stop. He has been known to have twenty and stop, while at other times he can't stop. El Caucho drinks what he wants, when he wants it, except before and during working hours. El Caucho is convinced that a given day is no sadder than another—and no more cheerful.

Leaning with elbows on the counter of the Sensation Bar, El Caucho finishes his tenth rum and Coke. He doesn't know whether he's going to stop. He never knows that. He's thinking. It has been at least two months since he made love—and the *moukère* wasn't great! Anyway, he doesn't think he is particularly inclined to make love today; he probably won't look for a girl. El Caucho is in the clouds for the moment; he's mulling over old memories, digging in his heart's cemetery, thinking about his life. He's here because he wants to be. He has money in his pockets today, enough to do anything he wants. His salary isn't great, but he eats modestly, has modest quarters, and only occasionally indulges in lovemaking. He wears decent clothes, but he never spends too much for his wardrobe. To be truthful, El Caucho has one vice, a big one: he likes to read. He reads anything—a telephone book or a novel—he likes to read everything, but he prefers books that are difficult to understand. In such cases, he can read them ten times in a row, until he has understood what they're all about, even stuff about philosophy. Of course, he reads them because in the course of his union and political activities he learned that an intelligent worker has to read and get an education, but especially because it pisses him off when he finds something that he can't understand or can't do. El Caucho is starting his eleventh rum and Coke.

Good thing today is Sunday. El Caucho wanted to enter this bordello when he saw that girl, so he came in. He's holding his own—he isn't drunk; he's drinking and doesn't feel a thing. In the bar's mirror, the first thing he saw was La Niña's shoulder, way at the end of the gallery. He knows what she's called: La Niña Estrellita.

"Estrellita? Estrellita? That's not her real name!"

Why not? Simply because El Caucho knows better. Is he called El Caucho because El Caucho is his real name? No! So? El Caucho saw La Niña's shoulder first in the mirror—her right shoulder. She raises her shoulder in an I-don't-give-a-damn way, as if she were cold. The round bump of her deltoid is perfect, but her clavicle juts out a bit, and the depression above it is deeper than it ought to be. She doesn't hide that; she's La Niña, which means she has a virginal side that is part of her charm. She must have played a lot when she was a kid. She is still playing, she is playing kind of awkwardly with her shoulder while all her other gestures are studied, just right, and they demonstrate that she has the art of lovemaking at her fingertips, the art of fierce lovemaking, the art of creating illusions. El Caucho can't hear her speaking—he would like to hear, but it does no good to turn his ear—he can't catch a thing. And yet she must be laughing. She must be laughing cruelly, as cruelly as she was lounging a while ago with her back against the palm. Everybody seems to be enthusiastic because of her liveliness, but basically nobody understands that this is not true joy. Nobody knows her. El Caucho can't see her any longer. She is hidden from his glance; he can't see a thing in the mirror. But in his glass, El Caucho can see a childish shoulder rising playfully.

La Niña must be at the end of the gallery, at a table with the marines. When a marine is all alone, El Caucho can talk to him. For him, a marine is a Yankee, a *gringo,* but he's a man all the same. And, in his life, every man suffers, every man loves. But when there are three, four, ten, twenty marines together, they stop being men and become Yankees, *gringos.* When they're face to face with a *colored* person, as they say, the marines are worse than animals. To those guys, a *colored* man, a Caribbean man, is a sort of *makak,* a monkey wearing clothes, but still a *makak.* La Niña must not be too crazy about the *white 'mericans,* less so than the other whores—that's clear. "Proles" like good work, work that's well done. On the job, they can't keep from putting their hearts into what they're doing, even if the boss is a bastard or not too honest. And a whore, in spite of everything, is a proletarian—she comes from the common people, and she usually goes back, at least back to her lair to expire. A whore does her task with a proletarian conscience, an innate love for work well done, even if she's at the end of her rope. Couldn't whores have their own kind of strike? Piece work! A union like that would be out of sight—to get a guaranteed minimum wage and old-age retirement! La Niña goes from table to table, rubbing against the men, letting herself be caressed; she hires herself out to earn her keep, just like workers. She works with her face, her eyes, her mouth, her buttocks, her cunt—after all, what's the difference between her and other workers? There are girls who become whores—people say it's their fault. For workers just as for whores, El Caucho tends to think that it's their fault. Maybe it's because he has become what he is on his own, painfully, losing sleep, fighting like a crazy man against himself, against life, against bosses, against bastards, against slackers and collaborators. He doesn't like feeling that he's a prisoner of anything, that's for sure, but what made him like that? Isn't it a lucky throw of the dice, a particular piece of luck?

In life's lottery, the "proles'" lottery, El Caucho drew a lucky number. His good luck was to have a mama like his. She had a Haitian father and a Cuban mother—she spent her entire life in Oriente, a simple and good woman. Even if she was a little narrow-minded perhaps, a little sanctimonious, El Caucho's mama had two exceptional traits: she had the determination of an ant and uncommon kindness. She was kind to the point of being a bit simple. El Caucho takes after her. If he has managed to become what he is, it's because he is the son of that woman, because of the capital kindness, the capital tenacity he inherited from her: the lucky number. . . . With that, El Caucho can take part in everybody's drama and comedy—he is his mother's son in every way and for everything, even if he thinks, acts, and lives differently from her. There are all types of miserable men—there are lifelong laborers, there are cops, there are spies, there are pimps, there are guys lacking in courage even when they are "honest," there are tramps, there are phoneys, there are drunks, there are whores. As for La Niña, she has to let herself be pawed by *white 'mericans*—that's her *job,* her work, her number in the lottery of life. Maybe she would have managed to become an atomic physicist at some other time. La Niña! A human being can do anything, commit any act—but, first of all, you have to know what you've got in your blood, what you've got in your guts, in your liver, in your heart, in your childhood, in order to decide. In spite of everything, you've got to send mad dogs to the dog pound. In a sense, everything a person does in life is done for the worms—you can't ever forget that when you think about human existence. You live and die—neither one of these things is a joke! But the worst is to be bored forever! At least, El Caucho is never bored. La Niña goes from table to table; El Caucho can't see her or even manage to hear her, but he can tell those who see her, who watch her, who speak to her, or who want to paw her. So he knows what La Niña is doing. She is getting plastered and luring her customer. But why is she getting plastered? Obviously she doesn't want to get called down by Mario, the boss—it's her job to promote drinking, but why is she getting plastered? By Mario's face, El Caucho sees that there's no reproach for what La Niña is doing, but it will be time for a change of the guard, in a while—she will have to go sleep with the marines. El Caucho is on his twelfth glass. If he could hear La Niña's voice, just her voice, he would know why she is getting plastered. He would learn a bunch of things about her, about her life and her personality, from nothing more than the sound of her voice. But try as he will, he can't hear her. La Niña. Nothing!

"Boss, another rum and Coke!"

There is a whole to-do in the gallery. A waiter has just come back to the bar with his tray. He's telling about it. . . . A girl threw the contents of her glass in a marine's face and then broke the glass on his head. Now she's squeaking like a baby mouse as she dances the rigadoon. The firecrackers are getting wild outside. He probably didn't stick a fork in her behind, manhandle her, or even slap her. The ruckus quiets down. In the distance, the Rara drums begin once more with renewed fury. Two waiters are dragging out *la loca,* the "crazy woman," who is howling and struggling. It's a run-of-the-mill thing, nothing more. A car has just stopped in the courtyard, pouring out another wave of marines. Mario shakes his head in frustration. He leans over toward El Caucho as if they knew each other. He likes this new customer—that's clear.

"That's nothing, just La Rubia. It's been five days since she had a fit. It had to happen. She isn't the worst one of the girls working in the club, believe me! She does her job well. It's unbelievable how La Rubia keeps herself in shape! She must be well past thirty-eight years old, but what a build! What style! You see, what's nagging at La Rubia is fear. She has a terrible fear of growing old. La Rubia hasn't ever looked toward the future or saved. La Rubia is a princess. She gives away everything she's got; she gives it to anybody, just like that, without a second thought. And then, she's in love—that's not good! She has a little *chulo*. She'd go throw herself in the Bois-de-Chêne for him in a second. I've known her for over fifteen years. La Rubia has always kept herself top-rate. It's a miracle! Never seen a girl with better breasts, and as for her ass, it's "ready-to-wear!" She's really sensational. She walks the way she dances, like a queen! I think she'll manage to keep going for some time. I keep telling her, but it's no use—she's afraid! She's not the jealous type, she's good to her friends, very nice—but I think she can't stand the idea that La Niña has become her equal, and she's playing the dowager queen. And yet, she likes La Niña a lot, protects her, cajoles her like a sister. For some time, every three or four days, when La Rubia is drunk, fear gets hold of her. The fear of growing old. She has a fit, but it doesn't last long. Out of pure viciousness, some of the girls are beginning to call her *la loca,* the "crazy woman," because of her fits, but they don't last long—you'll see! In five minutes, she will have taken her shower and be stone sober. She'll put on her best dress and come back into the hall like a queen. Half of the customers would like to sleep with her. That Rubia is something!"

Mario squints his eyes almost shut. Mario is intrigued by El Caucho: he likes this fellow. Something must be haunting Mario's memory—and La Rubia is probably part of it. Mario opens his eyes:

"Another rum and Coke, 'big fellow'? It's on me. I'd be happy if you accept. . . ."

El Caucho toasts the boss. Mario was surely a worker earlier in his life, you can tell. Maybe not one of the better workers— his mug isn't that of a fellow who likes to work hard or sweat, but he has certainly been a worker. He might have won the lottery. Unless he was an informer working for the bosses or a police spy. But Mario must not be a bad guy. El Caucho is wearing his overalls—yet Mario is paying attention to him and talking to him in a friendly way. From Mario's tone of voice, you can tell that El Caucho's presence reminds him of a lot of things and is bringing back memories, broad-winged memories that are sweet, tender, and bitter all at the same time—whatever the guy harboring them may be like. La Niña Estrellita is going from one table to the next through the crowd of marines, but she's getting closer to the bar. La Niña must not like the marines. If El Caucho did not know his own father, it's because he was shot by a marine rifleman under the Star-Spangled Banner, soon after the Cuban War of Independence against Spain. El Caucho's father was with Martí, but when the Yankee "liberators" who had come to help the Cubans chase out the Spaniards tried to take over from the former masters, turning Cuba into their own colony—the guerillas turned their rifles against them. El Caucho can neither see nor hear La Niña for the moment, but she's getting plastered, that's for sure. Why is she getting plastered? La Niña Estrellita. Which particular trait in this woman has sparked El Caucho's memory?

La Niña suddenly appears in the mirror behind the bar. El Caucho sees her back, a back with the curve of a swan's neck. La Niña is nervous. She must have been a nervous person before she began working as a whore. She is nervous like a thorough-bred racehorse! Her ears twitch at the slightest breeze, her jersey rustles at the least sound, her head pulls back constantly, and her neck and mane quiver at the mere thought of being spurred. Nervous people are incredible! Whether they're somebody or not, nothing they do is ordinary; exaggerated maybe, astonishing, admirable, crazy, grandiose, monumental, or simply outlandish—sure! Who knows? Moodiness, instability may be the essential traits of any strong personality, of any exceptional life, of any remarkable action—grand adventure, powerful creation, or great discovery. Their performance in any arena is often at such a price. The whole bet, for highly sensitive people, is the result of their aptitude for taming the stormy and delicate beasts that are their faculties. In the final analysis, their success depends on the freedom they have to rein in the wild beasts of their temperament in a productive, purposeful direction.

This is the back that La Niña Estrellita plops on the bed for hours, night and day, in the perpetual torture of false love and the ritual of coitus—no joy. La Niña's back makes slow movements, cat movements. In order to ape sensuality that way when a person is so tired, the tender gestures have their origin somewhere in the deepest part of the personality, where the soul has kept an immense reserve of untapped tenderness intact! That tenderness glides over La Niña's back, like a nice swell from secret springs, with an idle, prolonged shiver. It's a loving tenderness that promotes the fantastic play of her vertebral column, an uncalculating tenderness, a river with no estuary, no mouth, no goal, a gully of unused tenderness that the desert of endless days cannot absorb or exhaust. That tenderness originates in the hollow shell of her back, just above the cream-colored scarf, and flows, climbs, spreads over the lower part of the thoracic cage like an uninhibited breath. The tenderness runs out, stretches over her shoulder blades, those little wings that are barely visible beneath the skin, a ray of dark honey, spotted by the loose mesh of the red jersey. That tenderness glides, climbs with effort to the shoulder blades, and then suddenly spreads in waves from the slightly virginal right shoulder that La Niña raises with a tremor and naive grace toward her ear. On her lowered left shoulder, the delicacy of her back becomes bitterness, disillusionment, and her hank of blue hair gushes over the abandoned promontory. La Niña Estrellita, La Niña, what's your secret? Where is that mystery hidden? Your neck is that of an experienced woman, an expert at playacting in the arts of love—it spins around like a pot on the wheel, but her back itself is tenderness.

"Boss! Have a drink with me?"

Mario toasts El Caucho.

Caressing that Doric neck with his sweeping glance, El Caucho suddenly has a real sense that he was right to come into this bar. There's no doubt—something has linked, is linking, or will link him to this woman. What? Pickups are starting off from the Portail de Léogane toward Carrefour with their coughs and nasal sputtering. Kids are still setting off firecrackers. That neck is infinitely expressive. La Niña could communicate any thought with her neck. That's it—La Niña is speaking to El Caucho with her neck!

"I know you're there, man!"

Yes. He is really the one that she's addressing with that neck bent over to drink. She would like to get drunk but can't manage. The back of that neck uncovered by that twisted fleece falling over her shoulder is marked by a little furrow, a clear path that disappears into her dark hair. The little waves of the cerulean forest are straightened by the weight of the heavy, capillary cascade. La Niña's neck is not talking nonsense to El Caucho.

"Why are you there, man?" it asks.

And you, La Niña, why don't you dare come forward? Why are you trying to get drunk? El Caucho is quite sure that La Niña Estrellita is speaking to him with her neck. The city is one immense echo constantly broken by firecrackers, crazy noise, tom-toms, and trumpeting races. Suddenly, a hesitant hand scales La Niña Estrellita's left shoulder, emerges, stretches, perches its slender, nervous fingers on the trapezius of her back of dark honey. The fingers climb over one another, caress one another slowly.

"I'm nothing but a whore, you see? A simple little whore who is doing her job. I don't complain, I'm not happy, not a rebel, I accept my lot, and, in particular, I don't want to trouble my head with thinking. I'm a whore, you're a mechanic—that's life. Of course, I'm at the end of my rope, exhausted, but it's the same thing every day. I'm sitting here, and I'm drunk. You're unusually talkative, but you don't arouse anything in me except uneasiness. I drink because you put me ill at ease, you bother me, you're suffocating me! I'm an ordinary whore at her good age; leave me alone!"

Her fingers are moving like sad children; they come together in a bunch, separate, curve, flex, stretch out. They are delicate, long, nervous, thin, and so bitter!

"I'm finished, you understand? A whore becomes less and less of a human being with each passing day. I have nothing in common with you, you scare me; leave me alone, I tell you!"

Her palm is quite open, held above her left shoulder. That palm is an almost perfect hexagon:

"This palm does its slimy dirty business every day; it can't keep from it, you understand? This palm is degraded and can't avoid further degradation through gestures of unmeasurably disgusting degeneration. Who are you, man?"

It's true that in its manner, that palm is really a whore's palm. The wrist has a particularly dry and vulgar movement. Frightful! The whole degrading trade is revealed, set into this flesh. Even the delicate, long, nervous, slender fingers are not really sad children. And yet . . . There is some little remainder of innocence in those fingers, in spite of it all. They are children after all—perverted, corrupt, depraved, unfortunate, but children. Besides, it's not obvious that all of this is so visible. So, El Caucho, why do partiality, bold judgment, and a tendentious cruelty of spirit instill themselves so easily in the human heart?

Three women come back into the room. They have just finished with their share of brothel duties, their percentage of screwing. Now they are going to start dancing and promoting drink consumption. The marines are jabbering in nasal tones and calling out to the women who have finished their tour of love duty. Mario is moving around behind the bar. Other women have to go on duty—it's their turn to stretch out. Let's go, Lucrèce; let's go, Fernande; let's go, Luz-Maria; let's go, La Niña Estrellita, it's your turn to play. Suddenly La Niña's fingers begin trembling slightly.

"Why are you still there, man? I have to get down on my back. I can't get out of this chair, and it's your fault. You're keeping me from getting up! Get out!"

Luz-Maria and Lucrèce have gotten up. An enormous, red-haired marine is taking them off. Like a gorilla, he's hugging them against him with his huge, hairy, prehensile fingers digging into their sides and under their arms. He wants both of them at once. La Niña's palm goes up and down, nervously.

"The time has come, you understand, man? I can't put it off any longer. I've got to go. Get out, or I'm going to make a scene!"

In fact, Mario is scowling at La Niña, who is still sitting there. A flame-colored, sunny gold bolero of despair is making the hall jump.

*In the Flicker of an Eyelid*

*¡No quiero verte llorando!*
*¡No quiero verte su-u-frir!*
*Porque te adoro tanto. . . .* *

Mario is frowning and does not take his eyes off La Niña. El Caucho gets up slowly. He pays.

With his swinging, elastic gait, El Caucho hurries quietly through the gallery. La Niña Estrellita holds her palm open, displayed on her shoulder. El Caucho waddles past her.

"Hey, man! Look at the heart line on my hand—it's cut into ten branches; that means that I can't have anything in common with you. Look at the head line—it is very thin and twisted: I can't do anything with my head, I don't know how to think or choose, I don't act anymore—I'm acted upon. Hey, man! Look again before you leave! Look at my destiny line. At this moment, it doesn't show a conclusion—it disappears in the middle. . . . So, you see. Look at my life line, I will have a serious illness sometime in the coming years. It's impossible to tell whether I'll survive it. You see that we can't have anything in common—not yesterday, not today, not tomorrow. So long, man! Thanks for leaving!"

La Niña pulls out her compact, powders her nose, and as El Caucho leaves she follows his silhouette in the little mirror. She pretends to be powdering, but she is observing those shoulders as they move through the foliage. She stubbornly watches that foot with the heel that barely touches the stones of the walk. So long, man! La Niña Estrellita can only look in desperation at her compact; the man is gone—he has disappeared. Lost!

La Niña straightens up with a leap, shakes her head with salacious joy and sparkling eyes, breaking into a long, laughing neigh. She shakes her head wildly, and her laughter resounds like a waterfall crashing over a jutting rock. She continues to shake her head with the whirling blue skein of hair scattering wildly over her back, spreading over her shoulders, and rain-

---

*I don't want to see you crying!
I don't want to see you suf-fering!
Because I adore you so much.

ing down her breasts as it settles gently across her belly. Over
her face, La Niña has that sparkling mask of virginal vice that
makes men shiver and burn with desire. She is a lioness with
wild hair, a tigress with exposed teeth; she laughs, roars, twists,
and is always ready to spring. Her laughter bursts, explodes,
and scatters in a thousand shards of lively colors—reds, greens,
okras, indigos. La Niña has leapt into space and fallen back to
the same spot in rhythm with the hoarse merengue blaring from
the record player. La Niña has dropped to her knees, her body
stretched back on the ground. She shakes her hips and suddenly
makes her belly move to the atrocious rhythm of the merengue
and its lines of intertwined melodies. Caught up in the melody,
she stops breathing. A drum solo breaks into the lyrics. La
Niña's abdomen shakes in obscene spasms, gyrating and wob-
bling like jelly. When La Niña revels this way, stretched out on
the floor, the clientele becomes frenzied and goes crazy.

"*¡Ándale!*—go, La Niña! Niña Estrellita is on fire! La Niña,
give it to us! La Niña! Burn! Estrellita, give it to us!"

The drum breaks out in dry bursts, like a case of firecrackers. La Niña's belly mimics the rhythm, like a banner snapping
in a storm. The melody starts again. The belly reverses its gyrations, whirls, freezes suddenly, only to begin vibrating, twisting,
vacillating slowly, dizzily, then faster and faster.

"Burn, La Niña!"

"Whoopee! La Niña! *Well!*"

"La Niña! *See!* Give it to us! *See!*"

"Estrellita! OK!"

"La Niña Estrellita!"

The merengue stops. La Niña stops. She breathes deeply,
straightens up, still on her knees, then performs that unique gesture she does when the demon has possessed her: with her fingers frozen in a claw, she musses the strands of her hair, deeply
and nervously digging her fingernails into the thick hank and
scratching her scalp with a blank look. She is smiling. Her hair
is falling in a mess on all sides, waving around her hips. She
beams her icy smile over the hypnotized spectators.

"Ay! I want to make love!"
The marines leap forward and surround her.

❋

❋  ❋

Horns are yelping in the night. The firecrackers have almost stopped, but the Rara drums are going into maniacal fits in the distance. From time to time, more taxis come into the courtyard of the Sensation Bar, with its glaring lights. In staggering, bellowing bunches, the marines are invading the hall.

"Whoopee!"

The record player is howling "Gonna Take a Sentimental Journey." At the bar, a dozen clients sitting on the high stools are pumping rum with shaved ice and soda, Coke, or Canada Dry. The regulars are lost in the crowd of marines. El Caucho is there, wearing his fine white *guayabera* and light trousers of mauve-rose color. This noon, as he left the bordello, he went to eat lunch in a little restaurant on the Rue des Veuves; then he walked around. He jumped on a pickup headed for Léogane. He didn't want to follow the Rara processions and stopped at the road to Mahotières. There, he bathed in the river and took a siesta on the pebbled bank. When he got back to Port-au-Prince, he went back to his landlady's place and read for a little while. A difficult book. Published by a man with a funny name—Unamuno—who writes strange things. He didn't understand one iota. He will go back to the text as many times as necessary in order to understand what the guy was trying to say. He reread Nicolás Guillén's poem to the soldier. That's a poem, a real poem—alive with the existence of simple people. El Caucho likes stuff like that. A thinking worker must read, Jesús Menéndez told him one day. Since then, El Caucho has continued to read. He likes to read, but this evening, he told himself:

"I'm going to the movies!"

He got dressed and put on the white *guayabera*, which the landlady had ironed for him. That Cia is a *jouda*, a witch of an old gossip like nobody else—but for the business of ironing, she really knows how to do it. He hesitated between two trousers—

the khaki or the mauve pair. In the meanwhile, he went to have his shoes shined, and when he came back, he immediately grabbed the mauve trousers—an indeterminate hue between rose colored and blue, just like the human heart.

Why didn't he go to the Paramount Theater? They're showing a *serial, La Calavera,* and he wanted to see the next episode. That's a spine-tingling film. Of course, it wasn't that important to him. El Caucho is sitting at the counter in the Sensation Bar, the same place where he was this morning. He doesn't take his eyes off the mirror. Mario, the patron, is a bit out of sorts and has a bandage on his nose. Swaggering a bit, he's telling what happened:

"I go over to separate them right away. Then the big marine lets fly with a brass-knuckled fist right at my nose. He split one nostril open. If you had seen it! I didn't wait for the MPs. I wiped up with both of them. *No, sir!* None of that at Mario's! You could have picked them up with a coffee spoon!"

Mario turns to other clients as witnesses, points to his nose, and casts an angry glance at the marines sitting opposite him. El Caucho's forehead is lowered—it's his battering ram. El Caucho has barged in headfirst a number of times in his life. That's his weakness. A day comes when he's had it, and he takes action, something that can't be undone and that he'd never thought about before. You've got to think that it was simmering in his unconscious: the monkey never sleeps in front of the dog's door, says the proverb. In fact, El Caucho's impulsive acts have never sullied his honor as a worker—so he's not so crazy after all, this fellow. He is never comfortable near the marines. He stops frowning. It's crazy to get worked up because of them and to stay right there in their company. He could just leave. But he doesn't leave. He is watching the hall entrance.

From time to time Mario looks over at El Caucho. Exactly what does this guy want? He's very nice, but why does he stay at the bar like this, without getting drunk or fooling around with the girls? Clients like him who haven't come to the bordello looking for their ration of dreams or illusions always have some idea in the back of their heads. As long as there's no fight! Mario

stares at El Caucho's enormous biceps. Luz-Maria comes over
to sit at the bar. Luz-Maria is a tall beanpole with a coffee-cream
complexion. She has to be a good 5'9" with endless thighs and
big almond-shaped eyes—a girl built for love. Luz-Maria doesn't
think, she feels, she's alive—she's a fine animal who likes to purr
and loves to roll her eyes. She must be imitating La Rubia.

"Buy me a beer, *macho!*" she says to El Caucho.

She scratches his neck with crystal fingernails.

"*¡Déjame, puta!* Leave me alone, whore!"

Oh! It would be rough if he socked you! A man the way she
likes them! A *macho!* He doesn't mince words when he says
something. It comes out the way he feels it, and he's not likely
to be afraid of anything. She'd like a male like that for her *chulo*.
Even if he dusted you off from time to time—that must be great.
Luz-Maria hasn't had any luck for about two years—some kind
of bad luck sticks to her. And yet, she's a "guitar" who knows
the music. She's not bad. A handsome woman who knows her
trade, going through a bad period. No matter what she does—
whether she wears a *wari* seed in a gold setting, bunches religious metals on a chain, says novenas to Mary Magdalene, con-
sults Madame Pintel, or goes to see the hypnotists and sorcerers
—nothing works. Her bad luck won't go away. Luz-Maria is an
animal. She would like to get El Caucho to strike her. She
wouldn't flinch, and the next instant she would glue her lips to
his neck to give him a love bite. Maybe he'd be willing to be her
*chulo* after that? Luz-Maria is a bit tight-fisted, except with the
reigning *chulo*. She hasn't had a *chulo* for nearly two years. Bad
luck. . . . She rubs against El Caucho.

"Leave me alone, woman!"

El Caucho is grouchy and bends his head over his rum and
Coke.

"Give me a cigarette!" Luz-Maria asks El Caucho.

He doesn't answer. If you refuse money to Luz-Maria, the
drunkards say jokingly she will ask you to buy her a drink. If
you refuse, she'll go for a cigarette. If she still doesn't get anywhere, she'll ask for the time! She will pester you until you decide to give her what she wants: a good wallop! Luz-Maria is an

animal. She rubs her thighs gently against each other. "That's nice!" she keeps repeating. If she wanted to, she could go make love with any of the marines there, but she doesn't want to give pleasure for the moment—she wants someone to give her some. For two years, she hasn't had an official *chulo*. Bad luck. Luz-Maria caresses El Caucho's fingers on the bar. Mario chuckles; this game is relieving his bad mood. El Caucho raises his head, smiles at Mario, shrugs his shoulders, and lets Luz-Maria go on. She can keep on if she wants to. It doesn't make any difference to him. Luz-Maria gives Mario a spiteful look. When she's in one of those states, she is spiteful—she can be very mean. She can bite or try to scratch your eyes out. Mario is on the alert. Luz-Maria is an animal. But people are not fair! La Rubia is the one they're beginning to call *la loca,* the crazy woman! Oh, well! That's life! One of these days, the bad luck will go away, and Luz-Maria's rating on the whore market will go back up. She might become one of the queens of La Frontière since she's still young. That's the way the wheel of fortune turns. Luz-Maria should have a better life. She would stop being so mean. Luz-Maria sees that she's losing her time with El Caucho—he's a tough nut. She gets up and goes off to try her luck somewhere else. El Caucho straightens up and eyes the mirror.

A marine has just come back into the room through the back door. He is shamelessly buttoning his trousers. El Caucho doesn't take his eyes off that door. Some dancers are beginning to swing in the barroom. The marines are slapping their thighs and urging the couples to turn loose, to throw their arms and legs out as if they wanted to get rid of them:

"Hey, Ba-Ba-Re-Bop!"

Mario offers El Caucho a drink. He'd like to chat, but El Caucho isn't in a talkative mood. Mario can give up and stick his curiosity back in his pocket—nobody is more stubborn than El Caucho once he sets his mind to it. His eyes are glued to the mirror, but he seems to be staring into space. He takes sips, lapping a small piece of ice with his tongue each time—he savors the rum and Coke, then lets the piece of ice melt against his palate in a wave of absorbed freshness. The door opens slowly.

She's wearing a terrycloth robe and she's bare-footed. La Niña seems to be living in a nightmare. She is walking, her wide-open eyes are haggard, her face is livid. She walks through the barroom like a sleepwalker, reaches the gallery, and sits down at a table, opposite the bar, her arms dangling.

❊

❊  ❊

"Tell La Niña that she should go get dressed. She can't stay there like that. The customers don't like that."

François, the waiter, takes Mario's stare for several seconds.

"Go tell her yourself, boss! Why are you sending me? Didn't you see La Niña's face?"

Mario shrugs and lowers his head with a furrowed forehead. He goes over to the adding machine and, with one finger, slowly taps the keys to add up the bill of a customer who is about to leave. The adding machine clacks away. What a time for this to happen? Just as a bunch of customers are invading the bar! For the moment, nobody can speak to La Niña. Mario's hand is like a huge spider crawling over the adding machine keys. Nobody can go speak to La Niña—you have to leave her alone. Why did she do this today? How many marines were on her belly today? Why did she do that? She hasn't left her room since 1 o'clock this afternoon and now it's 9 o'clock at night. The adding machine jams—Mario removes his fingers and squints. There's nothing to be said; La Niña did her work, but why is she acting this way? She made love until she was ready to die! She's always ready to let out a moan, and she doesn't usually mind her obligations toward the clientele! La Niña has never had a *chulo*. The people who live close to her all know that love doesn't interest La Niña. She has never loved anybody. She makes love for money, and she always puts it aside, of course, but she doesn't seem to put too much stock in it. La Niña can't be unhappy. Why would she be? Hell! Why is she acting like that?

La Niña is slumped on the table, breathing hard, and she seems to be looking without seeing—she is dead. At the bar, El Caucho is petrified. Between his fingers, he's still holding the glass he was about to put to his lips, but he stops. He is frozen, can't budge. El Caucho has never felt such pain in his life. It's terrible to see that face. Not even the marines can stare at that face. Those who go by take a quick glance and move on or turn away a bit. La Niña's appearance hits you in the gut. Each feature is in place—just as it was this morning, but there's something worse than death in the expression on that maw. Her mouth is half open, and that little gold filling is sparkling on her teeth, like a fly on a scrap. The mouth is lifeless, with less expression than that of a cadaver. The corners aren't drooping, the lips aren't hanging—there's no frozen grin, grimace, smile—only the stupid shape of the mouth. Here's what La Niña really is, seen from the inside—here's what her soul has become. And they say the soul is immortal! La Niña is at dead center in her cardinal contradictions: she feels neither love or hate, for anything—just stupidity, complete indifference, an indifference and stupefaction that was never displayed or painted by any Watteau in the world. La Niña is at dead center between past and future; she has no history, no future, she is at the critical point in Time—the present isn't even flowing; maybe it doesn't exist. La Niña is suspended at an equal distance between sensation and image, she is crucified between perception and thought . . . she is floating. La Niña isn't even dead—that good fortune isn't hers. Her mouth quivers slightly, but her lips are moist, red algae or sargassum—just a shred of flesh. El Caucho knows the human mouth. The human mouth is the primary organ of thought, the one that produces speech. The human mouth is a marvel because it is the link between that chanting mass of galley slaves. There are all sorts of mouths. El Caucho sorts through the human mouths he recalls. He picks them out with his visual tweezers and places them over La Niña's mouth. Not one fits! That mouth is unlike any other in the world! El Caucho is sure now that he has known or will know that same living mouth in the rush of days and nights, in his dreams or his imagination.

There's the curve of her chin, her cheeks and her temples, the ellipsis—the mystery of La Niña Estrellita. At least ten curving lines fight with each other to define the shape of her face; that's because La Niña Estrellita doesn't really exist in space. She is material, sure, since men simply pay for pawing her, and yet nobody can define the working sketch of her face or her true contours. Just as she eludes analysis by the eyes, the most skillful of hands cannot discover or define her shape. El Caucho is holding his glass between his two palms, and his eyes are fixed on the mirror. He is caught between two sensations—the one gathered through his eyes and the other felt by his hands squeezing the glass to the breaking point. You might take one of the ovals of La Niña Estrellita's face for that of a sorceress, another for that of a Madonna or still for the purity of a young girl. You could find another ten ovals—one could be that of a bird in a dream, another could be a mask of torture, still another is that of the hard-boiled egg of everybody's bad conscience, another the arc of life, and that final and most vibrating loop, which is the swing of our daily wear: Death. Suddenly El Caucho stops. He thinks he's got the true ellipsis of that face in the palms squeezing the glass to the point of breaking it, but it slips away instantly. It flew away and lit on the chin, cheeks, and temples of La Niña Estrellita! Well, El Caucho, what are these jokes? You're not going off your rocker by any chance? That would be the last straw! You've had all kinds of adventures—hunger, thirst, solitude, imprisonment, exile, fights, the land of Absurdity, death breathing on your forehead several times—getting a taste of insanity is all that remains! You are trying to read books that are too complex, too clever for your brain. That's it, you're going off the deep end! El Caucho shakes his head in an abrupt gesture:

"Boss? Have a drink with me?"

El Caucho answers the boss in monosyllables and can't keep from looking toward the mirror. After all, the human cranium is a rugby ball, or more precisely, a sort of football that the Detroit *Giants* go after and grab away from the Dallas *Bobby Soxers*. And in that bullfight, every individual is a hammer; each one fights his opposite with his head! You get the picture?

"So, you work at the shipyard? Mechanic—that's a good trade!"

*Sight*

Mario squints and bends his head backward. Right, there's no longer any doubt—he has been a worker. If he had managed to become a mechanic, maybe he wouldn't have been either a spy or a police informant, and he wouldn't have ended up in the skin of a bordello owner! Mario is squinting. He can see himself once more. Twenty years and fire on his cheeks. Thirty years, three wrinkles on his forehead. Forty—disgust and fatigue. El Caucho is moving his lips, speaking to Mario, but he doesn't take his eyes off La Niña's face. He sees her jutting cheeks, at once a pitiful little creature blown by the winds of her dreams, a pirate flag on the top yard of her shoulders, a Venetian lantern in which a little chimera is flickering, a viscous medusa in the ambivalent sea of the bordello lamps. He can see the spiral shells of the ears, the nose, which is a hardy little jib still pushing through the blows and degradation that splatter Estrellita's pristine beauty with mud: leper, sorceress, madonna, adolescent, grasshopper, soap bubble, a wisp of straw, foam, life's vomit—all at the same time!

"So does it pay well—the shipyard?"

El Caucho doesn't answer because a strange saraband has suddenly begun to dance through his head. Shapes and images are leaping, crossing, recrossing, crossing between each other, and scrolling down the screen of his memory. The true shape of La Niña Estrellita's face has just appeared and is projected on the surface of his memory. A mouth is rising from an abyss and taking the place of the working sketch; the slender prow of a nose is emerging in turn and settling in the middle of the oval; two Venetian lanterns with little chimeras light the cheeks; the coal on two eyebrows is slowly rising from the ship's hold and accenting the sockets with a black line; and, finally, between the rays of the eyelashes two true roses are taking shape, the fresh roses of two eyes barely blooming, settling in their notches. In the flicker of an eyelid, the drowning woman has come back to the surface. Barely finished, the working sketch is disappearing, flying off—the innumerable mouths and eyes, the ophidian lines twisting and struggling, constantly negating each other among all the browns, ochers, golden yellows, and the honeys of

Caribbean faces. On the surface of the lake, there are still a few ripples, circles moving off to infinity. In the mirror, there is nothing more facing El Caucho but the stupid mask that nobody can bear to look at, that only he can stand. The face of the Sensation Bar's La Niña Estrellita is there—real, absurd, at the dead center of its contradictions.

*
* *

Smoke, sparks, dark curtains pass in front of La Niña's wide-open eyes. La Niña is haggard, stupefied, stupid, stultified, but she can see. She sees El Caucho's tense face in the mirror. A face that is nearly round, full of curves, beefy, thick, coffee-cream color. La Niña stares without blinking—she is anesthetized, paralyzed. Her pupils focus relentlessly on the man. His chin is round, firm, and imperious with little spikes of hard beard, those exuberant hairs that grow back the minute the razor has mowed them. That's vitality, life. Beneath his lower lip, just in the middle, a little cone of bluish hair is growing. Framed by two deep wrinkles that form the jutting part of the cheeks; his mouth is violet, moderate in size, a little thick, fleshy-lipped, voluptuous, topped by a short, bushy mustache like barbed wire. This mustache is a good half-inch wide, regular clear across, square at the corners of the mouth. The mustache goes straight along the lip, turns up slightly, and disappears for a quarter-inch, only to reappear and go back down to the other corner. His nose is round, shiny, jutting out with thick nostrils; it climbs a short distance only to spread abruptly into two slightly curving arches under the eyebrows. His brows are bushy and covered with the some coarse, lustrous hair; the two sides almost meet over the emerging nose. His eyes are profoundly set in their sockets, surrounded by a dark halo; they are large and round, with a filigree of veins, and are protected by heavy, wrinkled eyelids. His forehead is low and crossed by three deep wrinkles. His hair is frizzled but shiny; it comes down to his ears with thick, close-cropped sideburns. His skull is rather flat, in spite of the round cap of hair. Short ears, wide and flat, are attached to his mastoids. La Niña Estrellita stares at the man. She is lost in a fog, and yet she sees through the smoke, sparks, and dark curtains that obscure her view. His image is ingrained in her. No thought crosses her mind, she hears nothing, she feels nothing, but she sees that face. It stands out, well lit, in the center of the chiaroscuro that absorbs everything else. La Niña can feel the blood coursing through her temples in little spurts. She hears a low, muffled, pulsing din in her ears, confounding any perception other than that of the man's face. La Niña's mouth is dry, alkaline; heat flows from her frontal sinus down into the throat. Her nerves alternately tingle and quiet down. Haggard and confused, she doesn't take her eyes off the man.

Now, another face is superposed on that of the one she's looking at. A smaller face, a similarly shaped skull, with smaller cheeks and no mustache. The phantom image vanishes, replaced by another. The chin is wrinkled, the cheeks are faded and worn, the hair is growing thin and graying. God! How the man has aged! Here he is, instantly youthful again, cheeks gone, vibrant eyes, smiling mouth. What's this? Two virtual images play around the actual vision. Past and future are dancing with the present. La Niña is haggard, completely unconscious, stupid. The hopscotch of three faces continues for some minutes although her eyes are wide open. La Niña comprehends nothing. She gets up, supporting herself on the railing, and goes forward. She goes down the steps of the platform. All eyes are fixed on the terry cloth robe. The inebriated but shapely figure goes down the steps and her honeyed bare feet step on the white stones. Mario takes a breath.

✻<br>✻  ✻

A short while later, there is a terrible to-do in the courtyard, a sort of mix of shouts and angry voices, the barking of the pack and hunting horns. The waiters, several marines, and all the women run out. The hubbub of shouting and strident howls, calls, and swearing becomes a cacophony that continues for long minutes. The record player is bellowing a *canción cubana* at full volume. The black and red voice of Celia Cruz breaks out, wavering with guttural tones, and lowers again in fierce glissandos. A waiter comes in. Mario looks at him with anxious eyes.

"It's La Niña and Luz-Maria. They ran into each other in the courtyard. Luz apparently pushed La Niña, who lit into her with a fury. They were rolling on the stones of the walk when we got there. La Niña was banging Luz's head on the pointed stones, and Luz was trying to bite her. La Niña would have killed Luz-Maria if we hadn't gotten there in time. Luz is bleeding a little on her mouth and the back of her neck. Her clothes are ripped, but nothing serious. La Niña headed toward the pool and locked herself in. She must be taking a bath now."

At this, Luz-Maria comes in, raging, with her dress in tatters, breathless. Two waiters and several of the women are with her, dragging her along. She disappears through the door at the back, toward the rooms. At the bar, El Caucho is still drinking. Here comes La Niña again, with wet hair plastered on the back of her neck and her temples. She comes up the steps with a steadier step, but still drunk. A silence falls over the room. La Niña walks through the gallery and heads for the bar. She leans over and slides behind the counter. Mario doesn't look at her but lowers his head over the clattering adding machine. The waiters also pretend not to notice that La Niña is there. But El Caucho looks at her without blinking. Her neck is marked by scratches, the stigmata of the fistfight. She grabs a bottle of gin, glues it to her lips, and drinks. She has swallowed over half the bottle! She digs around in a drawer and pulls out a big cigar. She bites and spits out the tip. La Niña gropes, looking for matches on the counter. Mario and the waiters pretend not to notice.

El Caucho pulls out his lighter, lights it and holds the flame out toward La Niña. The flame burns the cigar. La Niña's eyes are glued to El Caucho's. Each is drinking in the shape of the other's face. La Niña watches the slight wavering of El Caucho's neck. El Caucho is looking into the withered roses of La Niña's eyes. La Niña comes out from behind the bar. She heads toward the door at the back. Mario lets out a sigh of relief. The women in the room let go, they *siguen,* go back to dancing, throwing their hips, jumping, bending, flexing their knees, shaking their shoulders, and twirling their breasts. Opposite the women, the marines stumble in the congo-merengue that the hefty red and black voice of Celia Cruz is belting out:

> *Gede-zarenyen, woy! woy! woy!*
> *Gede-zarenyen, woy! woy! woy!*[*]

El Caucho leans over his rum and Coke. He watches the little bubbles shimmering and rushing upward, breaking the reddish brown surface of the drink. Work begins at 6 o'clock tomorrow. A coastguard ship is in dry dock. As long as the foreman doesn't come to give the guys a hard time!

---

[*]"Gede-zarenyen" is the Gede spider, a mischievous spirit in Vodou, sometimes associated with Vodou; *woy* = woe.

# SECOND MANSION

Smell

Does the earth gravitate? Does not all matter
attract all matter?
—Walt Whitman, "Children of Adam"

hhhh. . . ."

La Niña Estrellita stretches for a long time with her arms bent over her head, her armpits wide open, her biceps contracted, her fists clenched, her mouth puffed out by a cushion of air held between her gums and lip. She opens one eye, glimpses the image of the Virgin of the Pillar watching her from the wall. She closes the eyelid, scratches her belly, but immediately lifts the other eyelid, which unwrinkles, opens, and lets a glance filter through toward the alarm clock vibrating on the night table.

"Damn! Eleven o'clock!"

La Niña sits up quickly, puts her feet on the floor, stretches again, and then sticks her fingers into her mop of hair, clear to the scalp. The room is dark since two heavy drapes are covering the shuttered doors with two closed wooden slats. La Niña gets up and glances around the room.

"OK!"

She goes to the doors, pulls the drapes, and opens the slats. A burst of light! She repeats her gestures at the other door. The room is invaded by the sun. La Niña takes another look at the disorder in the room.

"OK!"

She draws closer to the mirror and twists without moving her feet to see her profile and then a three-quarter view. She strokes her hips with rapid gestures, then goes up her ribs, and lifts her breasts in her cupped hands. Abruptly, she withdraws her hands, releasing her breasts to the pull of gravity. No, they didn't fall. They trembled lightly and her nipples quivered ever so slightly. She brings her face close to the mirror and examines it closely.

"OK!"

La Niña puts on her housecoat and slippers, takes a scarf with a steady hand, rolls her hair in a ball, and then with a quick gesture knots the square cloth around her head. She takes a broom.

"*Desesperación. . . .*"

She begins humming and then whistling with gusto, right in tune and very loudly, just like a man. La Niña sweeps the floor energetically and picks up scattered objects to put them back in place. She is really in a good mood and has the energy to deal with anything; this is the paradox of a cyclical temperament! At times—most often—the upward swing is slow and takes place in spurts interrupted with hints of new depression: a peak, a slump, a peak, a slump—more or less abrupt ladders. Yesterday morning after her bath, she thought it was all over and that she would have a pretty good day—that it was a new period, the triumph of vitality over anguish and the void. Then, everything suddenly fell apart. It was a roller coaster day! If she did not bash her skull against a wall, slit her wrist with a razor, or take rat poison, she must be fated never to commit suicide. What the human animal can take! There has never been a time when her moods have been so extreme during a single day. Sure, she has had some bad moments, some dizzying crises, but her mood is usually pretty much the same for hours at a time, either on the dark side or the light side—why this sudden change then? Ah! She will certainly remember this Palm Sunday!

What a thick layer of dust has accumulated in the room during this past week since she had her *break down*. Once she sweeps, it's more or less clean anyway. She just has to put a few things away, straighten her wardrobe, and do a little wash. She only has one pair of stockings left. She will wash a couple of pairs of panties too. She hasn't worn any underwear for about ten days—she has gone around with just a dress covering her skin, unable to stand any brassiere or underpants. When she is in one of those dizzy phases, the feel of nylon on her skin is worse than static horse hair—it burns like a hair shirt! This afternoon, the tide of marines is going to swell and flood the bar again. They'll be arriving any time now. Like grasshoppers! She has to be ready. What can you do—it's the season! Another two or three days, and the fleet will weigh anchor. In fact, when she has her crises, she is tireless in bed; an automatic creamer! How much cash did she make yesterday, without counting what she filched from the pockets of guys who couldn't see straight any more! This season, she has to get as much as possible. That's the price of freedom, and La Niña has more chances than the others of escaping. People will say:

"La Niña? What? Didn't you know she retired? Yes, dearie, she managed—she quit the trade! Now she has her own business."

To the extent that a whore can manage to get away from La Frontière. . . . Few of the girls manage to forget the neighborhood, even when they have managed to put aside a little money. The scene of the crime! Those who leave usually come back sooner or later to set up their own bar or bordello: to exploit their pals, in other words. When you have spent years at La Frontière, no place in the world has the same atmosphere, and you get bored. You can't forget your former fellow prisoners. You can't create relationships with people who have never known "the life." You miss La Frontière with its noises, yells, rumors, dramas, gossip, colors, and frenzied rhythms. Besides, after years of nightlife, even the succession of day and night has a different meaning. When you retire, you usually have two alternatives: either find a *palgo* who falls in love with you and keeps you, or else settle down for good with a *chulo* and support him. As for La Niña, she has never had a *chulo*. She will never take one! The worst types of human beings at La Frontière are the *chulos*. Even if they were able to do it, these guys would never have the guts to become whores. The job could be too rough for them. The *chulo* is a useless person who has nothing but his little ruffian's mug, his thug's swagger—he's a piece of shit. She will never take one! Why would she? To make love? No way! For what they're worth! To have a brotherly friend? Maybe, if they were real men. Of course, they know better than anyone what a whore is, how she functions—her heart—but a *chulo* is a guy who loves no one but himself. What whore has ever found a brother in her *chulo*? Not a single one! A *chulo* can't even play a role—he's a puppet by his very nature. Occasionally a girl finds a master in her *chulo*, and if she stays with him, it's not because she's afraid of his blows—phooey!—it's simply so she won't find herself alone at the hour of truth, the time when white hair is showing. Of course, the women who retire to settle down for good with a *chulo* are stuck-up. Here's what they say:

"Félicien's my guy. We've known each other for ten years. He was a taxi driver, but I don't want him to work any longer. The bar is doing good business—why should Félicien work?"

It suits them to belong to just one man. In the final analysis, whores are not much different in this respect from legally supported women, the great hetaerae of bourgeois marriage. Duennas, dames, demimondaines or trollops, they are all bitches curled up at the feet of a man.

"Lie down," he says.

They drop down.

"Give me your paw," he says.

"Pull it back."

"Lick my boots."

And the females obey cheerfully! Those who think they can escape the social laws of gravity are stupid, crazy women! Each one is playing the game in the different jobs the bourgeois regime has created. In our time, who isn't a slut? And ahead of all the others, the women who think they are free! Free will? A pile of shit. Besides, as long as they eat their fill without complaints, there are many women happy to be the puppy dogs of the men who think they're masters. Nobody really belongs to anybody else. When the time comes, the moment of wrinkles and white hair, retired whores who are not really well off almost always lose the *chulo* for whom they have sacrificed everything. He inevitably goes off looking for a younger, richer, and cheerier woman. Sure, it's easy to laugh, but who can smile during the final days of a smirking life? No! La Niña Estrellita will never take a *chulo*. She will never have a man or a master. So, alone to the end?

*Smell*

"¿*Quién sabe?*"

Who can know? La Niña casts a final glance at the Virgin of the Pillar. She knows.

"¡*O mi Virgen del Pilar! ¡Ve aquí tu Niña Estrellita!*"

La Niña holds no bitterness this morning—she is simply speaking to the One who knows. How curious! This is the first time in a long while that she has thought so clearly about the future. Sure, she has her nest egg like all the other *manolitas*.

"Another ten or fifteen years, then . . . ," she tells herself.

So? Nothing ever follows that "then" in her view or in her mind. On that point, La Niña Estrellita is quite the opposite of the other girls. She has almost forgotten she had a life before becoming a whore. Nothing of her past remains; nothing ever resurges in her memory. She has never felt the irresistible urge that gnaws at most of the girls: the need to recount her life to a customer, more or less whimpering as she does. La Niña never cries about her past; everything has been erased forever: her childhood and adolescence. She no longer knows how she got here. It's strange! For the first time, she is thinking about something beside the present.

"¡*O mi Virgen del Pilar! ¡Aquí está tu niña!* O my Virgin of the Pillar! Here is your little girl!"

She will have to save a lot of money. Money, that's what she needs, not a man! She will do what other whores have never done; she will travel for fun. Sure! Yes! Travel! That's not so silly. Why didn't she ever think of that before? That would suit La Niña perfectly. She will travel to distant lands, contemplate colors never seen, listen to unknown music, learn about strange customs. One day, some fellow—not a joker—told about a distant land where people bump bellies against one another in order to say hello! She will see the land of the Chinese. They're funny, those people. She will also visit the Arabs and speak with the women who live among three hundred other women in the dwelling of one man. That must be a lot of fun! They must not work their coccyx very hard, those slippery eels! All that would suit La Niña! Of course, she would return to La Frontière once in a while to visit her former friends.

"I've just returned from the land of the Papuans," she will tell them.

Luz-Maria will make a face! Can't stand her, that hussy! But La Niña will need lots of bucks to do all that—lots of cash! She will get it. Isn't she La Niña Estrellita? She can earn as much as she wants. Two or three days somewhere and bang! Pack her bags! That's what she needs, to be like the birds.

My God! She has forgotten the birds! She runs, opens the shutters, and brings the cage into the room.

"Coo, coo, my little beauties!" They haven't suffered too much—there are still a few seeds in the cage, but they're thirsty . . . ! My God! They're thirsty! La Niña opens the cage, and the two little budgies escape, making quite a racket and to-do in the closed but sunny room. A fluttering of wings. They really are thirsty. There they are at the washbasin. They're drinking. Drink to your heart's content, my darlings! Whoosh! The blue budgie flies off and lights, with infernal chatter, on the head of the brass bed. Brrr! The yellow bird flies off and lands at the altar of the Virgin of the Pillar.

"Not there, my beauty! That's where the great Virgen del Pilar lives, you see?" La Niña Estrellita runs around the room following the birds. She waves her arms, hops, growls, threatens, yells, laughs, prances, and, at last, captures the birds. She holds the blue budgie in her right hand and the golden yellow one in the other. The curved beaks bite at her fingers.

"Hey! Don't be mean, sweeties!"

La Niña presses the budgies against her bosom. What a good feeling, that little trembling in the palm of your hands. That warm little shudder of life that palpitates, ruffles feathers, hums, stretches—it's like silk, wool, cotton, feathers, clouds, air, dreams! The continual chattering of the parrots fills the room. The golden yellow bird is more sensual, more seductive than the blue one. The yellow bird must be a male. Is there really such a thing as a male budgie? She bursts out laughing!

"OK!"

She puts the birds in their cage and hangs it above the washbasin. That way, they will stay cool.

*Smell*

She feels fresh and ready to go this morning. It's extraordinary. She is relaxed and rested—not a shadow of fatigue—and she is alive with a kind of joyful exuberance. What a paradoxical character she has! What vitality in her little carcass. It's crazy! She feels like a balloon this morning! At times, she is in free fall, tumbling dizzily—the little balloon feels as if it were dying as it touches the bottom of the abyss, the depths of bitter anguish. Is it lost? Has it foundered? No! It's a miracle! A little puff of wind. . . . The balloon rises up, it's floating upward, upward into the blue sky. La Niña Estrellita rises by her own strength, inexhaustible like the force that drives the seasons. There are only two opposite forces—heat and cold that vie with one another and, in the struggle, combine in different proportions to produce the seasons. Why do people claim that there are four seasons? There are only those variable mixtures of cold and heat! Why should there be twelve months? Why not thirteen or, still better, fourteen? Fourteen lunar months that could be divided into two rainbows of seven colors, seven colors of months shimmering around the two poles of heat and cold? Why should there be twenty-four hours in a day? Why not thirteen, fourteen hours, twice seven hours that could be organized into seven periods of different color, about the two poles of light and its opposite, darkness—day and its opposite, night? That's all of life! Life, unique in its duality, in its fundamental duplicity, in its two nuanced irises, seven colors that blend variously, become iridescent, combine chromatically about the two dominant extremes. La Niña Estrellita is at the bottom of the hole, at the pole of negativity, and at other moments she is suspended, at equal distance, between life and death—she floats between vitality and annihilation, neutral, yellowing, flatulent, gaseous, stupid. . . . And then, finally, she manages to reach the zenith of life, sparkling, exuberant, joyful—as she is today. La Niña's mood may have seven different colors grouped around each of her two tendencies, the negative and the positive. La Niña doesn't love anybody or anything; she doesn't hate anybody or anything; but she knows that love and hate exist and that there are seven colors on each side. Will La Niña love or hate somebody, more or less, one day? La Niña is true to herself, simple, credulous—she believes in the Unknowable, in obscure forces, in the subtle spirits of the air and the wind, in the larvae, spirits of the dead, the simulacra—she is superstitious, she knows that the Virgin of the Pillar is always watching her. On her left wrist, La Niña wears a very small bracelet with the seven Golden Numbers attached—1, 2, 3, 7, 9, 13. . . . La Niña believes in the Golden Numbers. Is that as stupid as it sounds? Why shouldn't there exist an aliquot in the Universe, a perfect divisor of the sum of nuances of all realities? The Golden Numbers may have some relationship to the fundamental law of the world, the movement that makes the unity and duality of the existent?

For the moment, La Niña is in an exuberant state. She is humming, straightening her wardrobe; in a little while, she will go to the pool to take her bath and dress, and, afterward, will quietly and unrebelliously return to her whore's work. Men will desire her, and she will lie on her back to make love after turning the face of the Virgin of the Pillar to the wall. She will stare at the ceiling during the process. If it's worthwhile, she will simulate hysterical ecstasy and the exalted looks on the images of Saint Theresa of Avila—she will mew libidinous words to please her customer, and that way she will get an option on his wallet. And yet, something has changed from now on in La Niña Estrellita's existence. It happened suddenly, so suddenly that she did not realize when, nor how, nor why it happened. The woman with no past and no future has a dream from now on. She plans on changing into a migratory bird. But, is that really what La Niña desires—tell us, O Virgin of the Pillar, you who are all-knowing.

As for El Caucho, this morning, things aren't so hot. Things are not going well. Along with other things, he arrived at work late, and that hardly ever happens. The foreman yelled at him, and El Caucho yelled back and made a ruckus, although he felt he was in the wrong. El Caucho doesn't like the foreman, and this morning, things are not going well.

*Smell*

"Rafaël Gutiérrez," said the foreman, "is this the time to be getting to work? Then you're going to tell your stories about union problems to the fellows. The white man knows that, and he isn't happy. Don't worry, he'll find out everything in the end! I've had enough of seeing you swagger and play at being Louis-Jean Beaugé in the shipyard. If you can't act like everybody and keep your mouth shut, you can get the hell out! I'm the foreman, understand?"

El Caucho looked at the foreman without a word, and then exploded. "Come over here a minute and we'll see who has the loudest mouth. Come on, stick your spy's mug out this way, if you've got something you know where . . . ! Take one step this way, and El Caucho . . . ! As for your *white 'merican*, bring him here, and I'll tell him a thing or two. You run around the shipyard with your ugly mug, you turn people in, but I'm the one who makes the engines run, and they really run! Which one of us can they replace more easily? Does *your* boss have any reproaches about *my* engines? All the rest is my own business! And if you're not happy about it, stick your mug over here if you want to know who El Caucho is! *¡Maricón!*"

The foreman turned around and raced off.

He won't say anything to the boss for the moment. First, because he knows that the white man really is happy with El Caucho's work. And then, you never know with a man like El Caucho! He's no choir boy—he's capable of anything when somebody pisses him off: for one eye he takes two, and the entire mouth for one tooth! But, after all, the foreman knows that El Caucho doesn't hold a grudge. As soon as he has cooled off a bit, maybe in a little while, El Caucho will come ask him why he was looking for him, man to man, right in front of everybody. El Caucho is a funny guy—right in front of everybody he may propose having a drink with the foreman, no matter how much of a *maricón, cabrón,* or fink he may be. El Caucho knows how to get along with the guys, even with finks. If the workers are involved in a fight or a strike, the foreman knows that El Caucho won't show any mercy if he can "get him"; but he also knows that, in spite of all, El Caucho thinks every human being is a person. When the foreman's mother was sick, El Caucho really went out of his way to find some money for him, even if he considered the foreman a fink. He moved heaven and earth to help the foreman save his mother. All that bothers the foreman, that floors him, and bastard that he is, it makes him stop to think. If El Caucho manages to organize a union, the white will be unhappy, and that will upset the foreman's little schemes. On the other hand, El Caucho has to be careful because he is known as a foreigner in the country since he's Cuban, but he can't go back to Cuba for the moment *because* of a political affair. However, the Fédération des Travailleurs Haïtiens isn't an organization to trifle with and neither the foreman nor the white man can kick El Caucho out without a good reason. In spite of reservations, the government has to deal with the workers' movement even as it puts as many impediments in the path of the workers as possible. At the Labor Office, the FTH and the workers' movement have managed to place a few of the right fellows who do what they can. In fact, President Estimé isn't a bad fellow—he's a patriot. Oh, he has his weaknesses. There are things he doesn't understand, and his policies are often wrong, but that skinny little man whose eyes cover his entire face is haunted by a vague idea of national grandeur—you have to grant that. There are some real contradictions in life! It's funny that people don't catch on! The workers' movement has had its say, up to present. The foreman knows all of that, but in spite of everything, El Caucho has to be careful not to go too far, since he's a foreigner and runs the risk of being expelled. If El Caucho stays at the shipyard long enough, there will surely be a union. The foreman knows that, but El Caucho bothers him. The foreman has never met a guy like him.

Things are not really going well for El Caucho this morning. Fiddling around with a diesel engine, he broke the only good monkey wrench he had. A pal lent him his own, but things can't go on that way for long. El Caucho doesn't want to give the foreman cause to complain by asking for another wrench today. He has to be on guard if he wants to succeed with the plan he's been thinking about for some time. If he makes a wrong move,

## Smell

El Caucho knows that the foreman won't miss his chance—he suspects that El Caucho would show no mercy if he got him into a corner during a fight among workers. That's the way it is. It's the law of worker action, and El Caucho has learned that tune— ever since he has become a wanderer, he has learned how to dance! If things aren't going right for El Caucho this morning— if he got to work late, if he clumsily let the foreman have it, if he broke his monkey wrench—that's all because, in his pocket, he has a little note that is gnawing away at his heart. People say that El Caucho is made of solid rock, that he can take any blow without flinching, but people who repeat that are looking at him from the outside. You can't always see deeply looking down from the surface. Things are not going well for El Caucho this morning. His guts are churning. And that has nothing to do with the few drinks he downed yesterday evening—it's deeper than that. He is really suffering deep inside. His legs aren't doing so well either—he doesn't feel them, as if they had been chopped off. His chest is burning like a red-hot iron, his throat is tense, and his head is buzzing like a hornet's nest, and yet there's not a tear in his eye. It's funny! All of this because in the pocket of his overalls there's a tiny piece of paper searing his heart!

Oh! There are just a few lines scribbled on the paper. It begins this way: "Manzanillo, 22 January 1948 . . ."

The paper traveled for three months in search of its addressee. On the envelope are these words: Señor Gutiérrez y Faria. . . . That's El Caucho. He knew nothing of this news, and yet it happened three months ago. He had not heard a thing. There is not a tear in his eyes, and yet the paper is burning his heart. That's it! They put bullet holes in him! And that news has reached El Caucho during Holy Week! You understand, that's a blow! Jesús is dead, assassinated at Manzanillo on 22 January 1948. . . . Is that impossible? El Caucho wishes it were impossible, but it's true: Jesús Menéndez has been assassinated. Who is Jesús Menéndez? If he were just a great politician and labor organizer, El Caucho would be sorry for his death, of course, but Jesús Menéndez was more than that. He was a man, a real man. Of course, like everybody else, El Caucho had seen this Jesús work miracles on the plains of Cuba as the sugar workers were yelling and running after him by the thousands.

"Jesús, Jesús!"

That is not the reason that things are not going well for Caucho this morning. More than anybody else, Jesús Menéndez had embodied true brotherhood for El Caucho, a friendship as vast as a river, a man who was at once hard and kind, a man who had taught him all he knew. This Jesús showed El Caucho how to love, how to feel a beating human heart, how to laugh, to fight, to stand up, to suffer, to study, to go beyond himself, to believe, to live, and to empathize with every living being. Jesús Menéndez did not raise El Caucho, but, in truth, he had taught him to see himself as he really was. That's a lot—to see yourself as you really are. It doesn't matter if you don't believe in much of anything, if you don't go to church, if you no longer know or can't murmur a prayer, it's still a real blow to learn right during Holy Week that Jesús has been killed, that he is actually dead. Things are not going well for El Caucho this morning.

While El Caucho had his nose in his diesel engine, trying to get it to purr, a fellow from the shipyard came up to him:

"Hey, El Caucho?"

". . . ."

"Hey, El Caucho, listen!"

"What? What's up? What does anybody want from me now? Oh, it's you, Occide? Well?"

"It's that, El Caucho . . ."

"What? Let it out! Speak, for God's sake. My work can't wait! Speak up!"

"El Caucho, my kid was born. . . ."

"Born? *¿Nacido?* Bravo! A boy or a girl?"

"A boy."

Occide bares his teeth in a naive, enthusiastic grin.

"That's great, man! But couldn't you have waited for a better time to tell me? Are you buying drinks?"

"That's not what I meant. That is . . . Sure, I'll buy you a drink if you want. But, I've come to ask you to be his godfather."

"Godfather? Go to church?"

"Would that bother you?"

"Why would that bother me, as long as the priest doesn't chase me out? In any case, you must have taken him to the church, so . . . But I don't know any prayers, and I won't make the sign of the cross."

"So, you don't want to? You won't accept being his godfather?"

"That depends. . . ."

". . . ."

"I'll accept on one condition."

"One condition?"

"Yes, I'll accept if I have the right to choose the little fellow's name. If not, go baptize him somewhere else and get another godfather!"

"If that's all!"

"Do you know the name I want to give him?"

"What is it, El Caucho?"

"It's not a name that's known here. He'll be called Jesús."

"Jesús?"

"That's right! Jesús! That's my condition!"

"Jesús? Like the good Lord? How can you think of that, El Caucho? People would make fun of him. You're not really thinking about that name are you, El Caucho? You're joking!"

"Your name is really Occide—why shouldn't he be called Jesús? Jesús, or I won't be the godfather!"

"Really? Jesús?"

"Jesús!"

"If you weren't a real man, El Caucho . . ."

"Yes or no? Jesús?"

"Well, sure. I'll explain it to my wife. Yes, of course, El Caucho, but . . ."

"OK, you can tell your wife that I am the godfather. Don't forget, Jesús! And you can tell our pals that as godfather, I'll pay for a round!"

Occide gave El Caucho a funny look. If El Caucho hadn't done this favor for him, a great favor . . . The only compensation is to become friends—friends for life. Jesús as a name—

what an idea! What will Fifine think? Anyway! Occide tells their pals that El Caucho is becoming a little crazy. You can't imagine. In Haiti, you don't call a boy Jesús. There are girls who are named Jésula, and boys who are baptized Dieudonné, Dieujuste, Dieuhomme, but not Jesús. These Cubans are really something! They're always going overboard! Anyway, since that's what he wants. In the long run, it may be OK—it will be a bit unusual, and then it will perhaps bring good luck to the little guy.

At noon, El Caucho doesn't go with the fellows for lunch at Madame Puñez's place as usual. Things are beginning to go a little better, but he still can't accept the idea that *they* assassinated Jesús Menéndez! Anyway! That's the way life is! He's going to have a godson called Jesús. And he will carry out his duty as a man exactly the way his friend would have wanted. El Caucho, an *hombre total,* a worthy son of the Cuban people and the fraternal Caribbean, a fellow whose feet tread the right path because he is oriented by a simple heart in keeping with the practical necessities and the laws of life. El Caucho hails a pickup and climbs in, but he gets out way ahead of the Portail de Léogane, close to the École Ménagère in Martissant. He walks along the water, looking out to the open sea. He is treading on ground that is sunny, hot, an island, but, still better, a Caribbean island, the sister island of sugar-covered Cuba. Cuba and Haiti—the Flower and the Pearl of the West Indies. At the time of José Martí and Antonio Maceo, this was where thousands of guys from his country came to catch their breath and heal their wounds as they waited for new flare-ups in the great struggle for Cuban freedom. Latin America, Pan-Americanism, freedom, and equality first took up their arms on this Haitian territory and developed here before swarming from the North to the South. Twenty sister republics were born. These Haitian guys—all the same! They're real fanatics! They managed to go fight at Savannah for North American independence—for the *white 'mericans,* the Yankees! For one hundred fifty years, and more, by the thousands the people of this country have been going out to fight all the battles of Latin America. They went clear to Missolonghi, in Greece, to fight! The Mexican general

## *Smell*

Mina and Miranda or Bolívar may have walked right on this spot. El Caucho is walking in the sand where their footprints have been swept away by the trade winds. People here are a lot like him. They are warm people with eyes that know the meaning of color, with musical hearts and a head that lives rhythms, with senses that blossom in love and a body that is always dancing. Problems here and at home are analogous, morals nearly reflect each other, and there are fiery surges of the soul. In the vicinity of Oriente, there are tens of thousands of Haitian workers who have taken root and brought something to Cuban music. Yes, he is at home here, and he even has some drops of blood from this land in his own veins—and yet, today, there is still a little something missing here.

You can't reproach a man for having his own village, his own home, right? But he knows that the great Caribbean Federation will be born one day. A few men with vision are dreaming about it already. A free federation of men of the same race, the same blood, the same heart, who have gone through the same hell, the same servitude, the same combats. Freedom will only be achieved on the day that all the great individuals of the Caribbean will have joined their energy together, in spite of differences resulting from insularity and history. So, El Caucho himself, a son of the Caribbean, is first of all a fellow from Cuba, just a flat island, with flowing red and green hair—the emerald of sugarcane and that uncertain blondness of tobacco: he longs for it at times. Too many mountains here! When will El Caucho be able to go of his own free will to give a big hello to Havana, Camagüey, or Cienfuegos? When will he have the opportunity to go search for the traces of blood left by his friend Jesús in the rich soil at Manzanillo? It's unbelievable, but today El Caucho is feeling homesick!

Sitting at the counter of the Sensation Bar, El Caucho is a limp rag in the hands of memory. To begin with, the language is not the same here: you don't hear the machine gun bursts of Cuban speech. You can't find the colors and the brilliance here, the taste of the air, with a measure of saltiness in the breeze, a vibrancy in the atmosphere, distinctive qualities of light, smells, sounds. . . . If they heard that El Caucho was homesick, the fellows would be surprised, and they would heckle him, slap him on the back, and have a great time. At times like that, a thump or some teasing is the best thing—it does you good and gets rid of your depression. That's the way a man is made, and the workers have a particular dislike for showing their sympathy in words. A worker's life is rough, and he has to learn to grit his teeth, to laugh in all situations. How could you stand it otherwise? Today, seated at the counter in the Sensation Bar, El Caucho is almost falling apart. He is really homesick. El Caucho? Of course! El Caucho is like the others. His arms are dangling, his face is expressionless, his nose droops in his rum and Coke— they call the drink "Cuba-Libre" in his country. On this day, anybody could see things aren't going well for El Caucho. And besides, he's not doing anything to hide it. El Caucho is incapable of not showing what he's feeling. He's not here, he's far away—a piece of paper is burning his heart from the depth of a grease-stained overall pocket. They've killed Jesús! Hearing about that during Holy Week is a real blow! A brother who guided your first steps on a worker's difficult path. . . . Above all, a man who was your friend. A man who liberated your head and your heart from all constraints, who taught you that each man must be true to himself and not molded after some ideal model. That was it—Jesús Menéndez, a man of water and corn, this Jesús who worked miracles on the plains of Cuba. In the bar, Mario watches El Caucho. Who is this fellow? What does he have in his guts? What's he looking for?

La Niña Estrellita is going to take a bath—La Niña's in good form this morning, she is! Mario saw that right away. Business is going to hop today! Mario makes a happy gesture to La Niña. She replies with a friendly little wave. Curious, La Niña draws closer. Mario speaks to La Niña.

"Well, *chica*, you want to talk to me?"

La Niña nods yes and is about to open her mouth when a waiter comes hurrying up.

"Boss! There's a police officer in the gallery. He wants to speak to you, boss."

Mario frowns and hurries away. What kind of trouble can happen to him now? What's this all about? What's going to slap him in the mug?

"Wait, *chica*—I'll go see who this officer is."

La Niña hovers around the man slumping on the bar. He appears to be wrapped up in a distant dream. He must not see her. A curious perfume emanates from him, or rather, a mixture of four odors: heavy oil, thick sweat, tobacco, and depression. The man doesn't seem to notice she's there. La Niña breathes in this perfume, she savors it, she drinks in the smells coming from the man slumped at the bar. A strange intoxication takes hold of La Niña. She sniffs the man and joyfully takes in the aroma with a hint of exhilaration. That's it! She is like a bird this morning! First of all, this human scent leaves a general impression of someone who has lived a lot, rambling around all over with his scars and bumps, picking up something of the mustiness from each country. Some of the habits of each place rub off on the man, and El Caucho has a bunch of habits. Sure, at this season, the aroma of the Caribbean takes over everybody. With the hot weather beginning, it's a kind of rough, heavy valerian, something dense, varied, resulting from all the angelicas carried by the breezes, a germinating earthy musk, that humid scent of the mountains close by and the fragrances of the burning-hot sea, moaning, salting and resalting the skin—iodine, chlorine, soda, and magnesium. Along with all those aromas, La Niña senses some bouquets that are more personal, more pronounced. There are fragrances of breakfast avocados and bananas, the pungent peppery smell of the sesame that spices the little cassava cakes you dunk in the sweet, boiling-hot coffee in the early morning. This man must be a gourmand—sensuous and tender. With a profound love of life, a naive and fraternal physical delight in whatever the good Lord offers him as daily sustenance. You have to search and imagine the odor in order to find it—it eludes La Niña Estrellita's nostrils. The man is not a big eater—he's

*In the Flicker of an Eyelid*

frugal, and his love of food is unpretentious. There is no hint of those spicy salted herring from which you make sandwiches that take away your breath, none of those really suave, aromatic fruits—custard apples, soursops, mamey sapotes, giant apricots, sapotes, sapodilla plums. Maybe there's a hint of the subtle acidity of morning *akasan*. Thanks to all that, La Niña can picture this man when he wakes up—his calmness, his energy. He probably eats what is set before him, or whatever he finds, without willfulness, without demand, and without anger. She can see the little bites he takes, his manner of chewing, with the hint of a smile at the corners of his mouth. The fresh aromas of banana, avocado, sesame, and *akasan* float through the air. It must be good to live beside a man who has that odor. La Niña immediately rebels against such an idea, stiffens, and moves back.

That tobacco aroma? It's . . . Why, it's . . . , Cuba? Of course, Cuba. La Niña lets herself float away once more with the sensation coming over her from all sides, rocking her gently on the shores of the Flower of the Antilles. Ah! That tobacco, the very soul of the Cuban people! He doesn't smoke cigars—he is a simple, heavy-set, tough man—cigars are not part of him. Once in a while, perhaps. Yes, she smells something that she had almost forgotten completely. This is a man who smokes Cuban Delicados. To smoke that harsh, rich, syrupy, black tobacco, which is at once so brazen and innocent, you have to be a real Cuban, an *auténtico,* and you have to love Cuba with all your being because you have known all its byways and hiding places, have grown up and played there, and have known all the opium dens of the island winds. This man is not simply attached to the Cuban earth; he lives it, loves it passionately and patriotically. Cubans of his age who smoke Delicados these days are rare— blond tobacco is in style. Men who prefer Delicados are not aimless creatures subject to transitory fashion, weathervanes swinging with the taste of the day—they are persons of great loyalty, men of tradition, nonconformists; they may change, of course, but they are attached to their personal truth, which they know to be relative although as valuable as anybody's principles. These are men who believe with all their strength, without asking anyone else. For the first time in many long years, La Niña Estrellita envisions faces and silhouettes from the past, the silhouettes of old Cubans, Cubans down to the marrow of their bones, peacefully smoking that tobacco of colonial Cuba on Sunday afternoons. She sees old Havana, the brick arches of the old city, the sculpted porches along the sea front, the old stones, the port edged with the long buildings of the Aduana Central, the customs office, the inlet of the ocean, the promontory, the old fort—the Castillo Moro, eaten away by moss, rust, saltpeter, and grass, with its old cannons. And that little street near the old building of the ministry of national education where the men play chess in the open air, letting their dreams, reflections, gambits, sacrifices, schemes, and calculations mature—the calculations of both life and game, enveloped in the smoke spirals of the little cigarettes that they have to relight time and again. The Delicados. Who is this stranger? Who is this in front of La Niña? He is certainly an enlightened man, one with quiet strength, with calmness and fidelity! For a long time she has not seen any man like that in the shady atmosphere of the Sensation Bar. She had almost forgotten that such men existed! So there are still a few men like him?

Haiti! How he has adapted to this country! You can't tell from the rum he is taking in small swallows now. Rum, of course—Haiti whose rum has no equal. Any man who knows the Caribbean well and has really penetrated its spirit also knows that a person who has not savored Haitian rum does not know its rainbow-hued bubbles—subtle, sensuous, radiant, memorable—the whole art of living that can be hidden in that rum. Those who drink rum with water can only understand this with great difficulty. A *long drink,* whatever it may be, always alters the nature of rum. Cuban Bacardi, Dominican cider, and other spirits made from sugarcane—Jamaican, Martinican, Puerto Rican—they're all good, but the rum of Haiti is the very spirit of this land of Anacaona, Toussaint Louverture, and Dessalines. And yet, the Haitian aura that La Niña notes about this man is not the odor of rum, but something simpler, something more rustic, something almost folkloric! This man has been polished in the secret arcanum of this land! What Haiti imposes in that discreet and impalpable whirlwind of currents is that good aroma of *kleren tranpe,* the *bwakochon, zodouvan,* that citronella and absinth of the working-class suburbs, still trembling with the fragrances of pure alcohol. You drink it standing, your pockets filled with roast peanuts and, along with it, a little five-centime cigar that is also soaked in alcohol. Only real Haitians, the legitimate sons of the people rooted in their native soil, can drink this alcohol. But El Caucho takes it in stride. Looking for all of life's nuances, all its rainbows and meanings, La Niña has also drunk this alcohol at times, in moments of bitterness—to lull her heart to sleep. And yet, this man is no drunkard; he doesn't give off that offensive odor, the old sock smell of habitual drunkards, that incredible vapor of the unthinking drinker. He has slowly and consciously tried to understand the land where he lives. What gift for love is hidden within this enigmatic stranger! You can still discover Haiti in the pleasant aroma of peanuts coming from his pockets. Whew! You can smell the little skins of the seeds that you roll between your fingers, a bit of the vegetable balm that sticks and lasts for a long time. Haiti is still in that aroma of deep-fried pork and the smell of sautéed plantains, and fried sweet potatoes. There's Haiti at play at the end of that swing of aromas: ground corn with peas, *akasan,* cassava, and fresh *mabi.* La Niña is lost in the fraternal cradle of all these aromas coming from the slumped, silent stranger.

The scent given off by his hair is something different. It comes from farther away, from countries that La Niña doesn't know—but from which she has recalled the unpleasant odors from innumerable men who have pawed her—men from Central America—Panama, Honduras, Costa Rica. . . . Central America. All the ships of the world go through the big canal. In Central America, Indian blood is always nearby, and hair, in spite of mixed blood, is always straight, stiff, and falling into the eyes of people working in the winds that blow in from the Caribbean or the Pacific; because of this, many people have to hold their hair down with hair creams. Other people follow their example;

the habit is taken up and becomes the norm for the region. Almost everybody arranges his hair with "stuff" like that. La Niña imagines this life that she's often heard about. Many men have come from all Central and South America—Venezuelans, Chileans, Jamaicans, Puerto Ricans, Guatemalans, Columbians— more than you can count. There are lots of Haitians also. In those countries, the hair oil has that penetrating odor of beef marrow, of oriental valerian, and lavender. So this man has traveled, he has lived the hard life of Central American migrants looking for work and their impossible daily bread. He must have worked at all sorts of jobs. What an accumulation of experience comes from the fragrance of his hair! What a tough, experienced man she has in front of her! Maybe even . . . Yes, she manages to pick out the vague hint of an aroma of petroleum, a little pungency in the cocktail of aromas that the man stuck to the bar gives off in his melancholy reverie. They say that men who have worked with petroleum can never completely rid themselves of that benzine odor for the rest of their lives. It clings to them like a racial musk. La Niña has had proof with passing Venezuelans whose nostalgia, despair, and solitude she has cuddled in that bitter bed of a whore contemplating human misery. This man may have worked in Venezuela. Unless that smell comes from his present work as a mechanic. No. Well. . . . This smell isn't fresh after all, but lingering and light. Perhaps Venezuela or Mexico. Almost certainly Mexico—you can tell that from other things, from that perfume of papaya, for example. In Mexico, they really like papayas; at meals, they eat them as hors d'oeuvres or dessert, in fruit salads, cut into little cubes and chilled, almost frozen, and enhanced with salty, syrupy alcohol: pulque, tequila, *cargador,* and still others! Papayas have a resin, a sort of persistent turpentine, misleading and heavy. Yes, he has lived in Mexico, that's almost certain since he likes papayas. Besides, you can also sense the gentle spiciness of all those Aztec meals. *Muy indígeno mejicano,* authentically Mexican. In what emanates from the man, there may also be some presence of the little islands that form the tail of the Caribbean kite, connecting it with the southern continent:

Aruba, Guadeloupe, Saint Lucia, Trinidad, and others. The Dutch Antilles, in particular. In fact, the soil there is barren and nourishes only sparse vegetation: they prize coconuts. Oh, yes! This man has left traces everywhere, traveling around the Central American Mediterranean. Seeking what illusion? Looking for what hidden treasure? Pursuing what mirage, fleeing from what nightmare, urged on by what drama, by what stubborn combat? The clinging stench, all that mustiness of flesh, tanned by life and calloused by his obscure struggle with the angel—and with demons, too—smoked by the stations of his own path to Calvary, the smells of death and continual embalming—all of this cradles the great peace that La Niña has found in her heart this morning. What is this man for whom she has become a gentle steel magnet and who attracts her as well? The breezes he trails from all those shores contain the mystery.

The sharp odor of heavy oil entices La Niña's nostrils. These fellows work hard for a living, they dirty their hands as they sing, they roll around on the ground, lying under engines that dump disgusting waste materials on them—blue, viscous, faded, nauseating. In order to live, they have to make love to the machine, slide under it, cling to its body, match their body with the vibrating mechanisms of the chassis's belly, marry its radiator, caress its bowels, make its guts rumble with their palpitating pistons, transmission belts, universal joints, gear teeth, and let its Dantesque axles tremble. The exhaust pipes fart in their faces, the storage batteries piss acid on their arms, the valves ejaculate their thick, black, greasy sperm on them, the condensers and boilers let fly their gases, vapors, and streams of boiling water. Their numb, calloused, cracked fingers are impregnated for life or death with the thick, carburized tars that are so thick and musky. That odor of the struggle for life, that odor of the struggle to set mechanisms into motion from which the least groans, the smallest coughs, will tease the ear lovingly, an odor of struggle for the man who has set out to conquer power and glory, that odor from the immemorial struggle of humanity through the ages resounds for the first time in La Niña Estrellita's nostrils like a triumphal fanfare, a barbarian, an interloper, but it is so beautiful she is moved. Every love has two faces, the head and the tail, the spiritual side in which we can participate and the physical side, the coupling. Love, every love, contains in itself the possibility of prostitution. The same goes for the feeling awakened by that odor. La Niña Estrellita can finally smell the odor of human sweat—the sweat celebrated in the Bible! That perfume has just overwhelmed her olfactory sense. Inwardly she dives to a depth in her life that she had thought lost forever in the hidden, bottomless abyss of her personality, which has been buried by prostitution. Sweat for misery, sweat for the hunger of children crouched at home, sweat for lurking illness, sweat for the cracked roof and the worn-out shoes, sweat to elicit a fragile smile on a disenchanted face! This stranger slumped against the bar has the very odor of life, the odor of the march of humanity seeking a less despairing, less ugly, more dignified life, the odor of all those Agnus Dei from the masses for the dead! And yet, what arouses the little prostitute's olfactory sense the most is that odor of depression and despondency coming from El Caucho today. You know, that sharp odor, that bitter odor, that ever so subtle but penetrating odor of anguished men? That odor that can be detected in advance and from a distance by the dogs when a man is about to die in the neighborhood, the odor that makes them howl for an entire night, the odor that is not one of approaching death but one of human flesh sweating from remorse and an eternal farewell. She clearly senses that aroma about El Caucho. How he's suffering! A brother? His father perhaps?

"Hey, man? Are you asleep?"

Mario has come back to the bar. El Caucho sits up abruptly and sees La Niña Estrellita in front of him, almost against him, looking him straight in the eye. He suddenly understands what bothered his sense of smell for the entire while he was lost in a cloud, agonizing at the bar. What time is it? Damn! His work!

"Boss! Quick! How much do I owe?"

Before the owner can answer, he throws a bill on the zinc counter and hurries out. But, at that very instant, La Niña Estrellita who is close enough to brush against him, exchanges a lingering glance with him, a look that is at once insistent and uneasy.

❋

❋ ❋

"Hey! El Caucho! Hey! El Caucho!"

You give yourself a slap on the cheek. Whack!

"Hey, El Caucho!"

But you feel you're going to fall back into a dream and won't wake up. That's what El Caucho was saying to himself at the Sensation Bar, revolting against death, dumbstruck, tensed, paralyzed, prostrate. And yet, he wasn't thinking any longer about his friend Jesús Menéndez, who had fallen beneath the bullets of some unconscious captain acting under orders on the plains of Manzanillo. What are we anyway?

*Un poquitín y todo se pone al morado, un chiquitín y todo gira al rosado,* at the snap of a finger, everything turns mauve; then, for no reason, it all turns rosy. At a *pulquería* in Oaxaca, an old Mexican had once told him about the hundred colors. Their *cargador* is fiery, it's good all through the isthmus of Tehuantepec, which is why the people of the region always appear to be dreaming with their eyes open. They dream as they walk, they dream when they smile, they dream when they are working. They don't suffer much from their timeless hunger, almost not at all—they are dreaming. That's all the result of *cargador*! What a crazy *cargador* he took this morning, what a blow, when he opened that letter! He's *groggy* from it!

Mentally, El Caucho gave himself another slap on the cheek, a hard one, but it still did not wake him up. Jesús is dead—life is a pile of shit: some beautiful colors, but the stench of a dead dog!

That's really it! And you can smell the stench of this dead-dog life everywhere. You can smell it particularly in this disgusting whorehouse, this Sensation Bar, where his feet have brought him once more. What you smell isn't immediately nauseous, no, it's an aroma of cologne, disguised as Caron's "Nuit de Noël" (Christmas night) or Machin's "Air embaumé" (balmy breeze), but it stinks! It reeks of the sweat of fifty human beings gathered in one small bottle. Shake well before using! A perfect sample of life's real smell! You can notice that repulsive aroma of men who never have time to wash because they can't stop copulating—they love nothing but their own nether parts! Dogs! It's certainly the odor of the captain who brought down Jesús Menéndez on the plain of Manzanillo! Even burrowing animals don't have it—the muck of the pigsty is more pristine; and the proof is that there are people who lovingly care for their swine. Yes! It's a stench of iodoform. It comes from a careful guy, a guy who smears himself with chemical stuff before and after doing the horizontal fox-trot. Slam-bang! On with the music! Only from a marine can you get that persistent odor, mixing with a breath of aging marjoram—that's the perfume of the marines' hair! Their mint chewing gum! Why does he remain alone in the bar? Because he doesn't have the courage to move, first of all— he's beat, knocked out, washed up, blah, slumped against the zinc bar. And then, it's because life stinks everywhere. The living are only vultures, human-feeding flies—each one eating the others. Yesterday, he did not notice how much the Sensation Bar reeked. It must have permeated the stools, the cracks in the metal surface, the cash box on the counter, the walls, the floor, the still air. And yet, what he smelled wasn't the old odors, the dead aromas—it's still alive, it moves, it's advancing, it breaks into and penetrates the nebula where it's cooped up. It smells of the whore, the whore who has made love all night, who has a mixed residue of male sperm on her skin—who has made love unrelentingly, all night. Shit! They've made holes in Jesús! It smells like the fetor of a man with dirty socks; it smells like the fellow with a denture or the chauffeur stuck in his car for the entire holy day or the gentleman who gets a massage with lineaments—the individual who has taken his medicine before his arrival, the breath of the person who has eaten garlic pickles, the dude who has taken a tour of the fancy restaurants, the young cock who has waxed his mustache with "Gomina!" It reeks of the parishioner who did not miss the "Hail" of the Holy Sacrament, the Christian who has been to the sacristy, the parrot whose fish dinner wasn't too fresh, the strange bird who has a head cold, the duck with new shoes, the guy who just taken his suit out of mothballs, the old geezer who has gone to soak his rheumatism in the sulfur springs, the poor fellow whose eczema is getting crusty. It smells of the ordinary man, the flashy fellow, the pilgrim, the Haitian peasant, the biped. . . . It stinks! It reeks of the archbishop! The archbishop? Absolutely, the archbishop! A world where guys like Jesús can be knifed can only stink of archbishops! Shit! Men aren't interchangeable; every fifty years nature can only produce one Shakespeare, one Mozart, one Beethoven, one Goya, one Napoleon, one Marx, one Pasteur, or one Einstein—no more! That's the equation of life! No solution has yet been found for that. A little problem for the certificate of primary studies a hundred years from now:

"In a small country like Cuba, how many years did it take for nature to produce a Jesús Menéndez?"

A little problem for the diploma of contemporary police aptitude:

"How many seconds are needed for the proper killing of a Jesús Menéndez?"

Shit! El Caucho had never noticed that whorehouses stink so much. As whorehouses go, the Sensation Bar has a lot to say. The *manolitas* stink! He hates the *manolitas*. The bodies of the *manolitas* can pass muster—it must be their souls that smell up the whorehouses that way! No, maybe not! The *manolitas* don't have a soul—they don't belong to the human race. Their soul escaped through that gaping hole! Shit on the *manolitas*!

In the nebula, in his rage, in his hatred of everything, El Caucho heard a voice he knew better than all the others murmuring in his ear. It broke the shell of his stupor:

"That's what I can't stand in you, El Caucho. You didn't respond to the fellow the way you should have. Sure, he's someone you have to look out for—who would deny that?—but he spoke to you nicely. You never know! That's what I don't like about you, El Caucho, your anger. When you're angry, you're not yourself—you cease being El Caucho at those moments and become just any guy, a "secretary," a member of the organization. Anger is beneficial only if it is cool, and even loving, in order to be simply revenge—that is, anger that's realistic and measured. This morning, before the strike, you should have tried to explain to me something about that poor bastard's soul, but as soon as the fight broke out—so long, no more El Caucho, nobody but the guy "responsible," the "secretary!" The secretary and El Caucho should always be a . . . man! They should not be separable! Don't be that way! Remain yourself!"

That's Jesús Menéndez's voice in El Caucho's ear, and it was at Matanzas, after the meeting where *they* fired at the sugar workers!

"Ah! My friend! You're not really dead, then, since you can still speak to me? After that, who could believe that real men like Jesús are mortal? The ones who became men because all men have the power of gods, the only ones. Nothing passionately alive can die completely, it is perpetuated, passed on, transmitted from generation to generation—it outdoes itself. So man is immortal, as is life."

El Caucho's anger dissipated like that! All that was left was a speck of anxious astonishment mixed with bitterness that would not go away for several days. And yet El Caucho knew that the greatest funeral oration over the tomb of a real man can only be a great burst of laughter, a Niagara of really joyful laughter, unreserved, triumphal, free of suffering and without boasting. As they carry their dead to the cemetery, the peasants on the Cul-de-Sac plateau often dance, swinging the cadaver, and sing:

> *M di kriye pa leve mò!*
> *Si kriye te leve mò,*
> *Ounsi-kanzo yo ta mouri leve!**

---

*A peasant funeral song:
"I say don't wake the dead!
If weeping woke the dead,
The *ounsi kanzo* would raise the dead."

*In the Flicker of an Eyelid*

I say crying doesn't wake the dead; if crying could wake the dead, all of us and the *ounsi kanzo* would die and then return to life! Yes, El Caucho, there is something that you should learn from the illiterate peasants—that's humanism, culture. Humanism, culture—you will find only one aspect in the poetry of Rubén Darío, in José Martí's essays, in Marx, in Tom Paine, in Toussaint Louverture, in Stalin, Jefferson, or Lincoln. Geniuses don't make humanism or culture, El Caucho; they find it in collective creation and, with genius, distill it from the life lived by the people, their only true mentors in thought and love. However great they may be, El Caucho, geniuses have their limits—the limits of their own time, the lacunae in their own education, the weaknesses of what they have inherited from the past, the blinders placed on them by the all-out struggles that destroy our fraternal humanity. It's neither you nor them, individually, that should be made responsible, El Caucho, but each one of us. Barbarism and animal nature are in each of us—why look for a scapegoat? Without any doubt, you didn't approve of certain aspects in the personality of your Jesús either, and yet you loved him, you loved him in spite of his weaknesses. We need a great deal of culture in order that we never lose sight of our qualities as we count our weaknesses. Our greatness is to know that we are weak, all of us, so that we can struggle more successfully against the dross in our nature. El Caucho, we have to reconstruct the human heart, continually, but more urgently today than ever. We need to do that, and we have to get to it without delay. In spite of all the savage struggles of the times, progress is taking place rapidly, too rapidly for the human heart today—it has practically remained what it was yesterday. The heart has to go on, even if it cannot manage to be the first on the rope going up the mountain. Don't pronounce your passion for one person, but don't heap Jupiterian anathema on that other person—give only what each person deserves. Each one contributes what he can—take what's worthwhile from everybody, El Caucho. Inhale that whore's smell, friend, and tell us what good is hidden there.

El Caucho could not come out of his cloud so easily. That's

*Smell*

not how you rebuild a heart. The crouching cat of life and death is cruel! In his nebula, he still heard voices coming at him from all sides. What do you want—El Caucho is what he is, a knight-errant of the twentieth century, a diamond in the rough, a kid, a child of the Caribbean. His revolt and his anger have subsided, and a melancholy reverie has taken their place—El Caucho breathed more deeply, and the odors he has smelled struck him fully. Around that bar, lost in the mist of the whores' perfumes, there was an odor of putrid dog, but also fleeting, timid, tender, and persistent emanations of an angel. It was the perfume of that candle that La Niña Estrellita had lit a while ago below the image of the Virgin of the Pillar. The virgin wax had melted in her palm. It was the slightly baroque but sylvan and joyful scent left by the parrot feathers on La Niña's fingers. It was the spicy laughter of the sesame seeds that she had let flow through her fingers into the bird cage: a vegetal laughter that delicately enveloped her hands. And, finally, it was the bitter aroma of ecchymosis from bruises made on her neck during the night. All that was depressing, an infinitely depressing odor. It was also the little spark of his rediscovered peace of mind, the breath that had remained pure, sweet, mentholated, her calm respiration. God! All of that around a whorehouse bar! Of course, there had been the multiple exhalations of rutting males—putrid dogs—and in the middle of that awful aroma, there was the virgin wax, the sylvan and joyful feather, the spicy, laughing sesame, and the sad, bitter ecchymosis—all wafted about, saying that the human heart is diverse and that everything belongs to it. The *manolitas'* souls stink, true, but they bud and attract at the same time. Their souls "have not fled through the gaping hole," the way you said, El Caucho. Truth is always double-edged, iridescent, varicolored, subtle. A voice pulled the sleepwalker out of his shadowy closed universe.

"Hey, man! Are you asleep?"

El Caucho had leapt to his feet in order not to get to work late. At the very minute when he was leaving, he understood that what had been affecting him were not the aromas endemic to the place. La Niña Estrellita had been there right by him during his whole station at the bar. She was the one! La Niña Estrellita was all that, all that pestilence of dead dogs, but also a final, precarious dying but an ever precious little melody of perfumes of despair. That is why the look that passed between them was true, honest, dignified, intimate, timid, frightened, perhaps uneasy, but respectful and full of concern.

❖

❖   ❖

Night is falling slowly with soothing freshness. The air is filled with dew, and the sunset has not faded on the nearby sea. The March trade wind filters in everywhere, refreshing the people. The afternoon has been rough for the whores at the Sensation Bar. They have been forced to push drinks, dance, and make love without rest. And yet, the marines' frenzied pleasure is calming down a bit. They landed several days ago, and besides the fact that their money is running out, they are beginning to tire, to look for calmer, less delirious activities in this port of call. They will go back to sea tomorrow evening and would like to take some souvenirs back in their bunk: a mahogany statuette, some shoes with tortoise-shell heels for the distant girlfriend, a sisal handbag for mother, seashell necklaces for little sisters. For themselves, they'll take the memory of their tour astride a donkey or their photo with a little black boy in their arms. As drunken, wild, and racist as they are, they're like that. The delirious raptus, libidinous frenzy, and even their mental cruelty—everything mixed with sparks of light, charming childish acts, and idealistic gestures. And those are the least of the strange aspects of the good-natured and generous people of the Star-Spangled Union.

A great beanpole with light chestnut hair and covered with freckles is having a tête-à-tête with La Niña Estrellita. He's a marine who was with the invasion forces of Admiral Caperton at the time of the American aggression against Haiti in 1915. He has lived in the country more than fifteen years and speaks a bit of Kreyòl. He speaks with a singing, hoarse voice that is both amusing and annoying. He's a veteran of the *Marine Corps* of that well-known general Vandegrift. The fellow keeps on talking:

"At the time, she was almost a little girl. She saved my life during the fight at Marchaterre. I had brought her back to Port-au-Prince with me, and then I left. No more news. Since I came back, I've been searching everywhere. I've asked . . . *Nothing.*"

"Are you that attracted by that little Negress?"

"*What? No!* She isn't a Negress! *She is black, yes.* She's black, very black, but she's not a Negress! *Understand? No?* I know those Negresses."

"What are you talking about? A very black Haitian woman who isn't a Negress? You're kind of loony, aren't you?"

"*She is not a nigger.* She's not a Negress, I tell you! She is completely black, Miracía, but she's no Negress! I'm from South Carolina, and I know Negresses, I tell you. If you knew what she did for me! She didn't just hide me, over fifteen years ago! She can't be a Negress, Miracía! *Understand?*"

"So, my dear, you're in love! Maybe without realizing it!"

"*No!*"

"Then why have you been trying to find her for fifteen years?"

" . . . "

"And if you could take her back to South Carolina, would you do it?"

"*No!* She's very black, I tell you! They'd take her for a Negress!"

"And she's not a Negress?"

"*No!*"

"And you love her?"

"*Yes.* I have never found another woman like her! Miracía. She's no common woman. *Understand?*"

"And you don't like Negroes?"

"*No!*"

"And you come here telling that to me, La Niña? Haven't you taken a look at me? I don't know what keeps me from giving you a couple of slaps! And I bet that *monsieur* has already taken part in a bunch of lynchings of *niggers,* as you call them?"

"*I was born in South Carolina.* We can't love you Negroes. *But . . . But she wasn't really a nigger. I know niggers.*"

"But you *gringos* are completely loony! A loony nation—that's what you are! You don't love her, and here, after fifteen years, you're still dreaming about her, and you don't want to take her back home! She's very black, but she's not a Negress! What the devil have you got in that noggin?"

"Miracía's no ordinary woman. I will find her. *Help me.* Help me find her . . . and I'll give you a wad of dollars."

"Oh, pet! Are you going to leave me alone? Go look for a priest to make your confession, go to the police, go get fucked, but don't count on La Niña to play the detective. Besides, you bore me with your stories! You make my tits ache. Give me a cigarette, honey!"

La Niña is thinking about other things, in fact. She doesn't take her eyes off the porch. Something tells her that man is coming back this evening. Her heart is beating, and she's on the lookout. Pretty soon, she'll have to go to the room with her marine, and she might miss that man. See him. . . . If she can just see him, she'll be off to turn her trick. Her curiosity is natural. She's got a right, doesn't she? That fellow intrigues her, that's all. She is sure that he will come this evening. She doesn't want to miss him. La Niña gets up. . . .

"Wait, love. I'm going to take a bath."

"*Oh? You'll come back? It's true? You . . . come back?*"

"Listen, *gringo.* La Niña doesn't like for people to tease her! I'm going to take a bath, and neither you nor anybody else can stop me. You'll have time to drone on! I don't like to be pushed around! Hands off! And you're nice, in spite of all that. A little later, love!"

La Niña leaps up like a lamb and bounds through the room to run and grab what she needs for cleaning up.

❄
❄  ❄

La Niña is getting dressed. She'll put on her dove-colored silk dress, a sleeveless sheath—she'll wear it without jewelry over her bare body—it will make a supple autumn vine of her. She will twist her hair into one braid and tie it with red wool pompons that she snitched from a passing Mexican. On her right hip, she will pin the beautiful dark red rose she bought just last week. She won't wear high heels this evening, but she'll put on La Rubia's gold leather sandals. La Rubia wears exactly the same size she does. There you are, just a touch of mascara on her eyebrows, that's all—she won't wear makeup. She will let the burnt honey of her skin radiate like a soft, peaceful full moon. She would like for her rosy eyes to be smooth this evening, fresh—they should simply sparkle with the cool evening breeze that animates them. Her little jib of a nose is joyous and pure; her nearly violet curls can follow their natural curve. That's what she wants. This evening, she would like to be naked, clean, unadorned, without artifice, not a drop of perfume or a touch of lipstick. She would like to be a real *niña*. But can she still be a real *niña*? Her heart is beating this evening. La Niña, you are beginning to age and become soft. She smiles at her heart. In fact, she knows a lot about this man now. It's as if everything had been transcribed in a little notebook. First off, he's a man who has traveled a lot, for reasons she doesn't know, a man who has sailed all around Central America. A tough man who has worked at all sorts of trades, suffered, struggled, who passionately loves his work and the struggle, a son of the Caribbean. He has adapted to Haiti extraordinarily well, as has La Niña herself, assimilating the specific tastes of this people whose essence he has intuited. At the same time, he has remained a real Cuban, an *auténtico*. His love for Cuba goes beyond reason; he is faithful to her traditions and jealous of her. So, why doesn't he return to Cuba? It's strange. . . . At present, he is a mechanic. He sweats to earn his living, work that must be hard, but he loves it and does it with a kind of passion and idealism. His well-built body says that he is intuitive, sure of himself, and a straight shooter. His face is peaceful, but he is strong-willed, passionate—a being with a serene strength, knowledge, calmness, and faithfulness. The movements of his hand show that he is open, frank, fraternal, a bit mischievous, maybe a tease. He must like to dance—of course he dances well, like a cat, effortlessly, supplely, but he must improvise with a sense of fun—a dreamer, cuddlesome, sensuous, very sensuous. He has the tastes of a frugal man—he's not difficult, he likes good food, he's tender, naive, participating in everything that is alive. He has two superimposed facades in his rounded face. A young face, and then an older one, both enigmatic and impenetrable—idiot! What's she going off imagining now? She also knows that it would be good to live at his side, in the shadow of his strength, his experience, his courage, his sensuousness, his tenderness, and his camaraderie. That's a crazy thought, of course, but she can't get rid of it. In any case, he suffered a lot today, almost certainly because of some bad news, something serious. Perhaps there was a death. . . .

Why has she scrutinized the man this way? Where did she get her inquisitorial talents? What demon is motivating her? Isn't she La Niña Estrellita, a whore who, to her dying day, will remain solitary, friendless, without love or anybody close to her? So there's no more promise in her life? What does this man's mystery mean to her? Or is this need to understand something deep in her own being? This is new—nothing has ever intrigued her like this. It's a bit scary. A cloud has come over her joy. She knows that the man is going to come back in a while, *without fail*. She will immediately be in the grips of curiosity, irresistibly drawn toward him. She is afraid of this man! Yes, she's afraid, afraid of herself as much as she is of him. In a word, her life has been devoid of any drama until now—what's she doing, going off trying to complicate her petty, neurasthenic existence! Maybe it's nothing but sexual appetite, desire, hunger, vertigo? But what about her deadened senses, quite atrophied, dead forever? It can't be anything other than sexual desire—there's no other possible explanation. In that case, this man has to possess her, and quickly! She will tell him, but first she will have to make clear to him that she doesn't want his money. She wouldn't be free otherwise. This man must take her, at least five, ten times in a row, so that her senses recognize the stupidity of their desire. As soon as he has made love to her, she will become La Niña Estrellita again—the same indifferent little whore, as egotistical, selfish, and self-serving as before. She's only a whore, a girl who, with her vagina, earns the money she needs to continue her vegetative life during her old age. Nothing but money has any value for her—the rest is a pile of shit! But she won't take any money this time.

"¡O mi Virgen del Pilar! ¡Libra tu Niña Estrellita! Free your Niña Estrellita!"

And what if this man refuses to sleep with her? No man has ever spurned La Niña Estrellita—she can have any of them she wants. It makes her crazy to think that somebody might spurn her! But, in spite of everything, what if this man is the first to refuse La Niña Estrellita? Whenever one of the girls comes close to him, his face becomes impenetrable. But he won't push La Niña away. And didn't he give her a long, troubled look at noon? If he refuses, she will never get rid of those thoughts—he will haunt her forever. And what if she's not free of all that even after he has slept with her? What if, in spite of the certain, inevitable lack of satisfaction, the attraction is still there? There's a certain danger in making love with this man! She shouldn't go to bed with this enigmatic and withdrawn stranger!

"¡O mi Virgen del Pilar! ¡Ayuda a tu niña! ¿Qué hacer, mamita mía?" O Virgin, help your daughter! What shall I do, little Mama?"

And what if her senses should come back to life when she makes love to this fellow? That thought penetrates her like a stab from a dagger. She stops dead, speechless at the mirror in front of which she is combing her hair. Yeah, what if her senses come back to life in his arms? She begins trembling, her heart is beating fast and irregularly, her breasts quivering. All of a sudden, she lets go of the blue mass of hair and runs to the Virgin's prayer altar.

As she lit the candle now burning in front of the altar consecrated to the Madonna with the kindly eyes, she burnt herself slightly. She calms down a little, a hesitant smile appearing on her lips. In spite of everything, she is more sure of herself today—she doesn't show the least shadow of anxiety. She is

*In the Flicker of an Eyelid*

breathing easily. Why should she keep trying to torment herself? Her hair has fallen clear down to the fold of her crotch. Her hair is her greatest treasure. She twists the long, red-wool cord with its pompons around her bundle of hair, braided in a single long skein and throws it over her left shoulder. Twisting the cord, she makes diamonds in the long rope that strikes her hips. This is what Mexican women do. She saw it in an engraving. She knots the red pompons at the end of the long rope of hair and looks at herself in the mirror. With both hands, she smooths the sheath of dove-colored silk she's wearing over her hips. It's alright. She is supplely encased by her garment. She pins the red-velvet rose on her right hip and looks into the mirror once more. She smiles.

Her heart is really beating. That's it. She picks up her eyeliner and, there!—with a line, she darkens a brow. Then the other one. Good! She turns this way and that before the mirror. The dress shapes her figure. The black rope of hair lined with red swings over her hips. La Rubia's gold leather sandals cover her bare feet. She stops in midstride in front of the mirror, with her body in a three-quarters pose, her left leg bent with toes pointed downward. Her skin is fresh, cleansed, scrubbed with laundry soap. She is the way she wants to be this evening—clean, satin smooth, uncluttered, unadorned, without makeup, not a drop of perfume, naked beneath her fitted sheath of dove-colored silk—a real *niña*. Her heart is beating hard, but she smiles. With a decisive step, she heads for the door.

❋<br>❋  ❋

As La Niña comes into the barroom, there is not a single free table—the Sensation Bar is full to overflowing. An old bolero is playing softly on the record player. Miguelito Valdez's voice is wandering in and out of its meanders:

> *Y entonces lo dije, madame,*
> *¿Quiere Usted conmigo bailar?*
> *Y aquel cuerpito lindo y sutil,*
> *Lo pudo estrechar con loca pasión*

## Smell

*Muy cerca de mí. . . .*
*Su boca perfumada al champagne*
*Se abrió para decir no sé qué. . . .**

With half open lips, La Niña breathes in softly and abruptly through her teeth. The man is at the bar with his face turned toward the hall, and he is watching her approach.

"*¡La Niña! ¡Acá!*—come here, La Niña!"

"La Niña Estrellita!"

Pushing away the admirers who are trying to get close to her, La Niña heads straight to the bar. She walks lithely with a stride that is made lighter by the flat-heeled sandals. She does not waver in her initial course—she is sailing a stubborn course—like a steamer headed night and day toward its destination—straight toward the bar where the man is watching her approach. He is freshly dressed, as he was yesterday evening, in his purple trousers and white *guayabera*. La Niña looks straight into El Caucho's eyes but, as she gets close, her eyelids blink in spite of everything. She veers several inches, pivots lightly and goes to lean on the counter, next to El Caucho.

She moves right away and goes to stand at his right. She hesitates. She goes back to his left, hovering about him, with her legs weakened and her lips closed. She has completely lost her head and pulls herself together once she has chosen her spot. She does not take her eyes off the big, yellow marigold in the buttonhole of the *guayabera*. Suddenly, the man's virile odor invades her. She can no longer speak; she can't breathe, inhaling this musk of masculine flesh in spite of herself. Any work odor, any remaining odor has disappeared from his body. He must

---

*And then I said, Madame,
Do you wish to dance with me?
And that pretty, slender body
Was able to press with crazy passion
Very close to me. . . .
Her champagne-perfumed mouth
Opened to say something I can't remember. . . .

have taken a long shower. There is a powerful aroma that makes La Niña inhale quickly, an aroma coming from his armpits, from the back of his neck, maybe even from his crotch. His harsh, balsamic scent irritates her nerves. That scent provokes a thought that paralyzes her with fear, almost making her legs buckle. She has to lean against the counter. She thinks to herself that she's breathing the scent of _her_ man. _Her_ man is right there! She has recognized his scent. That's it. A hot, blazing mixture—something like _madanmichel_ grass in the summer, roasted all-spice seeds, or the pollen of St. Johnswort that the wind generously carries along with the butterflies. It smells like Indian pistachio, the sandbox tree seeds that kids roast when in season in order to crack them, and also the _nè towo,_ which they roast and drown in hot sauce. La Niña's throat is dry, contracted, her breasts are alive again, her clitoris is palpitating inside her panties; senses that have been dead for so many long years have been electrified, brought back to life!

And yet, she simply came to say something simple to this man:

"Come! I want you! I want you to make love to me all night, but don't come back tomorrow. You mustn't ever return. Take me! Let it happen now!"

She is more and more confused, mired down in her very silence, and she can no longer articulate a single sound. Like an animal straining at its tether, she's turning around the stake that holds her prisoner—she sniffs at him, continually taking in that male scent, smelling it, sequestering it, inhaling it, snubbing it—she is wracked with chills and fever. Suddenly she leans forward and breathes in the yellow marigold he is wearing in his buttonhole. Then something frightening happens. A vast field covered with marigolds looms before La Niña's eyes, an unlimited expanse that is all green and golden yellow. The perfume of the marigolds is terrifying. Everything collapses inside her, she runs away, shoving away dancers engaged in their duties in the hall. Tears completely blur her vision, she runs away, blinded, in the grips of a raptus, panic, and sudden agoraphobia.

*Smell*

❧

❧ ❧

As soon as she approached, El Caucho was taken with the clear perfume emanating from La Niña. It was a little glimmer of sunlight breaking through the gray vapors over his calm, controlled, silent, proud grief. La Niña had lost that parasitical odor, and her own aroma could be sensed. A shiver of astonishment ran through his despondent mood; his melancholy withdrew, crouching down somewhere deep inside, becoming a simple kernel at the center of his embittered sensitivity.

It was a fresh hot burst of milk, a bit sour, humid, the aroma of life when you lie down on your back in a meadow with your face close to the earth in order to milk a goat and make the stream from her udder flow directly into your mouth. As the ruminant bleats with impatience and stamps her feet, little drops of milk wet your cheeks, your lips, and even fall into your nostrils. That's what this bucolic steam was, mixed with leaves, the musk of red ants, and the stirring breezes from the *madansara* going crazy in the morning foliage. How clean La Niña was! She seemed to be cleansed of all the dross, lustrous, shining, and satiny in her sheath of aged ivory and with her single tress over her shoulder, the red flower, her carbon-black eyebrows, and the astonishing rosiness of her unwrinkled eyes! She was a gourd, a running calabash, a little cucumber, some unknown green pea, a budding reed—a veritable, Saturday morning garden cocktail in the bustling neighborhood of Oriente, where she had been born.

Oriente! El Caucho's mind remained captive for a second at that word pinned on this little wavering twig. Oriente! Then everything became confused; the word vanished as abruptly as it had risen from the depths of his subconscious. El Caucho let himself go with the wave of heat coming from beneath La Niña's arms. Wavering, shivering with cold, fear, and weakness, she couldn't keep from turning around him. El Caucho then saw into the most secret spectrum of La Niña's being. That animal scent was a spiced counterpoint to the cinnamon, star anise, and sage—a powder to sniff with cornmeal, chili peppers, oil of bitter oranges, and nutmeg. All of this was tempered with an incense of discreet intimacy, the valerian aroma of her wet, aroused vagina, the pubic hairs salted with oozing and magnetic liquids. He was burning, too! Then, she ran away. . . .

❊
❊   ❊

La Niña went running into La Rubia's bedroom. She stopped right in front of the bed—a momentary stop. La Rubia is lying entirely naked on her bed—noble like a great hetaera whose buxom, beautiful feminine flesh is displayed on the white sheet among scattered pillows decorated with orange peels, scattered matches, picture magazines, and a disorderly packet of photos. On a chair close to the bed there is a thermos bottle and a cup of pungent coffee. Smoking a delicate little meerschaum pipe, La Rubia is surrounded by spirals and clouds, and she's naked, her nudity generously displayed. La Rubia is a woman in love with her own body. She likes to admire herself. She often remains this way in her room, in view of the large mirror on the wardrobe, downing cups of coffee, smoking, stirring the cinders of her memory, in a state of reverie, exalted, contemplative, motionless. Age is catching up with her. This queen of La Frontière seems to sense at each instant that the cells of her body are dying; her smile is twisted because of the stabbing daggers. She knows that her summer is ending imperceptibly and that her glory is fading. Nobody is yet fully aware of that, but she herself has a vague intimation from all the little signs. When all the drunkards say, "La Rubia," they pronounce it the same way they say "Venus Farnese." La Rubia's no fool. So, in her refuge, the famous Rubia grows sad because of ephemeral matters, time seeping away on her wristwatch, the past fading in slow motion, and the future turning gray. It's a vision of the sunset! When La Niña bursts in, La Rubia raises up on her elbows. A sudden flame appears in her green eyes, and a prolonged shiver runs through her entire body.

After the brief, frozen instant, La Niña falls to her knees at the side of the disorderly bed, crushed. She is choked with sobs.

*Smell*

"What have *they* done to my *niña*? Always those men? Mario? Yes, of course it's men! How they can make us suffer, make us cry! Come here! Come, my *niña,* come quickly—come close to me!"

La Rubia offers the invitation in a trembling voice when she pronounces the word, "Come!"—a sort of meow from a lovesick cat. La Rubia's eyes are shining with a somber glow— her rosy golden skin is covered with goose bumps, and her lower lip is quivering. She leans over, slipping her hands under La Niña's arms, pulling her close.

"You don't go after them, and they hurt you! As for me, I still go looking for them, and they hurt me. That's our cross!" says La Rubia.

La Niña is still sobbing wildly. La Rubia tries in vain to raise her chin.

"Sometimes I wonder whether it isn't the pain they pile on me, the wounds they inflict that I'm looking for—that I love. But, I love your gentleness, too, Niña. You haven't come here for a long time. So my caresses don't mean a thing to you, Niñita? Now they've lost their power to ease the anger, anguish, cuts, wounds, and stigmata men give you? Where could we find a little comfort if we couldn't find it with each other? I'm not jealous, you see. What is there for us besides 'that?' Ah! Me too, I need a little comfort today. Come on, let me do it, Niñita. You'll see how sweet, tender, cuddly, how good I can be for you!"

As she cuddles La Niña, La Rubia slips her hand up her calves, but the tight sheath won't let her go beyond the knees. Then La Rubia sits up as she continues to soothe La Niña and to softly caress her legs and, at the level of her buttocks, she tries to get hold of the zipper pull that forbids access to the body still shaking with sobs. She skillfully and steadily pulls the zipper up to the neck. The dress falls open. With insistent, gentle pressure, La Rubia makes La Niña roll onto her back, undresses her, and throws the dress over a chair. With impetuous eyes, La Rubia lays her hands on this wonderful doe's young body as she contemplates it. La Rubia places her mouth against La Niña's round breast and takes the nipple between her teeth. With her left hand, she caresses the soft inner side of her open thighs and the cerulean clitoris. Her left hand has taken hold of one burnt honey side, smoothing and pinching its curves.

"Tell me, Niñita? Doesn't that really help to calm you down? Where could we find comfort after a rutting male has wounded us if we couldn't offer it to one another? Caress me, too. You've been to see the other women and not me? Niñita, give me a little tenderness!"

La Niña does not respond. She has let go, but she keeps on sobbing and biting her lips. She is nothing more than a marble statue—all the heat that was burning a while ago has vanished. It is only her heart that is hurting, terribly. From time to time, when she has been too bruised by the furor of rutting males, La Niña goes to let her smarting, poisoned flesh be caressed by La Rubia or one of the other women. Sometimes La Rubia or Lucrèce comes into her room, and if she is in a good mood, La Niña does whatever they ask. And yet, their slow, soft, smooth caressing has never aroused that overwhelming electricity of pleasure any more than the brutal, egotistical caresses of the customers. She has never had an orgasm—does she even know what an orgasm is? She told Dr. Chalbert that, but he has never been able to do anything for her. For many long years she has been looking for an orgasm in lovemaking, with men or women. Perhaps at the beginning of her sexual experience she may have felt, for a fraction of a second, a little fleeting spark—ever so weak and muted, without any definite sensation as her juices began to flow? Maybe that is only an imaginary memory, a memory that she made up a long time later? In any case, that quickly, almost instantly stopped happening. She never fails to remain lucid during her sexual relations, analyzing herself, examining herself as her lovers do battle over her. She has often asked herself whether it is for that evanescent and fleeting illusion that humanity gets worked up and crimes are committed. In La Niña's little head, all human actions, savage struggles, the thirst for money, hatred, and other horrors almost always have a deep motivation, directly or indirectly—love, lechery, the futility of sensuality or passion. But the experience of love she has had is so disappointing that she understands nothing about it. She had barely been deflowered by some passing stranger when she began right away to give herself to men for a crust of bread—she was then thirteen or fourteen years old—and she stopped feeling anything whatsoever.

She had talked to the other women about it. They had often told her about their own experience of the brutality and egotism of rutting males. Others had proposed lesbian love to her. Since she had never believed in anything much, except maybe in the Virgin of the Pillar, who, to La Niña's mind, understands, pardons, and even authorizes all the peccadilloes of joyless whores. She was not long in trying it out. She even made the first advances herself and went looking for companions given to lesbian inversion, bisexuals, women with strictly clitoridian sensuality, neurotics, or the rejects who are simply caught in the lone obsession of carnal pleasure, hysterical joy, the elusive pursuit of some new experience or even wholly imagined pleasure. No woman with a masculine, bisexual or extremely feminine character, whether sensual or an erotomaniac, has ever managed to arouse the least bit of true sexual pleasure in La Niña. She feels it when somebody touches her, but that's all—there's no color or sensation. La Niña has kept on with women who ask her, nevertheless, and occasionally she herself has even gone after some girl whose shape or splendid flesh has aroused her interest or curiosity. So, with La Rubia, it was La Niña who made the first advances. La Rubia is haunted at the same time by love for men and women. She has an insatiable dream of fusing with some being that she can't find. If somebody proposed that she make love with an ass or a gorilla, she would probably accept in hopes of achieving that impossible communion. La Rubia lives by her imagination. In the end, she is always in love with somebody. And yet, that wild pleasure that she seems to experience with this or that person leaves her unsatisfied deep down inside. Her insatiable sexual voracity, her cries, and her whimpering have always left La Niña deeply perplexed.

"I like the salty along with the sweet, *chica!* That's the way it is," La Rubia often repeats.

But for La Niña, there is nothing—neither salty nor sweet, neither bitter nor smooth, neither hot nor cold!

If La Niña continues this disappointing experience in spite of everything, it is for another reason. It's simply because it is satisfying to have somebody stroke her body with affection and kindness once in a while. That consoles her. Thanks to that little game, she can convince herself she is not completely alone in the world. When all is said and done, La Niña's lesbian love is a gesture like that of children who like to snuggle up on the lap of their parents to get their hugs and caresses. Even if she gets absolutely no sexual pleasure during these exercises, her partners are at least tender and maternal, especially the ones who have never had children. La Niña has gotten into the habit of this sport, this peculiar "love," a pretense that is not at all strange to her. Besides, without there being a bit of erotic arousal, she loves the beauty of the human body, whether feminine or masculine. When a new girl moves into the whorehouse, La Niña always makes advances to her. But La Niña boldly lies to all of them when she says that she gets pleasure from their caresses. She can imitate to perfection the sensual woman tormented by desire. That's her trade. Finally, the real reason that has led her into this incomplete and non-traumatizing "love" cannot be admitted— she has to pretend! Try telling her partners that they give her the illusion of having a mother! After all, she does not often look for women, just once every two or three weeks at most, particularly when she is in the grips of one of her depressive slumps. She tells herself that if she finds herself completely cut off from cuddling, with her alternately exuberant and neurotic moods, she'll go completely crazy. Solitude is dreadful at times. Enough to make you swallow rat poison some days!

"Niña. . . . ¡*Niñita mía!* Give me a little love," groans La Rubia. But La Niña is made of ice today. If she took refuge in La Rubia's room, it was simply to seek a human presence, someone to whom she could confide her utter confusion without even speaking. La Niña's sobs have subsided—they're shut off; she does not make the slightest gesture beneath the body that is pressing and hugging her with ecstasy. La Rubia's mouth slides down along her ribs, wanders over her belly, and the slobbery tongue slips into La Niña's groin in skillful titillation. The sucking, probing mouth envelops her vulva and clitoris. Neither hot nor cold. La Niña stares at the ceiling. She sees a vast meadow covered with strongly perfumed marigolds. She closes her eyes.

What is this meadow? Where? In what country has she seen it? Why did her breasts come alive a while ago in front of that enigmatic stranger at the bar? Why did her vagina begin to tingle, something that has not happened to her since puberty? She had not gotten through puberty when she became a woman. A woman! Well! A child-woman, a sexless tease, a frigid whore, paradoxically driving men crazy with desire. That's La Niña Estrellita! And this Rubia who, at this instant, is making all those fencing moves on top of her belly, who is breathing hard and trying to invent the most insidious and skillful new caresses! It's incredibly funny! Too bad you couldn't show this in a film! And that meadow of marigolds! It's disturbing anyway! As long as there's no sorcery in this whole strange adventure. Could that man be a sorcerer? It's as if the past darkness might be torn apart, as if her memory could return with a vengeance. Of course, La Niña remembers her real name, who she is, and where she comes from, but what will she become if really vivid memories begin to well up, rupturing the more or less black surface of her inner lake all of a sudden? What will her days and nights become if the past begins to haunt her at every second? Oblivion is so convenient! She wants it to last, to keep on! If her childhood were to come back to her clearly, she is sure that the Sensation Bar would seem like a prison worse than hell and its fires. The thought that sprang up uncontrollably in her mind a while ago is still there, beating at her temples like eddies from a raging sea. *Her* man is there in the bar! *Her* man is there. . . . *Her* man. . . . Why it's incredible! She is really and truly going crazy!

"Niña-a. . . . Niñita. . . . Niñita-a. Give me a little tenderness," begs La Rubia with feline cajoling.

With a distracted gesture, La Niña runs her hands over the vibrating guitar of La Rubia's body. Yes, that man has to take her!

Five, ten times in a row—all night! Only then will she be freed. She must not flinch. This time she will go right up to him without hesitation and hurl her request at him in a breath. But he must have left—he probably has. The flowery meadow of marigolds. . . . Who is this mysterious man who takes away her breath and her power of speech? *¡Virgen del Pilar!* Why is he haunting her?

"Niñita, are you sleeping?"

No, she isn't sleeping, but she pretends she is, and she does it well.

# THIRD MANSION

*Hearing*

*Estrujamos su voz*
*como una flor de insomnio*
*y suelta un zumo amargo,*
*suelta un olor mojado,*
*un olor de palabras puntiagudas*
*que encuentren en el viento*
*el camino del grito,*
*que encuentren en el grito*
*el camino del canto,*
*que encuentren en el canto,*
*el camino del fuego,*
*que encuentren en el fuego*
*el camino del alba,*
*que encuentren en el alba un gallo rojo,*
*de pólvora, un metálico*
*gallo, desparramando el día con sus alas. . . .*
—Nicolás Guillén, "Élégies antillaises"


We press his voice
like a flower of insomnia
and a bitter juice springs from it,
a wet perfume springs from it,
a perfume of biting words
that find in the wind
the way of the cry,
that find in the cry
the way of song,
that find in the way of song
the way of fire,
that find in the fire
the way of the dawn,
that find in the dawn a red rooster
of gunpowder, a metal
rooster spreading the day with his wings. . . .

adame Puñez? Do you believe in dreams? It's funny—
I've never believed in them, but I wonder whether I'm
not beginning to believe in them!"

"What did you dream about, El Caucho? If you dream about
flies, that means money; marriage, it means a funeral. If you
dreamed about death, it means that good fortune is coming your
way. But there are some people who have an accurate gift of
foresight, which means they see what's going to happen in the
slightest detail. In Caracas, I knew an old woman, an old
Quetchua woman, who had such a clear-sighted gift it was
frightening! If she told you, 'A gentleman dressed in gray, with
a cane in his hand and a red polka-dot tie, will arrive at 3:45
this afternoon,' you could simply set your watch by the man's
arrival! President Gómez himself, may the devil take that pig's
soul, had also heard about that woman. He sent for her once.
You're not listening to me, El Caucho—your mind is somewhere
else! So President Gómez . . . ! El Caucho! El Caucho, you're not
listening to me. OK! So, if you're not going to listen to me . . .
Forget it! What did you dream about, El Caucho?"

"That's not it, Madame Puñez—it's not dreams like that!
Madame Puñez, suppose you meet somebody for the first time
or that you go into a house where you've never set foot before.
You meet some old man there or you see some flower vases on
the buffet in the dining room. You fall into a reverie right away,
eyes wide open. This is a conscious experience, right? You see
your distant past—a gesture by the old man suddenly reminds
you of an old church where you had your first communion, the
flower vases bring to mind some little song you heard at age ten,

a perfume coming from the house reminds you of a suburban market from your childhood, of a walk you took at some time. . . . That's a conscious experience, right? And yet, you likely never knew that old man, the house, or the flower vases! There's something eerie about that! Why do you pay attention to the least flicker of an eyelid, a protruding chin, the color of a hair? You don't know, but everything recalls something, and you remember nothing! Do you understand what I'm trying to say, Madame Puñez? Do you know anything about dreams like that, Madame Puñez?"

"What are you talking about, El Caucho? Is there someone or something you think you recognize? Of course, I know about such things, El Caucho, but that has nothing to do with dreams. Those aren't dreams. In some cases you are completely mistaken, but in others there may be something you really recognize. That has nothing to do with dreams or the future—it doesn't mean a thing! Those aren't dreams!"

"And what if it meant something anyway? What if it had some connection to the future, Madame Puñez?"

"Do you want me to read the cards for you, El Caucho?"

"Madame Puñez, you don't know anything about those dreams. You could go on for a long time about waking dreams, the fantasies of a tired brain—and you would always find some great story to tell—you know about those things! But, real dreams, the ones that come to you when your eyes are wide open—you can't invent a thing!"

"I don't know about that? You still don't know who Señora Delia Abdón Canuelo Puñez e Ibarra is! I don't know anything about that? Let me read the cards for you, El Caucho, and you'll see the future as clearly as you see the daylight. Let me do it, and you'll tell me whether you don't understand what you call your dream!"

"No!"

"El Caucho, listen to your elders! Could you be afraid of the truths I might tell you? Not only about your dreams, but about your life? Listen, if you want, I'll even do a *chien de pique*. The *chien de pique* is great—you can see the future as if you were already there!"

"And all you have to do is put out your hand to grab the money you'll certainly get in the future? You can take it right away? That's it?"

"Could you be a miser, El Caucho? People say you are! Just one dollar, and I'll lay out your *chien de pique!*"

"A dollar? Do you think I'm crazy? If you were a dollar yourself, I'd pocket you right away, Madame Puñez!"

"Give me just three *piastras* then, and I'll do your *chien de pique?* You know, some people say they don't believe in hypnotists, they don't believe in cards, they don't believe in lines on the hand, but then one day they check out one of the methods, and they realize they have been fools for not having taken advantage of "science" before. The *chien de pique* is great, El Caucho!"

"Not interested!"

"El Caucho, I think they're right when they say you're a miser. Look here—you're tormented by what you call your dream, but you don't want to spend a red cent to find out! OK! I'll do your *chien de pique* for just six *gourdins?* Since it's you, and I don't like to see you so upset! Six *gourdins* for a *chien de pique,* El Caucho!"

"Not interested! What the hell do I care about knowing the future? Can you eat it? Would it let me get along better? No! Just suppose your *chien de pique* were right. You tell me that such and such is going to happen, but that I can't change it— so what good does it do me to know that? I always come out alright—more or less alright without a *chien de pique.* I'm not scared—I don't give a damn! If the time to die comes along, I'll always see how I react! And besides, I don't believe in your card predictions, with or without a *chien de pique.* Everything is always great with fortune-tellers, Madame Puñez! You're a crafty woman, Madame Puñez, and you know how turn a profit!"

"A miser! Yeah! That's what you are, El Caucho! A real miser!"

"Why don't you lay out a *chien de pique* to find out whether you'll get me to go along with your card reading?"

"Miser! Ingrate! You're a real Cuban!"

El Caucho smirks. He falls backward onto Madame Puñez's bed. *Chien de pique!* That damned Madame Puñez! She's got some good ones! But El Caucho likes Madame Puñez, and she's got a weak spot for El Caucho—that's obvious. Madame Puñez runs the restaurant where the shipyard workers come to eat. They eat well, and it's not too expensive, but Madame Puñez makes up for it in other ways: she lends money for interest to the workers—three dollars for five. Madame Puñez is a pitiless usurer, but, after all, she's not mean. She wouldn't forgive one penny of a customer's debt, but she always gives food credit to a guy who's broke. The minute they leave the shipyard, the fellows compensate by taking off without settling their accounts. In those cases, Madame Puñez storms, howls, pulls her hair out, and makes a sour face at the other workers in order to give them the impression that she is a pitiless usurer. She even calls herself "the old Jew," but, in reality, everybody lands on their feet in that little game. This "old Jew" imagines herself bloodthirsty, but, when it's all said and done, she's a tender-hearted person. She'd never admit that.

"Old Jew, I've come to borrow ten *piastras!*" the fellows say, trying to soften her up. When a worker is sick and doesn't have anybody to take care of him, she takes him into her own home and takes care of him like a mama. When there are baptisms and first communions, Madame Puñez's presents are never late. Madame Puñez is a daughter of the people, a daughter of the Caribbean. With a Venezuelan father and a mother who was half-Haitian, half-Dominican, Madame Puñez made some money and then got married to a Guatemalan mechanic working for HASCO—which is where she got the title of "Madame," which she doesn't forget. For new customers, she spreads her fingers to show her wedding ring, because such a distinction is pretty rare in her milieu. Her husband died a short time after their marriage, reportedly when he fell into a sugarcane shredder at the factory. El Caucho suspects Madame Puñez of having "lived it up" at a certain period of her life—she may have done a good deal of work on her back. She must have changed in time, as soon as she got enough money together to set up a little business, because she's a "worker," a real beast of burden, this Madame Puñez. By trading disorder for dust, she carried on an uphill struggle, cent by cent, until she owned two little rental houses and a restaurant. El Caucho knows that if, one day, somebody pries Madame Puñez's heart open, such an aroma of jasmine will pour out that the entire Portail Léogane neighborhood will be perfumed by it.

Madame Puñez has a weakness for El Caucho. She lends him money without interest and gives him a couple of packs of cigarettes from time to time, the ones she buys at a discount from passing sailors. She often keeps a little plate of food for him. So things are clear. And yet, as far as anybody knows, there is still nothing going on between Madame Puñez and El Caucho. She tries to convince herself El Caucho exerts some influence over his fellow workers and that he lectures them when they turn a deaf ear to talk about paying their debts. This is not a bit true. By fooling herself that way, the moneylender is only justifying to an "old Jew's" conscience her behavior with El Caucho. When the workers start bad-mouthing their favorite usurer to El Caucho, he simply smiles enigmatically. He does not get involved—he's just a thumb on the hand. It doesn't matter because, after all, Madame Puñez would like to "pull a fast one" by putting a leash around El Caucho's neck. She has planned well. She would sell the two houses, buy a little hotel, and run a "big restaurant" on the main floor. The big-hearted companion who would accept her would have a rosy life. And this would probably work well because Madame Puñez has a good head for small business, an unequaled talent for organizing things, credit with the important businessmen of the Bord-de-Mer, and plenty of solid political connections. She is a strong-willed woman who has more heart than she thinks she does. As long as the guy shows some tenderness—and in her thinking at this moment, El Caucho is the only man possible—as long as the man is fraternal, friendly, and takes interest in her feelings and dreams, she would ask nothing more. With respect to her sensuality, she thinks she "still has it"; she is having the last flushes of galloping menopause, and her desire might be nothing more than an expression of her ambition to "have a good life." But love is part of that, in any case—love that is calm like a great river with a potential for flood waters. Her conversations with El Caucho are the most human, the nicest, the deepest, the most intimate, the fullest experiences she has ever had in her life. El Caucho is a serious, unselfish, honest man. He is strong, gentle, and hard as millet—he is as true as the morning dew, he is as intransigent as the sun, as tame and understanding as a big dog, and he knows a lot of things—it's reassuring to hear him speak with that slow, rhythmical confidence.

"*La vida es sueño*," says Lope de Vega—life is a dream!

Madame Puñez thinks she is educated, and she displays it ostentatiously to El Caucho. Basically, she is just lamenting her fate and her unrealized hopes.

"Madame Puñez?"

"I thought you were asleep, El Caucho."

"Madame Puñez, are you going to Johnson's funeral?"

"You're funny, El Caucho. Delia Puñez is an educated woman—you've got to admit that! You can hate the dog, but don't say his teeth are black! Johnson was my customer, and an honest one. Just because he's dead and his debt will probably go unpaid won't keep me from going to his funeral. I even ordered a nice wreath with my name on it: Delia Abdón Canuelo Puñez e Ibarra, eternal regrets. I have my own sense of honor, El Caucho!"

Johnson Barrett was a Jamaican, a welder at the shipyard for repairs and refitting. He died yesterday, and his funeral will take place at four o'clock in the Cathedral of the Holy Trinity. This morning, El Caucho went to see the superintendent and let him know that the men would not work at the moment when their fellow worker, Johnson Barrett, was being taken to his grave. Johnson had a difficult personality, no doubt, *because of* his stomach ulcer, but he was a nice guy. At noon, El Caucho had gone to rent a black suit from Ticoolie, because he was supposed to be a pallbearer. That would be more dignified. Johnson had a right to a bit of dignity at his funeral. El Caucho also had an envelope in the pocket of his overalls. He wanted to take up a collection for the dead man's widow and kids. He had to scold some of the fellows who contributed only a pittance on the pretext that they had cool relations with Johnson, whose difficult character was legendary. But Johnson Barrett was more than a son of the Caribbean: he was an honest worker, and El Caucho was uncompromising, unyielding on that point. That was his own way. The fellows finally gave a decent sum.

"Delia?"

El Caucho is still lying on the bed. He is daydreaming. Madame Puñez knows that when El Caucho calls her "Delia," he needs money. In fact, she is unable to resist him when El Caucho pronounces the two syllables of her first name.

"What, El Caucho? What do you want now?"

"Delia, I need five dollars."

"I don't have any money, El Caucho! Everybody owes me, and because of the holidays nobody wants to pay me back! I've got responsibilities too! What do you want five dollars for?"

"That's my business!"

"When will you pay me back?"

"Are you going to give them to me or not? Since when have I been in the habit of not taking care of my debts?"

"Five dollars for seven and a half?"

"Go to hell, Delia! El Caucho doesn't go along with your kind of business!"

"Hey, El Caucho, you wouldn't be pining after some little woman, would you?"

"Are you going to give me the money or not?"

"Tell me if it's because of a woman?"

"No! Well, maybe it is!"

"And is she good-looking? Shapely?"

"Yes!"

"Better than me?"

Delia gives a little sample of how supple her pudgy back is. She lets out a crazy little giggle. Delia is amply blessed with flesh and fat; she is short, round, amply endowed, mature, but not unattractive. She has an amusing nose. Delia lets out a little chuckle from her bosom and rolls her abundant back with dexterity. There are fellows who like having an armful, but not El Caucho. In spite of everything, Puñez must be an experienced performer in bed. . . .

"Tell me, El Caucho? Is she better than I am?"

"Are you giving me the money or not?"

"Tell me first whether she's better built than I am. Look out, El Caucho—maybe she doesn't know how to do everything old Delia does. With me, what you see is what you get! A young woman will kill you, I tell you! So, she's better looking than I am? Young?"

"Yeah!"

"Tell me, El Caucho? Will you tell me how it goes?"

"So you're going to give me the money?"

"If you don't have a clean shirt for the funeral, I can wash and iron one right quick!"

"The money, Delia! You know that I can just leave you here with your money and go my own way. I don't have any more time to lose!"

"You've got to be clean when you appear if she's young. So, will you tell me?"

Madame Puñez finally pulls a wad of money out of her ample bosom and hands a ten-dollar bill to El Caucho.

"I don't have any change. . . ."

"That's OK!"

El Caucho sticks it in his pocket. Delia sighs and looks at him. Will she get this El Caucho? There are lots of men around, anyway! At his age, he ought to know the value of a secure existence! He would have all the money he wanted and wouldn't need to work! That wouldn't keep him from having all the girls he wanted. Delia knows that she isn't young any longer: fifty-four years old. It would even make her proud that her man was a *macho,* a man who gets around. She would ask him to tell her about his escapades. That way, she would be more certain of not losing him. In fact, the way she understands things presently, a man cannot be happy with just one woman: "It's physical!" she says. As long as El Caucho gave her a bit of satisfaction for those trifles once in a while, she wouldn't ask for anything more. She would even help him catch all the bitches he wanted as long as she remained the titular owner of the rooster, of course. She knows that it's five minutes before midnight on her clock and that she has to hurry up to find her companion for the hour of truth—a friend she can count on for old age. If El Caucho were only willing! She would have followed him anywhere, in spite of the demon inside him. She really has some business sense! With a couple of weeks in any Caribbean country, Delia is sure of finding a scheme, some *business* to get by with. El Caucho pretends not to understand, and Delia has her pride—she doesn't want to prostitute herself. After all, what's this guy looking for in life? Sometimes he talks about strikes and the workers' movement. The stuff he reads in books must be going to his head. Anyway! Delia is patient.

"I'm leaving, Delia."

"El Caucho? Skirt chaser! Will you tell me about it?"

She winks at him suggestively. El Caucho shrugs and rolls his shoulders—he goes out.

❋

❋  ❋

"Doctor Chalbert? What good is medicine if you can't help me have an orgasm when I make love? Tell me, Doctor Chalbert? Don't you think I'm about to go crazy?"

"You're completely crazy already, La Niña, how could you be crazier than you are? Give me a break and hold still!"

"So, I don't have 'syphilis' yet, Doctor Chalbert?"

"No. But I do have to examine you to make sure your working tools haven't picked up some infection. Stop wiggling your behind!"

La Niña keeps still during the rest of the gynecological examination. La Niña has an awful fear of germs; she comes to Doctor Chalbert twice a week for a checkup. Not a superficial checkup or a hasty interview: she wants to be examined every time "inside" and in all directions, and if Doctor Chalbert doesn't use the speculum with the lighted mirror on his forehead, La Niña refuses to get down off the examining table.

"Doctor Chalbert? Can a frigid woman desire a man?"

"That's a possibility, La Niña."

"Doctor Chalbert. . . . You're always saying that love is a joke. For La Rubia, in any case, it's no joke! Her *chulo* Gabriel is some pimp! He takes everything, and that idiot tells him, 'Here's more!' If love is a joke, why does La Rubia behave that way?"

"Damned if I know! La Rubia has a head full of garbage. She says that she can't live without Gabriel tormenting her. That's her imagination at work inventing all that. If you let your imagination go to work, there's no hope. And besides, what does that have to do with you, La Niña? You don't give a damn about love. . . . So? Since when did you begin worrying about people? La Rubia isn't your mother!"

Doctor Chalbert glances deeply into La Niña's tired eyes for a moment, shakes his head, and goes back to work. Doctor Chalbert is a round, chubby, stout man of medium height with a good nature and puffy cheeks. He is around thirty-eight to forty years old, a bachelor who doesn't drink, and he's not particularly given to running after women, although he likes the atmosphere of La Frontière. His only close friends are the colorful, simple people of the Portail Léogane, the *guajiros,* the drunkards, the *chulos* of the neighborhood and the workers from the outskirts, and particularly the tanner-leather workers. The little whores with their sad hearts are his friends. He forgives them many things because of their fresh sentimentality, their raw nerves, their openness, their naïveté, and their kindness. These little whores and the gutter people are the only ones who haven't disappointed him. The *manolitas* aren't pure gold coins, of course, they are *kòb,* copper pennies eaten by corrosion, but they never fool you—they ring true. Whenever they speak of love, gratitude, friendship, faithfulness, revenge, or hate, you can believe it and count on it. Doctor Chalbert seems to be burdened with some great sorrow, something very weighty. He says he believes in nothing—he makes fun of everything. He has become established at the Portail Léogane and will probably die there. When he earns three or four dollars in a day, he closes the door, gets into his old jalopy, and takes a tour around his little universe. He does not get upset, and he does not overextend himself, but he works hard when he feels like it, and he plays the banjo or a game of bezique when he's not in a mood to work. Sometimes he tours the bordellos during slack moments, around two o'clock in the afternoon. He plays lotto with the *manolitas,* who gather around him as soon as they see him— he plays the banjo for them, jokes around, or tells stories. The girls are crazy about him, but it's rare that he goes to bed with one of them, although he knows more about their state of health than anybody. He rarely takes a drink, and then not much, but he smokes like a chimney, and the banjo is his vice.

"Doctor Chalbert? You're a Rosicrucian—do you think that La Niña might have lived another life before being born? Could I have had another life before this one?"

"Who knows?"

Doctor Chalbert swabs La Niña Estrellita's behind carefully, but he isn't worried about her health—he doesn't see a thing. She didn't catch anything this week.

"Doctor Chalbert? Is it possible to completely forget somebody you've known very well? Can you 'recognize' somebody you don't know? Can you guess the past of somebody that you've just seen?"

"Anything's possible, La Niña!"

"Doctor Chalbert. . . . Why can't I easily remember my past life?"

The doctor stares into La Niña's eyes for a bit, signals for her to get off the examining table, sits down, and crosses his arms. He shakes his head.

"I think that's because you don't want to remember, La Niña. You prefer to bury the past because it's more convenient. After some years, you've more or less succeeded at it. On one hand, that suits you, but on the other, it's bothering you. You're out of humor lots of times—it's because of that. I've already explained that to you, La Niña—you've tightened up in order to live your little life. You're probably right to do it that way. With your character and type of work, it's probably far better for you not to have any memories. I've never asked you anything about them, La Niña—and that's the reason. You have to decide what you want, La Niña."

La Niña closes her eyes. She knows that Doctor Chalbert is right. Loss of memory has saved her. How did Doctor Chalbert guess that? After a serious illness, everything became simple once more. La Niña didn't fret any more. Her forgetfulness is a curious thing. She has nothing left but a skeleton of her past— everything else has vanished. Couldn't she uncover just one little corner? Just enough time to identify a face and then let everything fall back into oblivion. Could she lose her fragile equilibrium that way—it's an equilibrium that helps her live anyway? A face . . . just one! Something tells her that face won't bring bad luck.

"Doctor Chalbert? When you've got a man under your skin, can you get rid of him?"

"La Niña, I think something's bothering you today. Is there some way I could help you? What are you thinking about? What's eating at you?"

"Nothing, Doctor Chalbert—nothing at all. It's just curiosity. . . . So I haven't caught anything?"

The doctor shakes his head no and watches La Niña with her sad eyes. He thinks for a while and then asks her:

"Do you sleep well, La Niña?"

"Yes. . . . Well, more or less."

"Do you have an appetite, tell me?"

"Well, . . . I eat! Like everybody!"

"Except for your bad moments, you're getting along, right?"

"Yes."

"Well, do you want me to tell you something, La Niña? Shall I? OK. I'm going to tell you a story. I know somebody who always eats without wanting to, who drinks without any great pleasure, and spends his nights worrying—he has insomnia— and all this happens because he can't manage, he can't ever manage to forget the past . . . no matter what he does! That's memory, La Niña—when a person has missed out on his own life. I know what's bothering you, but in order to have a right to your memories, you mustn't depend on anybody else; you have to be able to live by your own means. The person I'm talking about used to have that possibility, but I don't think this would be easy for you in your trade. The person I'm talking about is worried, unhappy, and is a failure in life, but I'm sure that if somebody suggested taking away his memory, he would refuse. That's his nature. There are people who kill themselves rather than live like unconscious animals—there are others that commit suicide because they're tired of being conscious. Excuse me for being brutally frank with you, La Niña, but it's the truth: you've committed suicide, you have done away with your conscious life— it's just that your funeral dirge hasn't been chanted yet. Each person has a personality! Nobody can answer certain questions in another person's place! We are all alike, and yet we're all so different! What we really are is so different from our appearance. Each person has an individual truth, a cross to bear, a road that opens up. . . . La Niña, you have to have the will to face your truth with eyes wide open and to choose your own way consciously and deliberately. If you manage, it brings you joy. Go home, La Niña—I mean, go back where you live. You haven't caught anything—that's good. If something is going to happen to transform your life, it will burst all of a sudden in your head—in your heart first. At that point, you will know what's happening, but how can you know whether you'll have the courage to take the right path! That day might be your last if you get carried away without thinking it over maturely. Here you go—here's your prescription, but don't take too much Maxiton! Soon it won't work any more!"

La Niña lowers her head. She has to go. She leaves.

❊

❊  ❊

This evening, La Niña's mood is multicolored. She feels a tingle of exaltation, a desire to pinch, to scratch and meow, to muss up her hair—to do crazy things, and along with all that, a strange lethargy has come over her. A laugh with bitter aftertaste vibrates in her throat. She doesn't have that "cottony" feeling, no real anxiety, no interior void, no vertigo at all, no "knot" in her stomach—and yet, deep inside her something is stirring. That little seed of uneasiness may be melancholy—but not exactly— it's bouncing around inside the mug of her false joy like a bell with a deep tone. La Niña is like a woman refusing to recognize she is pregnant with the fetus squirming around inside her belly in such a wild manner that she might think she was about to give birth even without any pain. To La Niña's mind, giving birth inevitably implies terrible pain. But she is not suffering— she is afraid of a miscarriage, a premature child, the expulsion of a stillborn thought, some useless and excruciating cadaver, a powerless force with no life because it has no future. And since one can die from certain abortions, La Niña doesn't want to die. Without hope, she waits to see. Fortunately, in this phase of her mood cycle, she is spontaneously vibrant and exuberant. All she has to do is to let herself flow along with her own current so that nothing unusual comes out, for the moment. Later, maybe, but not now. It's better not to be a mother, to remain barren like the cursed fig tree in the scriptures, if the child a woman carries in her womb, against her will, may not be healthy. No passing maternity! This evening, La Niña is acting as if she did not know she was pregnant. It's easy—she only has to let herself be carried along by her multicolored mood.

During the night, the U.S. Navy squadron is supposed to set sail. *Good-bye! Good-bye, farewell!* Don't come back until you've got lots of dough, lots of dollars—not before. The prospect of soon being back out on the blue or gray solitude of the open ocean and setting back to the usual tasks, undergoing the sea spray and the perpetual meditation of the sailor—all of that satisfies and saddens the marines at the same time. The military procession gears back up in the great port where the evening sea breezes whirr softly, seeking sounds to carry about. In the suburbs and the nearby countryside, the Rara feasts are coming back to life also. For two days, the obligation to work has been vying bitterly to dominate the frenzied celebrations of the Indian carnival, but the joyful delirium has won out. For some, tomorrow will be Holy Wednesday: the crossroads of Ça-Ira will present a spectacle that seems to be a vision from inside a frappé. For others, this will be the Gulf of Mexico with its vicious sea, with the rolling and pitching of the heart over a capriciously unlimited space. The angry coughing and starting of motors and the bellowing horns have begun again on the avenue. A *rabòday* rhythm is wavering above in space:

> *Viv liks a! Viv liks a!*
> *Balanse debò,*
> *Balanse lamayòt!*
> *Viv liks a! Viv liks a!*\*

A few firecrackers go off, and there are cries from a few kids having a wild time.

"*Timoun!* Kids! Come look! The kids have set up a stuffed *gwo Jwif* at the corner of the street! Come quick!"

The yell echoes through the Sensation Bar. The girls hurry out following Lucrèce, a great beanpole—she's proud, fun-loving, and she's still living it up. With a big stick in her hand, La Niña leads the regiment to the attack. Screams, yells, laughter, and wild shoving. Too bad for the customers! Besides, almost all the marines head out with their Kodaks in their hands. The firecrackers are going off in bursts. Clusters of kids are letting out Sioux war hoops, pushing each other, stomping, and hiding the goal of all this to-do. The troop of *manolitas* from the Sensation Bar is getting close to the goal. Shoving with her elbows, La Niña has come close to the large straw-stuffed figure, which is supposed to represent all the Hebrew priests of the Sanhedrin who condemned Jesus. The strawman's head is made of an emptied calabash in which eyes, a mouth, and nostrils have been cut out; inside this head a little candle is lighting the face with its

---

\*Long live Luxury! Long live Luxury!
Shake it to both sides,
Shake the *lamayòt* (surprise box)!
Long live Luxury! Long live Luxury!

flickering flame. Solidly fixed on an old chair, which has been attached to the wall, the "Jew" holds out his left arm as if he were shaking hands while his other arm is extended at right angles, on a level with his forehead, in a gesture that is at once supplicating and protective.

With her stick, La Niña strikes the first blow, breaking the extended arm, which begins swinging in all directions. Blows rain down, and screams break out. The musicians of a jazz band are beating a *chalbari* on old pots and leading the *banboula*. The soloist lets go a furious *kata* beat, punctuated by riffs and somber responses of a *vaksin* roughly improvised from a piece of pipe. The entire crowd, consisting of kids, teenagers, whores, and urchins, with a few adults mixed in, has gone wild and is striking the *Jwif,* who is losing his insides and falling apart. Firecrackers are popping with a dry pop. The *bastreng* is nerveracking with its salacious rhythms. A very small harlequin, simply costumed in a short shirt made from different scraps of cloth sewn together, is standing facing the musicians and is awkwardly engaged in violent gyrations of his back. His stomach has an enormous belly button, an inflated balloon, and his ridiculous little bird is swinging in the wind. With laughs, yells, jeers, whinnies, the raucous bacchanal keeps breaking out as a series of firecrackers fills the air with the smell of saltpeter and smoke. The *Jwif* is cracking apart on all sides.

"Down with the *Jwif!*"

The poor, strange *Jwif.* He could resemble a big swollen and gawking Jesus more than the figure of Caiaphas, whom he is supposed to represent!

"Down with the *Jwif!*" bellows La Niña Estrellita, who is leading the noisy chorus. The calabash serving as the figure's head is broken into pieces, but it still remains miraculously in place, and with the rapidly approaching night, rays from the candle make its eyes and mouth give off a weird, terrified flicker.

"Down with the *Jwif!*"

The machine gun of the *kata* drum and the firecrackers explode, the whores and urchins are costumed and jumping, the rhythm crackles, and the *Jwif* gives up.

*Hearing*

As the kids go wild and the huge crowd continues its crazy scalp dance around the dummy, somebody, maybe a kid, hurls a long string of firecrackers beneath the feet of the crowd. People panic. People run every direction. La Niña runs off, still yelling, "Down with the *Jwif*!"

A child lies unconscious at the feet of the *Jwif*. Firecrackers are exploding around him. The *Jwif* catches fire. There is an abrupt, stupified silence, broken by the explosions of the string of firecrackers. The crowd is speechless, and nobody has yet dared go closer.

"Let me through!" trumpets a voice. It is El Caucho, returning from the funeral and still dressed in his black alpaca suit. He dives through the fireworks, takes the child in his arms and runs off with him.

❖

❖  ❖

El Caucho climbs the terrace of the Sensation Bar. Luz-Maria runs up to him.

"Look! Your jacket elbow is all burned! Come on, I'll repair it for you! I'll be quick—you'll see!"

Damn! He has ruined the rental suit. In the heat of action, he didn't notice a thing! There is a stinging pain in his elbow. Hey, he's burned, too. What luck! He didn't feel a thing! A bouncing merengue spins on the record player:

> *Dimasè Estime, roule m debò!*
> *Roule m debò!*
> *Roule m debò!*\*

El Caucho lets himself be led off by Luz-Maria. If only the damage can be repaired so that Ticoolie, the fellow who rented the suit to him, won't notice anything! At this point, El Caucho

---

\*Dumarsais Estimé, shake him to both sides!
Shake him to both sides!
Shake him to both sides!"

is neither inclined nor in a position to pay for a suit—he's had it!—a suit for which the old usurer would certainly ask an inflated price. Why did he need to go rent a suit for this funeral? With an innocent look in her eyes, Luz-Maria leads El Caucho away. They go through the dance hall where couples are wildly dancing. La Rubia is having one of her great days. She is all smiles in the arms of her *chulito*—Gabriel the chauffeur. Rubia really has style! El Caucho smiles, imagining her in a Cadillac. He follows Luz-Maria along the corridor. So this is where La Niña spends her work nights. He is going to see Luz-Maria's room. La Niña's must not be very different.

El Caucho has taken off his jacket, the black tie, the white shirt, keeping only his undershirt on. This is the way he had imagined their rooms—bare and with a few personal touches that can't relieve the shadowy gaudiness of the place. Typical! El Caucho sits on the edge of Luz-Maria's bed. He really does have a blister on his elbow—nothing too serious, but it burns a bit anyway. Luz-Maria rushes behind the screen that hides the dressing area. She comes back with a little bottle, but she has taken advantage of the chance to loosen her white silk blouse a bit, leaving her broad neck, decorated with a green ribbon, brazenly exposed at breast level. Her light coffee-colored skin is still fresh, and one side of the blouse has slipped, baring her right shoulder. But Luz-Maria is being cautious—she would not want to be too pushy and run the risk of frightening away the bird she has so adroitly managed to entrap. What an exploit. This gentleman isn't easy to handle. She has experience. Luz-Maria kneels in front of El Caucho and pulls his burned elbow toward her. She presses her hips against El Caucho's legs. He doesn't flinch. Luz-Maria is breathing lightly on the burn and letting her blouse gape open. El Caucho pays no attention.

"Does that hurt, my little cat? Wait, I've got just what it takes. Tincture of arnica—it's great for burns."

Luz-Maria is holding his arm carefully and giving little puffs on it. In fact, why is she blowing? As if by chance, her blouse has slipped down both shoulders—it gapes and exposes her trembling breasts. El Caucho is not paying attention—he is thinking about the ruined jacket. As long as this gentle little slut of a whore can really repair the damage! His elbow is generously swabbed with tincture of arnica. Luz-Maria is still working when she says:

"You'll see, my big rat—Luz-Maria knows how to sew. I was raised by the good sisters! Does that mean anything to you?"

She laughs and sits down beside El Caucho. Her hip is pressed against her neighbor's. She looks at the jacket. She is holding a needle with black thread in her mouth.

"It's not serious! You'll see what Luz-Maria can do, love. The good sisters know a thing or two. I would challenge anyone who hasn't been told to find the damage after I've repaired it!"

In fact, the elbow of the jacket is a bit ruddy, but the hole is not too big. El Caucho wonders why he is trusting Luz-Maria. He could have waited and asked Madame Puñez to do him a favor—that would have been less risky. What got into him? But, after all! He couldn't refuse! It was natural for him to want this repair work done as quickly as possible. It's not his jacket. Luz-Maria's left breast practically falls out of her blouse. El Caucho isn't paying attention—he's looking at the work the woman is doing. Luz-Maria has cut a piece of alpaca out of the jacket lining and has placed it over the reverse side where the hole is. Using the very thread of the cloth, she is making such a careful patch that El Caucho is amazed. He is watching her nimble fingers pushing the needle with consummate skill and touching devotion. There are really some surprises in this milieu! Luz-Maria is not patching, she is literally manufacturing alpaca fabric! What this woman needs is not a Cadillac, but the warmth of a cozy little home, even if it were poor. Luz-Maria's left breast has erupted from her blouse and is jigging a Saint Vitus's dance. Luz-Maria bleats a little laugh and looks El Caucho straight in the eye:

"You're looking at me, you lecher! And what a suggestive look you've got! I like it!"

Luz-Maria literally rolls her eyes. El Caucho doesn't say a thing.

God! How strange human nature is! This whore at his feet—

she would have crawled to reach him, she would even have licked his feet to get him for herself! A whore just like the others! And all of that—why, for God's sake? Because each human being is simply a prisoner, trapped in a shell, dreaming of reaching beyond personal limits and becoming one with all nature. That's solitude—dramatic, frightening, inexplicable human solitude! Everybody—bourgeois, tramps, workers, priests, revolutionaries, mystics, explorers, adventurers, intellectuals, beggars—everybody is desperately hunting for the same illusions: communion, fusion with something beyond themselves, of which they can glimpse the greatness. No! It's impossible that so much wasted passion on the long journey of humanity will not be crowned somehow. Something great will come out of it. Total love is a certainty, and that will be the ultimate divinization of humankind. Basically, this woman's exhibitionism is no more immoral than lots of other things—not at all! It's a kind of despair, you might say, pitiful, but human. She acts the only way she can—the way she knows how. How, in this world of predation and abduction, of children left on their own, abandoned in Babylon, Sodom, and Gomorrah—victims of every type of exploitation—how, with misery and deprivation all around, how could this pitiful Luz-Maria not have yearned and sought in her own way for a minute of communion since she lacked any harmonious life or shared happiness? In search of that, she is displaying the only property she thinks she has, the only thing in which people show any interest: her breasts, her flesh. How this woman wanted him to accept being the companion who would, from time to time, console her from the solitude of these maddening bordellos! With only a few stolen hours each week, she would have at least a small illusion of living like a normal person, a creature not totally deprived of companionship in life's galleys. For each one of us, life has only one deluxe edition—very rare and with only a single, printed copy; you can never forget that. Luz-Maria would have given everything for him to accept being her *chulo*. If he accepts, she will give him the right to beat her, slap her, take the money she earns by sweat and the mournful effort of her hips, as long as he consents from time to time to whisper something sweet in her ear, to make a comprehending gesture, to give her at least an apparently disinterested caress. Her billfold is lying on the bed, beside her, wide open with a wad of bills. She is showing her breasts and her money! All the women in this bordello are crazy—outrageously crazy!

In this way, all through the ages, man and woman, that immutable expression of the unifying duality of life—man and woman, a brusque demonstration that the harmonious unity of opposites is possible in spite of the apparent contradiction—man and woman have frantically searched for love. Up to now, only a caricature has been realized, and likewise only facsimiles of intelligence and fraternity. Luz-Maria will probably not find the *chulo* of her dreams. And if she were to find him, the contemporary world would endeavor to ruin or destroy that fragile communion, to empty it of any meaning, to emasculate and sully it. In the final analysis, Luz-Maria's breasts are a witness to humanity! By means of a thousand small, prophetic signs, this era is announcing the possibility of great changes. People often perceive the social or political import of these signs, but how many understand their meaning for the individual heart? All those who are actually alive are links between two concepts of humanity and life; in all realms of thought and action, they carry within themselves, at one time, the past and the future, reaction and revolution! The movement will come from apparent stagnation and virtual ugliness; love is already beginning to change; it is throwing off the constraints and imbalance that have been imposed on it, up to now, by barbaric societies. It is simply necessary for a few great visionaries to set the example, for them to raise the banner of love by their uplifted arms. This evening, El Caucho senses that he has the soul of a volunteer for the journey to the moon of that great, human love. Fraternity will not really be achieved on Earth until the day when men and women will rise to the level of their historical task, loving with true love, with the fusion of their hearts, senses, and minds, going forward, becoming a harmonious cell of humanity finally liberated from animality.

"It's hot, don't you think, my little cat?"

Luz-Maria takes off her blouse. Another bleating little laugh. With her torso bare, she bends her body, letting her swinging breasts give off the aroma of strong coffee. As she plies the needle, she snuggles up to El Caucho and sighs:

"Take off your undershirt, darling. You must be hot too. Are you afraid of showing me your build?"

El Caucho is not staring at this body—so frantically, stubbornly, and repeatedly offered—but at those busy hands at work. The body is bending, unrolling, opening, palpitating, sighing, almost liquefying—as if seeking to be absorbed in a ravishing symbiosis. It's so depressing! Her eyes are those of a crazy woman retaining nothing that is human, but the hands of this animal in heat and the fingers that are lovingly finishing the repair, showing that the spark of conscience has not completely disappeared. Yes, we are really in a house of crazy people. The women are all crazy, every one of them—La Niña Estrellita like the others.

El Caucho hears the delirious yell that La Niña was uttering in the street a while ago.

"Down with the *Jwif!*"

El Caucho can see himself in the crowd of onlookers, watching the scene when the cry stabbed him. He hadn't yet noticed La Niña in the confused mob; he hadn't yet heard her voice, but he had immediately understood that she was the one bellowing. That voice had nothing in common with what was happening on the street. Under the guise of collective exaltation, this was an intimate cry, a cry that took every opportunity to break out, taking advantage of a situation where it was legitimate to yell. How much, how many things had she kept quiet about for so long, how many things of which she herself was not even aware, how many forgotten things came out in that voice. A captured beast, a trapped tiger, a tree struck down by lightning, a crushed dog—they all howl that way!

"Down with the *Jwif!*"

No, that is not really what La Niña was trying to say in that almost inarticulate bark of distorted sound emitted not from her throat or torso, but from her belly and guts. She wanted to say that she cannot take it any longer, that life is frightful; she was pleading for mercy, imploring. That voice had risen into the sky like an immense tongue of flame, throwing off sparks of all colors at every level—pink, yellow, blue, green, white, nearly black, ultraviolet. With that yell, La Niña let out her bile, howled her resentment.

"Down with the *Jwif*!"

Her hatred for everything, for this life from which she cannot escape, her hatred for the botched world, her hatred of hatred, her hatred of filthy love, her hatred for the lack of love, hatred of herself. With those blows of a billy club, she was punctuating her resentment on the arms, legs, and belly of the *Jwif*—and on his head that was as hard as fate. Wham for money! Wham for the responsible social organization! Wham for the right-thinking bourgeois! Wham for the bordellos! Wham for the whores! Wham for La Niña! La Niña's howls split the air—obscene, fierce, stiff. Those howls were aimed at children, the only truly innocent people who willingly participated with her in this strange game of assassination. With indecency, she was asking them to look at her, she was begging them to humiliate her, she was imploring them to never forget what she wanted to leave them as a legacy:

"Down with the *Jwif*!"

You could notice little quivering notes in that howling, echoing like little farewells. Farewell to the Frontier, farewell to the neighborhood, farewell to the sea, farewell to the Caribbean, farewell to all those who know that La Niña exists, to all those who have condescended to worry about her, even a single time. La Niña is leaving! La Niña is disappearing! La Niña is sinking!

"Down with the *Jwif*!"

La Niña exposed her inner self with that howl. The sounds she unleashed, shapeless and sticky, were vile. This was her way of telling the world about all the pestilence, the vice, the desire for vice, that were corrupting it, and deep down inside, she couldn't accept them. She was speaking of her ennui also. She was revealing the world's carrion, its putrid offal, its teeming worms, its fetid gases. That very disarticulation of syllables was hateful:

"Down with the *Jwif*!"

But El Caucho could also discern the vibration of sobbing in this heartrending yell. Yes, she was crying at the same time. Because of this, her voice kept a nuance of humanity, the edgy innocence of a little girl with some tremendous grief. It was coming from far away, very far away, but El Caucho could sense something familiar. Who is this mischievous girl who was crying? What have they done to her? El Caucho can see himself wiping the eyes of this woman whose face is surrounded by a mist. The explanations of the girl he is consoling, her stammering. . . . There is an imperceptible lisp in her speech. Where does that come from?

"Down with the *Jwif*!"

In fact, La Niña's yell is not completely inarticulate. You can hear some of her punctuated words and a slight lallation. At that very instant, some firecrackers had provoked panic, clearing away the square. It was then he saw, at the feet of the burning dummy, an unconscious child lying in the middle of the sparks and the projectiles falling there. Shoving the people out of his way, he yelled too and hurtled forward.

"I'm hot!"

Luz-Maria unhooks her skirt and takes it off. El Caucho doesn't budge. Completely naked, she is trying to catch his eye, as she twists like a cat, exposing her womanhood like a ripe fruit. With a sigh, she picks the jacket up again, pretending to take a few more stitches, then she throws it down and lets out a groan.

"Ah! You ungrateful fellow! Come on over here!"

She pushes against El Caucho, holding on to him, trying to bite the powerful pectorals bulging from his undershirt. El Caucho holds her shoulders, keeping her gently, firmly at a distance. As she struggles to get loose, an iron grip presses increasingly on her deltoids and paralyzes her. He looks calmly and cooly into her eyes. He lets go and looks at his jacket.

"What work! But you are magic, ¡*guajirita*! ¡*Verdad*! You

can't tell a thing! What can I do to thank you? That's not easy. I'm not sure. . . ."

What can he really give her to express his warm feeling? He has a little money, but, all the same, he can't offend her that way. He has nothing valuable to offer her. Yes, he does! His chain. And his tiepin, a little black pearl that his mother left him, the only thing left from that gentle creature who made him into El Caucho. His hand hesitates, twice. The chain? No! So, the pearl? What is that piece of jewelry, after all? Luz-Maria has curled into a ball, waiting for his decision, watching him with the eyes of a miserable little puppy. This is a cruel affront for a woman! El Caucho turns his head, takes his shirt and puts it on. Her stare hurts! There are tears at the end of her eyelashes. El Caucho throws his jacket over his shoulder. This is a real crucifixion! What can he give her? He goes over to the bed, extends his index finger, taking a tear on it and drinks it; then taking the girl's head in his two hands, he speaks to her.

"*Guajirita.* . . . My name is Rafaël Gutiérrez, but people have given me the nickname of El Caucho. That's curious, right? El Caucho offers you his friendship. Do you want it?"

He places a kiss on each cloudy eye. She keeps them closed. She is ashamed. The tiepin? He hasn't got the courage! He heads toward the door. But the chain, why didn't he give her the chain?

La Niña is displaying her pig look. This *Jwif* business has left her in a bad mood—nervous, capricious. She is looking for something at which she can direct the malicious laugh that is choking her, some vicious teasing, a scapegoat that she can yell at, that she can *salanbe,* as she says—some foolish thing she can do or, better still, someone she can hurt. She is sitting at one side of a table, alone, spread knees, a somber look, a sardonic smile at the corners of her mouth, torturing her scalp with her claws, voluptuously scratching her occiput. The marines are flooding into the Sensation Bar. La Niña notices one at a distant table, a young fellow with a pretty vacant stare. On the little finger of his left hand, he has a white metal ring with a green stone that keeps intriguing La Niña. The stone gives off striking rays beneath the reflectors of the hall, a kind of intermittent glance, the rays of a lighthouse lamp. La Niña has the impression that the little green stone is signaling her, calling her.

"La Niña! Come here! Come see!"

Mario, the boss, goes by within reach of La Niña. With a flick of her wrist, she pinches his buttock, hard. He turns around, speechless.

"Hee, hee!"

La Niña smirks with a stormy glance and wrinkled brow. Mario shrugs, turns on his heels, and heads toward the bar without a word. The little green stone is sparkling on the Marine's finger. La Niña can hear it.

"Hey! Come here, La Niña! Come see!"

A waiter goes by. La Niña surreptitiously grabs a bottle of beer from the tray he is carrying. The waiter did not see a thing. La Niña downs the bottle in several gulps and leaves the empty bottle among the plants growing by the railing. What a face the waiter makes when he does not find the right number of drinks on the tray! La Niña is exultant. Mario does not joke around; he will make her pay for that pinch!

"Hey, La Niña! Look! I'm green! Come here!" says the little stone on the ring.

La Niña gets up. She heads toward the table where the marine with the ring is drinking with his pals. She stops, leans on the fellow's shoulder, takes the cigarette he is smoking, and blows smoke in his face with an enigmatic smile on her lips.

"La Niña!"

"La Niña Estrellita!"

The group is delighted. La Niña settles down on the marine's lap, settling in.

"What are you having? A Pabst? Phooey! Jocelyn! Barbancourt rum for everybody! And bring the bottle!"

She takes the glass from the marine with a disgusted pout, and holding it with her fingertips, she lets it fall into the planter. The marines applaud and raucously imitate her.

"Hurrah, La Niña! Hurrah!"

"La Niña Estrellita! Hurrah!"

"Jocelyn! Rum! Hurrah, La Niña!"

The marine with the ring has a cigar in his jacket pocket. La Niña takes it, bites it, spits out the tip, and sticks it in her mouth.

"Give me a light, fool!"

Jocelyn brings the bottle that was ordered. La Niña is smoking furiously.

"At my order, everybody drinks! Ready! Fire! Reload!"

A joyful mood takes over at the table and, every four or five minutes, La Niña gives the command "Fire!" After some time at this game, La Niña gets up.

"I'm going to dance for you," she says. "But I want the floor clear. I want to dance alone!"

At the news that La Niña wants to dance, the dance floor empties. Somebody puts a furious *guarracha* on the record player, and La Niña gives a sample of her talent. She twirls her behind, legs, hips, and makes a little swing of her belly, advancing with her knees bent in little hops, only to fall back into the rhythm, swaying, shaking her shoulders like a plum tree and letting her limbs dangle even more freely. She bends her waist backward, and then quickly flinging herself backward, she touches her occiput to the floor and straightens back up immediately. The hall is going wild. And yet, La Niña has finished astonishing them. She stands still, marking the beat slightly with her feet, but not moving, and makes her buttocks dance. La Niña's buttocks can really do the *guarracha*! It's hair-raising, fabulous, funny, downright dirty, and lascivious. One buttock rises as the other one descends and then stops way down and begins vibrating wildly as the other one remains frozen; then that one takes off and the right side tenses. She falls down in a full split, and in that position, she does a disjointed jig, doing a bumpy dance on her vagina and belly, before she returns to her place in the gallery beneath thunderous applause. She straightens up, perches on her marine's lap, sticks her tongue out at the fellows demanding an encore, and throws grimaces left and right. La Niña gives the order again.

"At my order! Ready! Fire! Reload!"

The guys are rolling their eyes, but La Niña is on a roll, with her pirate's eyes, her mutinous mouth, and her joyful nostrils, as fresh as the morning.

At the instant when El Caucho came in, climbing the terrace of the Sensation Bar, La Niña was commanding a battery of zombies who, in a desultory manner, were obeying her orders, "Attention!"

The marines' chins were beginning to fall down on their collars. La Niña stopped cold when she saw that man. When she saw Luz-Maria lead El Caucho off and saw that El Caucho was going right along and disappearing in the direction of the rooms, she did not understand right away. She was astonished. Then she felt something like the stab of a dagger that left her breathing hard. She would have liked to run after them to slap Luz-Maria and take El Caucho away to her own room. She simultaneously underwent an irrepressible urge and complete paralysis—she did nothing but lower her head, thinking. But coming back to life immediately, with fierce eyes, and a smile on her lips:

"At my command! Ready! Fire!"

The battery is not responding any more.

"Fire, I said!"

The battery responds listlessly. The little green stone on the marine's finger gives La Niña another glance. She lays her head on the shoulder of the fellow on whose lap she is resting, kisses his neck, bites it at the nape, and skillfully slips the ring off his finger. She glances around and, without letting on, throws the ring among the green plants growing along the railing. She empties her glass. Nobody is the wiser!

"I want to dance some more! You're going to see something you've never dreamed of!"

Her samba is a real triumph, but as soon as her dance is over, La Niña goes to sit at a different table.

❋

❋  ❋

For the moment, La Niña is leaning on the bar with a glass in her hand.

"Let me through!"

What a voice El Caucho has! It's a deep baritone that re-sounds as if it were in a cathedral! What a man he is! He had dived into danger as everybody was running away, and he saved the kid. For the rest of her life, she will be able to hear him yelling those three short words:

"Let me through!"

He is really Cuban. He spoke in Haitian Kreyòl, but he ut-tered the sentence with the dizzying and explosive energy that only Cubans have: a passion for speech, a passion for life be-neath the appearance of tropical indolence, a passion for fleet-ing time. She almost thought, one of the fellows from Oriente. It is true—there is something from Oriente in El Caucho's ac-cent, that guttural roll of the final *r* without accenting the *r* in the middle of a word. And yet a final *r* is almost non-existent in Kreyòl. Could anybody who has not lived in Oriente have that accent? Some other person might not have noticed this pe-culiarity, but she could not miss this typical guttural *r*. This man, who has really been around, could not have kept that accent if he had only lived in Oriente for a short time. Maybe in child-hood? Oriente. . . . La Niña hangs suspended on that word for a minute, trying to capture its juice, its salt, all the mysteries the word could hold for her. Her heart beats faster.

"Let me through!"

There is a chill in the energy with which the sentence was ut-tered. There was no reflection in the intonation, but there was ever so much self-assurance, moderation, determination, quiet estimation of the risk in his tone. To all appearances, that man always knows what he is doing and why he is doing it. An in-fernal gambler would not have spoken differently.

"Let me through!"

In that tone there was a taste for danger, the intoxication of action, and yet so little exaltation! What can give the human voice such an accent of self-confidence? The tone was that of a prophet, a visionary. As if he were stating that nothing could happen to him! And yet, in the first word uttered, he had expressed a sort of fatalism, a sort of sharp but unconcerned hoarseness that expressed a lack of fear for either life or death. The word *me*, referring to himself, was detached from its context, as if he were adding: "Because I am alone, truly alone, always alone."

His only worldly goods then were his confidence in life and in himself, a confidence that is clad in iron but simply shielded by sunlight and incorrigible hope.

"Is there a tree to uproot? A mountain to move? A human life to save from its fate?"

That was indeed what he had yelled—that and nothing else! That voice was hoarse, gentle, vast, serious, solemn, disinterested, loving, passionate, pure, full of appetite, caressing, kind. . . . *¡Virgen del Pilar!* What color in three little words uttered by a simple human voice! And now that voice is shut up in one of the whorehouse rooms, in dialogue with Luz-Maria. Luz-Maria! A real animal! That voice is not modulating for La Niña at this moment! That rainbow voice! Luz-Maria took away the only true iris from heaven, La Niña's only iris! Has it gone out forever, Virgin of the Pillar? Because if he did "that" with Luz-Maria, Virgin of the Pillar, the earth has forever fallen away beneath La Niña's feet—her memory, her stubborn dream, her secret and obstinate hope are lost forever.

"Mario! A rum and Coke!"

❖

❖  ❖

That is El Caucho coming up to the bar with his swinging step, asking for a rum and Coke. Mario gives him a knowing look. El Caucho smiles and shrugs his shoulders.

"Well? The kid? Did anything happen? Is it serious?"

"Uhh. . . . A firecracker struck him beneath the eye. That's what made him lose consciousness. Several burns here and there. It won't be serious."

La Niña slyly gets into the conversation. She wants to know!

*Hearing*

She wants to hear him speak again. The conversation takes a triangular turn. La Niña makes a comment to Mario, but her words are directed at El Caucho. When El Caucho speaks to Mario, he is really reassuring La Niña. For his part, Mario is feeling talkative. El Caucho seems alright to him. Mario chats with El Caucho and answers La Niña. This has been a good week, and the squadron is leaving tonight without having done any great damage to the Sensation Bar—not many fights, no serious injuries, no police interventions, nothing broken! That's OK! And Mario is glad to be speaking to a man of the type that's hard to find these days. A guy like this brings back memories. El Caucho is drumming on the bar with his thick fingers. La Niña's tinny little voice crackles, her syllables rising and falling on the counter with an Argentinian ring. Periodically, El Caucho rolls out his phrases in his rough, dark-hued voice that echoes in his chest. La Niña scratches her scalp with her claws. Mario laughs heartily and tells anecdotes about last season. El Caucho rubs his knees against one another, making the alpaca of his trousers rustle. La Niña is tapping her foot nervously on the crossbar of her stool. A rattle lost in that Argentinian register. Fingers drumming. Mario's big laugh. A muted intonation in that thundering voice. Scalp scratching. Rustling alpaca. The tinny voice. A big laugh. Foot tapping on the crossbar of the stool.

No! He didn't sleep with her. His voice wouldn't resound that way. Besides, Luz-Maria would have been sure to come back in with him, holding him like a dog on a leash, ostentatiously, triumphant. The man's voice is clear, unhesitant—the elbow of his jacket has been repaired. He did not sleep with her. Oriente. . . . Yes, he is rolling those final *r*'s. It makes you think of a great blaze burning in a muted song. It quivers, crackles in a Cuban way: a sort of great sail that a tricky wind is making snap with approximately the same sound. The voice is metallic—a heavy metal. He is drumming. He is nervous. Who would tap that way with his fingers? His voice is a winding river, a continual and serious current bearing salt, heat, tenderness, and intelligence. A touch of malice. It must be great to lie awake, pressing against him in a state of semi-consciousness as he whispers "things" in your ear, with those crackling syllables that continue to hum. That rustle of alpaca sets your teeth on edge, but it means something. That means that he is nervous—he excuses himself, says he is sorry. No, I did not do what you might think. . . . La Niña's heel is tapping out Morse code against the crossbar of the stool:

"Good. I'll believe you this time. Fine! You didn't do it."

That guttural tone. One word comes back often, giving an affirmative and interrogative punctuation to each sentence:

"¿No?"

Particularly in Oriente, they talk that way. He laughs for the first time. Good heavens! That laugh! Why, it's . . . it's . . . It's what? It's funny, it's like a kid's laugh! There's a chorus of short little breaths, drawn in with whistles, humming, like a diamond ringing, delighted. She knows that laugh. Drumming, rustling alpaca. No! This is too awful, too stupid—she can't remember! It's on the tip of her tongue, and it goes away. She knows that laugh. Virgin of the Pillar, why that crazy idea? How could she know that laugh? Virgen of the Pillar, why that crazy idea? Here's another one—even crazier—that keeps coming back: "This man sitting beside her at the bar—it's 'her' man!" He laughs. That guttural vibration as he laughs. His voice twists. No, Virgin of the Pillar, no!

El Caucho is a little ill at ease. He is inwardly ashamed of that. He coughs to clear his throat. In spite of himself, each one of his coded messages means that he did not do what she might have thought he did. He is there only for her, just for her! And what if La Niña had come into the room a while ago and seen him with Luz-Maria naked? But, after all, does he owe an accounting to anybody? He has the right to sleep with Luz-Maria if he wants to! La Niña's voice is the sound of a fountain flowing, unconscious of its own origins. It's a fresh sparkle trying to find forgotten music. The guttural way he speaks! Oriente! It's almost certain. What naïveté in that rattle that crackles and then rings! He knows that voice! A long time ago, there was a similar voice ringing over the broad, marigold-covered meadow. That voice has deepened, become more serious, less joyful? The scratching of her scalp reminds him of something also. It whispers four or five times and then stops. That voice breaks into droplets of rain. The nervous, anxious foot tapping that is calling. . . . Where has that come from in his complicated, adventurous life? He seems to recall everything—the timbre, the gestures, that relentless nervousness. . . . In that voice, there is something stubbornly and desperately pure, in spite of the influence of this milieu. Is it an affectation? A game? No! It's so different from her braying a while ago:

"Down with the *Jwif*!"

There was something animalistic about that, while now, this sparkling flow from a spring inspires confidence.

There is a sudden to-do. Angry voices resound across the gallery. A nasal uproar. Jocelyn, the waiter, is answering. Somebody is fighting in the gallery. A violent blow resounds, and a table cracks and falls onto the floor:

"*Somebody stole my ring, I say! I know it! Robbers!*"

La Niña lowers her head. Somebody gives a blow on a different table, which noisily falls on the floor. Mario runs from behind the bar. They are fighting in the gallery. La Niña lowers her head. El Caucho turns to watch the scene.

✻
✻   ✻

The protest is getting louder. Jocelyn and two other waiters are fighting an entire group of drunk marines. Seeing Mario come toward him with sleeves rolled up, one marine breaks a bottle against the railing and waves it, pointing the broken end at the approaching boss. Mario turns pale and steps back. The marines are breaking chairs against the walls and arming themselves, yelling, howling, demolishing tables. Arming himself with a chair as a shield, Mario retreats further. He is obviously scared. A marine has gone around him. El Caucho steps in.

He heads right for the marine waving the broken bottle; he keeps his eyes on the fellow and slowly walks directly toward him. Suddenly he leaps and grabs the marine's arm. There is a brief scuffle. El Caucho twists his antagonist's wrist so abruptly that the fellow lets out a howl of pain. El Caucho grabs the broken bottle and hurls it into the courtyard; then turning back to his adversary, he gives him a powerful uppercut. The marine is literally thrown onto his back, unconscious. El Caucho lets out an awful roar. All the marines turn toward him. El Caucho retreats. Mario has run to the bar and taken the telephone off the hook. The marines are headed for El Caucho. He backs off further. La Niña cannot say a word.

El Caucho has his back to the wall and is hitting out with volleys of his fists to hold his assailants off. They step back also, but they are laying siege. El Caucho is watching the marines with a kind of sensuous delight. One big fellow tries to get close. With one left hook, the marine crumples. Another comes up. A terrible swing—the man stumbles and sinks to a seated position with his head *groggy*. It's a general assault. El Caucho is launching veritable volleys of blows with impressive roars. The marines retreat. With each new aggressor who has the daring idea of coming close, El Caucho punctuates his fall with a number in Spanish. His eyes are shooting fire.

"*¡Cuatro!*"

Another victim.

"*¡Cinco!*"

El Caucho is worse than a bull.

"*¡Seis! . . . ¡Siete!*"

El Caucho is laughing and letting out little yells. The marines surround him but do not dare come too close. They do not take up arms—it's *fair play*—these are real Yankees. They are on the alert, waiting, and pretending to attack—looking for their adversary's weak point.

"*¡Ocho!*"

The marines are really stupefied by this furious bull who doesn't miss his assailant.

The military police invade the Sensation Bar. They strike the marines with long nightsticks. In an instant, the hall has been cleared out.

The marines are carted off to a police wagon, waiting for them at the terrace. El Caucho wipes his forehead. Mario and the waiters hidden behind the bar finally stick their heads out. La Niña has not moved during the entire scene, sitting like a statue. Finally she can breathe. El Caucho comes over to the bar:

"Boss, give me a *grog*! A couple of healthy fingers! That makes you thirsty!"

El Caucho takes a deep breath. He laughs. Mario looks at him with admiration.

"That's really some 'Hello, Mister!' *¡Hombre!* What work! Are you a boxer? Frankly, I've never seen anything like that!"

"A boxer? No! Have to admit that it grabbed me just like that. The marines killed my father in Cuba a long time ago. I never knew him. So, you understand that now and again the desire to settle accounts with those bastards takes hold of me. Another *grog*, boss. I'm thirsty!"

"Well, from now on, you're at home in the Sensation Bar, *¡chico!* Mario's word of honor!"

El Caucho gulps down the rum. There is a still drop of blood on his lip. La Niña's hand reaches over and wipes the bleeding mouth, touching it with a handkerchief. La Niña lowers her head. She gets up. She goes over to the gallery. El Caucho watches her. La Niña searches among the green plants. There is an emerald sparkle. Only El Caucho saw it. La Niña climbs back up the steps, crosses the hall, and heads for the rooms. Her right fist is closed on something. She turns around. Would she dare? El Caucho does not know what he would have done in that case. La Niña disappears through the door, which recloses automatically.

# FOURTH MANSION

*Taste*

*¡Platero, qué grato gusto amargo y seco el de la difícil piel, dura y agarrada como una raíz a la tierra!... Ahora, Platero, el núcleo apretado, sano, completo, con sus velos finos, el exquisito tesoro de amatistas comestibles, jugosas y fuertes, como el corazón de no sé que reina joven.... ¡Qué rica! ¡Con qué fruición se pierden los dientes en la abundante sazón alegre y roja! Espera, que no puedo hablar.*
—Juan Ramón Jiménez, *Platero y yo*

Platero, what a pleasantly bitter and dry taste the tough skin has—it's tough and clings like an earth-bound root! Now, Platero, the concentrated seed, healthy and full with its delicate fibers, the exquisite treasure of edible amethysts, juicy and hard as the heart of some young queen. Delicious! With what a sensation the teeth sink into the joyous and abundant red ripeness! Wait, I simply cannot speak.

This morning, a true, living peace has descended over the Bord-de-Mer. No more sailors, no more wild scenes, the harbor is clean, no more furious Hertzian storms, and there is a tranquil atmosphere enlivened only by the ordinary activities of the commercial zone. But in the distance, a few muted series of explosions announce that the popular celebration of Holy Week is going to vibrate around the peasants' carnival, the Rara, which will not spill out beyond the limits of the suburbs. In the city, the fancy neighborhoods in particular will progressively halt their activities as the tragic and admirable Mystery of the Passion heads toward its culmination. La Niña woke up this morning in a groggy, icy, shivering state. Could it be that old tropical fever—which she had overcome if not completely cured—is reawakening? Who knows? In any case, she does not have that bitter taste nor the rigid feeling through her back, the ordinary signs of a new malaria attack. This must be something else. She is seated on an armchair in the glow of sunshine in front of the opened door with shutters, staring at the courtyard with its scattered plant tufts, green bushes, and fronds. In their cage suspended from the slatted blinds, the parrots are making a deafening uproar. La Niña looks at the birds, but she only sees them from the corner of her eyes. She is not really exhausted, not even feeling pain, but she simply feels that sort of languor that robs her of any desire to move. Besides, she is getting warm—the shivering is calming down to an occasional spot of gooseflesh. She is watching the film of the past three days rewind. The spectacle begins with images from the preceding evening and goes backward to Palm Sunday, which has changed the habitual flow of her life. It's stupid! If she hadn't been standing in front of the gate Sunday morning, nothing would have happened! Can she be sure of that? If she had not been in a critical phase of her life, what happened could never have taken place. Maybe she has even seen that man a number of times in the neighborhood without noticing him, without any spark igniting between them? Apparently, they were struck by something that had been brewing inside and had finally emerged only because of the earthy aspect of existence. In the end, everything that happens comes from our innermost selves: a part of our character that is always on the lookout for chance, just as a lightning rod tends to attract lightning. A delay of one, two, several days does not prevent events or whatever is prescribed in the inner logic of our hearts from taking place.

Up to now, she has lived by one basic principle, by the preconceived idea that her entire life would proceed in linear fashion according to a scheme established by some crazy god. She has seen her life from the exterior, proceeding in a straight line, and she has defined it as nothing more than the norms of the "pleasure" profession or the collective image of all the little Caribbean whores: a difficult apprenticeship, admission to a seraglio, the struggle for notoriety and "glory," the days of fame, and then the slow decline until finally, according to whatever the individual has managed to put aside, the final days in the gutter, the role of procuress, or a sad and nostalgic little retirement. In the harshness of facts, that is so, but seen from an individual perspective, is life the same thing for each woman? La Niña thought so, or at least she pretended to think so up to now. She has tried to base her inner life on her profession, and that has been the source of her suffering, her inalienable disequilibrium: that solid ukase coming right out of her own adolescent self-sufficiency. She thought she knew everything that was awaiting her in this profession, and she never bothered to show any interest in what other women thought; she had never paid any attention to their human drama. Today, she finds herself right up against a wall because she is not prepared to face the problems that were bound to plague her sooner or later. She had not been willing to see that the other whores had managed to find some balance in their lives, if only through a dream life, an inner mirage, an illusion perhaps, but one to which they cling with all their might. In her presumptuousness, she has repeated to herself that it is silly to base one's life on something false and unobtainable. She has engaged in a kind of reasoning that is logically accurate but humanly false: since it is impossible for a whore to find and live true love, she is not free, and all her acts are invalidated by social morality, which condemns her, and by the practical exigencies of a false rebellion in her struggle to exist—and, consequently, the chimera is futile. Q.E.D.: no utopia for me! Alas! But it is that chimera that, for us humans, gives our moods and psychic health some equilibrium—we bear our cross thanks to our mirages. Like other people, whores are less miserable in that way, and they even have occasional good periods; for La Niña, who has wanted to believe that she is exceptional, life has oscillated between maniacal excitation and nervous depression. Some result! That is where she has gotten through pride. So much the worse for women who think they are superior to others!

La Niña? Just a lovemaking machine, an obscenity-producing machine, a machine for laughter and nervous activity. You insert the right coin, and the machine does what it is designed to do! This is simply monstrous pride! Why hasn't she committed suicide, why hasn't she struggled desperately to find a job as floor polisher or caretaker of purebred dogs? Didn't those jobs seem dignified to La Niña either? She should stop complaining! Ultimately, what is killing La Niña is morality. She wants to believe secretly in true love and in beauty—that is why she has refused the luxury of taking a *chulo* like the others, somebody who would flatter her and give her a moment of illusion.

Faced with this dazzling truth, La Niña remains bewildered. With her hand shaped into a claw, she tortures her scalp. Yes, Dr. Chalbert is right: you always discover the truth by yourself when you resolve to examine closely your own personality; but it is often too late to turn back. Two days ago, she decided to choose an illusory dream for herself—that of becoming rich and taking a tour around the world—and in that way she admitted the failure of her gratuitous affirmations and logical concepts. But now, here is her pride, her monstrous pride, insisting on the selection of another mirage, one more unattainable than the illusions of the others. In order to avoid a commitment at this time, putting it off to some distant future, she has created an alibi. That way, she will not have to change anything in her present life and will be able to continue living as she did before. But now here is the point of rupture with her past conduct. In a word, there are two Niñas—the one she has gagged, and the other she has canonized: Saint Niña Estrellita, queen of whores, an exemplary lady of the night, a perfect *manolita*—pray for us! But the first Niña, that little Eglantina Covarrubias y Pérez, a native of Oriente, is finally getting her revenge. And what revenge!

Can she still make up for it, in spite of everything, and follow the others, taking a pimp, dressing him, feeding him, and putting money in his pockets by straining her own back? She would have to. She has to do it quickly before it is too late! She must kill that incorrigible faith in love, destroy the very last stone of that hidden little sanctuary that she has constructed in the depth of her own heart, dedicating it to sublime feelings, to beauty, to purity. Without any delay, she must bring that Eglantina Covarrubias y Pérez into line. La Niña must manage to derail that sentimental little retard and prostitute her heart as well! By recovering her memory of everything, it will finally be possible for her to put the little girl from Oriente in her place and combine her with La Niña—to adopt her skepticism, her corrupt heart, her wandering senses, her degraded, unhealthy spirit. In fact, that man has simply acted as a catalyst for a reaction that inevitably had to take place in her. As for this El Caucho whom Mario believes to be a real man, *un hombre transcendental,* La Niña will demonstrate that he is as spineless as the rest of humanity. She must manage to sully him. Only then will everything become simple once more.

La Niña gets up from her armchair. Good! Her maneuver? She will do it in a little while. For the moment, she has to go take a bath and regain her calm, fresh, and spontaneous mood.

She has made up her mind—now she simply has to carry out what she decided to do. La Niña lets her red satin robe slip off and stands completely naked in front of the mirror. "This" has been at work for twelve years—all of "this" has been pawed night and day, bruised, trampled, contorted in the most obscene positions by maniacs in vice, and it's still viable! Her flesh is perfectly elastic, her breasts still have their pert shape, aimed forward, tense, shiny, without a tarnish on their burnt honey surface. She is still physically attractive in the general curves of her figure—a real woman, and yet there are some persistent signs of aging, scattered here and there over this body of the professional bed companion! On the clavicles, the hollows, the shoulders, even the belly, and clear down to the clitoris, there is still something innocent, adolescent, and naive. What man can, through the gift of joy and sensual equilibrium, finally help this body achieve its full feminine potential? Who will be able to harvest this remnant of virginity that has paradoxically been preserved by any possible means? This is the spiritual aspect, the strength of that stubborn dream, a secret: it is a secret virginity of the heart that has protected the elasticity of that flesh, the shiny marble of those breasts, and the mature grace that persists in the entire eglantine of that miserable body. Oh! El Caucho! Will you be a gentle, demanding *chulito*—kind, tender, firm—for this La Niña who has waited for you? For, you see, her spirit is not dead. Eglantina Covarrubias y Pérez—you see, most horizontal professionals have something that is at once scandalous, obscene, and vile in the carnal beauty that covers them; but La Niña Estrellita is nearly virginal, and your life's breath salvaged that from the shipwreck and preserved it all this time! Our soul sculpts our bodies and colors our faces; the spirit, a strange electricity that distinguishes human from animal origins, is a marvelous cosmetic surgeon. Vital breath is capable of miracles in defiance of the usual laws of matter. And yet, as material and powerful as the living matter from which it comes, the human spirit is a true natural force! Thus, when it is pure and sure of itself, the spirit struggles mightily with disease, the most virulent germs, and perhaps it even combats to a certain extent natural aging—and the least little cell obeys its law. Yes, La Niña is totally the work of Eglantina Covarrubias, that immortal being. Thanks to Eglantina, you can still have something else to offer to the man you are waiting for. You can put your fluffy orange bathrobe back on, you can go out of your room, quickly or slowly—life carries you along! The hall of the bordello is almost empty. With great bursts of vulgar laughter, three or four women are "holding court" in the gallery.

La Niña Estrellita is at the pool. She is bathing. She is floating on the surface, with her face out of the water.

"¡*O mi cielito del Cáribe! ¡O Virgen del Pilar, aquí está tu Niña Estrellita!* O my little Caribbean sky! O Virgin of the Pillar, here is your Niña Estrellita!"

The Caribbean sky is blue, without the slightest leukoma, wrinkle, or crack in it. The sun is made of spun gold, orange-hued in this month of March as only Caribbean Marches can make the sun orange. The water is refreshing, and La Niña lets herself float. Her eyes—those two faded flowers on her face—lose their wrinkles in the dark honey of her complexion. Like the suffering brown Madonna in those old churches of the time of the conquistadors, silent, gentle tears flow down La Niña's cheeks. The salty tears fill her mouth, but her lips are moving gently. Where is that melody coming from? Yes, it's coming! The words of that little song she used to know come back to her lips:

> *Capullito de alhelí,*
> *Si tú supieras mi dolor,*
> *Responderías a mi amor,*
> *La, la, la, la la, la la. . . .*\*

Tears are streaming from those roses, La Niña's eyes. Tears are a good dew. La Niña is humming and crying at once.

---

\*Little bud of the gillyflower,
If you knew my pain,
You would respond to my love,
La, la, la, la la, la la. . . .

*Taste*

✤

✤  ✤

With an abrupt gesture, El Caucho throws his monkey wrench down. Without warning, he pushes everything aside and walks away from the motor he was working on. He goes looking for the *foreman,* and when he finds him, says in an angry tone:

"*Foreman,* I'm not feeling well, and my head is spinning—put me on the sick list. This won't disturb the work—the motors are running fine, and besides, tomorrow is Holy Thursday: there won't be much to do!"

El Caucho turns away before the *foreman* can answer him. He goes to get his clean clothes and stalks out. His pals call to him, but he doesn't answer. He leaves. On the road, he signals to a truck, which stops, and the passengers squeeze together to make room for the new arrival.

"Go on! Let's go!"

The truck is headed toward Portail Léogane. Traffic is flowing smoothly now—really moving along. The Portail is already in sight. They go past it. A little further, El Caucho climbs down at the Avenue Républicain and takes the Rue de l'Hospice-Saint-François on the right.

"Hey! El Caucho! Hey! It's really him! Where are you headed at this time of day? You're not working? You're some big chief! I'd like to do what you do, but I can't find any work. They promised me a job preparing the grounds of the Exposition, but that remains to be seen! What are you doing today, El Caucho?"

Ti-Djo is speaking. Not a bad fellow, but he really knows how to lay it on thick—he should have a degree in that. In the Bord-de-Mer neighborhood, Ti-Djo almost always manages to collect at least two or three *goud* in a morning spent mooching. What do you expect? When you've spent two or three years out of work, "on the merry-go-round" as they say, and without any unemployment compensation, it's not easy to get back into the habit of work. In spite of everything, El Caucho feels a little sympathy for Ti-Djo. That guy really has talent! And even if he's a sponger, he is always ready to be helpful—and especially to help a friend in need.

"Are you really in a hurry, El Caucho? Are you headed home? Things aren't going too well? Here, have a cigarette. Ah! My poor El Caucho! If you only knew how thankless *business* is these days at the Bord-de-Mer! I had put all my hope into a little motor that somebody gave me to tinker with, but it's really not in shape. If you're not in too much of a hurry, El Caucho, maybe you could take a look at it—that would really be helpful to me. Oh, I'm not asking you to fix it, but just to tell me whether it can be fixed. You know, El Caucho, things are not really good for your pal Ti-Djo. I'm wasting away, man! If work doesn't begin soon on the grounds of that damned Exposition, I don't know what's going to become of the poor men in this country!"

El Caucho lets himself be led off. In fact, he has time to deal with what's bothering Ti-Djo and then to take a rest. Besides, well . . . what an idea! Ti-Djo's place is not too far away—it's on the Cour des Miracles, next to the Wesleyan Temple, right across from the French Center.

"El Caucho, my little brother! At the house, I've got a bottle of *tranpe,* some Péterplancher—good stuff, really great! Don't you think we could buy a little something to eat together? We'd feel less lonely that way!"

"OK, Ti-Djo! Let's go to Delicia's."

Delicia, who really lives up to her name, runs a restaurant. She prepares meals to take out or to eat in the restaurant. Her place is located in a little courtyard beneath a huge soapberry tree.

"Delicia's Place—Cleanliness and Gastronomy" says the sign nailed to the tree. As she squats in front of her little grills, Delicia's face, floating above the tumultuous swells of her breasts, her wrinkled belly, and her monumental thighs, is concentrating on her work over the coals. El Caucho and Ti-Djo have served themselves in no time: chicken and rice, decorated with golden butter beans, goat jerky in a spicy sauce, a lot of fried plantains, and fried ripe bananas in a cream sauce for dessert. El Caucho is quiet and unexpressive, but Ti-Djo does not give a damn. Sponging off his friend, he is going to eat like a bourgeois—he doesn't worry about El Caucho's mood and leaves him alone.

After lunch, El Caucho repairs Ti-Djo's motor, and the two companions make the best of the Péterplancher. El Caucho is staunch enough to put away quite a few shots. Today, he has laid everything aside, he isn't very talkative, and he "downs" the glassfuls at a pace that has sent Ti-Djo hunting for more bottles.

*
* *

It is relaxation time at the Sensation Bar. Two o'clock in the afternoon. The ladies are holding court in the garden. There are a good half-dozen *manolitas* from the neighboring bordellos, accompanied by their *chulitos,* two of the hostesses, and two or three apprentices seeking work. Mario is managing the lotto bank. The waiters are coming and going with their platters. Off by himself with his chair against a tree, Doctor Chalbert is strumming the banjo. The unnoticed flow of hours continues in this unusual moment of tranquility and joie de vivre.

La Niña is sitting astraddle a chair, attentively observing the lotto cards spread out in front of her. She is caught up in the heat of the game and is hardly participating in the disorderly conversation that echoes and brings explosions of laughter to people's lips. The ladies have thrown off their professional masks—they are wearing little makeup and are casually dressed. This is the most agreeable moment in bordello life. It would not take much to give an illusion of complete happiness. Only Luz-Maria is ill at ease. Since Julio left her to take up with Felicidad at the Magic Bar, Luz-Maria has been in pain—it's rotten luck. The aspiring *chulitos* present make no great impression— they are starving, young delinquents who, at first glance, give no sign of security. These ladies prefer a mature man, one who is around thirty-five years old, a bit corpulent, and endowed with a prominent, sensuous belly. They have little taste for the unstable dandies who are penniless, like all the others, unless, of course, that rascal Cupid plays one of his tricks on the sentimental Messalines. In that case, there is no Hermione who can be their equal. Too bad for Luz-Maria! Today, she'll have to settle for one of these youthful fellows, but just for the night. She will let him understand that. Besides, when they are in training for a career as pimp, these whippersnappers have a sturdy professional conscience, great tenderness, and touching zeal in their trials at the horizontal fox trot with the "little mamas" on whom they've staked their claim. Which one will choose Luz-Maria? In any case, she will warn him right away and with extreme clarity: after a skirmish of lovemaking, he can't count on anything more—never knew him, so long!

La Niña is having a terrible streak of luck. That is not surprising since, in spite of her apparent watchfulness, her mind is wandering all over the place. She wants to play and wants to win, but her mind is as erratic as muriatic acid—it comes and goes off in all directions. Damn! She has to find the answer! At noon, she was waiting for El Caucho, and he didn't show up at all. In the afternoon, a man like him must be working. She can't count on him coming. What a strange man, all the same! La Niña is throwing caution to the wind, playing to pass the time. It irks her to lose constantly—she persists. She loses.

Lucrèce, a woman whose fortune is in her eyes, her attractive and ambivalent smile, and her filly's gait, is winning everything she could want this afternoon. Her *chulo*, Carlos—a little *grimo* and a political spy from the ministry of the interior, a real ace in deceptive denunciation—is seated beside his female companion with his revolver showing, looking conceited and happy. From time to time, Lucrèce waves her hand as a sign of victory. Without batting an eyelid, Carlos stuffs her winnings in his pocket. Lucrèce is lucky. Doctor Chalbert is plucking away on his banjo, playing a romantic merengue—an old-time merengue, "*Lisette quitte la plaine,*" Lisette, leave the plain—and Violetta from the Magic Bar is leaning familiarly on Doc's shoulder.

"... 24 ..., 87 ..., 5 ..., 49 ..., 18 ..."

Mario is calling out numbers. In spite of her stubborn persistence, La Niña is distracted, mixes up everything, and finally throws it all on the floor. She gets up from the game table and ambles listlessly around the players who are being watched by the tireless and concerned eyes of the three aspiring *chulitos*.

"Nyahh!"

La Niña makes a face at the little shits. Disconcerted, they look down and pretend to be interested in the game. Maybe Carlos is trying to find a way to get closer, gently of course. He has a way of making a poker face that is funny as can be. That's it! Go ahead, fellow! You make me laugh. I don't like informers, understand? Your boss, Gros René himself, has failed to sink his teeth into La Niña—it's no oddball like you who can shake her up!

Fernande comes in arm in arm with a tall, skinny woman—a long plank of pitch pine, a mulatress with a bony, yellow face and hair sticking to her temples like molasses. This big log's getup is pitiful, not to mention the black velvet chamber pot she is wearing on her head, like the dowager Queen Mary.

"Good morning, Madame Pintel!"

The *manolitas* hover around Madame Pintel. Clavellina, from the Democratic Bar, gets up from the game table and hurries over to the old trollop. She sits down in front of a console that has been placed to one side and pulls out her pack of cards. Luz-Maria also abandons the lotto game and goes over to her.

"Are you reading cards or palms, Madame Pintel? I like the lines on the palm—they always reveal the same thing!"

Madame Pintel turns toward La Niña.

"What about you, La Niña? Now are you ready for me to read the cards for you?"

"It's the lines on the hand that interest me. People say that you can also read lines on the feet. What I'm telling you is true, you silly geese! No joke! Don't you know how to read lines on the feet, Madame Pintel? Now that's something that would intrigue me! The only thing is that you mustn't tickle me; I warn you—I don't like that."

Doctor Chalbert is getting ready to leave, in spite of the concerted protests from the *manolitas*. He puts his instrument in the jalopy, which begins coughing, farting, and sneezing before it starts with a tubercular wheeze. Firecrackers are beginning to pop in the street again. The kids must have come back from school. Easter vacation begins this evening—and the neighborhood will soon be unbearable. It won't take them long to put a new *Jwif* together.

"... 47 ..., 53 ..., *el número uno* ..., 73 ..., 69 ..., 20 ..."

Mario continues his litany and the lotto players keep throwing money on the table. Madame Pintel calls to La Niña, who has fallen into daydreaming.

"La Niña? Are you coming for a palm reading? It's your turn."

La Niña doesn't budge. She can't take her eyes off the gate. In fact, El Caucho has just made his appearance. His gait is a bit heavy, but he heads straight for the group with his firm step.

"La Niña? Are you coming?"

El Caucho is now close to the game tables. His eyes are red, and his forehead is furrowed. He must have been drinking. He is really "loaded," but he can take it—he stands straight, calm, and dignified. Mario looks up.

"Hey, *hombre!* What's your name again? Oh yeah, El Caucho. El Caucho, come sit beside me! I'll offer you a drink! He's no ordinary guy, you know. Last night ..."

Mario tells about the fight the evening before. El Caucho sits down in silence beside Mario. He has red eyes, but he keeps looking straight into La Niña's pupils, and she seems to be hypnotized by him. Madame Pintel is losing patience.

"OK, La Niña? You're not interested any more? Besides, my poor eyes can't see any more here—I'm going to sit in the gallery. La Rubia, are you coming?"

La Niña has taken La Rubia's place in the lotto game.

" ...75 ... the two little ducks ... 3 ... number zero! ..."

La Niña is gambling everything. She is winning. She is winning everything she wants. She keeps her eyes glued on the lotto cards. El Caucho does not say a word—his red eyes are focused on La Niña. What he must have drunk! And yet, he remains really steady—he can really hold his liquor! He's not saying a word—just sitting quietly, not even blinking. Fortunately, it is beginning to get dark, and nobody seems to notice that he isn't taking his eyes off La Niña. La Niña is risking everything like mad. Shivers run down her spine. She wins every time. The critical moment is coming—it is now or never!

"...13...,6...,81..."

"I won!"

La Niña again! She gathers up the winner's stakes with a triumphant glance. Now she has a little pile of bills in front of her. Mario gets up.

"It's almost night. Game's over! It's time to get ready for work. Put away the tables and chairs. Jocelyn, François..., and you too, friend! Hurry up! Coming with me, man? I'll offer you a drink at the bar."

Everybody gets up. El Caucho stands up, but he stays where he is. Jocelyn, François, and Camille carry the equipment off. La Niña is on her feet, too. She is caressing her green and white postiches. Jocelyn takes the last two chairs and disappears. La Niña and El Caucho are alone.

El Caucho is standing with his eyes glued on La Niña. La Niña is trembling; she steps closer to him with her winnings clutched in her hand. She is very close to El Caucho. She hesitates; he does not flinch. La Niña moves closer. Their breathing mixes. La Niña hesitates. Her lips barely touch El Caucho's mustache for a second. Their mouths come together. La Niña kisses him passionately. She eats, nibbles, feasts on that big lip, finally feeling its contours; she caresses it with her tongue. She passionately kisses that meaty double fruit. She takes a breath. He returns her kiss! If she could just die during that kiss! Let it last, let it last—let it go on forever! Let the stars come out; let the moon rise! Let her lie down! Let the dawn redden the sky, let the sun rise, let the day be one endless second; let the sun drown in the sea! Let it make way for the stars, for the moon, for the other eternal comets! But El Caucho has interrupted the kiss. Why? Oh, why did he do that? With his thick fingers, he has discovered the shoulder sticking out slightly from La Niña's blouse. He kisses it—another carnal kiss, as fiery and enchanted as the first. Let it keep on! Let it be extended to the boundaries of space! La Niña is devouring the back of the neck that is close to her mouth—she smells it, plants her teeth in it, drinks it. In a similar way, she discovers the man's shoulder and lets her tongue glide along it. She is furiously tasting that spicy flesh. The pectoral muscle, the bud of his nipple. She would have liked to undress him and give herself to him right there in the crushed bushes. He resists. He recovers himself.

"Take this!" says La Niña. "Take it all! Take it all and take me!"

El Caucho draws away from La Niña. He glances at what she has just slipped into his hand. She has handed him the whole wad of bills she won.

"Not that, woman! Not that!"

El Caucho's feverish eyes are burning La Niña. She'd like to sink into the earth! She suddenly begins trembling.

"Not that, *chica!*"

Anger distorts El Caucho's voice. He is rumbling. He throws the wad of bills at her feet in a gesture of anger.

"Not that!"

La Niña has turned to stone. She is paralyzed. She wants to speak, explain, but not a word comes out. El Caucho bends over and picks up the bills. He puts them in La Niña's palm. He bends his head. He turns on his heels. He leaves. His toes touch the floor, but his heel hardly comes down. El Caucho . . . is gone. . . .

This is La Niña's little world.

La Niña is sitting at a table with Habib, an important half-Syrian, half-Haitian businessman, along with several of his companions. Habib came this evening with some other companions that he has just imported from Puerto Rico—deluxe gallantry. That does not mean that these women are superior to the others in any way, but they are the darlings of their slave master for the moment—that's all. When he has had enough of them, he will drop them the way you throw dirty laundry aside. At that point, the women will leave for some other spot in the

Caribbean, if they do not stay to increase the population at La Frontière. The future success of these little whores is a different story, and it's a matter of chance—their way of dealing with people, their savoir faire, their inclinations and talent for the profession. At Habib's table sits Urbain Tancrède, a big politician of the moment and an official of the ministry of the interior. At his right is a young mulatto and on his left, a young fellow with alert eyes—he is a black. Urbain Tancrède's guardian angels, Gros René and Carlos, Lucrèce's pimp, are also there. Lucrèce is there, too, of course. Further on, there is another fellow that La Niña doesn't know. At a neighboring table, there are two mulatto ephebes, fair-haired youths. These two are well-known homosexuals who come to the Sensation Bar to sneak pecks at each other. There are not too many customers in the hall this evening—just a few habitués who cannot get along without the shady atmosphere of the bordellos. Mario is behind his counter—unexpressive and meticulous as ever.

What is Mario looking for in life? Fortune? He already has a substantial living. He must tell himself that he is after riches. In fact, Mario has become part of the milieu. He eats well, drinks quite a bit, does not sleep much, has plenty of everything he needs—but, in the final analysis, what he really wants is the spectacle that he watches from behind his counter, taking in the whole raucous scene, yelling at the waiters, stopping the music when something catches his attention, putting on frenzied records and promoting the bacchanal when the pantomime slows down. Mario has the impression that he is the deus ex machina of the carousel he has put together through patient effort. He firmly believes he is the one who makes the puppets dance on his stage. Mario has achieved what he wanted. He has money, and now he can take it all in, take in with wide-open eyes the bitter comedy of life. He has finished being an actor himself. At midnight, at two, four, six o'clock in the morning, when there is nothing more to watch, he will close the place, put the dolls back in their boxes, and go home. He will lie down beside his wife, who begins snoring without ever asking a question. His daughter is in a boarding school with the good sisters of Saint-Joseph-de-Cluny on Lalue Street. One day, that gentle little creature will have a bourgeois wedding—that's almost certain. Toward one o'clock in the afternoon, Mario arrives at the Sensation Bar with the bearing of someone who makes the world turn, and the bordello comes to life. Some day, Mario may turn to politics, but only after he has left his post at the counter. Then Mario will have found a bordello of another dimension, a more ignominious form of prostitution that is more fun to contemplate and manipulate. That's what the Caribbean is like.

La Niña does not want to look at herself this evening, so she is observing other people. That keeps you busy. Big Habib, calmer and with a more protruding belly than ever, is probably planning some surprise that will floor all the big shots in flour or coffee—that is probably why he is with these politicians tonight. At least with Habib, you make no mistakes—red head that he is, he has a sort of nostalgia for the lot of have-nots. He seems to have chosen making money because that little game amuses him, but more than anything he wants to prove to himself that he is capable of becoming a multimillionaire in dollars like everybody else. You just have to choose the right direction. Habib does not give a hoot about "good society"—he hangs out with prostitutes, *chulos,* pimps, and, once in a while, the politicians he needs. By his own example, he demonstrates that money is stupid. Evenings, he heads for the bordello, after spending the entire day giving the great bourgeois from the business world a hard time to his heart's content. Habib is an anarchist millionaire. Of course, he pulls some pretty good ones— he takes an innocent girl and places her on the road to prostitution; he takes a bourgeois with a high collar in the palm of his hand and throws him up in the air two or three times, only to let him fall into the garbage can, great guy that he is. Habib seems to despise the human species—he pulls some really filthy tricks, and then, all of a sudden, he makes a gesture of such nobility, such generosity, such tenderness, that you are flabbergasted. If, some fine day, Habib is called to do something great, he is capable of throwing everything aside and throwing himself, heart and soul, into making the human condition more beautiful, more joyful, and making all humankind shine with such a sparkle that he himself will be amazed, to all appearances. Habib is capable of the worst and the best—if he does not have the time to turn completely rotten as a victim of his own game. What is it that Habib wants to avenge?

Urbain Tancrède is the unthinking, wily bastard. He is working for Estimé's government today, but there will be someone else tomorrow. After going through hard times for years, Urbain Tancrède has "arrived." He does not like to strain himself and does whatever is demanded of him. He is the executor of important affairs. If an assassination is needed, Urbain Tancrède is there; if there's some torturing to be done, Urbain Tancrède volunteers; if it's a bit of espionage, Urbain Tancrède cleans his spy glasses; if it's necessary to betray somebody, Urbain Tancrède won't miss the boat. As long as he keeps eating! His henchmen, René and Carlos, are simply less educated, more stupid copies of Urbain Tancrède. Gang law is simply grub, sex, and the take. The two petty bourgeois, the mulatto and the black man, are another matter. The mulatto comes from a family that lost its position—for him, politics is the only way to regild his coat-of-arms. On a political level, color is the principle—the so-called struggle against the mulatto bourgeoisie is what pays these days—and so, the impoverished little mulatto bourgeois starts howling with the others:

"The blacks are right! The mulatto bourgeois are a bunch with no country—they are full of prejudices, racist, and exploiters! Support the people's policies of President Estimé!"

As soon as he has earned a few hundred thousand dollars by denouncing the mulattoes, he will return to the governing council of the Cercle Bellevue, and nobody will have more social prejudices than he does. So, to the attack of the state and financial rewards! For his part, the little black politico is dreaming of passing over to the other side of the barricade. He has finished secondary school and has a *licence en droit*—he knows what the good life is; he has read a few books:

"Down with the mulatto bourgeoisie! Get out so I can take your place!"

When he has his factory, three or four hundred *kawo* of land, a $50,000 house, what will distinguish him from the other mulatto bourgeois that he is vilifying today? His political demagoguery? Maybe! In fact, the color question is an excellent weapon that can still serve for a few years to disarm the people and to divert them from their essential objective. Thanks to that, it will be possible to cut to pieces the competing bureaucrats from the mulatto bourgeoisie. Long live feudalism! How long will the people let themselves be taken in by this little game played by the black and mulatto ideologues? In the meanwhile, the issues of state and society remain unresolved. Long live the "majority class," gentlemen!

The two little faggots at the next table are spending money papa skimmed off in politics, in the black market, or in other shady affairs—along with a few other delinquents here and there in the hall, and the cycle is complete! There you have La Niña's little world. They are all here in the Sensation Bar this evening, looking friendly, but they are playing the infernal game. One evening, they are slapping each other on the back, only to stab one another in the back the following morning. But something will nevertheless bring these parasites of the people back together: their animal needs and their filthy money. While they are there, the Earth keeps turning, the Sensation Bar is brightly lit, the whores are braying, the *chulos* are getting themselves taken care of, the *palgos* are making the rounds of the fancy restaurants, the peasants are trading their bits of nothing for dirt, the workers are grinding, hundreds of thousands of the unemployed have only their knuckles to gnaw on, the so-called Marxists are gargling with words, and the stench is spread out beneath the sun. There you have the little world of La Niña Estrellita!

Her future days and nights will be spent in this company. Her youth will not last long, maturity is lurking, and decrepitude awaits her at the end of the tunnel.

As for El Caucho, he was drunk, and yet he turned away from the woman offering herself to him; he refused her money. El Caucho is crazy. That guy refuses to be a *chulito;* he threw the money down. He is not eager to come to the Sensation Bar to offer his ration of illusion to a woman he likes and who is ready to relieve him of all material need. El Caucho is always himself—fit to be tied, whether he's drunk or not. He bends over, picks up money he doesn't want, and slips it back into your hand before leaving. He is practically begging your pardon for his angry gesture—he is begging your pardon for having insulted you, since he tells you that he mistook you for somebody else. If he had not been drinking, perhaps he would not have thrown the money down, but he would have refused it just the same. Alcohol unleashed that gesture, but his behavior surfaced from deep inside. He's never coming back. That vast meadow with its yellow marigolds is gone forever! That feline suppleness and those inspired gestures are gone! That living speller in which she was relearning the ABC's of real life is gone. That stocky, tender hand that tapped while recounting his heart's story, that rough male aroma of leafy vegetables, herbs, peanuts, roots, and so many, many spikenards is gone!

"Not that, *chica*!"

The sinuous voice, loud and thundering, his gutteral articulation has disappeared; the warmth has dissipated, and the kiss is gone. That kiss!

His lip is a hard guava, a bit alkaline, salty, rough, causing a kind of itching, pecking, making you want to prolong the contact. That man must let the sea breeze drop the seaport spray on his lips. Enamored of the suave trade winds, he must love this salt that is the soul of the insular Caribbean. At any moment, in the creases of his lips, there must be that bitter delight from the ocean air, that cerulean blue, the sole azure in the world, which extends its sapphire elixir from the Bahamas to the Guyanas, from Puerto Rico to Tampico, Veracruz, Panama, Cartagena, and La Guajira. El Caucho's lips are the sea, sky, lagoon, the Étang Saumâtre, just like the Azuéi and the Caguani loved by Cacique Enriquillo. The penchant for that biting taste—primal alkaline—is something ancient with men of these islands: Lago Dulce, sweet water lake, Enriquillo said when speaking of those waters with an aroma of sparkling water. The carnal spice of that blue lip, like the most beautiful blue in the world, is witness to the salty ardor hidden in that body.

Savoring the velvet of the mucous membranes, you have the impression of quitting the sea to head into the estuary and suddenly arriving in the river. Far from altering or emasculating the sapidity, the bouquet of the alcohol he drank, the Péterplancher, heightens the sensation. The satin interior of his mouth is glazed with an almost pure fructose, slightly bitter, a scintillating *godrin*, an ardent, spirited wine. Ah, that sensation gone forever! So, where, in what dream, in what country beyond the tomb, in what paradise can it be found again, Virgin of the Pillar! That pearled fruity taste of the mucous membrane with the sparkling essence of the gums, what a surprise, what titillation! The juice of virgin tobacco—and a Cuban "Delicado" to boot—the hint of lemon peel, the sharpness of mint along the biting edge of the teeth. And then, entering that cavern with its humid vaults, finding that gelatinous, sneaking, lively monster crouching, lurking! Ah! To marry that wet, sensitive beast, covered with taste buds—that sweet and sour beast! That crazy kiss with that long, fleshy, Venusian tongue, that sticky lizard, rising, fleeing, running, rolling up, and constantly embracing its prey, its polypary mate! Then the rain inundated these two entwined animals, ecstatically sucking, a warm, acid autumn rain, the rain of two salivas, one the heavy syrup of citronella, the other a piquant anisette. And all of a sudden, the desiccation of desire swells, a fizzy surge of electricity, and everything has been changed into a torrid and earthy desert on which two sodden jellyfish, rough and dehydrated, are in the last throes of death beneath the burning sun of pleasure!

Lips half open, eyes almost shut—La Niña relives her lost ecstasy. From now on, this man is her whole life, everything that she will no longer have. Will she ever be able to forget those minutes? Forgetting her past life is easy, on the other hand! That kiss, the joining of those two mouths, stopped only because the human heart has limits, breath must continue, but another kiss followed that one immediately. On the nape of his neck, she discovered a pepper shaker; the cinnamon of hard flesh, balsamic;

the resin of that coarse pineapple, his neck; the spicy salad of hair. His shoulder is a ripe tamarind that sets the teeth on edge, a more biting tamarind flavor than all the citrates continually sought by Caribbean children in search of a mouth-tingling surprise. The fold of his armpit is the sum of all the sensual fruits of this archipelago where paradises are countless, exalting, terrestrial, lordly. As for that pectoral muscle, pulled away at the instant she was discovering the fleshy bud of breast at the onset of her exploratory adventure, the scents she had already inhaled from the body of this man suddenly became real like a salami or salt pork. Better than all other aromas, this has given hope once again to her long anesthetized senses. Ah! Wrested away! She is all alone now!

Her table companions keep jabbering. For them, keeping company with these women is nothing more than an occasion for their schemes. The high official is pontificating:

"President Estimé. . . ."

La Niña leans over and whispers something in Lucrèce's ear. The two women get up without attracting the gentlemen's attention. They head for the rooms. La Niña follows Lucrèce into the dark room. Lucrèce leans over her bed, uncovers a corner of the mattress, searches, and pulls out a package with two cigarettes, which she hands to La Niña. Lucrèce goes back to the barroom alone. La Niña goes back to her own room, bolts the door, and then undresses. She gets in bed and lights one of the cigarettes. She inhales deeply, filling her lungs, not losing an ounce of smoke. This is the only solution left: artificial paradises. She conscientiously draws on the cigarette, in spite of the nausea rising in her throat. She waits for the liberating takeoff, the delightful sensations of a bitter nirvana in which pleasure or a stupefied trance will titillate and lull her frightened heart. Why didn't she think of this earlier? It's stupid. She has to try everything—opium, marijuana, Demerol, and all the rest. At last she will be free, freed forever from consciousness, freed from her dreams, freed from her senses, freed from that man who left carrying with him that last firefly of her twenty-sixth year.

"La Niña, you're dead—you're already dead; it's just that the funeral chants haven't been sung yet!" Those are Doctor Chalbert's exact words. She did not invent them. So what does she have to lose?

*

*   *

The clock at Saint-Anne's peals out midnight. El Caucho goes back to bed. He keeps squirming, looking for his favorite position, but he cannot sleep. What woke him up? It was not that clock, because it is always ringing in this neighborhood, and he never wakes up at night. His head is heavy. What got into him today? To begin with, this was not the time to stop work. Sick? That's a joke! El Caucho is never sick. He hasn't been thinking much recently; he has spent more money than he has ever earned in a week, not even counting the ten dollars he borrowed from Madame Puñez. In fact, El Caucho has a small deposit in the Royal Bank of Canada, but he mustn't touch that. That's a kind of health insurance, a guarantee in case of some unforeseen catastrophe, and catastrophe is always hovering over El Caucho's head because of his mania for reform. And then, if by some chance the political situation changes in Cuba, he will have his nest egg—he won't be held back for lack of money. He mustn't be a fool; he no longer has anybody in this world. Where could this affair with a prostitute take him? He's aging. He will be thirty years old in a few months; he has relentlessly struggled against this bitch of a life; he has painfully tried to maintain the course he set out for himself: he has exerted greater effort than any of these megalomaniacs hunting power and fame to achieve their goals; and now, after all that, what? He's thirty years old and has his first gray hairs, relentless solitude, no real friends—just companions, good companions at best. True friendship may be more difficult to find than genuine love because, with real friends, there is no sexual attraction to complicate the relationship. It is easy to find somebody who has more or less the same opinions you do about important things, but somebody who has the same basic approach to life's problems, the same heartfelt reactions, someone who is more or less like you, come on! Someone who would feel your heart beating, someone who could see inside you with a sixth sense! That isn't easy! At times, people who are different in almost every way may be closer, more capable of being sympathetic, of participating in somebody else's drama or comedy than the people to whom you are linked by some agreement in ideas. More than anything, friendship is seeing somebody with your inner eye, taking part in the thrill he gets from a blade of grass, from the onset of springtime, from a woman, from a glass of alcohol, from disappointment or happiness. Of course, if there is that accord of ideas also, if existential beliefs are similar, this friendship can go a long way—but, above all, friendship is a sixth sense. It is rare for two human beings to have their antennas set on the same wavelength and to connect right away with one another. You look for that for a long time before finding it—it takes time. The battle of life has never left El Caucho time to discover that friend. If he were an ingratiating person, a good bourgeois, content with his slippers in the evening, he might easily have encountered another spineless friend just like him, but El Caucho knows that he belongs to the kind of people who are storming the universe. El Caucho does not want to be ashamed at the moment when he is facing death. He doesn't want to have missed any mark that he could have hit. He will tell himself:

"I haven't had any real friends; I haven't known true love; but whose fault is that? It's not because I didn't try. I searched passionately. The brutal struggles of the time didn't allow me to make that discovery, and others weren't prepared to encounter me. Too bad!"

Whether people do justice to El Caucho or not, let them remember that life did not keep him from doing the best he could. He will have contributed in his own way to the advancement of humanity, even if it was only by a few millimeters on the long march forward. He will have helped history to function. He will have given a hand to the flowering of great human love. That is something! El Caucho is an authentic son of the Caribbean. When he has to "sign off," he will say:

"I've done a lot of foolish things, but I did them in an honest, human way. I did a little something, even if it wasn't enough! Anyway, what a joke life is! So long, sun!" And he will offer a broad smile to the great blue sky.

El Caucho has a headache. He gets up to go after a tall glass of water. He does not turn on the lights, so he stumbles, hits several pieces of the miserable furniture in his rented room. He finds the pitcher in spite of all that. He drinks directly from it and goes back to bed. He will see the fellows tomorrow and explain to them that they have to organize a union. He will lay out his political ideals. He will go for a walk, he will listen to the sea singing, he will lie down in the grass and breathe, and he will suck on an alkaline blade of grass. Tomorrow, he will read a book, even if the subject is hard to understand. Tomorrow he will continue looking for a true friend to share the drama and the comedy of his life. Tomorrow, he will look for a woman made for him. Back in bed, El Caucho can't sleep. He sees his clothes hanging, phantoms of his boredom; he sees the table, he sees the chair, he sees his toes beneath the sheet. The night is luminous, and the light comes into his room through the half-open blinds. You can see. El Caucho measures the blood coursing through his temples. He feels his heart quiver and jump. The heart, that ticker—some curious machine! What could he drink to get back to sleep? He has to sleep! He will have things to do tomorrow. What about turning on the lights? No! Must sleep! What if he turns on the lights anyway—he can read a page of his book, just one page. What a fellow—El Caucho!

El Caucho remembers. Her eyes make her look as though she were magnetized. *Aimant*—magnet? *Aimer*—love? The words must have the same origin. Why did he drink himself into a stupor today? Say, El Caucho, why? Some guys would not understand. There are some fellows who would have said:

"Comrade El Caucho was drinking today—he was drunk. Comrade El Caucho needs to be punished. When you have the union responsibilities of comrade El Caucho . . . When you have the political education Comrade El Caucho has . . ."

"Shit!"

*Taste*

Comrade El Caucho, as you call him, is not made of wood. Jesús Menéndez said that once. Comrade El Caucho is allowed his bad moods like everybody else. Doesn't that ever happen to you? If you don't understand that, you may be "comrades" as you say, but you're not friends. When comrade El Caucho is depressed, are you inside his skin to feel what he is feeling? So! You're not friends! He doesn't have any friends. In fact, however, the comrades are right. Everything they say is true, but it's their way of saying it, right? Pay attention to controlling your moods next time, El Caucho. Everybody has moods, but just the same! Look at that woman—you threw down the money she handed you! Is that fraternal? You insist that everything should be explained to the fellows! Theory and practice. . . . That all happened because you had been drinking, comrade El Caucho. Comrade El Caucho!

"Shit! Haven't you finished that song? That's enough of that . . . , OK?"

Ah! If he could find a guy who would be a brother, a real friend who wouldn't need a picture to understand, to sense everything right away. A guy who would be discreet, even though he was close to you, and who might chew you out once in a while, of course, but one who would understand. Not a guy to give you lectures or offer absolution, but a guy who could get inside you. A guy who would smile and be able to express everything you're feeling with the rainbow of his smile. When things were not going well for you, for no particular reason, a guy who would stay with you without asking for anything, even if he had a date with some little darling. A guy you could talk to without him looking at you wide-eyed as if he were asking whether you weren't a little loony. A guy like that, just one—you ought to be able to find one all the same?

El Caucho remembers. She came very close. Their breath mingled. Then, like a butterfly lighting on the mouth, trembling while walking around, it changed—it was transformed. A long tongue darted about and licked his lips—God, that was good! Like a little barley sugar cane—or rather, like a little candied violet, a candy without sugar. The tongue penetrated his mouth

and the taste of violet disappeared. It was a lively little animal—
a lusty little animal covered with sea spray, iodine—soda and
sugar all at the same time, something like playing in the sea on
a hot day. When you open your mouth at the surface of the
water, your tongue will taste the top layers. El Caucho went off
once with a little neighbor girl. . . . Maybe that is only his recollection of a dream? Now who was that little girl? Which one
of them had egged the other one on? Did she, or was he the one?
In any case, it happened in a broad meadow covered with
marigolds; and rascal that he had always been, El Caucho had
kissed the little girl! The whole Caribbean sea was in that
mouth! Since then, he has been looking for mouths with the
same taste! El Caucho, you can look around, search the entire
Earth, lift all the stones, spread all the leaves apart, climb all the
trees, run along all the beaches, the ravines, dunes, savannas,
valleys, lagoons, plains, mountains—and you know you will
never find a human mouth with that same taste. That mouth
was your whole youth, El Caucho. Youth is stubborn and does
not forget!

Then that tongue went up and down along his gums, brushed
along his teeth. It changed into something mentholated, fresh,
with a soul of its own that ran like an April fountain over the
niches between his incisors. Then, the mucous membrane of
your mouth fused with that of the other mouth: it was a
*kayimit,* a star apple, the fruit of the ancient Caribbean! A fruit
with living flesh, violet-colored flesh, juicy and succulent, cool.
It's a gelatin, a fruit that will never have its like again on the
Earth! The joining of two mouths preceded the miracle. The
miracle happened. It appeared in the form of that fleshy, vene-
real animal, hunting the sticky protuberance of your tongue—
and the two beasts struggled, rolling and unrolling. One beast
was ravenous, the other was dancing—and it was as good a
dancer as La Niña—a savage, ferocious, voluptuous beast looking for its bride: tracking, cornering, taking the other one prisoner, holding it, ravishing it, enchanting it with its own magic.
Then the rain fell, a heavy spray like the Caribbean rains of November—a warm, gaseous, ozonic rain made of those two com-

bined salivas—citronella and anisette. There followed the drought that was as severe as when the peasants speak of the *sèk,* that torrid desiccation of the desert. The two beasts rubbed against each other, seeking each other out in that earthy taste of the desolate savanna, burned beneath the sun. The two beasts were in agony for a long time, dead from exhaustion.

El Caucho remembers. He himself broke off the kiss to look for another contact, another kiss. That hairless shoulder, openly protruding, seduced him. He put his hungry lips to it, and all the little petals of Cape flowers with their spicy juice stuck to his palate. His lips remained attached to the softness of that shoulder with its carnal taste, the taste of blood at skin level, a taste of coursing blood, the savor of flesh hiding all its balms, all the animal musks that the body of a beloved woman can hide. Then, the pleasure of that mouth sucking on his nipple became too terrible. And at that very moment, something inhuman was slipped into his hand. He looked. It was money. A word escaped from deep inside.

"Not that, woman! Not that!"

El Caucho sits up abruptly on his bed. His face is hardened. For the first time, he has failed in his task as a human being. He condemned without trying to understand. Maybe it was that kiss taking him back to a distant past to rediscover his former, innocent heart? El Caucho is trying to remember. Why did that woman kiss me that way? Who taught her to calculate and to explore a mouth with that degree of languor and perfection? How did she discover all the gestures used by El Caucho himself when he kisses a woman he likes, all those gestures that he learned in his precocious adolescence and kept all through his life of wandering, looking for the mouth of his dreams? El Caucho is trying to remember.

"Good Lord!"

He brusquely turns on a lamp and leaps from the bed. Where did he put the key to that old suitcase? There, in the box on the table. He takes the key, opens the suitcase, and delves inside. There is that old packet of letters and photos that every man gathers over the years. He throws it on the bed. It scatters. There is his old mama's yellowing face. His father in military uniform. First communion, friends, relatives, strangers, girls he had an infatuation for, holidays, strikes, the union, former comrades, passing fancies. . . . Old memories! The whole litany of images that he has kept during his pilgrimage around this Antillean Mediterranean. What did he do with that photo? He goes back to bed.

No! He can't recall the forgotten face. If he could bring it back to mind, he would remember the name, and all the details would come back to him. El Caucho's face is hard. This is the biggest wager of his adventurous life! If he can find what he's looking for, if he can build a future on his past, he will take the bet. Everything must be built on the past. You add up your chances, you look at the realities, you consider the difficulty of the route, and without a second thought you leap, impetuous like the raging torrents hurtling down the precipitous mountainsides in this Haiti of light!

# FIFTH MANSION

Touch

*Emerge tu, recuerdo de la noche en que estoy*
*Era la alegre hora del asalto y del beso,*
*La hora del estupor que ardía como un faro.*
*Ansiedad de piloto, furia de buzo ciego,*
*Turbia embriaguez de amor. . . .*
*Cementerio de besos, aún hay fuego en tus tumbas,*
*Aún los racimos arden, picoteados de pájaros.*
*Oh la cópula loca de esperanza y esfuerzo*
*En que nos anudamos y nos desesperamos.*
*Y la ternura, leve como el agua y la harina.*
*Y la palabra apenas comenzada en los labios.*
—Pablo Neruda

Appear, memory of the night in which I am . . .
It is the joyful hour for attack and kissing.
The hour of wonderment burning like a beacon.
A pilot's desire, a blind diver's impatience
The confused ecstasy of love. . . .
A cemetery of kisses, although fire remains in your tombs,
Even the fruited clusters burn with pecking birds,
Oh, the mad coupling of hope and strength
In which we entwined and despaired.
And the tenderness, as light as water and flour.
And the barely formed word on the lips.

This makes four times in a row that Lucrèce has knocked on La Niña's door. Lucrèce is uneasy. She heads for the bar, rummages around in the drawers, and finds Mario's keys. The key for La Niña's room must be there. Must be this one. Lucrèce knocks again. No answer. She sticks the key in the lock and turns the bolt with some difficulty—the door opens.

La Niña is just sleeping. Her sleep has been heavy and nervous. Cigarettes. . . . Lucrèce takes a chair and sits down at La Niña's bedside. The bed is a mess, and La Niña is half uncovered, with one breast bare. A deep snore escapes her lips. There is such an expression of pain on her face! Her forehead is wrinkled, her lips are moving, her almost hairless arm is constantly moved by muscle twitches, and her legs keep shifting. She is dreaming. Some terrible nightmare must be tormenting La Niña. So much suffering is chiseled into her features. The heavy, bluish bush of hair flows over her uncovered shoulders. She is moving her lips. She is dreaming. How beautiful La Niña is with that tormented look! How beautiful that honey-colored breast is! Lucrèce reaches over and caresses her bare shoulder and the nascent swell of breast—running her two fingers lightly over that palpitating bare breast as it quivers from La Niña's nervous, beating heart. Lucrèce rises slowly from her chair, her face illuminated by her sparkling eyes. Lucrèce's hand wanders over the delicate body beneath the covers, in search of that delicate mound. She places her palm over the pubic area. The sleeping La Niña moans. How beautiful La Niña is with her half-open mouth and her flickering eyelids! She is sleeping. She needs gentle care. Desire makes Lucrèce's equine body shiver. She lets her robe fall, revealing her slightly masculine anatomy. She is a trotting mare, a beauty of a woman whose borderline endocrinology places her between male and female modes, often buffeted by the impulses of intersexuality, and she has the great lanky body of a freemartin looking for every sensation, seeking by turns to dominate or be dominated. She gropes the sleeping body, leaning over more and more. La Niña jumps and brutally pushes away Lucrèce, who is virtually on top of her.

"Not that!"

Her cry snaps like a whip. Lucrèce pulls away, speechless and shocked, and she puts her clothes back on. La Niña rubs her eyes:

"What are you doing here? What were you doing? What did you come here for? Leave me alone!"

"La Niña, I knocked several times. I was afraid, so I went to look for Mario's keys and I opened the door. . . ."

"But what were you doing?"

"You were having a nightmare, La Niña. You seemed so unhappy, so beautiful, that I wanted . . . Oh! La Niña! Don't you want me? Tell me? Don't you want me to give you a little tenderness? It's been a long time since you came to me, La Niña!"

With a dark look, La Niña scratches her scalp with her fingernails.

"No! You disturbed my sleep! That's a kind of rape! You didn't have my consent. I don't want that! Not you or any of you! Never again! You disgust me, all of you! I don't ever want to do that again!"

Lucrèce's face clouds over. In a huff, she knots her robe's belt.

"Well, give me back my cigarettes!"

"What cigarettes?"

"My cigarettes, whore! What do you think? I know that a man has caught your eye. But what can you be except a whore? You're just a bitch, like all of us! A whore! So, I disgust you today? OK, give me back my cigarettes! Spit them out! Vomit them up! So, I disgust you!"

La Niña turns red as she leaps up, stopping at the edge of the bed, furiously scratching her scalp. She has a nasty look on her face, and her mouth is tense and battle-ready.

"First of all, get the hell out of my room before I yank your guts out! Get the hell out, quick! And as for your cigarettes, you'll be lucky if I don't turn you in to the police! Leper! Go on! Get the hell out! Outcast! You bitch! Hysterical woman! Syphilis! Pile of shit! Get out you woman-man! Orangutang! Get the hell out if you don't want me to turn you over to the police! That's what I should do! Let Colonel Panangrenn hoist you by a pulley and beat your rotten cunt! Go on! Get out! You walking infection!"

Lucrèce is nonplussed by this avalanche. She extends her hand toward the beautiful body that electrifies her.

"La Niña. . . . What's wrong with you? Listen. You made me angry. Why don't you want to do it? Tell me, don't you want to? I'll be gentle with you, La Niña. Just like before. I want you, La Niña!"

"No way! None of that! Never again! Not from any of you!"

La Niña rushes forward. With all her strength she pushes Lucrèce toward the door, shoving her and making her trip. She frantically hits Lucrèce on the back, pushes her through the door, and closes it.

"Never again! Not that! Not that!"

She collapses face down on the bed. She will search for that man through the entire city. She will find him. She will tell him that he drove her crazy, that she cannot live without him. She will give it all up! She will do anything! She will become a washerwoman, a cook, a coffee sorter, she will go to work at the textile factory, she will become a sisal weaver, she will be a vendor at the market. She is no longer La Niña. Eglantina Covarrubias y Pérez, yes! She's not La Niña any more!

Rolling her body into a ball, La Niña is thinking. And what if the expected miracle does not happen? What if her senses do not come back to life in the arms of that man? What if she's simply left with her dead vagina, her cadaverous breasts, and what if, after the first great days, that man turns out to be just like the others: brutal, blind, lying, lacking in tenderness, egotistical? What if she is no longer speaking to him after several weeks? What if he cheats on her with other women in a search for flesh that vibrates on the same frequency as his own? What if she finds herself still alone, sad, and older one fine morning? She will kill him! By stabbing! And she will kill herself afterward! Yes!

But what if she does not manage to kill him? What if she does not have the guts to kill herself? What if she cannot adapt to a workingman's hard life any more than she already has? Spoiled as she is from her life in the bordello, what if La Niña starts luring men again in order to avoid the life of a salaried worker, in order to satisfy the needs and whims she has effortlessly developed? What if she is disappointed by a man who forgets the miracle of their love and finds herself forced to beg for a bit of maternal tenderness from some hustling Lucrèce, Rubia, or Felicidad? O Virgin of the Pillar!

La Niña gets up and wallows about like a foundering schooner. With unsteady legs, she heads for the altar of the Madonna of the blue veils. She falls to her knees.

"¡Ay, mi Virgen del Pilar! ¡Mira aquí a tu Niña Estrellita! O my Virgin of the Pillar. Look at your Niña Estrellita here!"

Kneeling, she lowers her head to the ground. She is crying in desperation. Raising her head, with a look of hatred, she yells at the Virgin.

"I've been praying to you without stopping, night and day, Virgin! What have you ever done for me? You're the one who wants me to be trampled, tormented, ashamed of myself, and incapable of standing up? You're not a true virgin! No, you're not! All women are whores! You're no virgin! And besides, what right would you have to be one?"

She spits. She insults the Virgin of the Pillar, who smiles at her. She lets herself fall back to the floor. She has blasphemed against the Virgin, her only succor! She is crying. She is abashed. She prays. She is crying. She blasphemes again. The firecrackers keep going off outside, along with explosive shouts rising to heaven. In the distance, the epileptic crisis is at its highest pitch—the Rara drums let out a *rabòday* to high heaven. A ringing like church bells can be heard. The vesperal mass of Holy Thursday is about to begin at Saint-Anne's. La Niña listens, gets up, and wipes her eyes. She feels a stabbing void deep in her stomach. There it is! It's her depression coming back on, the black hole, the abyss. She has had only four days of respite! No! It's not right! With that kind of obstacle, how can she undertake the delusory task of becoming a normal woman once more? In life and death, she is La Niña!

"La Niña, you are already dead! Your funeral hymn simply remains to be chanted!" Doctor Chalbert said that. Yes, she'll always be La Niña! Neither heaven nor men will ever forgive her. Lucrèce is right—she is only a bitch, nothing but a whore! She walks over to the night table, takes the bottle of Maxiton, swallows two tablets, heads for the washstand, and takes several swallows of water right from the pitcher before sprinkling her face. She straightens up. She's going to deal with this. It can't go on! She looks around, quickly grabs a pair of panties and slips them on. Bra, skirt, blouse. A hat? She doesn't have a hat! She smooths her hair with a quick stroke and arranges a chignon with her heavy mop of hair. A scarf will do. She knots a turban around her head. This evening, she will find out whether she is to remain La Niña forever. She is going to try her luck. Who knows?

As she walks out, she meets Lucrèce leaving her own room. They glance at each other.

"Lucrèce. Come here! Excuse me for what I did a little while ago. The cigarettes upset me, you understand?

"Well, where are you going, La Niña? Are you coming back?"

"Yes. I think I'm coming back."

"You think so? Will you come to see me then?"

"Maybe. Well, yes. Yes, I'll come."

Lucrèce uneasily watches La Niña leave. At least, La Niña won't do anything stupid? Poor Niña! Lucrèce is scared. A whole world of pain and despair is showing in La Niña's look. Lucrèce is a slave at the oars of the same galley—she knows all about it. Her eyes follow La Niña as she goes out the door.

❋

❋  ❋

El Caucho is bending over his diesel engine. Damned machine! *¡Caramba!* Hell! It works perfectly and then suddenly stops for no reason! He bends over. He fiddles around, pours some oil on it, tightens a bolt, loosens a belt, and then straightens up. And it still doesn't want to keep spinning. He wipes his hands with a rag to remove the excess diesel fuel staining his fingers. But it should work. He takes a step and restarts the engine.

"Come on! Turn, damned machine!"

It snores, sputters, coughs—it's turning! A wide smile spreads across his round face. He inclines an ear with delight, listening to the machine.

"Come on! Better than that! Give me the right sound, damned engine!"

The engine produces the sound. It is working well. El Caucho laughs.

"I knew there was nothing wrong with you, old top! You were trying to play a dirty trick on El Caucho, devil?"

El Caucho stops the engine and pats it on the back.

"There you go, old girl. Take it easy now, calm down!"

The foreman comes up.

"I told you there was nothing wrong with it. It was being stubborn because I wasn't the one who started it."

"El Caucho, you know I wasn't trying to give you a hard time—it's just the "white man"—he likes the machinery to be ready to go, even when there's no work. That's normal, no?"

"Maybe it's normal, but I should get my overtime. That's normal, too. A good hour and a half of extra hard work!"

"That's none of my business!"

"Don't worry, it's my business! El Caucho knows how to take care of himself! An hour and a half of overtime is two hours of work. No work this afternoon, right?"

"You take care of it!"

"I'll take care of it alright! I'll take care of it the same way you will take care of getting paid for the time you spent hanging around me without doing a thing. OK, bye! *So long!*"
*"So long!"*

El Caucho stretches his shoulders and extends his great duck feet. The toes, the heel glides over the ground, and, there you go! The rubber man leaves. Work finished. Off to dreamland!

*Touch*

❖

❖  ❖

El Caucho goes into Madame Puñez's restaurant.

"El Caucho? You're coming here to eat now? You can see—all the fellows have left."

"OK! If you want, I'll leave too—see you!"

"You can really be difficult! Come on, sit down! Cornilia! Bring Monsieur Caucho's food! It seems you had to do over-time?"

"Yeah!"

"What's wrong now, El Caucho? There's something strange about you!"

"Unusual? You women—you think a man is always the same! Is life the same every day?"

"I think so! The same old grind every day—meals two or three times a day, according to how much money you've got, a little outing in the evening, and sleep every night!"

El Caucho shrugs his shoulders.

That's what we want to see! And we refuse to see the rest! Do you think what you said is all there is? Last year, there wasn't an Exposition; this year there will be one. The FTH ordered a general strike last year after the Gonaïves affair; this year, there hasn't been one. President Estimé launched an internal loan pro-gram today to pay back what we owe to the "'mericans." The wharf workers got a raise one month ago. The government has ordered maneuvers on the Dominican border to geld Trujillo. The tanners and leather workers have made a statement of claims. Aren't those some changes? Don't you see things are looking up? Winter is over. The rains have come and gone. Life's outlook is changing slowly, imperceptibly, but one fine morning you're surprised not to see something that was there before. Not just years, but weeks and hours are no longer the same. El Cau-cho is surprised to see how times have changed. He is astonished to see that he has become another El Caucho.

In the long run! God is our sole master! Maybe you're right—maybe those are only bookish ideas. In any case, Madame Puñez, she's still an old harpy that nobody listens to!

El Caucho is eating. He is grinding his teeth. He licks his lips.

"Delia? Your meat pies are great. I could chew your fingers right off with them!"

"Now what are you going to ask me for?"

"Always joking!"

"So?"

"Well, I left a package of old photos here with you—do you remember?"

"But you took them back a long time ago! What would I do with old, yellowed photos?"

"You were really interested in them, for some reason! You showed them to your cook—and here's El Caucho at the age of ten months! Here's El Caucho's mother showing him off to a neighbor. El Caucho's mother was a beautiful woman, right? And you told Cornilia, 'Here's El Caucho at his first communion. Look how he seems to be mocking the Good Lord he has in his heart!' Anyway, all joking aside, I can't find some of my pictures any more."

"El Caucho, love, you've got some nerve! That's too much! Me, Delia Puñez? Would I steal your photos? When you play with puppies, they always give you fleas! Come on! You can search everywhere—you'll see whether you find any of your old pictures in my place!"

"OK. If you don't have them, I believe you, but there could still be one or two that might have slipped into a bundle of laundry in your chest. That wouldn't be your fault!"

"First of all, why do you need those pictures today? To go show to some little whore who has been making you dizzy recently? You'll see where these affairs lead, El Caucho!"

"That's my business!"

"So, that's all I get, El Caucho? You just give me a few promises? Since we've known each other, I thought that we could always count on each other's friendship. And I thought I had a faithful friend! Thanks, El Caucho, thanks a lot!"

"That's enough, Delia!"

El Caucho has finished eating. He gives Delia a look to pacify her. But she has already calmed down and regrets her anger.

"Go look in the chest, El Caucho—maybe you'll find what you're looking for after all. You never know! You're a clever man! You need money?"

"No, thanks, Delia. So I can go see?"

El Caucho hurries to the stairway. Madame Puñez shakes her head in frustrated resignation.

❋

❋　❋

El Caucho makes his way through the port, where activity has slowed down. He goes along the Rue du Quai, heads for the Place de la Commune, comes back. He heads for the provincial bus depot; the late buses are rushing to leave, half empty. What could he have done with that photo? The last trolley of the Mac-Donald Railway Company, the "motorcar" as they call it, is about to head for Saint Marc. El Caucho hurries into the little station, mingling with the crowd around the ticket and shipping windows. The conductor of the motorcar, a tall, lanky fellow with a slender mustache, is friendly with El Caucho. He waves at him.

"Hey, El Caucho! Do you want to leave with me?"

The vehicles are moving. El Caucho waves. Suddenly, he leaves the quickly emptied station. Why not go play a game of checkers with the women at Gabriel's? The usual people must already be there. No! He ought to go by the FTH headquarters, after all. Somebody had told him they needed him. Not today. They'll drag him into a political discussion, and their politics isn't very Catholic these days. They've begun following the petty bourgeois ideologues who are being manipulated by the big feudal landowners from the North and other places. That would lead to another rumpus. El Caucho goes by the docks. The rail cars of the Compagnie du Wharf are moving off one after the other. The men are working energetically; things are humming along. Bravo, fellows! You've carried on a good class struggle! You've won a great and deserved victory! That's union work! Here's the dock for coastal freight. The sailing vessels are dancing at anchor—the aroma of *Fransik* mangoes embalms the sea breeze. Hi, brother! Hello, *Dieu-Protège*! A beautiful sailing ship. Hello, *La Sirène*—hi, sailors: I wish you a stiff breeze, good sailing! El Caucho walks on. He has to make a decision finally. What should he do? She's a funny woman, anyway! It's some wager! If he could find that photo. . . .

Here are the first shacks of La Saline. If people simply gave dynamic support to government policies instead of philosophizing and letting themselves be dragged along in the wake of the petty bourgeois civil servants—if they gave conditional support, constructive criticism, made proposals, came up with projects, conducted campaigns to resolve the most important problems of the day, it would be better than all their abstract talk. Such actions would bring results. Estimé is no fool—he's got blinders on, but you can't take away his patriotism. If the working class were on the alert, watching over their affairs, making noise when necessary, the government would be forced to walk a straighter path. An Exposition! What a stupid affair! Some fifteen million dollars thrown away in unprofitable construction! Why not fifteen factories that would give jobs to thirty thousand workers? A garrison town at Belladère? What for? Maybe labor policies deserve to be reconsidered in all the underdeveloped countries of Latin America? In any case, there is at least something wrong with the tactics—it doesn't fit the realities at all. When was the last time he had that photo in his hands? Try to recall. No, he just can't remember. Work must be created for all the semi-proletarian unemployed workers in this area. La Saline stinks; those kids running around in mud and sewage—a good half of them are done for! They are dying like flies! That's urgent! It's not enough to build a bunch of more or less hygienic shacks. The problem has to be yanked out by the roots. Give men work, and the habitat will automatically change as a consequence. Physiological misery, verminosis, malaria, rickets, tuberculosis. . . . With all that going on, the petty bourgeois are thinking about a Universal Exposition in order to promote tourism, they say. As if tourists would come to look at some twenty more or less presentable buildings! If they come some day, it will be for something completely different—to see the savagery of a little island several hours away from Miami. Factories are needed right away to absorb unemployment! You could produce paper with bagasse from sugarcane, glass, furniture for export from precious woods, a light industry for aluminum and so many other things! That's true revolutionary action in the Caribbean—creating an economic base, an industrial base for national independence. All those stupidities about the presumed struggle of one class against another simply amount to playing the game of two principal enemies—retrograde feudalism and foreign imperialism simply engage in empty talk and edge the bourgeoisie out of the fight and right into the arms of the entire nation's enemies. Letting ourselves be led by the pseudo-revolutionary verbiage of the petty bourgeois civil servants is to betray the main struggle and maintain the country's backwardness.

Now what is he headed out to look for? All of this because of a woman! There he is, tormented, knowing that in his own heart he is immensely dissatisfied with his two types of dreaming—collective and individual dreams. He has to make up his mind: El Caucho will never really be a hard and shining force until he has squared the circle—until he has established an equilibrium in his own personal life. Life is a game, an adventure, an exploration. What can he lose by taking hold of this wispy and unbalanced woman's life? After all, Cuba and Haiti are curiously similar. Of course, over there, the working class is bigger, they struggle better, they're more experienced in some ways; but the penetration of imperialism is deeper there, and things balance out in the end. Here, people have more revolutionary traditions, and the other social classes are less conservative and less organized. There are lots of jokes in both places: the questions of color and the *authentiques* in Haiti and, in Cuba, the *auténticos, revolucionarios, ortodoxos,* and worker divisions. If we were united, we could have gotten a Grau San Martín to accomplish a host of things. Oh, well! Of course, the political independence of the working class must never be sacrificed, but it's obvious that large unions and agreements must be created. That tactic is really in line with theoretical strategy. Then, hell!

*In the Flicker of an Eyelid*

The final flashes of youth are quietly disappearing. In any case, youth will disappear whether there is immobilism or some crazy adventure! So, what is there to lose?

Ah! If he just had that photo! In spite of everything, he decided to take the difficult road. Comrade El Caucho, in your love affairs, don't forget the Caribbean, waiting for you and hoping for the action of millions of El Cauchos. Ah! If only the energies of the federated Caribbean peoples could be joined together, they could jostle bad luck and the course of history! Each person would have only to advance with his brothers, friends, and loves toward the conquest of life! But that's still an illusion—morning hasn't yet broken over the Caribbean! Patience! Ah! If he could embrace the past of that face in order to resculpt it in the clay of a simple, combatant, and mutually enriching love. A life for two begun over, hand in hand. El Caucho, you have to recognize that your heart doesn't want to continue alone as it did before! You can't walk alone any more, fight alone, suffer alone. The time for you to find a companion has come. You're afraid, El Caucho—it's fear that is making you hesitate. What the hell! You are doubting yourself, doubting love, doubting life, doubting the movement!

El Caucho is walking along the port. As he passes, he caresses the heads of hungry little black kids. He breathes in the salt air from the sea and lets the spray settle on his lips. He extends a finger to the butterfly of life, flying off this instant. He eats a snow cone. He glances at a pair of shapely legs, a disappearing compass. His eyes light birdlike on the balcony of a pair of quivering breasts. He listens to the Rara drums growing more energetic in the distance. He exchanges a friendly glance with a stray dog that stops, injured paw suspended in the air, to look at him with soft, tearful eyes. El Caucho picks up a trampled old photo, he looks at the humped back of a little old woman heading off, he pats the shoulder of a candy vendor. El Caucho's forehead is creased. Ah! If he could only find that photo! The firecrackers begin popping again.

❊

❊　❊

*Touch*

The Church of Saint Anne is all draped in black and silver hangings. The censers are swinging in the chancel where the assembled chapter is moving slowly in the vesperal rites of Holy Thursday. Surrounded by the heavy smoke of perfumes from the Orient and the noise of the rattles, the crowd kneels and rises again without tiring. Gregorian chants fill the nave and echo through the lateral vaults—sad, suffering, anguished—with the nasal tones of voices that bleat the psalms and lamentations. Jesus is with his gathered disciples for the last time before his Passion, speaking to them, giving his final messages for the blessed. The foot-washing ceremony is being conducted in front of the great altar. La Niña has collapsed against the balustrade of the small altar over which the statue of the Virgin is camouflaged beneath a great purple hood. La Niña knows that the *Mater Dolorosa* is there, with her stricken heart, ravaged by the inexorable march toward the conclusion. The most terrible week in the mythology of modern times! The Virgin is there, as despairing as the little whore lying at her feet.

La Niña is not praying. She is not reciting either the "Hail Mary" or other litanies—she is not even paying attention to the hymns echoing beneath the vaults. She has simply come to visit the Virgin. She has taken the trouble to come tell her story to the Mother of Sorrows. She is a little whore from La Frontière—everybody knows that. It isn't pretty——her life is not shining, and her heart is leprous; that's no secret for anyone. Someone told La Niña a long time ago that, like her Divine Son, the Virgin has no fear of cadavers, crazy people, lepers, criminal, syphilitics, or whores. Only humans, with their morality, are expected to condemn this unhappy little chain gang of untouchables. If La Niña had received what it takes to become a nun, saint, or virgin, wouldn't she have done that? She is a whore, and people say that is her fault. Is it true that she considered that calling and chose it with a light heart? After all, the Mother of Sorrows knows all the commemorations of history. If La Niña took the liberty of appearing before the Mother of God, it is because something serious has taken place.

A man came along. After some hesitation, La Niña had

resolved to take him as her *chulo,* as a companion in her hell—something she had refused to do up to that moment. But the man refused.

"Not that!" he said.

He does not want to be a whore's companion. So La Niña ran to see the Virgin—something she had never dared do up to now, being aware of her degeneration, in spite of the difficult times she has gone through in her life. She has not come to ask for money, success, fame—she has just come to inquire about one little thing. To have a simple question answered. When you're a whore, is it because you were born to do that? Can you stop being one? If that's possible, she is ready to leave the Sensation Bar this very day, but at least she has to find out whether she isn't going to land in between Charybdis and Scylla. La Niña wants to hear the answer clearly. Card readers, palm readers, hypnotists, and *bòkò* all speak with great authority about everything, but La Niña doesn't trust them. She isn't convinced of their honesty—but if the Virgin reveals her destiny—not her future, but her destiny—she will believe that. The Virgin knows what suffering is. This moment is the culmination of suffering for the Mother of Sorrows. It is the most terrible week of suffering that a mother can endure. This week has also been a true Passion for La Niña. It has been atrocious, and the entire future hinges on it. She wants to hear the answer clearly. She is ready for whatever is necessary—candles, masses, ex-votos, contributions, penances, and this and that. For her entire life, La Niña has been devoted to the Virgin. She has never stopped speaking to her. This is practically the first request that she has ever made of her. So she has a right to have an answer.

La Niña is desperately clutching the balustrade, leaning her forehead against the cold forged iron. Her eyes are closed, her hands joined as she has seen in pious images. La Niña will wait until the Virgin has a minute. She wants to hear the answer in a clear, audible voice. If, somewhere in the azure sky, there is somebody who cares about Niña Estrellita, she knows she'll hear an answer. She is waiting.

The vaults resound with the separate, modulated voices of the plainchant. A thousand opposing voices are vibrating, cries and lamentations—grave, urgent, anxious appeals—are mingling, conflicting, and producing a great polyphony. Amid the aromas of incense, the smoke from the candles, and the profound harmonies of the church instruments, an immense and unique interrogation is tendered in all its forms. There can be no mockery. The entire history of planet Earth is covered with these psalms, hymns, and lamentations. Humanity continues its interrogation. Its question is grave, lofty, tragic. There must be no mockery. Humanity has been supplicating for millennia. We must listen with hats off if we want to understand where we are and whither human nature will take us tomorrow. A great part of humankind no longer believes itself to be of Adam's lineage but rather finds it shares the quality of *homo faber*—that is, that they have abandoned their animal nature. That segment of humankind is beginning to take a different direction while the rest of the human race—still a majority—has not lost all hope of receiving an answer. From this time onward, the question is urgent—it is ever more uneasy, anxious, but its lamentation continues to resound in the church naves. That mass of humanity is ill at ease, it hesitates and loses hope from hearing, as the unique answer, only the unctuous voices of priests who untiringly repeat that the Earth must be a vale of tears, that it is enough to continue imploring across the centuries. Is that supplication the only path to salvation? Is waiting in resignation for eternal happiness the only possible attitude? Beethoven has already stated that question dramatically in his grand *Missa Solemnis*, the *Mass in D*:

*Dona nobis pacem!*

Even now, humanity no longer believes blindly as it did before. It is tired, and fists are raised. If it has not already set out on a new path, it is turning more and more toward new temples and those new assemblies that were already praised in the past century by a certain Ozanam. Prayer becomes action.

During that most terrible week in the mythology of all time, Divine Paraclete, Lamb of God, and you, Virgin and Mother of

Sorrows, La Niña Estrellita, along with millions like her, has collapsed there and still hopes for an answer. Will she leave without obtaining it? Think of that! In fact, if La Niña does not get a crystal clear response this evening, the very columns of heaven will fall, and there will be little value in those grandiose and venerable buildings bearing witness to human grandeur and affirming a certain success—earthly success—of the gigantic adventure begun by the first primates. How many minutes will La Niña Estrellita wait during this twentieth century? Exhausted, La Niña desperately hangs to the balustrade. Jesus is with his assembled disciples one last time before his Passion. The noble, severe, dramatic ceremony of the foot washing is taking place at the Church of Saint Anne. The canons, vicars, and children of the choir are splashing each other's feet. The bells have been quiet since morning. The crick-crack of the rattles rasps along with the advancing hours. The censers are swinging in the chancel. Prayers die away and begin again. Hymns die, and the church empties. La Niña is still there, sobbing. She cries for a long time.

It's Holy Thursday and Mario gives the girls the day off. It's not worth opening. La Niña is coming back. She is walking with her head lowered and the scarf that was wrapped around her hair a while before is hanging from her fingertips, dragging in the dust. It is night now, a night filled with firecrackers, drums, stars, and asteroids burning high on the mountain. The scarf drags over the tiles in the courtyard. It sweeps the steps of the terrace, the gallery, and then stops. El Caucho is sitting with Lucrèce at the bar. He seems to be interrogating her. Seeing La Niña, Lucrèce calls to her in a friendly voice.

"La Niña, we're waiting for you. OK, I'll leave you!"

This Lucrèce is not a vicious woman. She suspects something. Lucrèce is undoubtedly the most intelligent person among the women at the Sensation Bar—that may even be the source of her conflicting moods? The business at noon finally enlightened her.

Basically, she would be happy if some luck came La Niña's way because, unless she's mistaken, something out of the ordinary is taking place at the Sensation Bar. If La Niña experiences a miracle, it will be a memorable date in La Frontière. It will be one more reason for each woman to take hope. It will warm the heart of all the *manolitas*. Lucrèce disappears with a friendly glance toward La Niña. Go on, La Niña! Try your luck—none of us can begrudge you that. Don't play the fool—work it right, sweet-talk him if you have to.

La Niña sees El Caucho. She is afraid of going up to him. She doesn't believe it. She's weak, without strength, and without a voice. In spite of it, she walks forward by reflex and lets herself sink onto the stool next to him. She is still La Niña. She raises her timid eyes to the man, with her eyelids trembling, afraid to let hope shine and yet unable to stifle it. El Caucho speaks quietly, in an irregular voice. His gutteral *r* crackles.

"In general, I don't beat around the bush, *chica*. I'm that way, right? Life has pushed me around—I'm no choirboy. Do you have time to hear me out? It may take a while. If you can't, I can come back another time."

La Niña's eyes suddenly display terror. She is trembling. Her anxiety is at work. His crackling voice.

"So? Yes or no?"

La Niña nods yes. Lucrèce has returned on tiptoe. There may be a bunch of girls with attentive ears behind the door in the hall, but neither La Niña nor El Caucho pays any attention. Lucrèce turns on the record player and disappears. It is La Niña's favorite song, *"Desesperación."* No, La Niña—you can't let go of yourself. Things like this can't happen to a girl who has led a life like yours. Come on! Keep your nerve!

La Niña raises a finger, approaches him timidly, and slowly caresses El Caucho's left wrist. How can anybody have a wrist like that? She follows the trajectory of a vein. The curiosity of discovering such a body suddenly grips her. Her anguish is gone. So, who is this man? La Niña grabs both wrists abruptly, quickly.

"Come! Come dance!" she says.

She can hardly put her fingers around a wrist. They have all the strength, all the tone, and all the tenderness of which she has dreamed! She holds it and presses the elastic flesh. El Caucho looks at her and lets her lead him. They stand. She slips her right hand into that large palm. The hand closes. It raises La Niña by her waist. She is carried away! She lets her left elbow fall over that broad, enormous shoulder. Ay! La Niña! You're leaving! Where are you, La Niña? Rising, rising!

La Niña is a feather, a leaf, a bird, borne away by the musical breeze. La Niña is floating between two heavens—a snowflake hovering in a cottony dream, scattering, dissipating, disintegrating to become space itself. What a void embodying space! Her flight loses speed although it has not seemed rapid, just vertiginous. La Niña is on the edge of vertigo. So this is what it's like to be really alive? A movie fade-in; the slow return of consciousness. So slowly! Her weakness starts in her imprisoned fingers and the elbow braced on that shoulder. Two great streams of weakness flow and then join together to become the affluents of a great, warm torrent shooting from the imprisoned hip to flow through her genitals and thighs. La Niña's entire lower body is nothing but weakness and languor. La Niña is returning from a great distance! La Niña's body is coming back to life. Is it her right thumb that she can feel? Yes. It is receiving life from the hairy wrist on which it rests. Her pulse is throbbing. La Niña's right thumb has become nothing other than the pulsing of this man's blood. Now La Niña's other fingers are coming to life—the index and middle fingers, which are caressed and pressed by the square, calloused, spatula thumb! La Niña's hips are coming to life. Everything is coming back. She looks at El Caucho, smiles at him. It was him!

He has swept her away so quickly with that bolero that everything is swimming in her head. It was nobody but him. He is holding her tightly. Tenderly. She does not know how she manages to follow the direction that he is giving, and yet she is doing what he wants. That palm placed on her hip is virtually carrying her—it's a slow, undulating, feverish walk.

*¡Desesperación!*

Who is talking about despair? Why speak of despair when his step is so clear, when the momentary hesitation is nothing more than the insidious calculation of an untamed rhythm to allow the hips of two people to meet, sense each other, and adhere. She masters the harmony easily, thanks to the racial intuition of a brother coming from the same dancing people as she does, through the natural intuition of a companion born in rhythm and living by movement, through the intuition of a partner needing no choreography because of his knowledge of everything heavenly, earthly, and alive. La Niña moves with him, yielding her hips and body over to the powerful architecture of this man. La Niña gives and she takes. Her whole body measures each of his angles, the hollows and rounded parts of this beast who now belongs to her. She is finally able to explore that body! How could she have imagined such calm strength in a real torso, such delicacy in those powerful arms, and the same palpitating strength and tender intensity in a man's belly? Before, she has never known anything but the brutality and debilitated violence of those gorillas in their hollow love, the deceptive vigor of crazy, lusting geldings thinking only of themselves while making love—the tetanic and laughable nanism of those pleasure gnomes. From now on, how can she face that immense task, surpassing dream and memory: discovering in that herculean body a tangible model of her persistent dreams? Ah! Reality has intervened more quickly than dream! La Niña is the bride of this living strength. She is the fiancée of his breasts with their adamantine pectorals. It is the robust joining of that lily-white thigh slipping between the solid spindles of those powerful limbs, it is the marriage of two waists, the union of two sex organs, the alliance of two shoulders, the bed of two bellies, the blessing of her umbilical and the receding musculature of his flat abdomen. They soar. Le Niña lets her dream swell, she tries to extend her dream to match his immense dimensions. She is trying to cast the statue conceived by every human being into a warm, living, and unreal being that her hope has returned to her.

We, the peoples of the Caribbean, are children of truth and light, children of water and corn, children of the surging sea, children of an old trade wind that is at once a bolero, merengue, calypso, beguine, rumba, *kongo payèt, mayi,* and eddy. The sun, our father, is a round whirlwind of clarity. In the empty hall of the Sensation Bar, the *bolero-son* continues at the whim of the knowing grammophone that tirelessly repeats the lesson given by a *manolita* called Lucrèce:

*¡Desesperación!*

Who dares speak of desperation? El Caucho and La Niña are dancing—serious and candid, conscious of the sacrament taking place. It is the step of their renewed life, barely sketched and carrying them off as if their own *bolero-son* had been composed only for discovering each other, for that instant of eternity. No learned gesture. La Niña is carried off by a hardened but gentle man, one who knows the force that makes the stars spin and the round of the seasons. Églantine knows everything about this élan that makes buds appear and flower on branches. She is dancing.

La Niña says in a clear voice:

"Stop!"

The man stops as she speaks. La Niña says:

"Come!"

The man follows her into the hall leading to the room.

La Niña enters the dark room. She turns on the light. El Caucho stands at the entrance and casts a glance around the space. La Niña hurries over to the unmade bed, brushes it with her hand, pulls on the sheets, and arranges the pillows to give the bed a more decent appearance. She is ashamed of the disorder in her room. She picks up scattered clothes from the tiled floor, empties the ashtray through the blinds and lowers them to let in the frolicking trade wind. She remains standing with the little ceramic saucer in her hand. In front of her are the table, the nightstand, another table, an old armchair, the altar, the shutter-doors, the sleeping parrots, the wardrobe with its mirror topped by two tired suitcases, a chair, and finally the door where

## Touch

El Caucho is standing. That's all. This is La Niña Estrellita's ultimate refuge, her torture chamber. There is the trade wind that keeps her company here when she is alone. Reeking of age, the room has its odors, its silence, its nocturnal resonance, its black butterflies fluttering about the paper shade on the ceiling. So, from this instant on, El Caucho knows everything.

He comes in, closes the door, takes off his jacket and hangs it on the back of the chair. He rummages in his pockets and takes out a handful of marigolds, throwing them on the bed. This is a blow that La Niña takes head on, right on the breast. She goes over with buckling knees and sits on the edge of the bed, looking at the marigolds scattered on the sheets. She looks at El Caucho and runs her fingers over the flowers.

"Do you like marigolds? People say they bring bad luck, but I don't believe it."

The words float slowly into La Niña's heart. She gets up, goes over to bolt the door, and sits back down. She scatters the yellow petals and the pollen fallen on the bed. She is dreaming. El Caucho is concentrating. He paces about the little room with a heavy step and then stops.

"I've already seen you. Not here. That's why I'm here. You know? What's happening is really unbelievable!"

She stares at him. He comes over, takes her hands, and sits down beside her.

"I can't really remember," says La Niña.

El Caucho puts a finger on his lips.

"I'm the one who has to remember. Don't talk. I've got to find it!"

He turns her little hands between his fingers. You would say they were two grape leaves. He caresses her fingers, one after the other, with the reverse side of his right thumb. He closes his eyes. Each finger is a little spindle, slightly marked by a vague, raised fold, just before the first articulation. On the middle phalanx of the third finger on her left hand, there is a little scar, barely perceptible. He rolls her fingers. He turns her hands over to the palms and skims over them with the back of his hand—then he places a kiss in the hollow of each palm. He lets his lips wander. Those palms are almost perfect hexagons. The head line is quite thin, twisted. The heart line is cut into twenty sections. There is a half line for luck. The life line stops at midcourse and then reappears. El Caucho brings her fingertips to his mouth and holds them against his lips.

"You've got long nails," says El Caucho.

La Niña pulls her left hand away, searches in the drawer of the nightstand, and pulls out a pair of scissors.

"Cut them!"

El Caucho looks at her.

"Cut them, I said!" La Niña repeats.

El Caucho takes the scissors. La Niña places her head against his shoulder. He cuts the nails without arguing. For El Caucho, a man has to act on his word. The ruby-lacquered clippings fall one after the other. Without hesitation, El Caucho presses the little scissors hard and detaches the hard crescent with one movement, right at the flesh. There, it's done! She takes his great paws in her palms and squeezes them. Two great sandy paws, big mitts, calloused creatures that are alive and struggling. Two tears are hanging like pearls at the tips of La Niña's eyelashes.

"Shouldn't I have cut them? Well, it's done! I've got great paws, I should have . . ."

Lacking any petty vanity, La Niña shakes her head in a kind of nostalgic negation. She stops him, putting a finger on her lips.

"Don't talk! I'm trying to recall. . . ."

In spite of the tears rolling down her cheeks, La Niña is radiant and smiling. The Virgin did not answer, but life is beginning to become clear. Beginning now, she realizes that humans are alone, that there is no God, no rose-bearing rain falling from heaven, no manna, no flood. Humans are alone and control their daily destiny through efforts completely justified by the grandeur of our species' adventure, the marvels of the universe and of life, the satisfaction of a pure heart, and the respect of the natural laws of existence. Remembering will be the first act of freedom by which La Niña will defy the fatality of inhuman social structures and turn in her own favor the rigorous but pliable laws of that nature, which are matter, movement, impersonal force, life and thought, eternal reality. La Niña is crying, but that is an act of struggle and insurrection—she is joining that uncounted army struggling humbly, stubbornly, and without useless posturing or shortsighted rebellion. True, valid heroism lies within the obscure existence of the humble, who reconcile sedition and patience, individuality and solidarity, resistance and impulsiveness. The tears are dropping—swift, large, round, bitter. This is bitterness disappearing. And it is at that exact moment that a large hand touches down on La Niña's shoulder with the delicacy of a bird—the great fingers stroking her contours, trying to discover the secret, the arcanum of every existence. Eyes closed, La Niña lets him continue.

La Niña and El Caucho are in bed. On the nightstand, the lamp projects a circle of ultraviolet light. Nothing has happened so far. They are simply lying in bed, quietly, almost without moving—their naked bodies touching. Their love will be consummated only at the moment of discovery, without calculation, like drawing water from a fountain. They are aware of this. They are waiting, unhurried. La Niña has placed her head on El Caucho's shoulder. Her mouth presses on a little meaty nevus that she has found at the edge of his clavicle. Her left arm is wandering beneath the sheets, exploring his back and loins. Between the tips of the first three fingers of her right hand she is holding a little star-shaped scar marking her companion's elbow. She is thinking but does not let go of the hardened star. Five points? On the left elbow. La Niña is holding onto that slight rough spot as if it were a family jewel. She is thinking.

El Caucho is also stretched out on one side, holding the back of La Niña's neck in his hand. He is rubbing his fingers over her flowing hair, which is even darker beneath the lamp. The little waterfall rustles, flows, and bursts forth beneath the light over his thick phalanges. With his free hand, he strokes her still thigh and the curve of her hip. Their bodies remain joined, tranquil, peaceful, happy, but with no burning desire. Each one is searching—one feeling the bud of a breast, the other the supple bulges of two breasts pressed against the relaxed muscles. A heart transmits a steady, continuous vibration to the thoracic cage—vibrations moving outward in larger and smaller circles—evanescent, but reappearing at the epicenter of life. Another heart is beating, a sempiternal flick against a lukewarm torso. One epigastrium is breathing in, the other exhaling. The silk of a belly is rubbing against the satin of a body section that is infinitely and variably molded. The hollow of an armpit acts as a suction pump on the other's armpit. The skin on the thighs has welded together in long, sweaty curves. Four legs are at play. Twenty toes grapple, loosen, and reengage; two of them tickle a sole, go back up the ankle, but they are stopped by tight pincers that immobilize them and then release them at once. Nails scratch the hollow of a malicious limb. At the bottom of the memory lakes, flotsam is freed from moving sand, silt, and sargasso—they bump against each other and shake on their keels, trying to regain the surface. La Niña is afraid. Afraid of the act that is going to take place. What if . . . , what if. . . ? But there is a paradoxical calm inhabiting her and pacifying her at the same time. She is sailing. He is thinking.

"That star on your elbow? You fell out of a tree? A mango tree or . . ."

A hand clamps over her mouth.

Why, yes! It was a mango tree. That was so long ago! How did she manage to. . . ? Silence. The parrots let out their confused chatter and then fall silent. The Rara drums are making the atmosphere vibrate so much that the air in the room seems to be pulsating with the *rabòday.* Have the Rara bands dared penetrate the concrete of the suburbs? Let the police beware! Cars are coming down the avenue in a such a frantic herd that the entire building is shaking. At the Ça-Ira crossroads, there must be delirium. The silence is vibrant with a thousand distant sounds. One mouth is pulling on the other, just to capture the swollen fold and taste the saltiness. A crazy alarm clock begins chortling in the neighboring room. Somebody muffles it quickly. This morning, Luz-Maria must have wound up her Chanteclair by habit. The lovers shudder. Their thoughts guide the bodies toward a position that would make it easier to bring back the past.

"What time is it?" asks El Caucho.

La Niña covers his mouth and her free hand tries to turn the clock out of sight. On the nightstand, the unnoticed tick-tock is becoming obsessive.

"Why, I hadn't thought! You must be hungry! I . . ."

El Caucho quickly frees his hand and covers her mouth. Her breath filters through his fingers. He progressively relaxes his hold. La Niña takes advantage of that right away.

"I'm sure you're hungry!"

Gagged again, La Niña breaks into laughter. Eagerly, she squirms loose.

"You're hungry, I said! Your stomach is growling! Wait, I've got something!"

She tries to disengage her body from his. El Caucho holds her.

"Don't you want to eat—tell me? It'll only take a minute? Please! Let me do it! I don't want you to go hungry!"

El Caucho anoints himself with the burnt honey of her epidermis. He relaxes his hold. They tremble and sigh as their bodies separate. Two bellies exchange a final kiss. La Niña suddenly pushes the sheets away, jumps up and escapes with a triumphant laugh.

Painfully cut loose in a bed that is too vast, El Caucho misses her, and in the violet chiaroscuro, he watches her silhouette quickly disappear with its virtually prepubescent feminine grace. Beneath the blue swath of hair, the back appears like a gilded lizard and undulates above the twin curves of the buttocks, as it bends toward the tiled floor in the corner, below the oratory to the Virgin. In the blue-yellow glimmer of the burning alcohol lamp, La Niña looks like a little frog crouching beneath the trembling disk of a hesitant moon in the rainy autumn.

❖

❖  ❖

El Caucho has rejoined La Niña. He is seated on the ground beside her in front of the alcohol lamp, which has just gone out.

On either side of the couple, two saucers bend upward, one holding large crackers and the other filled with jam. La Niña is buttering the crackers. The coffee is burning hot. They are eating the crisp crackers covered with jam and fresh butter. Aromatic serpents of steam from the coffee swirl around La Niña and El Caucho. Her head has fallen against the powerful shoulder. She's dreaming.

"Here, eat some more. Eat, I tell you!"

He is eating. With his arm, he is trying to pull her down on her back, parallel to himself.

"Wait!"

She bends over, stretches out her arm and pulls over a little rug. They lie down shoulder to shoulder, hip to hip, and their feet mingling on the warm spot left by the alcohol lamp. They stare at the ceiling in silence.

"I think I'm about to remember," says El Caucho.

La Niña sighs and taps her fingers on her companion's thigh.

"It was really difficult before you got here, you know," says La Niña.

El Caucho places his rough palm on La Niña's belly. She is trembling. She is afraid. Her heart is beating wildly.

"I'm afraid," she stammers. "I'm not a real woman, you know. I don't like love. I'm afraid."

El Caucho is putting slow, firm pressure on La Niña's abdomen. He places his other hand on her left breast, making her heart jump.

"I'm afraid!" says La Niña.

El Caucho places his hand over her genitals, which are alive, warm, humid, swollen. El Caucho doesn't move.

"I'm really afraid," murmurs La Niña. "I've never had an orgasm making love. I tell you I'm not a real woman!"

La Niña's heart is pounding like a crazy, wild beast. It charges without stopping—a mechanical ram.

"Calm down," El Caucho tells her.

La Niña remains still, but her heart has gone wild.

"Calm down. You can slow your heart down. Take a breath!"

La Niña is breathing erratically. Is her heartbeat slowing? No, it isn't. El Caucho's hand is still holding her moist pubis.

"Breathe slowly!" says El Caucho.

La Niña breathes deeply. She breathes in and exhales slowly. Is her heart calming down? No. Well. . . . Maybe!

"I'm afraid. I don't like making love. I've never felt anything."

On the ceiling, like on a screen, La Niña thinks back over her countless and painful series of joyless sessions of lovemaking. She is breathing deeply since El Caucho asked her to. Who can this man be? La Niña breathes.

"I've never felt anything, never. It must be an illness. I've never . . ."

"Quiet! Don't say anything!"

Her graceful pubis is alive, swollen, humid, warm, in spite of everything. El Caucho is serious. He is afraid of this heavy responsibility handed to him by life. What is the power of memory? What is the power of love? Maybe it will still take a long time to give back to this woman that ecstatic cry to which every human being has a right. Can such anomalies be reversible? After all, what does he know about physical love? What does anybody know about physical love, what can anybody know as long as the person has not truly loved someone else, body and soul—two inseparable poles of a unique existing entity? He is afraid, he doesn't know, but he will struggle just as he has always struggled against every obstacle he has ever encountered. Who is this woman?

"It must be an illness. I've never . . ."

"Shhh!"

Heart calmed down. Oriente. An elastic gait. A meadow covered with marigolds. A guttural sound. The aroma of a Delicado. That saline lip and the *godrin* of his mouth. A star-shaped scar on his left elbow. An image is stirring in La Niña's head. She is afraid. The tip of a finger slides over the tender mucous of her vulva. The index finger wanders over the bud of her clitoris. It takes over.

"I . . . I've never, never . . ."

*In the Flicker of an Eyelid*

"Shhhh!" murmurs El Caucho.

He doesn't move his hand. Is that apparently live mucous really dead? What does it mean to live? Isn't living to experience? What is sensation, what is pleasure, what is death? El Caucho hasn't particularly experienced pleasure over the course of his rough, joyful life as an insurgent worker. How could he formulate responses to such questions? Ah! Humans are ridiculous to cast a shadowy veil over the more attractive parts of the handsome body of the human being, the sexual organs that experience life more intensely than the rest! Under the pretext that it is immoral and pornographic to talk about that, humans have been kept in almost complete ignorance about the arcanum of carnal pleasure, which may hold the key to all emotion. The act of love has to be celebrated as the greatest expression of the human being, a conscious and reflective being in the conservation and flowering of the species. In the fierce battles of the working world, the Suffering Army—as the glorious peasant collectivists in the Haitian Revolution of 1843 called it—in its battle for humankind, wasn't it specifically this ignorance that limited the victories, occasioned serious defeats, and brought about so many blunders, errors, and stupidities? The errors that El Caucho commits every day often come from those lacunae about what the motivating principle of life and action is: pleasure, joy, the pain of human suffering. That stupid prudery is responsible for a great part of all the contemporary pathology of sensuality, of sexual neuroses, and the aberrations that lead to inversions. Where is the boundary between sensation and pleasure? Isn't it the entire human body—living matter and psyche—that feels and is moved to give an agreeable or disagreeable color to the physical sensations we perceive? When he learned about the death of Jesús, didn't he experience an undeniably physical pain in his chest and his entire body? Don't laughter and tears punctuate pleasure and joy, a tickling sensation, pain, and suffering whether they are physical or moral? How can it be explained that certain physical tortures bring paradoxically carnal enjoyment in poor, abnormal creatures? It is clear that the psyche is the premier orchestra leader of emotion. The act of physical love, copulation, may then be spiritual acts of beings who cannot cease being spiritual? Human love, of whatever type, is at once ideation, idealization, and the willful trembling at being confronted by a radiant being that is esteemed and desired for an ongoing electrical contact. This may be the reason for which we cannot separate the intimate personality of the beloved from the charming fleshly envelope. La Niña has never experienced the pleasure that guarantees the perpetuation of the species and of a well-balanced self! And he has perhaps only a single night to try to resolve that problem! La Niña may escape from him tomorrow if he fails. He will fight! The prime condition of their union is to make the admirable and radiant cantilena of the two attuned sexes resound from their lips. Like a conscientious worker, a man of the Caribbean, and a lover, he will fight all night until the sun breaks forth in laughter!

"I'm afraid!" whispers La Niña.

"Shhhh! Shhhh!"

✳<br>✳ ✳

El Caucho and La Niña are in bed, in the dark. La Niña is letting her frail hands wander over the receptive muscular body. She does not want to let him down. She would like to be happy with the same rough joy he feels. Yes! She would like that! It's inhuman to think that she might not. . . . How gentle he is! Why isn't he trying? He could try, if only once. He doesn't dare. He is afraid. He is afraid of hurting her. He mustn't be afraid. Even without the dehiscent delight of the flesh, his presence would be enough for her. Let him simply be there, be there forever—she asks nothing else of life. La Niña would be content enough. She has never been happier than now. No greater happiness can be imagined! As long as he has a triumphant orgasm, she could live from now on just to bring him satisfaction and pleasure—she would derive her pleasure from that. His gentleness is enough for two—she is being cleansed by her contact with him—his gentleness is radiating within her. The sensation of one person must be able to provide the happiness of two beings united in life and death. Yes, she thinks so! La Niña caresses his enormous limbs, presses on the rough plain of that pubescent chest. La Niña is dreaming. This man can belong to her! What can she do to keep him? Why can't she recover that lost image? Who is this man?

He moves.

"Well? Are you still afraid," asks El Caucho.

"I don't know!"

"Come on! Don't you want to tell me?"

"I want to! But I'm not sure. I don't think so."

"Don't be scared by what I'm going to ask. Have you ever been pregnant?"

"I think so. Yes, two or three times. But I've always gotten rid of it."

El Caucho lets his head fall on the pillow. What did he used to do on Sunday when he was younger in Oriente? Who was it that he made love to the first time? Does this woman really like him? A spark seems to have passed between them in the Sensation Bar. If he could just find that lost photo! He won't go to work tomorrow.

"You mustn't be afraid. You'll see. I think that awful nightmare will be finished. You needed me."

He has spoken seriously and deliberately. The words have spurted from his lips spontaneously—already shaped by his subconscious. He is frightened by what he has just said. What a commitment! La Niña has raised her head, trying to look into his eyes. He lowers his forehead. He places his lips on her temple. He lets his mouth wander behind her ear to the back of the neck. He surprises La with little unexpected licks.

"Hey, you're tickling me! Stop!"

"That tickles?"

"What do you think? When I'm tickled, it makes me laugh like everybody else! That's not the same thing! I'm telling you—stop! I don't want any more!"

El Caucho breaks out laughing but keeps on.

"So you're ticklish?"

"Of course! That doesn't stop me. . . . But, all that aside, I don't feel anything when I make love. You found the spots where I'm ticklish right away! Wait! You'll see yourself!"

She goes to it, searches over his body, but El Caucho controls himself. Ay! What a grip he has! He pins her motionless. She struggles. They wrestle, but she is quickly overcome. El Caucho keeps on. He goes down. His tongue and hands wander over La Niña's entire body—along her neck, her breasts, the ribs, her hips, up to the point where they turn into the loins. That mouth!

"Stop, I tell you! No! I don't want to! Stop!"

El Caucho keeps on. That tongue! La Niña breaks out in nervous laughter and tries to scratch him—she twists and tries to escape. In vain. El Caucho's wet lips are exploring La Niña's entire body.

"That's not fair! Stop it! Stop it!"

La Niña pounds on El Cauco's chest with both fists. It resounds, but he doesn't seem to feel it. He keeps on with increasing ardor. El Caucho shows no mercy. La Niña's laughter is spasmodic like Luz-Maria's alarm clock.

❊

❊   ❊

Why did he stop? He doesn't dare go any further? He should. That wouldn't bother La Niña—she's used to it. She is breathless, but she would be happy to give him pleasure. She would show him what she knows. He must be tired.

"Are you asleep? Do you want an orange?"

"No!"

"I'll peel one for you!"

La Niña turns the lamp back on. They share the orange. She looks at him closely.

"Aren't you from Oriente, like me? That's right, isn't it?"

El Caucho nods yes. La Niña rests her head in the hollow of his shoulder.

"Aren't you sleepy?"

He shakes his head no, but he doesn't take his eyes off her—observing each line on her face, each movement of her body.

"You can go to sleep," says El Caucho.

"No!"

She is looking for the hollow of his shoulder—the place where her cheek fits so well. She is tickling his pectoral with her tongue, taking the tip of his breast between her teeth and biting him gently. She feels beneath the sheets, caresses his thighs, strokes his penis, flattens the raised hairs. She is delighted with his excitement. She grabs his erect penis.

"No," he says.

She stops and tries to catch his glance.

"You don't want to?"

"I want to remember," he says. "I have to remember first."

She hesitantly continues to caress his great body, which belongs to her more and more as the minutes pass. She stops.

"I knew that I would find you," she declares. "Find you, or find you again."

He pulls her raised, wide-eyed head against his shoulder. She lets him do it. A meadow covered with marigolds. That sensual smell of haymaking, which is better than the freshest air she ever breathed! She breathes calmly and deeply. She is calm. El Caucho caresses her shoulder with the back of his hand. La Niña sighs. Her breathing becomes more and more contented. She is asleep.

❖
❖  ❖

La Niña rubs her eyes. She was sleeping but her dream woke her up.

"You're not asleep?"

"No."

"I think I was asleep. Did I sleep long? I was having a nightmare."

She lays her head on his chest. She dreamed that she had a fight. She was on a street. A bunch of guys attacked her. She faced up to them, but there were too many of them, and they were stronger than she was. There was heavy rain to the horizon. She was hitting back, blow for blow. They were striking her head, her eyes, her nose, and in particular her mouth. She was yelling and struggling. She was crying. Then a boy came up, dressed in a shirt with big blue, orange, red, and green squares. He let out a great yell. Then she dropped the bloody star she had between her fingers. It was his yell that woke her up. La Niña is thinking about her dream, trying to concentrate.

"Listen! Did you ever have a checkered shirt?"

"A checkered shirt?"

"Yes! With blue, orange, red, and green squares?"

"I don't remember!"

"When you were a kid!"

"Kid?"

"Yes!"

"No. Well, maybe. I don't remember!"

La Niña's throat tenses suddenly, and her eyes are flooded with tears. She sobs. El Caucho has raised her neck and is looking at her. He caresses her slowly. She is sobbing. Then he slips her head onto the pillow and kisses her. He kisses her right on the mouth. Her tears have salted his lips. She is stifling. He moves his mouth and begins to kiss her neck, breasts, and entire body. She calms down bit by bit. She returns his caresses. She pulls his body and rubs herself against him. He caresses her slowly. She is smiling. She gropes for him. She finds him and grabs hold.

"No!" says El Caucho quietly.

"I want to!"

"Not yet. I think I'm about to remember."

She lets go and falls limp, trembling. So, he doesn't want her? Ah! If he could just remember that checkered shirt! She curls up in anxiety. She hasn't been anxious for several hours! Maybe it wasn't the beginning of a real crisis? A false alarm? She has to calm down. Didn't her mother have a godson? What was the godson's name? Bah! Everybody has godsons. She has to calm down. She breathes deeply, the way he told her to. It's true that it's soothing. The minutes go by. She sighs. She moans. She goes to sleep.

El Caucho is thinking. He is searching his memory—the faces of friends, relatives, their friends. He raises each blade of grass, each stone, each old box, every toy he once had. A checkered shirt she said? He half sees a shape, but can't manage to tie it to any specific memory. He can't give it a name. If he just had that photo! He has to find it, come what may! He is going to find it. How she's sleeping!

❊<br>❊  ❊

El Caucho turns the lamp on. He shakes her gently.

"Come on! Wake up!"

Half-conscious, La Niña mumbles an unintelligible answer.

"Come on, Eglantina! Wake up!"

La Niña snores and tries to go back to sleep. He shakes her more vigorously.

"Come on, Eglantina! You have to wake up! Eglantina!"

"What?"

"Eglantina? Are you awake? Eglantina?

"Yeah, what do you want?"

She rubs her eyes; then she jumps. She is trembling.

"What did you call me? Repeat it!"

"Eglantina. That's really your name? Eglantina Covarrubias y Pérez?"

She looks at him with wide-open eyes.

"Be quiet!"

She is crying on El Caucho's shoulder. Oriente. Eglantina Covarrubias y Pérez. What forbidden world is he daring to evoke? She has been La Niña for everybody for over twelve years! It's rare that she even thinks of that name inwardly. What right does he have? Who is this person daring to break the taboo? Who is this person that has come to bring her back from the dead? She takes his face between her hands and rubs his face this way and that with her palms.

"And I can't think of your name! I was little, certainly. But I know, too. . . . I know, and I can't manage to remember."

"I had a photo, a photo of you and me, with my mother and your parents. I think I lost it. If I had that photo, I think that you would remember, too."

*Touch*

"A photo, you say? Wait!"

La Niña sits up abruptly. She hurts her toes on the tiles. No matter! She turns the light on. She heads for the wardrobe, and there on the top shelf, behind some old, worn-out shoes and heteroclite objects, she pulls out a dark little wooden chest with broken hinges. She goes back to lie down and hands it to him.

"Look! Hunt for it!" she says.

El Caucho rummages in two packets tied with ribbons. Letters, identity papers, a lock of hair, a dried marigold, a little stub from a communion candle. La Niña is watching intently. So many cadavers! The ones that lie sleeping in each person's inner cemetery, that great cemetery with neither sun nor moon, where in spite of everything, oblivion never manages to emasculate a tomb completely. When those phantoms awaken from their death, the weight of joy, shame, pride, remorse, and emotion weighs their shoulders down! At the bottom of the chest, there are some old photos. That little Eglantina who flowered in the suburbs of Oriente is there. There she is at every age. Here is the rose of those eyes that La Niña has not managed to destroy. El Caucho takes a photo. The one that he lost. He holds it out to La Niña. She takes it. She looks at it for a long time, propping her head against the shoulder offered to her.

"I had lost myself," she says.

El Caucho caresses the body, which lets itself go. She puts her hands over her face. Does she remember? La Niña shudders.

"Come!" she says in a hoarse but relaxed voice.

He lets her pull him to her. Then, with gentle concern and tenderness that he hardly ever had the chance to use, he tries to reanimate that beautiful, ailing body that has been handed over to him. What is the power of memory? What is the power of love? El Caucho is trembling. He is afraid of this new responsibility that he is assuming. How much time will it take to bring forth from this poor being the cry of ecstasy to which every human being has a right. He thinks he loves her, but apart from satisfaction, what does he know about physical love? Satisfaction! What satisfaction? Up to now, he has only had passing affairs of illusory love. Never before has he participated with his whole heart and soul in the intimacy of another being. He is afraid. He doesn't want to violate that body; he puts off as long as possible the moment of pure, ecstatic consummation. He obeys each inspiration, each impulse of his beating heart. In spite of this fear, his ignorance and his faith discover each necessary gesture for La Niña Estrellita's first night of love.

With spontaneous trembling, upturned eyes, and chattering teeth, the young virgin, Eglantina Covarrubias speaks to him.

"Rafaël! Rafaël! I think I'm in love. . . ."

It is her first time. She was in love all night. The roosters crowed their hearts out over Port-au-Prince as the night stole away. With him, she can remain in love for her entire life without the least miracle if, at least, both of them are able and willing to tend with all their energy that most fragile and marvelous plant known in nature: the love of a man and a woman, living by and for the universal fruition, that radiant human love.

The Sixth Sense

. . La nuit, je m'étendrai à tes côtés, tu ne diras rien mais à ton silence, à la présence de ta main, je répondrai: «Oui, mon homme!» parce que je serai la servante de ton désir. . . .

. . . C'est comme une complicité de coeur à coeur, ça vient tout naturel et tout vrai, avec un regard peut-être et le son de la voix, ça suffit pour savoir la vérité ou la menterie.
—Jacques Roumain, *Gouverneurs de la rosée*

. . . At night I will stretch out beside you. You will say nothing, but, to your silence and the pressure of your hand, I'll respond: "Yes, my man!" because I will be the servant of your desire. . . .

. . . It is like the complicity between two hearts: it flows naturally and quite truly, perhaps with a look and the sound of your voice—that's sufficient to discern truth or lies.

**B**road daylight. He is still asleep. Eglantina has already prepared coffee. Sitting beside him, she is playing with the gold chain he wears around his neck. She is serious. Through the partition come the sounds of somebody washing: Lucrèce is carrying out her morning washing ritual. Eglantina is fingering the gold chain. What now? What's going to happen? He is snoring lightly, gently. What will come of her joy? If she continues working as a whore in the Sensation Bar, joy will soon be a dead bird—her cantilena of love will not live as long as the cicada, and the big, relaxed body beside her will slip away with her dream, absorbed by the voracious horizon of the future. She is virtually certain of what he is going to ask her shortly. What can she answer? Not a thought comes to her. Nothing but images, clear images, of stupefying, terrifying clarity. She is afraid. She doesn't know. From this day forward, who is she? La Niña? Eglantina? Or nobody? She is at a loss. To her surprise, the images she thought were destroyed come flooding back before her eyes just as yesterday's sounds strike her ears—those morning sounds of the bordello's promiscuity. She is no longer a nobody. No longer does she know anything about her own heart, her will, her orientation. She now embodies a great passionate love, but in such ignorance and uncertainty! She certainly loves him, but that is all she knows! What can she answer?

He's really sleeping! He's snoring gently. Lucrèce is sweeping. Eglantina is playing with Rafaël's chain. His chain! The images are flooding before her wide-open eyes. She has lost nothing, not a feature of those distant faces, not a single old piece of family furniture, not a day of her childhood loves, not a blade of grass in the marigold-covered meadow. It's incredible! It burns within

*In the Flicker of an Eyelid*

her breast, worse than anxiety! That's it! Her anguish is coming back! What can she do? To whom can she turn, since heaven does not want to, or is unable to reply? It's a hole, a black hole, the abyss. So La Niña is still alive! This returning crisis, that's La Niña! Will Eglantina be able to kill La Niña? Oh, my God! She is bitter, cold, hot, delirious, dizzy, and at the same time, all those images are pushing forward like a herd of horned animals in a passageway that is too narrow. Die! Can she die to stop that anguish from coming back! While her memory was out of service, she used to have alternating crises of hysteria and *break-downs*—but she has regained her memory, and nothing has changed! Oh, Rafaël—you are my only certainty. Can you help me? Who can help anybody else? Doctor Chalbert used to say: "Nobody can answer certain questions for another person!"

He is sleeping. He is snoring gently. She is choking, sinking! She no longer has the Virgin of the Pillar to whom she can pretend to turn or offer a prayer. She doesn't know exactly what will come of her tomorrow. She loves him. She thinks she loves him, but what can he do for her? He definitely gave her something extraordinary—that delicious and excruciating wave of royal pleasure. He made her groan, whimper, scream her cantilena in tones she had never experienced. She wanted to die and then asked to die again from that unexpected miracle. Yes, he gave it to her. He gave it to her ten times. It's unique, unthinkable—he gave life back to her, and yet he couldn't take La Niña out of her body. La Niña is still there. La Niña is that anxiety, that terror, that bitterness with no cause, the hole, the vertigo. And yet, at the moment when that disheveled springtime of royal pleasure was burning, searing, overwhelming every little cell of her body, she had thought that her king had killed La Niña. Let him wake up then! Let him tell La Niña to die again. Let him kill her! He is all-powerful. La Niña could not kill Eglantina—how can Eglantina kill La Niña by herself? Oh, Rafaël! She is bitter, she is in love, and she doesn't know!

He is sleeping. His black mustache is slightly ruffled when he breathes. He is snoring. He snores gently! Eglantina's fingers are clasping the gold chain. This crisis is horrid! It has never been this strong, this beastly! How can she enjoy the life that has been restored to her if that Niña keeps haunting the days and nights of reborn Eglantina? He's going to awaken soon and find her flatulent, gaseous, bitter—in the grip of a neurotic crisis. He is going to say, "Come!" with that ardent, firecracker staccato characteristic of his speech. What can she answer with this wild beast's claw gripping her chest? What happened before, that unlikely discovery of her real self, is almost nothing beside the immensity of this new task: to become the woman she wants to be. Her love is a bed of coals that stirs and burns at the same time, but she knows La Niña is threatening her treasure.

"Oh, Rafaël! I don't want what you've uncovered to die! How can I prevent that Niña from ruining the only possession of an Eglantina who is still only eleven years old! Oh, Rafaël! My crazy tastes, parasitical tendencies, sick dreams, neurotic thoughts, and instability came from lack of satisfaction, futile struggles, and the daily routine. Wasn't I killing my only treasure, that fragile love of a hysterical street girl! I love you, Rafaël—save me from myself, from the usurper who took my place and has been riding me mercilessly! Save me!"

The firecrackers are starting to pop again. He is still asleep. The dry, loud, good-humored salvos are resounding. He is sleeping. La Niña's breast is a dizzying void. Jubilant shouts from the neighborhood kids, the rush of the trade winds and the sea. He is sleeping. Nothing wakes him up. He is sleeping in the arms of Eglantina, who is all fear, bitterness, and anguish. She is looking at him. Her king! She loves him intensely. The neighborhood has gone wild. If she could only reach the Maxiton pills in the drawer of the nightstand without waking him up. . . . She moves slightly. She reaches out and manages to get the bottle. His eyes are open! He is looking at her!

"Good morning!"

"Good . . . , good morning."

"What are you doing?"

"It's . . . it's . . . my medicine . . ."

She shows him the pills.

"Why are you taking that medicine? Are you sick?"

"Well, it's . . . Oh, Rafaël!"

"What is it? Why are you crying? Why that medicine?"

Crying and shivering, she is holding two pills between her thumb and index finger. He caresses her slowly.

My God! He knows. He knows everything she thought about a little while ago! He can guess everything! She is crying. He raises her head. She resists him. He takes her mouth. Ah, my God! That voracious animal! It's good, good, good! He takes the pills away. He takes the box and looks at the directions included.

"Eglantina, do you think this medicine is really necessary now? I love you, you know. Don't take it!"

He said the word! He loves her! Two little suns break forth in the room. Eglantina's rosy eyes climb upward toward Rafaël. She smiles ecstatically, but that beastly puncturing claw is still there. A beast mercilessly ripping her to pieces. . . . She smiles.

"Do you want to put them back in the box?"

She nods yes. She is afraid. He lays her backward. The imprint of that gentle, weighty male strength! Again! Again! The excruciating wave of regal pleasure runs through Eglantina. She hums the spring song that makes her hair stand up and brings ecstasy to every last cell in her body.

"Oh! My king!"

❧

❧  ❧

"You see, Rafaël—I haven't ever told you this. Do you remember the day when I gave you this chain? That happened in the meadow where the those great red bulls I was so scared of used to go. The meadow with the marigolds. When I went home, they beat me because I didn't have my chain any longer. But they believed what I told them—that it was lost. I cried, and I was happy to be beaten because I had given it to you. That was my secret. It was so simple at that time!"

"And yet, things weren't going so well at your home at that time; I remember that clearly. As for me, I had hidden the chain because I couldn't tell my mother. I hid it beneath a big rock but each time I went out or was going to meet you, I wore it. I was ashamed to admit to you that I was being secretive. Since that time, it has never left my neck."

"Do you remember the shoemaker?"

"The shoemaker?"

"Sure, the shoemaker. He was a relative of yours . . . your uncle, I think. He was deaf. Evaristo? Don't you remember? We met at his place. We went there to play."

This is the ecstatic rhythm of the soaring memories, interrupted by brief, joyful salvos, firecrackers, and the voices of kids going wild around a new *Jwif* that they are attacking at the corner. Bodies joined, Rafaël and Eglantina are living a moment of fullness, vibrant and gentle—they are stirring up their beginnings, their childish love; they see everything again. The nearby sea and the trade winds blow all around and create the aria of this romance from their past. Their very voices seem to marry the raucous percussion of the *ráboday,* which makes the atmosphere in the room crackle. The *Rara* drums continue proclaiming the jovial enthusiasm and boundless joy of the Caribbean on this Holy Saturday. Eglantina and Rafaël recall happy and less happy days. In their wild charge, the neighborhood kids destroy the mournful silence from the distant bourgeois city, which is enshrouded in the Passion of Jesus.

"What's that? Listen! What's that?"

Eglantina listens.

"Ah! That's Lucrèce!"

Eglantina bows her head. She can feel the spasm returning, slowly knotting in her breast. She tries to smile, but the intrusive noise coming from the neighboring room accentuates the anguish that had disappeared during their electric embraces.

"But what is it?" asks El Caucho again.

"Do you really want to know?"

Eglantina is serious, her head lowered. A cynical wrinkle appears at the corner of her mouth.

"What is it?"

"Well, it's Lucrèce. She and Luz-Maria, for sure. They're rubbing each other's back with brushes of couch grass. They whimper, but they love it. Do you hear them? Well, now you know!"

*In the Flicker of an Eyelid*

Filled with reflections and tension, they fall silent. My God! What if he were to think that she, too . . . Then what? If he questioned her, wouldn't she, too, have some difficult confessions to make? What will she do if he insists on knowing? Lie? Doesn't she have the right to lie so nothing will affect her only treasure, her miserable neurotic love? A man is clear-headedness itself! But what if deception, perpetual duplicity, lies, or even simple mental reservations slowly undermine the feeling that is her guiding light from now on? Isn't that confession beyond her strength? Even if she wanted to, maybe the words won't come out!

As for El Caucho, he isn't even thinking about such things. He is thinking about the mutual desires that will have to be allowed from now on. He is meditating on the inevitable hopes and disillusionment ahead. He is considering the difficult social constraints that will undoubtedly affect their fragile communion. He is a conscientious, responsible worker—and he has found her once more after years of separation. Sure, the idea came to his mind that all the women in this bordello are crazy. Eglantina is crazy, too! Will love be able to survive and take root in the depths of their personalities, a little more deeply each day? If love remains simply sexual harmony and shared memories, if the inclinations of their changing personalities don't grow in their hearts, if love remains only what it was at the moment of its crystallization, it will inevitably wither and destroy itself. Every day, with tiny, repeated flicks from all sides, life slowly but surely remolds the hearts of every human couple, their senses, their consciousness, their aspirations, their loves. An abyss tends to appear spontaneously between two people as soon as their respective evolution stops growing in agreement and confrontation. Will she be able to guess. . . . Oh! He doesn't ask much of her; he doesn't ask her to change instantly into what he wants her to be, what every human being should be; he only insists on her living, that is to say, changing, moving imperceptibly each day toward a more certain equilibrium, so she will free herself slowly but continually from what her horrendous life has imposed on her. Without an evolution parallel to his own, not identical to his but parallel, devised and deliberated through intuition, Eglantina's love will soon become inert, a poor crawling thing incapable of renewing surprise, joy, and the poetry of human relations that people are always looking for. A human being demands constant renewal on all levels, going beyond that divine sense of the unknown—that's a law! With the sense of things already seen, known too well, the most beautiful colors become boring! One fine day, love dies from stagnation. If the rose of her eyes loses its insight, if the five intimately linked senses stop learning life's secrets, the attractions of the body fail, pleasure changes to banal perception, indifference, disharmony, opposition, spite, and animosity. If personalities are in disaccord, growing apart, if they no longer commune with one another before the bread on the table each day, a flower, a bird, the springtime, illusion, chimeras, and action, love follows its inexorable path of devaluation and is transformed into repulsion, scorn, hatred. Slipping, sliding, bumping, everything loses its dignity and becomes degraded!

Eglantina is bitter; anguish is tightening her throat; that beast's claw is ripping her heart in spite of the body closely joined to her own. What is he thinking about?

"Rafaël? Listen to me? If you don't want me any more some day, if you've had enough of me, even this morning or in a little while, don't wait, don't hesitate: leave right away. Even then, you would still be right. I know that you will always be right— I know what I am, Rafaël! Leave when you're ready. But always tell me the truth, whatever it may be, do you hear? I will never stop thanking you, however long I may live. Whatever you do, you will always be right. Only . . . , I . . ."

He hugs her until she's breathless. Heavens! She has understood. She has guessed, guessed everything! Could everything be possible?

"What about you? Will you always tell me the whole truth?"

That question is worse than the stab of a dagger! Eglantina pales, she's stifled, she has a knot in her stomach. He pushed ahead too quickly. He caresses her.

"I'm talking about the truth of your heart, not about the

banal, absurd truth of facts—I'm not asking for anything more, Eglantina. I don't even want to know. Don't ever tell me anything. It's up to me to guess, right? We'll last together on one condition. You already know which one. That, I could never. . . ."

Eglantina breathes more easily. Her anguish is relaxing its grip on her. He knows!

"Oh, you! You!" she murmurs. "Come!"

Ah! That lithe, muscular, rhythmic body! The miracle is renewed!

✤<br>✤  ✤

The shuttered door half opens, cautiously and gently. Who's there? What's this? A surreptitious hand pushes a platter through and closes the door. On the platter is everything they might need for lunch. And what a lunch! The little *manolitas* of the Sensation Bar are saying that they have understood the miracle and that they salute love. Eglantina opens a questioning eye toward her companion, and a hesitant smile appears.

"That was Lucrèce's arm," she says. "They know."

He squeezes her shoulder hard enough to crush it. God, he's strong! Of course he understood! He understands! That gesture is a sign of enlightenment. They understand, too. He caresses her forehead.

"What time can it be?" he asks.

"Don't leave! Wait. My God! Twelve-thirty! Shall we eat? Do you want to eat what they brought? Oh, if you don't want to, I'll . . ."

"Of course, silly! Why wouldn't I? We'll have to thank them before we leave."

She looks at him. Before leaving? My God! When does he want to take her away? Where? Right away? Eglantina is worried. How will she react in that future when he has taken her away without warning? He speaks, he decides, but does he know everything? Eglantina is in the grip of doubt, and she's overwhelmed with dizziness.

"Shall we get up?"

He jumps out of bed, grabs her, and carries her to the wash basin. Like a feather! This sudden, brutal tenderness takes her by surprise. Anguish! She lets herself go.

He stands her up against the wall. She looks at him with the trembling roses of her eyes. My God! How gentle is that massive body that weighs you down, that crushes you, that wrests you from the earth to replant you in another soil, that seeks you, that caresses you, that reenergizes you. If she lost that, my God!

"Eglantina, do you remember what you did to me once? Ah, you don't remember! I won't forgive that, you'll see!"

My God! What's he going to do? What's he talking about? What . . . The whole pitcher of water suddenly splashes over her. Oh! Why did he do that? Of course! The bucket of water! He hasn't forgotten that! Still burning with the heat of the bed, Eglantina shakes herself and rubs against him to get him wet too. He hasn't forgotten! She laughs.

"Up to now, I've really been a big liar, you know!"

They're sitting at the table. They're eating. My God! Maybe the chicken isn't spicy enough! She doesn't have any hot sauce, any relish, any pepper in her room. Will he like it? He doesn't like it! Maybe he does, after all. He won't tell her. He is eating hungrily. She looks at him seriously. It's just as she thought. He takes little bites, with a smile at the corners of his mouth. Did she guess that or did she already know it? He is sensual, likes good food, and is tender, but he's not a big eater. Maybe he's ashamed? No! Everything in him is balanced—he's open, frank, spontaneous. He really eats whatever he can find. Eating is a couple's primary ritual. Giving her man something to eat! She, La Niña! The void in her breast makes her eyes open wide. When you've been a whore, do you remain one for your whole life? When she was twelve years old, Eglantina gradually fell into a mysterious sleep that has lasted almost fourteen years. During that entire period, La Niña has reigned—so if, once more, she becomes the girl she was at age twelve, with no experience, letting herself be carried away by the first man to come along, she will certainly not be suited to this man. Does she have to transpose La Niña's experience? How? What should she keep? What should be thrown away? Will she be able to choose? What if yesterday's vices, faults, and problems come back in furious waves to assault her? What can she do? Lie? What if she can't adapt to a new life?

Eglantina sits straight and forces herself to eat; she tries to smile and struggles with all her strength against her anxiety. She is seriously contemplating this first rite of the couple. She passes the bread, the rice, the peas. . . . She is totally icy and is struggling. Isn't this a crazy, illusory dream? Wouldn't it be better if this comedy were stopped immediately? My God! The dish of ice cream is soft! It's beginning to melt. No, it's only the top that's beginning to drip a bit. What if she killed herself? She watches him gravely. He is eating slowly, with small bites. He is smiling behind his mustache.

They are still in bed in the afternoon. Eglantina is slowly smoking the Cuban *Delicado,* which she had never tried before. Within the slow spirals of that colonial Cuban tobacco, a serious conversation is taking place, interrupted by the frenzied staccato of the pagan populace that is drumming out the ominous darkness of Good Friday on the quarter hour. It is time to consider the true law of life. Christ is going to Calvary today, says the legend—the dead will be hurled from their tombs, lightning will cut through the sky, and thunder will resound through space. The veil of the temple is rent from top to bottom. The kids in the suburbs bring back to life the myth of the poor, candid, and enlightened man who gave the Sermon on the Mount. They beat on their *Jwif* and celebrate the Sabbath. They wanted to make a God of a man who was fraternal and candidly idealistic. Did he believe it himself?

"*Eli, Eli, lama sabachthani,*" he cries.

"My God, my God, why hast thou forsaken me?"

## The Sixth Sense

Jeanne d'Arc was also heretical on her funeral pyre.

With the harsh words she hears, Eglantina Covarrubias y Pérez wonders whether there is a force capable of assisting her in the impossible combat that she is being urged to undertake. As for him, he believes only in himself, in human companionship—everything seems possible to him.

"Do you know that I have been in prison and that I may go back?" he asks. "We workers have our honor and our duty—we have difficult battles to wage, I have to warn you. If, by some chance, I were to leave you alone after some time, you would simply have to go to find our comrades. They would help you."

She doesn't reply. Her anxiety is tearing her apart, but her companion's hand is covering her wet, throbbing pubis. Where can she get the strength for such a struggle? What if she brought shame to him some day? Does she know how to share with someone else? Does she have the gift of heart, the gift of clear-sightedness, the sixth sense necessary to foresee the needs of this hard, gentle man—serious, passionate, committed, disinterested, honest, stubborn, strong, as true as the morning dew, as generous as the rain, as intransigent as the sun, intimate, understanding, demanding, and tender as a great dog?

El Caucho is speaking—he is speaking with that deliberate confidence. He claims that all love is difficult in these times. He says that love in our time is blind, limping, paralytic, irrational, and mystical because humankind is still all of that—hovering between two types of existence: semi-animality and future humanity. He maintains that one day there will no more *manolitas*, that one day our socially organized species will reach the age of reason and will throw off the last paroxysms of bestiality, irrationality, and illogicality that still affect us. He wants her to be his companion through the tempest blowing across the universe. Does he know her? Eglantina looks at him hard. From time to time, she brings her hand to her head, but stops before she finishes, with her claws immobile under Rafaël's frowning brows. Eglantina is tortured with cold and anguish—she is trembling. The firecrackers keep exploding outside. They hear

Mario's voice. He has come to take a look at his puppet show. It's terrible to see a man possessed by his own fantasy to that point—it's stronger than he is. The car starts up. It has gone.

What if she committed suicide?

❊

❊   ❊

Evening has fallen. Eglantina and Rafaël are still in bed. People are dancing and cavorting somewhere far away in the lively joy of the Indian carnival. The woman who was La Niña is listening to the description of the difficult, combative life that her companion is proposing. The sun died a little while ago in the wild phantasmagoria of this room with its copper, enamel, crystal, nickel, and beasts of light. They are still intertwined and questioning each other.

"Did that little star inserted in your tooth give you your name?"

She nods yes. She is aflame with contradictory feelings, fears, anguish, intoxication, revolt, terror, fright, love, and controlled tears. She looks at him.

"And what if, in spite of everything, I happen to bring shame to you some day?"

She slowly articulates the syllables with uncontrolled energy. She scratches her scalp with her sharp fingernails. Rafaël glues his eyes on Eglantina. She stops, with her head bowed. He places his hand back over her moist, throbbing pubis. He embraces her.

"I don't know what I would say or do in that case, but you would be responsible for whatever I might do."

His look is at once tender and harsh. La Niña is trembling. Is he threatening? Whom is he threatening, himself? Her? What is he talking about? My God, if she could simply escape from this man before it is too late! But can she escape him? It's already impossible to disengage herself from this Rafaël with whom she roamed the meadows in her childhood. He was like a cowherd, as taciturn as the young bulls in the enclosure. When she was frightened of the cattle, he would tell her:

"Come with me! Come see!"

And his fist would close over her hand. She had to follow him whether she wanted to or not. As long as she had not gone up to the nervous beasts, she couldn't escape. Will it be any different now?

A wave of music comes from the bar. The girls are beginning to dance with each other. Don't they ever get enough?

"Sunday, we'll go see the *Rara* at the Ça-Ira crossroads," he says.

La Niña is burning with fever. She wants to run away, to go far away, somehow, very far away.

"I know that you will not bring shame to me," he says. "You couldn't!"

This reassurance is irritating! She is trembling. He takes her mouth. Ah! That *godrin* on his mouth! She yields. . . .

❊

❊  ❊

Night has fallen again. They are still intertwined. They are sleeping. They wake up to make love again. They go back to sleep. They are two lost children of the radiant Caribbean. They will be first at the top of the rope in humanity's climb toward the age of reason, the time when the contradiction between feeling and reason will have been left behind, the age of love. What does that mean? Eglantina opens her eyes in the dark. The table, the old armchair, the altar, the corner of the wash basin, the chest with the mirror that belonged to La Niña Estrellita. . . . She sniffs all the old smells of this torture chamber. La Niña was all alone—that's why the phantoms of her memory have survived in her inner cemetery, that great cemetery with no sun or moon. With her companion at her side, can Eglantina forget La Niña? If Eglantina was able to hide for such a long time, why won't La Niña disappear? And yet, just as Eglantina imposed so many secret but invincible impulses on La Niña, maybe La Niña will be able to do the same in spite of this new companionship.

How can La Niña be prevented from slowly killing the only thing left to the rediscovered Eglantina, her fragile and unstable love? What if she can't break free from this persistent neurosis? Who will deliver her from this conditioned but real neurosis that's gripping her breast this very instant? He gave her an excruciating wave of pleasure, a harmonious orgasm, the dazzling springtime of joy mingling heart and body, a royal joy, a delightful, tentacular octopus sucking on every last cell in her body; yet is it possible for her human antennae to tune in to the same wavelength as his? Will this man ever divine the contradictory feelings that are torturing Eglantina?

He abruptly raises his head to look at her. Just as he thought! Her eyes are wide open. Rafaël lets out a great laugh she has never heard. He takes her mouth. She is afraid, but her fear disappears; it's almost gone. They roll in a wild, breathless embrace. Does Eglantina have the necessary sixth sense to maintain love forever?

They fall asleep, exhausted.

❋

❋　❋

The wild bells and alleluias have broken out: it's the deafening jubilation of the Saturday of Holy Water. El Caucho awakens with a start! Damn! He shakes her. Eglantina is calm and smiling—she opens the rose of her eyes before the five senses of this hard, tender man.

"I have to go!" he exclaims. "So, get ready—don't say anything to anybody, and I'll come to get you at one o'clock, as soon as work is over. Agreed?"

Eglantina lowers her head.

"Well? Agreed?"

She can't raise her head.

"You promised," he says. "OK, agreed?"

"Agreed," she says.

He jumps to his feet, goes quickly to get dressed behind the screen. He comes back. He has dressed in no time. She looks at him with wide-open eyes, leaning on her elbow. He is ready.

"One o'clock?"

## The Sixth Sense

She nods, then jumps from the bed, choked by her sobs. She goes to him, kisses him, covers him with her body.

"One o'clock?

"Yes. . . ."

He hugs her again. He leaves. He's gone!

CODA

In the Flicker of an Eyelid

Siento un anhelo tirano
por la ocasión a que aspiro,
y cuando cerca la miro
yo misma aparto la mano.
    Porque, si acaso se ofrece,
después de tanto desvelo,
la desazona el recelo
o el susto la desvanece.
—Sor Juana Inés de la Cruz, "En
que describe racionalmente los
efectos irracionales del amor"

I feel a tyrannical desire
for the encounter to which I aspire,
and when I see it close,
I pull my hand away
    Because, if it is offered perchance,
after my long and difficult insomnia
suspicion and doubt make it bitter
or fear makes it disappear.
—"In which [she] rationally
describes the irrational effects
of love"

She has dressed and is cramming her underwear and things into an old suitcase—there is the box of souvenirs, shoes, and various little objects. She's frantically trying to finish. She will leave everything else. How can she get those big suitcases out and not attract attention? Oh, yeah! Antoine, the candy vendor! She'll ask him to come. There's a hall at the back of the courtyard. He'll put her suitcases somewhere in Clémente's shop. Clémente won't say anything, and Antoine won't talk about her leaving if he gets a little money. Not right away, at least. There she has finished. Everything's there. The chest! She goes over to the altar, takes down the image of the Virgin of the Pillar and places a board against the wall to hide a mark. She takes down a little heart-shaped chest, with rose-colored shells on it. She goes to the bed and sits down.

Her entire fortune is there: $977 in new bills, fourteen twenty-dollar gold pieces, three gold tiepins, two men's watches, ten or so rings, one with a square stone set in platinum, a fiery emerald—that's all. After fourteen years of work, she has this treasure because she has never taken a pimp who would take the profits from her work. Most of it she has gathered during the last two years with her success and reputation, which have never failed her. Somebody is knocking at the door. Who can it be? My God!

"La Niña! La Niña!

"I'm busy. What do you want?

"Open up!"

My God. She mustn't see those suitcases. She empties the contents of the little chest in her black handbag.

"Right away!

She puts the suitcases behind the screen.

"Who's there?"

It's Lucrèce.

"La Niña come on! You know, we didn't see you yesterday, but it seems that Gabriel has dropped La Rubia. He has taken up with Concepción, you know, the girl who just came to the Kangaroo Bar. La Rubia went to the Kangaroo yesterday evening. She came back in one of those fits! You know how she is when something gets her? This is worse! We've been knocking at her door since morning, but she hasn't answered. We're afraid to open, but you know her. If you don't mind. . . . You're the only one who can go see—she won't say anything to you."

❖<br>❖ ❖

Lucrèce has Mario's keys. The girls are all standing back a little, behind the door in the hall. La Niña sticks the key in the hole, turns it, opens, and steps back immediately. With a yell, Lucrèce pushes her aside and rushes in. . . .

La Rubia is hanging above an overturned stool in the middle of the room. There is a letter on the floor: "To Mario." La Rubia has hanged herself. She's completely naked—swinging, turning slowly at the end of the rope, her eyes bulging out, her tongue protruding from her mouth. Her suitcases are packed. Four of them. Each one has a tag: "For Luz-Maria," "For Fernande," "For Felicidad," "For Lucrèce." On the nightstand, there is a big can of black hair spray with a carton: "For La Niña Estrellita." La Rubia was a great lady; she has ended her life as a great lady. Nobody will ever pronounce "La Rubia" again with the accent used to say "La Vénus Farnese." The girls begin yelling; Lucrèce pushes everybody around.

"Come on! Take the suitcases. Can't leave those for the police; we'd never get anything back. Get out, all of you! La Niña, you don't stay here either; you're so wrought up you'll get sick. Come on! Out! Don't stay. I'm going to telephone Mario."

❖<br>❖ ❖

## Coda

La Niña has gone back to her room. She is sitting on the edge of the bed, shaking with a spasmodic shiver. Her teeth are chattering. Her sharp claws are ripping her breast. She opens the carton. There is a wad of bills, some jewels, some photos, papers, finally a large envelope with La Rubia's large, curling handwriting: "To La Niña." La Rubia was educated. On certain evenings when she was drunk, she would recite resonant poetry that flowed out with a slow Aztec rhythm. It seems that she had "worked" in Acapulco for a long time. She would recite strange poetry that nobody understood. La Rubia was a very great lady, even if she was a whore. Who had La Rubia been before she became what she was? La Niña's wrist is shaking with great jerks. She opens the envelope. It is a sheet of paper with faded writing. This letter was written a long time ago, with that same tall, curling calligraphy. It is poetry. The title is *"En un abrir y cerrar de ojos,"* "In the Flicker of an Eyelid." At the bottom of the page, the ink is still fresh.

*Niñita,*
*As you see, my good-bye has been ready for a good*
*while. I simply waited too long. Keep this paper and the*
*others as long as you are alive. Sometimes, when you*
*have the time or when your heart has become too heavy,*
*try to read these lines—you'll see what all of us are and*
*why I had to do what I've done. If, by any chance, you*
*meet a human being who is worth the trouble and might*
*be interested, show what I've written or give it to the per-*
*son. It wasn't possible to go on! En un cerrar y abrir de*
*ojos.... La Rubia has left before it is too late. You know*
*how we all end up. I loved you, Niñitita, and that's why*
*I'm leaving a bit of my perfume. La Rubia has had*
*enough, she is going to sleep. Nobody should cry. Let*
*people at the Sensation be joyful, lively, and cheerful after*
*my departure. Courage! Keep on.... Bravo!*
                                        *Just an old Rubia.*

✽
✽  ✽

El Caucho enters the courtyard of the Sensation Bar. He is wearing his khaki trousers and his white *guayabera*. The police have already been there for a while, and the ambulance has taken the corpse away. There's nothing complicated: a whore killed herself—the letter is there to prove it. Everything is clear. Who knows? Maybe the students at the School of Medicine are dissecting La Rubia this very moment on the necropsy table. Mario is behind the bar, as usual. His mouth seems a bit stiff all the same. It seems that at one time there was some connection between him and La Rubia.

El Caucho comes on in. His shoulders are rolling, his neck moves back and forth in its persistent nutation; that same rhythmic, elastic gait. He places one foot forward on the toes, the heel barely skimming the ground, and there—the rubber man is in. He is determined. Three or four girls are talking with broad gestures at the bottom of the terrace. As soon as she sees El Caucho, Lucrèce runs to him.

"*Hombre*! What hasn't happened at the Sensation Bar today! La Rubia killed herself—they found her hanging by her gullet! And then La Niña left—nobody knows where.

"Left?"

"Yes. She left this for you. She begged me to put it right in your hands."

"Left?"

"Yes."

Lucrèce hands a little packet to El Caucho. The three horizontal wrinkles on his forehead rise. But he is a hard man, tanned by the sun, salted and peppered by the Caribbean trade winds. In his opinion, she couldn't have left. A promise is a promise. He opens the packet at once: a watch, some photographs, and a hastily scribbled letter.

La Niña's writing is not broad and curving, not tall and relaxed. Everybody will tell you that La Niña is not educated as La Rubia was, and yet, in spite of her poor downstrokes, her scrawls, and her awkward characters, what she wrote is thought provoking. What's in this letter—maybe El Caucho wouldn't agree—is the message of an enlightened woman. You can argue:

she should have, she shouldn't have; but that's the way it is. Four sentences. Yes, she loves him, she loves him more than she can say. He gave her a flush of royal pleasure. She had never imagined that could happen. He is her king, but she is leaving, she is going away. She has to try to become a real woman, a worthy companion for him; she is going to struggle to see whether she can get rid of La Niña. It will last as long as it takes—a month, six months, a year, but she is going to work in order to live; she is going to try to kill La Niña. If it works, she will come back to find him of her own free will; if not . . . Perhaps she has made a poor calculation but, in any case, her act is an enlightened act, a highly conscious and responsible act.

"*¿Chica?* Can you take me to her room?"

Lucrèce looks at him, astonished. Oh, well!

❋<br>❋  ❋

El Caucho sits at the bar. In the room, nothing is left except the furniture, outright disorder, a little bit of displaced dust, that's all. He couldn't pick up the image of the Virgin of the Pillar, ripped into pieces. It's really true—she didn't lie—she's going to struggle like a woman of the Caribbean to regenerate herself. El Caucho clenches his fists.

"Boss, give me a *grog*. Two good fingers."

"*¡Hombre!* What are you saying? Do you know the news? La Rubia . . . What a week."

El Caucho lowers his head and doesn't answer. Oh! He's not a man to give up like that. What she did is foolish—she'll learn to know El Caucho! Once this rascal has made up his mind, the sky can fall if it wants, but he'll still carry out his decision.

"So long, boss!"

El Caucho leaves the Sensation Bar. Two o'clock resounds from the tower of Saint-Anne's. The old Mexican was right:

*Un poquitín y todo se pone al morado, un chiquitín y todo gira al rosado"*—at the snap of a finger, everything turns mauve; then, for no reason, it all turns rosy!

The noises of the city are picking up in the distance—the

firecrackers, motors starting, the sudden squeal of brakes, the enraged barking of horns, the exalted Rara drumming, and that obsessive breathing of the sea, resounding at the whim of the Caribbean trade winds. El Caucho believes that he will find her again—he believes it as sure as he breathes—he has not lost the roses of La Niña's eyes. Perhaps . . . *¡Quién sabe!*

# *Glossary*

For convenient reference, we list non-English words and expressions (some of which are translated in the text of the novel). The following abbreviations are used: F (French), K (Kreyòl), L (Latin), S (Spanish). English terms italicized in the text of the novel were in English in the original text. Spanish terms in the original text remain in Spanish, and the marks of interrogation and exclamation are inverted before the beginning of the relevant word or expression.

With regard to pronunciation, consonants are roughly as in English, keeping in mind that *t* is always hard (never *sh* as in "nation"), *g* is hard in Kreyòl but either *g* or an aspirated sound in Spanish (before *i* or *e*). A *ch* is an affricate in Spanish, like "*ch*alk"; in Kreyòl, it is a voiceless sibilant /ʃ/ like "*sh*oe." The voiced sibilant /ʒ/ is similar in French and Kreyòl.

Basic vowels are similar in Kreyòl and Spanish (symbols of the International Phonetic Alphabet between slashes):

> *a* /A/ as in "*fa*ther"
> *e* /e/ like French *é*, "b*ai*t"
> *i* /i/ as the double *ee* in English, "f*ee*t"
> *o* /o/ as "b*oa*t"
> *ou* /u/ in Kreyòl, as in English "b*oo*t"
> *u* /u/ in Spanish, like "b*oo*t"

Where standard French has four nasal vowels, Kreyòl has only three:

> *an* /ã/ like French "t*an*te" or, roughly, English "d*au*nt"
> *en* /ɛ̃/ like French "p*ain*" or English "r*an*t"
> *on* /ɔ̃/ like French "m*on*de" or English "w*on*'t"

## Glossary

*abrazo* (S)   hug

*akasan* (K)   cornmeal pudding or porridge

*¡ándale!* (S)   go (on)!

*banboula* (K)   the smallest of the three Vodou Rada drums; a dance (also *kata*)

*bastreng* (K; F: *bastrengue*)   a small music group; a popular dance hall

Beaugé, Louis-Jean   A historical personage of Haiti, famous for his intransigence, his touchiness, and his legendary bravery (JSA). Monseigneur Beauger (note historical spelling) was the first Haitian bishop (translators' note).

*bwakochon* (K)   the hogbush; used to flavor Haitian alcohols

*cabrón* (S)   a he-goat; a "bastard" or a pimp (slang)

*calor* (S)   heat; *¡hace calor!*—it's hot!

*canción* (S)   song; *canción cubana* refers to the popular songs of Celia Cruz in the novel

*cargador* (S)   a loader or docker; slang, a slightly salty, strong Cuban alcohol (note by JSA)

*chalbari* (K)   a public outcry; a drum rhythm

*chico, chica* (S)   small (boy, girl)

*chien de pique* (F)   a sixteen-card spread in tarot (see the afterword)

*chispa* (S)   spark; drop (rain); crumb; *echar chispas*—to throw off sparks, to be furious

*chulo, chulito* (S)   insolent (familiar); a pimp (slang)

*coño* (S)   (vulgar) cunt; (expletive) shit!

*desesperación* (S)   desperation; a favorite song (a *tango* or *son*) of La Niña's

Dona nobis pacem (L)   Give us peace (Latin mass)

*equivocado* (S)   mistaken, confused

*godrin* (K)   a wine made of fermented pineapple skins

*grimo* (K)   a mulatto with light-colored hair and light skin

*gringo* (S)   a foreigner; commonly, a Yankee

*guajiro, guajira* (S)   a Cuban peasant (masculine, feminine)

*guarracha* (S)   a lively Spanish dance

*guayabera* (S)   a Central American pleated shirt-vest (JSA)

## Glossary

HASCO   the Haitian-American Sugar Company

*jouda* (K)   a highly curious person; gossip (from "Judas" in the New Testament)

*Jwif* (*gwo Jwif*, big Jew) (K)   "Jew"; in Rara, specifically, the symbolic Jew of the Sanhedrin, blamed for supporting the Crucifixion of Jesus; kept in Kreyòl to avoid confusion with the common ethnic or religious meaning of "Jew."

*kakakòk* (K)   literally, "chicken shit"; a coconut fritter

*kasav* (K)   the edible root cassava

*kata* (K)   the smallest of the three drums in the Vodou Rada rites; a specific drum rhythm

*kawo* (K)   a Haitian measure of surface area; equivalent to 3.19 acres

*kleren* (K)   a cheap Haitian rum or alcohol; *Kleren tranpe* is flavored alcohol

*kòb* (K)   a Haitian penny

*kongo payèt* (K)   a sensual dance

*loca* (S)   a crazy woman

*mabi* (K)   a Haitian peasant beer (JSA)

*macho* (S)   male; a man who parades his virility

*madanmichel* (K)   an aromatic grass

*madansara* (K)   a black and yellow mantled weaver bird; from the name of the bird, the term is used to refer to roving market women

*makak* (K)   a monkey

*malicón, maricón* (S)   a homosexual (pejorative)

*manolito, manolita* (S)   a young man or woman; a prostitute (Caribbean)

*mayi* (K)   a rapid Vodou dance

*mierda* (S)   shit (used literally and as an expletive)

*moukère* (F)   a woman (a pejorative word in Algeria; from S, *mujer*)

*muchacha* (S)   girl

*nètowo* (K)   plant seeds roasted and eaten with hot sauce (JSA)

*niña* (S)   girl; whore

*Glossary*

*ounsi kanzo* (K)  a Vodou initiate of the second degree; assists the *oungan* or *manbo* (priest or priestess)

*palgo* (S)  a bon vivant who is especially generous with women (JSA)

Péterplancher (K)  a strong alcohol (*tranpe*)

*pulquería* (S)  a bar where people drink *pulque* (a Mexican alcohol made from agaves)

*puta* (S)  whore

*rabòday* (K)  makeshift, shoddy; a lively dance in the Rara

Rara (K)  carnival festival taking place during Holy Week (JSA)

*rubia* (S)  in the Caribbean, usually a mulatto woman with roughly blond hair (JSA)

*salanbe* (K)  to insult, swear at someone; to beat up

*siguen* (S)  to follow (continue a wild Caribbean dance) (JSA)

*tranpe* (K)  a cheap Haitian alcohol

*vaksin* (K)  a bamboo flute

Venus Farnese  The Naples National Archaeological Museum contains a number of statues of Venus and Aphrodite, including a "Callipygous Venus." The Farnese collection of sculpture is in the Museo e Galleria Nazionali di Capodimonte, above Naples.

*wari (ouari)* (K)  a variety of tree, Caesalpinia, used for dyes and various medicines

*zodouvan* (K)  nakedwood tree; a flavor for alcohols

# Letter to Jacques Soleil

"I have to tell you that I think about you a lot as I would think about a great slice of sun illuminating my life. I am going to do something you will one day see as necessary and important. When you have even one drop of black blood, Haitian blood, you remain a child of our country whatever happens."
—J. S. Alexis, Anvers, 24 December 1954

"All countries are beautiful, my little Florence, but one land will respond like no other to the ardor of your blood: a land of flame and unheard-of beauty, made for your feet, arms, and heart. Because of your blood, expressed in your fiery dances, no country will ever replace the land of Haiti, from which you come.
—J. S. Alexis, Lisbon, 28 December 1954

"Alas, I won't have much time, from the great distance where I am, to keep up my inalienable paternal duty. My little daughter, I can give you something I know quite well because I've desperately sought it and found it even as I continued to look for it—that is a sense of purity of heart, love of life, and human warmth. I've always tackled life with a pure heart. It's simple, you see, Florence. . . .

And especially, never forget that a human being is not merely arms, legs, and hands, but, above all, intelligence. I wouldn't want you to let your mind slumber. When you let your mind slumber, it rusts, like a nail, and then you become vicious without realizing it."
—J. S. Alexis, Havana, 11 January 1955.

"Letter to Jacques Soleil" appeared as the preface to Éditions Gallimard's 1983 edition of *L'espace d'un cillement*.

This is your child, your elder daughter who has become a woman, writing to you from beyond the boundary of your endless absence. We have been deprived of one another for over twenty years, and today I want to speak to you about the book you left behind before returning to the stars, *In the Flicker of an Eyelid*. You know, it's my favorite book, the one that appeals to me more than any other and through which everything in me comes together—and, in my own poor words, I'm going to try to tell you why.

In order to understand the fascination this text holds over me, I've had to gather over time the scattered debris that you left behind you, to decode the mysterious signs you willed to me—for my hunger, for my thirst—and to break through the hereditary exile by facing my own fear, walking toward our agonizing and broken island.

"La Rose des Yeux" (rose of the eyes), "L'Églantine," or "La Quadrature du coeur" (squaring of the heart): for a long time, you hesitated in choosing among those titles. The third one clarified your project. You wanted to undertake that enigmatic geometry, the eternal challenge, and the hypothetical solution of love between a man and a woman in a universe, the Caribbean, where those relations are often carried to a point of absolute caricature. A world that has been tetanized, marked by steel, shaken by the traumas of slavery, genocide, and the slave trade—a world in which each of us is condemned to the perpetual and violent conquest of one another, imprisoned in primal and paroxystic relationships that leave us thirsting. This aggressive and derisive love game engenders a society that is infernal in all aspects. These pathological relations with the world, politics, the nation come hurtling back like a boomerang at man, at woman, at nature, at childhood.

People persist in caricaturing you as a rigid communist, a venerable leader, a pure Marxist, a relentless theoretician, a man bound by his own reasoning—a personage that our generation totally mistrusts—but you manage a lightning escape into the rainbow, and you break the sharp steel collar, letting us glimpse a path unknown at the time. It is a royal way to be explored with delight, a window looking out on man and woman and still to be opened: on life, the open air, our world.

> The first day, as they will see, it will be sight. The second day, they will hear voices—it will be hearing. And so on with smell, taste, touch. From the five senses, I would like to create a sort of suspense. All of this in the terribly exciting atmosphere of a slightly crazy city, with carnival erupting from the suburbs and with marines everywhere. (J. S. Alexis, "La rose des yeux")

The decor is set. Little by little, the mansions will throw light on this or that element of the landscapes of hell and heaven that are being built before our eyes.

In order to miss nothing, let's not look at your finger—as so many others have done blindly or perfidiously—but at the star you're pointing to.

In this novel, *In the Flicker of an Eyelid,* the characters do not meet each other at just any street corner, on just any mountain slope, or on just any shore of our Caribbean. According to your own expression, they are

> the leaders at the head of the roped party on the mountain of Radiant Human Love . . . (J. S. Alexis, "La belle amour humaine")

To begin with, she is a caricature, the parody of a woman, a female, abandoned and confined to her role. She has all the attributes that are usually bestowed on the "eternal woman": her bitchiness, her hypersensitiveness, her sex appeal, her unique vocation for pleasure, traits that alternate with her exceptional beauty, her fraternal relations with her fellow galley slaves, her basic, suppressed uneasiness, her recurring neurosis, her desperate true nature. Accustomed to this parody of love, she knows how to play the slut, the tease, and she goes along with all that by lacerating her own heart, crucifying her senses. She mutilates herself. She is neither Pasionaria nor Penelope, and yet, without realizing it, she has everything needed to become an exceptional being. Here we are at the very antipodes of the usual story: the repentant prostitute.

> Woman is strong; she bestrides torrents, she overturns thrones, she stops the passing of the years. Her skin is of marble. When such a woman exists, she is the dead end of the world. Where do rivers, clouds, isolated birds go? To hurl themselves into woman. But she is rare. (Jean Giraudoux, *Choix des élues*)

La Niña Estrellita is not the Virgin, she is the little Whore. In Haitian society, she has been relegated to the servants' quarters. She is a taboo character about whom little is said in our literature, which most often speaks only of a few high-class "courtesans" trying to climb the social ladder—which is permitted rather easily—by means of money quickly gained and squeezed out of high-ranking men. This woman does not run around among the rich and powerful, who are unaware of her existence—she lives among the obscure people, without a *chulo,*

> in that bitter bed of a whore contemplating human misery. (99)

Helpless, she witnesses the individual and collective drama, which is her own. She exists outside of society, crushed by social morality and prudish hypocrisy. In Haiti, the "intellectual elite"—poorly named—made no mistake in neglecting with nearly total silence this marvel of a novel, which disturbed literary conventions, the social code, rigid structures (death), and ambient prudishness, and in spite of the bluntness that kills language, its haunting disarray, and the terror of impotence. But because she is "out of the game," our little whore is more capable than anybody of freeing herself from this absolute slavery. Since she is nobody, she has nothing to lose. She will accept this challenge that only exceptional women—not even Messalina or the Maid of Orleans—can accept. And she has a "privileged" observation post for recognizing the destruction left by love-

---

*"Letter to Jacques Soleil"*

lessness, and she will perhaps be able to find the remedy in her own manner, later.

This woman is Cuban by origin and, thereby, incarnates the nomadic swarming of her people throughout the fragmented and radiating Caribbean. But La Niña is frigid and willfully amnesiac. Her life can be summarized as giving pleasure without experiencing it. She gives and does not receive. And in order to survive in this nightmare, she has obliterated, dissimulated, her past. She no longer wants to know anything about herself in order to survive, come what may, in the present. And the present is chaotic—she swings between hysterical jubilation and a tide of anguish that disarticulates her, body and soul.

From the very first lines, we encounter La Niña Estrellita in her room at the Sensation Bar, with a customer, an American marine—plying her trade in bed.

That bed, in La Niña's universe, is the vessel of her perdition, the instrument of her alienation.

So she has to leave that bed, to abandon it in order to set out on her journey of rediscovery, in order to try to rediscover herself. And that is exactly what happens: the text says so openly. . . .

Leaving her bed, La Niña is ready for the journey of rediscovery. But she is disoriented and does not know where to find the road: her head is spinning.

She needs the intercession of a traveling companion, a ferryman, a navigator who will be able to find the right direction.

Meanwhile, she finishes preparing for her departure; she achieves the rupture.

So La Niña leaves behind the somber room where she has been tortured, without a single regretful glance at the marine who is there. In front of her door, she has to "push back" and "even shove" (10) her way past the other marines waiting for their turn in the hallway.

These sailors are really not the Argonauts she needs for

her journey, to accompany her in the quest for the Golden Fleece. . . .

She walks through the bar: "The record player is blaring a bolero of passion, despair, and golden sun" (10):

Me *siento morir-r-r!* I feel I'm dying!

That dying, passionate bolero is the golden sun, the disappearing sun, as it sets.

So La Niña Estrellita is that dying bolero as it becomes the Golden Sun.

Yes, because gold, the metal of the gods, is the very sweat, the sun's poop.

Gold is Death.

But each death is a return, a renaissance; it is the sun that dies each day and is reborn the following morning in the land of the Rising Sun, in Oriente. . . .

She is going to set out on the road of rediscovery.

She is in the gallery of the bordello.

She "bends her waist, projects her breasts": she is a ship at sea, La Niña hoists her sails;

She projects "her tired breasts": she is a vessel setting its course;

She "makes her hips sway": she is a frail bark, her sails swollen by the wind; La Niña pitches and wallows;

She "walks down the entrance steps of the terrace": this is the departure! La Niña the ship has left her dock, the wharf. At sea, La Niña the vessel has not yet mastered the helm, her rudder. She needs a helmsman . . . (Jacques Rey-Charlier, *Rap-Track*)

It is clear that our Niñita is the entire Caribbean, handed over to the pleasure of others, making a living with her body, sterile and exploited (touristically, since that is nearly all that remains to devour). From the first pages, she is going to be forced to plunge "into the saline ocean of memory" (Rey-Charlier) in order to survive.

In 1957, your vision was assuredly one of astounding lucidity. La Niña's frigidity and her quest for sensual pleasure are cer-

---

## "Letter to Jacques Soleil"

tainly that of all women. Haiti remains a creature possessed by aggressive powers (internal and external) that rape her after having forced a parody of consent. The Caribbean and its peoples live by tourists' enjoyment of the hundred thousand beauties of our land. While others are sated, these peoples are powerless and frustrated in their losing battle for survival—an omnipresent neurosis, a disguised and multiform prostitution in order to continue struggling, or, alternatively, a ruthless and nightmarish exodus that leads from Hell to Hell (Jean-Claude Charles, *De si jolies petites plages*).

For our benefit, you boldly explore a way to get us out of this tunnel—like a real *natif-natal,* with consistent, ferocious humor, you explore this farce as if it were a drama in which the sun bursts out laughing.

For us black and mulatto women of the Caribbean, you meticulously avoid any concession to exoticism—whether it's new-look or everlasting—in this perilous adventure in the land of women; there is no torrid or sophisticated swooning, none of those elegant and vacuous adventures of sexual prowess.

Now, you know, young people are positively or negatively fascinated by the couple. Our generation wanted to get out of politics, out of arrid dogmatism, in order to enter life and the relationships that direct it. We wanted to examine experience in detail, in its daily aspects. In this book, you give a hint of what we would discover later: the transformation of our relationships. The stalemate of some will be the stalemate of others—a life's stalemate; woman's stalemate will be that of man.

And here comes the man: She "has noticed a man in blue overalls. He's coming toward her" (13).

"An incredible marvel!"
Yes! He had to arrive now since "things are really not going well," and he is a mechanic! He also had to be dressed in blue! Of course! Since El Caucho is that vibrant ocean that was not visible and who is bringing life to La Niña!
Here is that being whose "breathing makes her melt."
Here is that navigator of the Rising Sun who is going to

help her find her childhood Oriente, the Oriente of her resurrection!

Here he is: El Caucho—the rubber man, the cat with
seven lives and seven deaths! The man who bounces back!
The sailor of the solar mechanism of life! He is the one who
will bring her motor back to life, who will make it hum.
(Rey-Charlier)

He walks through life with his elastic gait—he, too, is a wanderer. He has knocked all around the Caribbean "Mediterranean." He is a mechanic and a union worker, the "positive"
character in the novel whom we find somewhat irritating in our
times, but with nuances of vigilance and good humor.

He is at once a man of solitude and solidarity, adaptable and
stubborn, tender and severe, occasionally brutal, self-assured,
and uneasy; he likes to drink a lot and reads continually. He is
not perfect, not virtuous. He is not made of one lone piece. He
is a real man, in fact!

He is a man who does not run with the pack, who doesn't
conform absolutely to the criteria allowing his fellow men to
give a peremptory definition of what a woman is; a man who
behaves "differently" and who is able to examine his own
words, actions, anger. A man who tries to respect a woman, in
strict contrast to the habits of those around him; he challenges
the evasiveness of other men.

But he is, in particular, a "noble man who knows his origins—
that imperceptible first movement—and who acts immediately"
(Confucius). He sees beyond appearances and it is not La Niña's
beauty that strikes him first. It is her eyes, closed in a look of exhaustion and disorientation; it is her fragile, arched feet, the very
roots of a human being: he measures their "hidden strength and
great tenderness." He perceives the vitality buried beneath her
fatigue. He accepts sharing that load.

Without knowing it, he immediately recognizes the Caribbean
and La Niña. He quietly assumes his role as the ferryman between life and death, between death and life: he accepts the challenge of fecundation. He is going to "orient" her.

*"Letter to Jacques Soleil"*

We are at the end of the 1940s, under the regime of President Dumarsais Estimé (1946–1950)—the period when the ideology of color emerged, when the question of color was being tossed around: blacks against mulattos.

On the dark side, it is the tragic Holy Week, "the most terrible week in the mythology of modern time" (189), at the gates of Port-au-Prince: Christ's Passion, which begins on Palm Sunday, the palm and olive branches, to finish on Holy Saturday, the eve of the Resurrection. Six "mansions," a "coda"; seven chapters, seven days.

On the side of light, it is the peasant carnival: the Rara groups carry carnivalesque, subversive chaos throughout the suburbs and the countryside. Countering the Christian Lenten celebration, they prolong the carnal festivities.

> During this same Holy Week, the author invites us to witness a True Passion: the True one. A feast of the senses. Including a True Resurrection. Yes, the one that happens through the real miracle of palpable, universal love—true, liberating love—which finds its human expression in the natural gesture of carnal delight, the body of man and woman. The High Mass of eroticism.
>
> And it's a whorehouse in Carrefour where that Passion is played out! In Hell.
>
> It is the Passion of La Niña Estrellita, her Calvary, the Resurrection of Eglantina. (Rey-Charlier)

This is one of the rare times that a woman is found as the central character in the novel, a woman in the process of becoming and who is crucified, like our Caribbean, because she has killed her senses. Her memory will be brought into the world by the true man who brings them back to life. Delight reborn.

The encounter takes place gradually, and you narrate it to us in crescendo, musically. Against the background of an old Afro-Cuban melody, a black bolero that is sparkling and scarlet from the good old times—music being rediscovered today, when a man and a woman reveal themselves slowly, and the shock is so strong that the feelings are taken apart, one by one, in voluptuous, cinematographic slow motion, pure sensations. They take their time, and we are forced to perceive "from inside," a technique that has since been much used. The form of the narrative is thus transformed since we easily, imperceptibly enter into that sensual universe where there are no more implacable facts or linear events, into that subtle, fleeting and delicate feast of the minute trembling of human beings.

By slipping from one sense to another, from one chapter to the next, La Niña/the Caribbean/Haiti awakens little by little from her nightmare, and each day and night of her Calvary is a long, painful march that is at once blinding, intoxicated, palpitating in its progress toward the liberation of her senses and of her life. At each station of this Way of the Cross, she is upheld and supported by the man. At long last!

But in the quest that you sketch for us, she is leaning on the past, carried along by it. Initially, young rebel that you were, you thought you were the first to carry out the revolution. But when you publish this book, you are thirty-seven years old, and you know full well that to continue existing, exerting the will to keep existing—"one has to tie the old rope to the new one." That is why La Niña's memory and its agent, El Caucho, are salvation.

Eglantina is going to be reborn, and through the death of La Rubia, her sister in servitude and former queen of the whorehouse, it is La Niña who dies. The little prostitute catches fire, burns up, and goes out in a red glare. When the past appears, she is a new being—companionship and infinite tenderness are going to propel her into orbit. Now that the Caribbean has a memory, let her recognize who she is, that she can change and exchange, and that everything is possible.

You ask: "What is the power of memory? What is the power of love?" (20). Let's remember it is immense and revolutionary. Since that very memory and that very love allow me to speak to you today beyond the laughter and tears of a child, beyond your blood and my adult tears.

But a woman knows that there must be maturing after fecundation—it's her role not to forget that. In _The Absinth Star_ (the unpublished sequel to _In the Flicker of an Eyelid_) she sets sail.

---

*"Letter to Jacques Soleil"*

She is going to reconstruct herself with boldness before she joins the man in building. For me, she does not flee: she takes hold of herself, a firm grip on herself, and prepares herself for action in order to join that action. Here is what you said a few months before your death:

> I am preparing a tetralogy devoted to the adventure of a couple's life—*In the Flicker of an Eyelid* will be the first volume. Afterward, there will be the flight from responsibility, the refusal, and then the acceptance.
>
> They will look each other "in the whites of their eyes" (announced in 1959 as a title in preparation) for several years. The couple has begun to exist. There is the wear of daily life—one watches the other living, one watches the other without saying so. Usually they are not satisfied—for you can't be satisfied when you contemplate, but only when you act.
>
> The inner process has to be the same one in the eyes of the world and one has to be of the same "breed" in action.
>
> Then there is the rupture, which will not be definitive— that is the subject of the fourth volume: the description of everything lacking in the earlier stage.
>
> But the heroes, who are Cuban, will meet again in Cuba and their love will become a little more possible.
>
> Because Cuba is the Caribbean adventure. Trial by fire for all men and women of the Caribbean.
>
> There is the endurance of humankind in this country or that setting, but if the structure changes, opportunities for individual change are created for humankind. (J. S. Alexis, "Le couple aux Caraïbes")

1959: the publication of *L'espace d'un cillement;* the triumph of the Cuban Revolution, which evoked the enthusiasm of an entire region and an entire generation that was thrown into activism far from their own country—where Che Guevara becomes the archetype of the guerilla fighter, at once a romantic and a martyr: that is the hope that sweeps away the last reticence and mobilizes young people everywhere.

## "Letter to Jacques Soleil"

Today, in light of the events of the last twenty years, our hope is more nuanced and somewhat faded because of the failures. But at that time—the socialist nature of the event had not yet been proclaimed, but it would be after the U.S. blockade—it is simply immensely comforting and offers a half-envisioned, promising path. This is the ideal frame for "another life."

In spite of the loss of my innocence and my political certainties, in spite of my skepticism in the face of destructive facts, I love the wholehearted manner with which you plunge into innovation.

People have always wanted to separate the man of action from the artist. But in this novel, precisely because it is no longer a strictly "activist" book, you strike me as coming together. That is crystal clear since the work carries on, surpasses, and fully tests theory. The theoretical and esthetic basis that you set out to affirm for yourself and your people was in gestation and was, therefore, perfectible—it would probably have evolved and become richer and more subtle by confronting implacable reality. Through the secret coursing of our blood, I know the precious material you were made of; you, my leopard of a father, I know that you had "hitched your plough to a star" and that your honesty and determination would have certainly led you to face Stalinism with wide-open eyes, the "good" with the "bad" imperialism in the full light of the evidence.

Your work is a diamond in the rough: in all senses of the term. It realizes a complete cycle, and I feel that you were free of dogma here, infinitely richer—you were taking off. Here, you no longer need to bend ideas in order to make them fit helter-skelter into some reductive system of thought. You have no more imperatives, and you are creating something organic that bears its own regenerative force—pistil and pollen—that decrypts the past and holds up the future with both hands. Memory is in one, Love in the other—you embrace the Caribbean as you cry and laugh.

You wrote this book that brings everything in me to culmination—you "engraved" it on the eve of your final voyage. This last novel, more than any other, is marked by the genius born of urgency and in the paroxysm of your own Passion. You wrote it in a few weeks, working like crazy, after having let it mature over several years. You undoubtedly thought that you would have no more time to write. You made hats in order to feed us, you laughed, you danced—like a good konpè jeneral dansè [dancing Comrade General]—you "played the clown," you leapt around, you fought like an incomparable pirate. In a world peopled by the irresponsible, you were a tireless and responsible man—like El Caucho—without ever sinking beneath the load: creation, reflection, conceptualization, vision, action. In unheard of solitude!

So, as the incorrigible daughter of a father-dreamer of realities, "your *gwo-mechan-kriyèl,*" your child has begun dreaming. And I imagine what you would have written afterward: *L'Églantine* or *La quadrature du coeur, Dans le blanc des yeux, L'étoile Absinthe.*

On your sixtieth birthday, I have just experienced a close and sumptuous encounter with you. Destiny is being fulfilled. This letter from the daughter-woman, neither a conqueror nor a victim, will make the "voyeurs" smile, it will make those who psychoanalyze life smirk, and it will make certain men in rusted machinery grit their teeth—it could be entitled: "How to return, from beyond the tomb, and be reborn in your own child." I say to you, *"onnè"!* [honor], and I hear you answer *"respè!"* [respect]. I say to you "Love," and you reply "Memory!"

Let's listen to the shrewdness of each one of your words, each one explosive since your voice was silenced abruptly.

*Florence Alexis*
*Paris, January 1983*

# Afterword

French and Haitian critics enthusiastically greeted the appearance of Alexis's first two novels: *Compère Général Soleil* (*General Sun, My Brother*) in 1955 and *Les arbres musiciens* (The Musician Trees) in 1957. For *L'espace d'un cillement*, published by Gallimard in November 1959, Georges Jean-Charles notes simply that "the critics greeted [it] with great coolness" (232). Among the most favorable comments on the third novel were critics who knew Alexis. Jean-Claude Charles (quoted by Florence Alexis in her introduction) said that the novel demonstrated "the search for a new creative perspective": "Beauty of form, beauty in itself runs through the tragic obscurity of the human and social condition" (Charles, x). Ghislain Gouraige said that "the milieu in which the novel takes place, the atmosphere of vice, perversity, and obscenity, is a challenge" (297). In a brief review, Henri Amer praised the poetic aspect of the novel: "[It's] impossible not to be caught up in the inexhaustible verbal richness of J.-S. Alexis. To enter his novel is to dive into a tempest of colors, sounds, and perfumes. A true poet offers us something like a wild synthesis of the miserable, ardent, multi-colored life in the Caribbean of his childhood." He goes ahead, however, to deplore the "tired plot" of the novel: "The prostitute with a big heart regenerated by her profound love is nothing new" (969).

Paul Laraque wrote in "Camarade Soleil" that the novel presents two fundamental themes: "on the one hand, that of the sexual relationship between man and woman on the individual as well as the social level; on the other, that of the necessary solidarity between peoples, particularly in Latin America, the

Caribbean, and underdeveloped countries faced with oligarchy and imperialism. Like an orgasm in love, revolution brings that full satisfaction of need and desire in the social domain."

In his prologue to the 1978 edition of the Spanish translation, José Alcántara Almánzar says that Alexis's principal thesis is that "love is capable of humanizing man and liberating people who are enslaved to themselves or to their milieu" (v). In the same edition, Pierre-Charles writes that Alexis had unlimited faith in man. "This faith illumined his life. By it, writer and revolutionary were combined. That faith runs through all his characters. And unrestricted optimism can be felt in the heart of this marvelous, fantastic, and critical realism" (xiv). Robert Manuel felt that "a man living in a society dominated by a macho ideology" needed "true sensitiveness to the emotional world of a woman and a certain comprehension of the spiritual life of a prostitute" to write such a novel (98).

In his 1957 essay "Où va le roman?" Alexis himself gives an extensive list of major literary influences. He mentions first Tolstoy and Dostoevsky, as predecessors of the Soviet writer Maxim Gorky. He goes on to list a series of the "great French realists": "Balzac, Stendhal, Flaubert, Zola, Maupassant, Roger Martin du Gard, etc." Next come the North Americans—Steinbeck, Hemingway, Caldwell, Albert Mast—followed by three Latin Americans—Jorge Amado, Ciro Alegría, and Miguel Ángel Asturias, and finally Jacques Roumain, Haitian novelist, politician, and ethnographer (99).

Apropos of *In the Flicker,* Georges Jean-Charles notes particularly three nineteenth-century French novelists who portrayed prostitutes and courtesans in their fiction: Alexandre Dumas fils (*La dame aux camélias*), Émile Zola (*Nana*), and Guy de Maupassant (*Bel-Ami*) (215). Several of Dostoevsky's women may well have exercised some fascination for Alexis, among them Sonya (*Crime and Punishment*) and Natasha (*The Idiot*).

While literary precedents for the sympathetic treatment of the prostitute were not lacking, Jean-Charles underscores Alexis's own familiarity with the working-class areas in and around

*Afterword*

Port-au-Prince: "Let's remember that from his adolescence to adulthood, La Frontière was always one of the Port-au-Prince suburbs that most attracted Alexis" (215).

## The Political Context of 1959

Although Alexis may have finished *In the Flicker* prior to Castro's assumption of power on 1 January 1959, he certainly had knowledge of worker unrest in Cuba and of growing opposition to Batista. Alexis's novel, foregrounding the organization of sugarcane workers in Cuba and foreseeing an eventual union of Caribbean states, appeared some ten months after Castro's assumption of power. On 24 May, President Duvalier suffered a heart attack and was incapacitated for four months (Ferguson 42). In October, Alexis and several friends organized the socialist PEP (Parti d'Entente Populaire/Party of Popular Accord), and Alexis published a "Manifeste Programme" ("Le marxisme"). Hector states that this manifesto is evidence for "situating Jacques S. Alexis, along with Jacques Roumain, among the most prominent leaders of the Haitian workers' movement" (109). On 30 August, a small Cuban invasion force, led by an Algerian national, landed at Les Irois in southwestern Haiti (Diedrich and Burt 144). Former president Stenio Vincent, openly caricatured under his own name in Alexis's first novel (*General Sun, My Brother*), died in Pétionville on 3 September. Alexis's son, Jean-Jacques (named after ancestor Jean-Jacques Dessalines), was born in Haiti. Late in the year, Alexis left Haiti to participate in the thirtieth Congress of Soviet Writers and continued from Moscow to China, where he was greeted (and photographed) with Chairman Mao.[1]

On the international scene, Charles de Gaulle had assumed the presidency of France in June 1958. The European Common Market was instituted on 1 January 1959, just as Castro came into power. Other major events included the continuation of the Algerian struggle for freedom from French rule and preparations for the independence of former French colonies in West

Africa (including Burkina Faso, Cameroon, Sénégal, and Togo—Guinea had already declared its independence in 1958).

## Labor Unrest in 1948

*In the Flicker of an Eyelid* takes place during Holy Week, 1948.[2] Alexis inscribes in the text a number of historical and cultural references that anchor the love story of La Niña and El Caucho in the time frame of 1948 with complementary references to the decade of the 1940s.

We can agree with several critics that Alexis foregrounds the geography of the Caribbean in his third novel. Laraque wrote that "the Caribbean is substituted for history, and eroticism for the marvelous" (cited by Jean-Charles 210). The statement by Michael Dash that the novel "is not as closely linked to particular political events" as Alexis's first two novels (191) may be literally true to the extent the love story dominates the novel. The statement is misleading, however, in that Alexis takes such care to inscribe the novel in the historical and cultural context of the 1940s and, more specifically, that of 1948.

## Cuba in 1948

There is a series of references to earlier Cuban and Caribbean history. El Caucho's father fought with José Martí in the second War of Independence, an attempt to prevent the United States from replacing Spain's colonial power in Cuba (38).[3] Reflecting on the reciprocal relations between Cuba and Haiti, El Caucho thinks that, at the time of José Martí and Maceo, "thousands of guys from his country came [here] to catch their breath and heal their wounds as they waited for new flare-ups in the great struggle for Cuban freedom" (72).

President Ramón Grau San Martín was in power in the spring of 1948 (Carlos Prío Socorrás took over in October). In addition to communist backing of Cuban workers' demands, Juan Bosch and other Dominican leaders residing in Cuba were organizing an expedition to "liberate" the Dominican Republic from the dictatorship of Rafael Leonidas Trujillo Molina. President Harry Truman had even dispatched his chief of staff, General Dwight Eisenhower, to see that the expedition was disbanded in the summer of 1947 (Thomas 755).

Alexis repeatedly stresses the "Caribbeanness" of his two protagonists. Alexis spoke of Eglantina (La Niña) and Rafaël Gutiérrez (El Caucho) meeting once more, in Cuba, in the fourth volume that was supposed to follow *In the Flicker*. After years of facing the difficulties of everyday life and their differences in character, "their love will be a little more possible." Replying to the question why that love would be more viable in Cuba, Alexis replied categorically that "Cuba is the Caribbean future" ("Le couple," Vilaine interview, 23). He foresaw "a prospect for all Latin America, in particular for the Caribbean—a revolution similar to that in Cuba."

The most important historical date of *In the Flicker* is 22 January 1948, the day on which Jesús Menéndez Larrondo (born 1921) was mortally wounded by army captain Joaquín Casillas Lumpuy at the railroad station of Manzanillo (southeastern province of Granma, Cuba). Menéndez had just been working for an agreement between workers and the management of a sugarcane-processing center. An agreement had been reached for workers to resume work on 23 January. Headed back to Bayamo, Menéndez and Captain Casillas, who had been following him, got off the train briefly at Manzanillo. When the officer attempted to arrest the labor organizer, Menéndez pulled away. Captain Casillas's shots mortally wounded Menéndez before he could reboard the train (García Galló 145–53).

In historical fact, Jesús Menéndez had risen quickly from work as a local labor organizer and leader to national and international prominence. He presided at the International Conference of Sugar Workers, held in Havana, 20–26 November 1947, in which workers from Hawaii, Puerto Rico, the United

States, Mexico, and Cuba participated. Following that meeting, Menéndez was named vice-president of the International Committee of Sugar Workers, based in Washington, D.C. (García Galló 69).

Jesús Menéndez's importance in the novel is that of having been not only a courageous defender promoting the organization of sugarcane workers but also a mentor for El Caucho. El Caucho began a program of reading and self-education under Jesús's encouragement. Like Jesús Menéndez, El Caucho is a "man of water and corn" (74, 193), a transparent reference to the 1949 novel *Hombres de maíz* (*Men of Corn*), in which Miguel Ángel Asturias showed the devastating effect of agricultural commercialization on the Guatemalan peasants, the "men of corn."[4] Without specifically mentioning it, Alexis was probably aware of the fact that Jesús Menéndez's career as a labor organizer was underway at least by the age of thirteen or fourteen, in 1934–1935. This would coincidentally be close to the very period when the adolescent Rafaël Gutiérrez (El Caucho) fell in love with Eglantina Covarrubias y Pérez (La Niña) in the eastern province of Oriente, since she has been working in Port-au-Prince for some fourteen years (235). El Caucho would likely have met Jesús and begun working with him in the late 1930s or early 1940s, before being forced to go into exile to avoid arrest. It is likely that Alexis's nickname for his hero is based on descriptions of Jesús Menéndez. One of the testimonies collected by García Galló describes Menéndez as having an "elastic walk": "Empezó a andar con su paso elástico" (he began walking with an elastic step) (152). Rafaël Gutiérrez's elastic walk is also the provocation for his nickname, El Caucho, the rubber man: "The toes land, and the heel barely touches the ground. El Caucho. They're right to call him 'El Caucho,' the Rubber Man. He likes to be called El Caucho" (19).

El Caucho makes the connection between the Cuban *auténticos* and the *authentiques* of Haiti (185). Grau had organized the revolution party of the *auténticos* in 1934 (Leonard 28). In 1947, as the Cold War and fear of communism began to loom in international politics, the "Auténticos" "had successfully established themselves as the dominant force among the sugar workers" (Thomas 752). In the March 1948, the main opposing parties in Cuba were the "Auténticos" and the "Ortodoxos" (757), prior to the general elections and Prío's takeover from President Grau.

## Haiti in 1948

Roger Dorsinville writes of Haiti that the events of 1946 led to the baptizing of the young opposition as "les Authentiques" (136). President Dumarsais Estimé had been in power since late 1946, after his predecessor, Élie Lescot, was thrown out of office in January 1946 following a student-led strike in which Alexis and other young Haitian intellectuals took part. The development of labor unrest had been pretty much held in check by Lescot during World War II and under Estimé since the end of 1946. As the Haitian economy continued to falter, Estimé hoped to bring Haiti back into international prominence through the organization of an International Exposition on the occasion of the bicentenary of the founding of Port-au-Prince (see Corvington, pp. 326–43). The novel alludes to expectations that the Exposition would create new work for the unemployed, but the rushed dedication of the Exposition took place only on 8 December 1949, with the official opening of the entire grounds deferred until 12 February 1950. Although the Exposition drew some international attention to Haiti, the government was left with a debt of nearly 34 million gourdes, considerably higher than the estimated budget of 19 million gourdes (332, 337, 342n).

Alexis is less critical of President Estimé than he had been of presidents Vincent and Lescot in the two previous novels: "Estimé is no fool—he's got blinders on, but you can't take away his patriotism" (184). Faced with the refusal of the United States to renegotiate the Haitian loans of 1922–23, "Estimé launched an internal loan program today to pay back what we owe to the 'mericans" (181). National sentiment was strong in favor of the internal loan to liberate Haiti from this burden, and the debt was resolved on 1 October 1947 (Corvington 104–5).

Labor unrest is an explicit and important part of the backdrop for *In the Flicker*. Following the strike by students and workers against the Lescot government in January 1946, there were numerous strikes by leather workers, dockers, railroad workers, and numerous others through 1946 and 1947 (see Hector, 186–87). Daniel Fignolé led a general strike on 30 October 1947. A strike of electrical workers, begun in 1947 in spite of the government's decree against strikes by state workers, was repressed by the government in January 1948 (72–73, 187). On 19 February, a resolution was presented to the Senate to consider "communist activities or demonstrations of a nature to subvert public order and tranquility" as "conspiracies against the Constitution and state security" (Corvington 106). In early March 1948, the work of the communist-oriented Haitian union, Fédération des Travailleurs Haïtiens (Federation of Haitian Workers) was undermined by the formation of a government-supported union, the Fédération Haïtienne du Travail (Haitian Federation of Labor) (Hector 80–81). These events are an important part of the social scene forming a backdrop to El Caucho's reflections on the defense of workers' rights and the repressive attitudes of industry and state.


## Cultural Background


*In the Flicker* depicts the prostitutes constantly singing or listening to Cuban music. Miguelito Valdés and Celia Cruz are among the famous singers associated with various genres of Cuban music in particular—the *son*, the *bolero*, the *tango*.[5] Then there is "Sentimental Journal" brought to the top of the hit parade by Doris Day and Les Brown in December 1944 (Tiegel). Lionel Hampton's "Hey, Ba-Ba-Re-Bop," a famous thirty-seven-second riff, was first played in Los Angeles in December 1945 (Hampton 203, 208). At one point, El Caucho thinks of *La Calavera*, a serial film he liked (*In the Flicker* 145).

---

*Afterword*

This is most likely an allusion to Luís Buñuel's comic adventure film *El gran calavera,* which came out in 1949 when Alexis was still a medical student in Paris (Buñuel). There is a distant thematic parallel between Buñuel's film and Alexis's novel in portraying a worker as a reflective protagonist who stands up for his rights.

Epigraphs play a significant role in announcing the major theme of each part, but Alexis apparently wanted them to be seen as closely connected with his "mansions," so he takes liberties with the texts by changing words, switching the order of the extracts (in the case of Roumain), and even substituting different titles. A citation from Walt Whitman's *Leaves of Grass* announces the theme of the entire novel: "You prostitutes, flaunting over the trottoirs or obscene in your rooms, / Who am I that I should call you more obscene than myself?" Alexis mentions the title "Autumn Rivulets" from *Leaves of Grass,* but the extract is the second stanza of the poem "You Felons on Trial in Courts." The first mansion is preceded by an extract from Apollinaire's "L'amour, le dédain et l'espérance" in his *Poèmes à Lou.* The epigraph for the second mansion is from "Children of Adam" in Whitman's *Leaves of Grass.* For the third mansion, Alexis uses an excerpt from Nicolás Guillén's "Élégie a Jesús Menéndez."[6] A beautiful excerpt from Juan Ramón Jiménez's "La Granada" (The Pomegranate, from *Platero y yo, Platero and I*) introduces the fourth mansion.[7] Preceding the fifth mansion, there is a series of isolated excerpts from Pablo Neruda's "La canción desesperada" (song of despair), rearranged into a non-strophic text.[8] Alexis places excerpts from Jacques Roumain's *Gouverneurs de la rosée (Masters of the Dew)* at the head of the sixth mansion, without specifying that the two quotes are taken from different chapters—the first is by Annaïse (chapter 9) and the second by Manuel (chapter 6). Finally, the epigraph of the coda comes from Sor Juana Inés de la Cruz. "En que describe racionalmente los efectos irracionales del amor" (In which [she] rationally describes the irrational effects of love) is the title of section 86 in her long poem, "De amor y de discreción" (*Redondillas* in *Obras completas*).

Each epigraph has clearly been chosen to highlight the explicit sensory thematic of a given mansion. Alexis felt free to re-arrange or cut the source texts to fit the dominant theme of the mansion.

## Religion: Vodou and Catholicism

The dual framework of Vodou and Christianity is in evidence throughout the novel. Alexis ironically places this major en-counter in the life of his two Cuban exiles during Holy Week. This automatically brings in the carnivalesque events of the Rara celebrations and the "Killing of the Jew," in which, by Thursday, the people erect a stuffed figure that will be attacked and destroyed. Elizabeth A. McAlister notes that the Jews are seen as the "Christ-killers": "According to this ritual logic, Judas, who betrayed Jesus, is conflated with 'the Jews' who 'mis-treated Jesus', making all Jews into 'Judases'" (211).

There is irony behind the fact that La Niña, the most popu-lar prostitute in the Sensation Bar, has a little altar dedicated to the Virgin of the Pillar. For a while, this seemed to be a casual reference to La Niña's naive faith. Later in the process of trans-lation, it was discovered that an important movement is asso-ciated with María of the Pillar, who appeared in the flesh in Zaragoza, Spain, at the beginning of the year 40 of the Chris-tian era. The Virgin's appearance in Spain was to be associated later with the discovery of the Americas by Columbus. In 1939, the annual commemorative services began in Zaragoza, and in 1982, Pope John Paul II declared the Virgin of the Pillar to be the "Reina de la Hispanidad," the Queen of Spanish peoples in the New World.[9] A small statue of the Virgin Mary is honored on a pillar in the basilica of Zaragoza.

The narrative constantly recalls the concurrent and sometimes conflictual Vodou and Catholic celebrations of Holy Week. As Good Friday approaches, the quiet and mournful contemplation of the Catholic faithful is increasingly disrupted by the raucous passing of the Rara bands, the firecrackers, and the "killing of the Jew." For Eglantina and Rafaël, the gradual process of recognition and awareness of their latent love after those four-teen years of separation begins and reaches a point of culmina-tion from Palm Sunday to Holy Saturday.

La Niña maintains her altar to the Virgin of the Pillar. She turns the image of the Virgin to the wall when she is in the grips of the marines astride her (166). The rediscovery and renewal of her childhood love for Rafaël Gutiérrez during Holy Week 1948 sends her back to the church seeking a clear answer from the Virgin to her question: "When you're a whore, is it because you were born to do that? Can you stop being one?" (188). In a reflective parallel to the anguished thought of La Niña, the narrator suggests that a "great part of humankind no longer be-lieves itself to be of Adam's lineage but rather finds it shares the quality of *homo faber*" (189).[10] This allusion to Bergson sug-gests a liberation from religious belief and individual assump-tion of responsibility for freely creating one's own life. The nar-rator goes on to consider the necessity of freeing oneself from clerical exhortations to accept suffering: "Is that supplication the only path to salvation? Is waiting in resignation for eternal happiness the only possible attitude? Beethoven has already stated that question dramatically in his grand *Missa Solemnis*, the *Mass in D*: *Dona nobis pacem*!" (189).[11]

This brings in an allusion (made by the narrator) to Ozanam: "Prayer becomes action" (189). For the moment, La Niña re-mains in tearful distress as she waits for a response from the silent Virgin. As she is entering into the new love relationship with Rafaël, however, Eglantina will choose the heroic path—she will overcome her doubts as to whether she can kill the little whore, La Niña, in order to become her true self. She will leave Rafaël behind as she goes in search of her own identity.

Although Vodou is present primarily in the ongoing Rara cel-ebrations of Holy Week, the presence of Ezili Freda is implicit in La Niña's cult of the Virgin of the Pillar. This Vodou spirit is the light-complected female embodying love. She is ferociously jealous of the human who becomes her mystical husband. At the same time she is all-compassionate for abused, exploited women: "It is frustrating to give oneself to men one does not know, that one detests, men who exasperate or disgust you. Ah, the life of a prostitute is terrible. You understand why I, Grann Ezili, bestow kindness and good fortune" (Déita 117).

Apropos of her painting *Game of Love* (in which the spectator looks through an open door at an altar in honor of Ezili), Marilene Phipps writes that love is a "risky affair." Phipps notes that the rooster standing at the door to Ezili's altar is the symbol of Ezili's husband Ogou (a warrior spirit). "The ruffled-up and somewhat plucked and bared rooster in the painting alludes to the risky affair mentioned above and to Ezili's consort" (personal communication, 3 May 2001).[12]

## Composition of the Novel

*In the Flicker* is divided into seven sections: six "mansions," designating the five senses plus the "sixth sense," followed by a brief coda. In what sense was Alexis using *mansion,* which was not current French usage in the twentieth century? In her preface to the 1983 reprint edition, Florence Alexis uses the term simply in her father's unusual sense of a chapter-like division of the novel: "Little by little, the mansions will throw light on this or that element of the landscapes of hell and heaven that are being built before our eyes" (243). I suspect that Alexis's usage relates to the expression in the King James version of the New Testament, "In my Father's house are many mansions" (John 14, 2). The Louis Second translation of the Bible uses *demeure* (one obsolete meaning of *mansion* in French). French *mansion* was also a relay station along the main highway from Rome (used by Roman officials as rest stops)—the Sensation Bar is in fact a stopping place for La Niña in her journey toward love. The astrological sense of the twelve *mansions* (now *maisons*) of the zodiac was almost certainly another nuance for Alexis: the prostitutes are always preoccupied by their future and various divinatory systems. Madame Púñez is insistent on telling El Caucho's fortune by means of a *pique de chien:* "you can see the future as if you were already there!" (109).[13] During the Thursday afternoon recreation at the Sensation Bar, Madame Pintel offers to do a card reading for La Niña, who responds that she is more interested in the lines of the hand or the feet (155).

The first four mansions are devoted to the slow process of attraction and recognition between La Niña and El Caucho. It is only in the middle of the fifth mansion ("Touch"), on Holy Thursday, that La Niña's "vraie Passion" (true Passion; 188) reaches a crisis level. Mario, the bartender, has given the whores the afternoon off. After wandering around town, El Caucho comes into the bar and quietly asks La Niña if she has time to listen to him. She impulsively leads him to dance. They kiss and disappear into her room. In bed, toward the end of the mansion, they begin to remember, and El Caucho identifies her as Eglantina (208). The sixth mansion ("The Sixth Sense") takes place on Good Friday into Saturday morning: the process in which each explores the other's body and character as they reexamine the past.

The bordello is reputedly a house of "pleasure." The pleasures noted in this novel are extremely limited: the pleasure of solitude and sleep after a night of work; the pleasure of bathing alone in the little pool behind the Sensation Bar; the pleasure of seeking palm readings on afternoons off in hopes of a brighter future. Sex with the clients brings no pleasure for the whores: La Niña's back is fixed on the bed "for hours, night and day, in the perpetual torture of false love and the ritual of coitus—no joy" (38). Her enticing, wild dancing may bring an enthusiastic response from the marines, but for her, it seems to function as a kind of paroxysm that numbs the nerves before she undertakes a night's work and, toward the end, an act calculated to attract El Caucho's attention. For La Niña and El Caucho, that dance promotes, rather, the process of recognition.

The sixth mansion and the coda present testimony that the newly awakened Eglantina can experience pleasure that she thought had been lost forever to La Niña. Anne Marty's summary assertion that "the place of action remains a fundamental space for pleasure" has to be taken with qualification. Recognition brings a renewal of earlier sensual attraction for the Cuban couple and the discovery that the whore has not killed forever her ability to reach orgasm. Marty is perhaps justified in seeing the reader colluding with the novelist in an act of "voyeurism," but the novel can hardly be characterized as simply an "erotic novel in which the Marxist discourse of a revolutionary ideal follows its own path" (88).

As La Niña passes from table to table, inciting the clients to drink, there is a narrative development on the whores as "piece workers," members of a proletariat: "A whore does her task with a proletarian conscience." It would be great to have a union in order to obtain a "minimum wage" (34).

If El Caucho seems to reflect the partially macho standpoint in spite of his ideals, Alexis also presents the theme of lesbianism with sympathy, in particular when La Rubia attempts to obtain tenderness and sympathy from La Niña in the second mansion (98–104).

Literary critics should be cautious about the symbolism in this novel. La Niña may be undergoing her own "Passion" during Easter week. In her preface to the novel, Florence Alexis also alludes to La Niña's "Calvary" and to her "Way of the Cross" (250). Her departure is a kind of "Resurrection" (249) but this should not lead us to conclude that she is simply a female "Christ." Alexis is too specific that Eglantina rejects the mysticism of the Church, although he may be touched by Beethoven's *Missa Solemnis* and even by the sincere anguish to be found in that music, as he is by La Niña's years of blind faith. Eglantina's disappearance in the coda, however, suggests an acceptance of life, the "game of love." She has left in an attempt to find herself and to make her own way in life. According to his own vision, Alexis would have shown Eglantina and Rafaël meeting again to continue waging the eternal struggle between Ezili and Ogou, the give-and-take of true human love.

# Notes

1. Fuller biographical details on Alexis and his family are given in the introduction to *General Sun, My Brother* (ix). Jean-Charles remains an important source of biographical information and an exploration of the Haitian political context. See also Gérard Pierre-Charles.

2. By the actual calendar, Holy Week 1948 extended from 21 March (Palm Sunday) to 28 March (Easter). In the novel, El Caucho receives the message with the news of Jesús Menéndez's death three months later (69), which would have been late April. It is not clear whether Alexis forgot the actual date of Easter in 1948, or whether he might simply have been indifferent to such detailed historical accuracy. He stresses in any case the lengthy time the note took to travel from Cuba to Haiti.

3. The first Cuban war of independence against Spain took place between 1868 and 1878. The second war began in 1895 and was interrupted by the U.S. invasion of Cuba in 1898.

4. According to Prieto, "Asturias conceived his 1949 novel as a palimpsest of myths set forth in the *Popol Vuh*" (92). "Maize is both divine (the god Hunahpu is maize incarnate) and fundamentally human" (93). In the novel, the peasant maize growers resist the government's attempts to impose commercial corn growing.

5. Miguelito Valdés (1912–1978) moved to the United States to sing with Xavier Cugat's band in 1940. His most famous song, "Babalu," was later taken as the theme song of Desi Arnaz. Celia Cruz (born 1924) studied at the Conservatory of Music in Havana, where she began her career on radio and television. She settled in New York City in 1960. Coincidentally, as this afterword was being finished, she appeared at the J. F. Kennedy Center on the program to honor Whoopie Goldberg with the Mark Twain Award for Humor, on 21 November 2001. There are useful Web sites on Celia Cruz and Miguelito Valdés: www.si.umich.edu/chico/salsa/ and www.slipcue.com/music/cuba/valdesm.html.

6. All translations of epigraphs in French and Spanish are ours, although we cite published translations under the author's name in the bibliography.

In the French text, Alexis says the Guillén extract comes from "Élégies antillaises," a title that might have been suggested by another group of poems entitled "West Indies, Ltd." (Guillén, *Obra poética*). The extract actually comes from the final (seventh) section of a long elegy, "Elegía a Jesús Menéndez," in the section "Elegías." In line 5 of the

Spanish text as given in *L'espace* (159), Alexis substitutes "olor de palabras" for the original, "agua de palabras." We have corrected this and one missing accent in the translation.

7. Alexis made two relatively small cuts in the original text. Following the first suspension points (after "la tierra"): "Ahora, el primer dulzor, aurora hecha breve rubí, de los granos que se vienen pegados a la piel" (Now, the first sweetness, dawn made into a small ruby, of those seeds that come stuck to the skin); and, after "reina joven": "¡Qué llena está, Platero! Ten, come. ¡Qué rica!" (How full it is, Platero! Here, eat. How delicious!).

8. We retain Neruda's text as adapted by Alexis. The relevant lines of the original text are as follows:

> *Emerge tu, recuerdo de la noche en que estoy.*
> . . .
> *Era la alegre hora del asalto y el beso.*
> *La hora del estupor que ardía como un faro.*
>
> *Ansiedad de piloto, furia de buzo ciego,*
> *turbia embriaguez de amor.* . . .
> . . .
> *Cementario de besos, aún hay fuego en tus tumbas,*
> *aún los racimos arden picoteados de pájaros.*
> . . .
> *Oh la cópula loca de esperanza y esfuerzo*
> *en que nos anudamos y nos desesperamos.*
>
> *Y la ternura, leve como el agua y la harina.*
> *Y la palabra apenas comenzada en los labios.*

9. The Associación "La Virgen del Pilar," based at the Basilica of Zaragoza, maintains an extensive web site from which we gleaned significant information: http://members.es.tripod.de/caballerosNSdelPilar/hispani.htm.

10. Because Alexis capitalizes the expression *Homo faber*, there is a possibility he is also alluding to the novel by Swiss writer, Max Frisch, *Homo faber*, published in German in 1957, just two years before *In the Flicker*.

11. Alexis wrote that "three artists who were not novelists have always exercised great attraction for me. In Shakespeare, Michelangelo, and Beethoven, I have gotten the taste for placing on stage masses of human beings, entire societies" ("Où va le roman?" 99).

---

*Afterword*

12. A detail from Marilene Phipps's painting *Game of Love* is used for the cover of the paperback cover of *In the Flicker*.

13. Information on the *chien de pique,* a Tarot spread, was located in www.geocities.com/twelveofhearts/chiendepique.html. This is a sixteen-card spread in which a "significator" is chosen to represent the questioner. The spread is a search for four cards: the significator (the questioner's circumstances), the seven of the significator's suit (questioner's thoughts), the jack of spades (questioner's fate), and the ace of hearts (questioner's love and home life). After reshuffling the deck, each of the cards sought and its partner are placed in four vertical rows. When the four cards are found, the deck is reshuffled and the spread continues until the maximum of sixteen cards is reached. The last eight cards fall in two outer vertical columns. Cards falling in the same row as one of the four key cards help to interpret the various realms of the questioner's life.

# A Note on the Translation

The original text of *L'espace d'un cillement* is essentially trilingual: the base narrative is French, but with a number of words and expressions in Haitian Kreyòl and in Spanish (see Jean-Charles 213–14).

For Haitians who read the original version, the intermingling of Kreyòl with the French poses little or no problem. The co-translators disagreed on only one major point: Edwidge argued for fidelity to Alexis's personal spelling of Kreyòl, but Carrol was insistent on using current standard Kreyòl orthography in order to underscore the distinction between the Kreyòl and the French languages.

Given the fact that Alexis frequently footnotes Spanish expressions, the language constitutes a minimal problem for francophone readers, as for many Haitians. In the English version, Spanish words and expressions used by Alexis are preserved. Where it did not seem too obtrusive, English translations of both Kreyòl and Spanish have been worked into the text, although a glossary is included at the end of the novel for handy reference. Translations of the texts of songs or poems in Kreyòl or Spanish are footnoted. Kreyòl has been retained in the Rara songs and in expressions where there is no common English equivalent. The Spanish of the Cubans reflects working-class and peasant-class discourse and, in particular, the milieu of the sex industry where they live and meet.

# Acknowledgments

There is always a debt to willing friends and colleagues who respond to urgent calls for help. A big thank-you goes to Melanie Hersh, who read the first draft of the translation and picked out a number of typos and infelicities even as Edwidge Danticat worked with it concurrently. Florence Alexis and Dora Polachek both read the translation of the former's introduction, giving useful commentary and corrections. Conversations with Paul Laraque brought a sense of the presence of "Jacques Soleil" (Alexis). Salvador Fajardo graciously took time to look over translations from the Spanish. Roger Savain is an ever-ready consultant on matters of Haitian Kreyòl.

On numerous and varied details, Nello Barbieri, Elizabeth McAlister, Rosemarie Morewedge, Bernard Mulligan, and Lili Van Vranken also offered needed assistance.

# Bibliography

## Writings by Jacques Stephen Alexis

### Fiction

*Compère Général Soleil.* Novel. Paris: Gallimard, 1955. (Reprint, 1982). Translations: *Mi compadre el general Sol.* La Havana: Casa de las Américas, 1974. *General Sun, My Brother.* Trans. Carrol F. Coates. Charlottesville: University Press of Virginia, 1999.

*Les arbres musiciens.* Novel. Paris: Gallimard, 1957.

*L'espace d'un cillement.* Novel. Paris: Gallimard, 1959. Translation: *En un abrir y cerrar de ojos.* Trans. Jorge Zalamea. México: Ediciones Era, 1969.

"L'Amourette." Novella. In *Le Nouvelliste* (Port-au-Prince), 23 Dec. 1959.

*Romancero aux étoiles.* Novellas. Paris: Gallimard, 1960. Translation: "The Enchanted Second Lieutenant." Trans. Sharon Masingale Bell. *Callaloo* 20, 3 (summer 1997): 504–15.

#### POSTHUMOUS

"L'inspecteur d'apparences." Story. In *Anthologie du fantastique*, ed. Roger Caillois, 2:287–311. Paris: Gallimard, 1966.

"Dieu premier." Excerpt from "L'Églantine," an unpublished novel. *Nouvelle Revue Française* 235 (July 1972), 49–67.

### Other Writing

"Of the Marvellous Realism of the Haitians" (including "Prolegomena to a Manifesto on the Marvellous Realism of the Haitians"). *Présence Africaine*, June–Nov. 1956, 8–10: 249–75 (English version). "Du réalisme merveilleux des Haïtiens." *Présence Africaine*, June–Nov. 1956, 8–10:245–71.

"Les littératures noires et la France." Conversation de Jacques Stephen Alexis, René Depestre, Ferdinand Oyono, Mongo Beti. *Optique* 34 (Dec. 1956): 31–42.

"Une lettre religieuse de Jacques Alexis à propos des *Arbres musiciens*" (a reply to R. P. Salgado, 1957). In *Une négritude socialiste: Religion et développement chez J. Roumain, J. S. Alexis, L. Hughes*, by Claude Souffrant. Paris: L'Harmattan, 1978.

"Où va le roman?" *Présence Africaine*, no. 13 (April–May 1957), 81–101.

"La main dans le S.A.C." *Le Nouvelliste*, 11 March 1958. Reply by René Depestre, "Le Nègre démasqué," *Le Nouvelliste*, 18 March 1958.

"Florilège du romanesque haïtien." 1959. Reprinted in *Étincelles*, supplément littéraire, May–June 1984, 8–9, 13–21.

"Le marxisme, seul guide possible de la Révolution haïtienne [Manifeste Programme du PEP]." 1959. Reprinted in *Présence de Jacques Stephen Alexis*, ed. Gérard Pierre-Charles. Port-au-Prince: CRESFED, n.d.

"La belle amour humaine." *Europe* (special issue on Haiti), 49 (Jan. 1971): 20–27.

## Interviews

"La Rose des yeux." Interview by Sophie Brueil. *Les Lettres Françaises*, no. 658 (14–20 Feb. 1957).

"Le couple aux Caraïbes." Interview by Anne-Marie de Vilaine. *Afrique Action* 11 (26 Dec. 1960): 23–24.

## Studies on J. S. Alexis, *L'espace d'un cillement*

Alcántara Almánzar, José. "Prólogo." In *En un abrir y cerrar de ojos*, i–viii. Santo Domingo: Taller, 1978.

Amer, Henri. "L'espace d'un cillement—Romancero aux étoiles." *Nouvelle Revue Française* 8 (1 May 1960): 969–70.

Dash, J. Michael. *Literature and Ideology in Haiti, 1915–1961*. Totowa, N.J.: Barnes & Noble, 1981.

Gouraige, Ghislain. *Histoire de la littérature haïtienne*. Port-au-Prince: Imprimerie N. A. Théodore, 1960.

Jean-Charles, Georges. *Jacques Stephen Alexis, combattant et romancier d'avant-garde,* ou *L'humanisme de Jacques Stephen Alexis.* West Palm Beach, Fla: LQ Editions, 1993.

Laraque, Paul. "Camarade Soleil." Unpublished talk given at the Jacques Stephen Alexis Festival, organized for the Department of Black Studies, City College of New York, 1982.

———, ed. *Rencontre,* no. 3 (1992). Special issue on Jacques Stephen Alexis.

Manuel, Robert. *La lutte des femmes dans les romans de J. S. Alexis.* Port-au-Prince: Deschamps, 1980.

Marty, Anne. *Haïti en littérature.* Paris: La Flèche du Temps, 2000.

Pierre-Charles, Gérard. "Sobre el autor." Afterword to *En un abrir. . . .* Mexico: Era; Santo Domingo: Taller, 1969.

———. "Biographie de Jacques Stephen Alexis" (with Haitian friends in Mexico). *Rencontre,* no. 3 (1992): 68–71.

Séonnet, Michel. *Jacques Stephen Alexis* ou *"Le voyage vers la lune de la belle amour humaine."* Toulouse, France: Archeopteryx, 1983.

## Related Literature and Studies

Asturias, Miguel Angel. *Hombres de maíz.* Madrid: Losada, 1949. Translation: *Men of Corn,* trans. Gerald Martin. Pittsburgh: University of Pittsburgh Press, 1993.

Buñuel, Luis (director). "The Great Madcap/El gran calavera." Notes for videocassette. Water Bearer Films, WBF 8035, 1993.

Charles, Jean-Claude. *De si jolies petites plages.* Paris: Stock, 1982.

Confucius. *Yiking: Le livre des transformations.* Paris: Librairie de Médicis, 1981.

Corvington, Georges. *Port-au-Prince au cours des ans.* Vol. 7: *La ville contemporaine, 1934–1950.* Port-au-Prince: Deschamps, 1991.

Dauphin, Claude. *Musique du Vaudou: Fonctions, structures et styles.* Sherbrooke, Qué.: Naaman, 1986.

Déita. *La légende des loa du Vodou haïtien.* Port-au-Prince: Bibliothèque Nationale d'Haïti, 1993.

Diedrich, Bernard, and Al Burt. *Papa Doc and the Tonton Macoutes.* Port-au-Prince: Henri Deschamps, 1996.

Dorsinville, Roger. *Marche arrière.* Vol. 1. Montréal: Collectif Paroles, 1986.

Ferguson, James. *Papa Doc, Baby Doc: Haiti and the Duvaliers.* Rev. ed. New York: Oxford, 1988.

García Galló, Gaspar Jorge. *Esbozo biográfico de Jesús Menéndez.* Havana: Editora Política, 1978.

Giraudoux, Jean. *Choix des élues.* Paris: Grasset, 1939.

Guillén, Nicolas. *Obra poética, 1920/1972.* Vol. 1. Guadelajara, Mexico: Universidad de Guadelajara, 1978.

Hampton, Lionel, with James Haskins. *Hamp: An Autobiography.* 2nd ed. Discography by Vincent H. Pelote. New York: Amistad, 1993 (1989).

Hector, Michel. *Syndicalisme et socialisme en Haïti, 1932–1970.* Port-au-Prince: Deschamps, 1987.

Jiménez, Juan Ramón. *Platero y yo.* Ed. Michael P. Predmore. 2nd ed. Madrid: Ediciones Cátedra, 1979. Translation: *Platero and I.* Trans. Antonio T. de Nicolás. San Jose, Calif., and Lincoln, Neb.: toExcel, imprint of iUniverse.com, 2000. (New York: Paragon House, 1985)

Juana Inés de la Cruz, Sor. *Obras completas.* Vol. 1. México: Fondo de Cultura Económica, 1951.

Leonard, Thomas M. *Castro and the Cuban Revolution.* Greenwood, Conn.: Greenwood Press, 1999.

McAlister, Elizabeth A. "'The Jew' in the Haitian Imagination: Pre-Modern Anti-Judaism in the Postmodern Caribbean." In *Black Zion: African American Religious Encounters with Judaism,* ed. Yvonne Chireau and Nathaniel Deutsch, 203–27. New York: Oxford University Press, 2000.

Neruda, Pablo. *Veinte poemas de amor* y *Una canción desesperada.* 6th ed. Buenos Aires: Biblioteca Contemporánea, 1958 (1924). Translation: *Twenty Love Poems* and *A Song of Despair.* Trans. W. S. Merwin. San Francisco: Chronicle Books, 1993.

Prieto, René. *Miguel Ángel Asturias's Archaeology of Return.* New York: Cambridge University Press, 1993.

Rey-Charlier, Jacques. *Rap-Track: Mondes interlopes.* Unpublished manuscript.

Roumain, Jacques. *Gouverneurs de la rosée.* Rev. ed. Coconut Creek, Fla.: Educa Vision, 1999. Translation: *Masters of the Dew.* Trans. Langston Hughes and Mercer Cook. Intro. J. Michael Dash. London: Heinemann, 1978.

Thomas, Hugh. *Cuba; or, The Pursuit of Freedom.* Rev. ed. New York: Da Capo Press, 1998.

Tiegel, Eliot. Program notes to "Les Brown and His Band of Renown." Hindsight Recordings, HCD 252, 1994.

Whitman, Walt. *Complete Poetry and Collected Prose.* New York: Library of America, 1982.

# CARAF Books

## Caribbean and African Literature
## Translated from French

A number of writers from very different cultures in Africa and the Caribbean continue to write in French although their daily communication may be in another language. While this use of French brings their creative vision to a more diverse international public, it inevitably enriches and often deforms the conventions of classical French, producing new regional idioms worthy of notice in their own right. The works of these francophone writers offer valuable insights into a highly varied group of complex and evolving cultures. The CARAF Books series was founded in an effort to make these works available to a public of English-speaking readers.

For students, scholars, and general readers, CARAF offers selected novels, short stories, plays, poetry, and essays that have attracted attention across national boundaries. In most cases the works are published in English for the first time. The specialists presenting the works have often interviewed the author in preparing background materials, and each title includes an original essay situating the work within its own literary and social context and offering a guide to thoughtful reading.

## CARAF Books

Guillaume Oyônô-Mbia and
Seydou Badian
*Faces of African Independence:
Three Plays*
Translated by Clive Wake

Olympe Bhêly-Quénum
*Snares without End*
Translated by Dorothy S. Blair

Bertène Juminer
*The Bastards*
Translated by Keith Q. Warner

Tchicaya U Tam'Si
*The Madman and the Medusa*
Translated by Sonja Haussmann
Smith and William Jay Smith

Alioum Fantouré
*Tropical Circle*
Translated by Dorothy S. Blair

Edouard Glissant
*Caribbean Discourse:
Selected Essays*
Translated by J. Michael Dash

Daniel Maximin
*Lone Sun*
Translated by Nidra Poller

Aimé Césaire
*Lyric and Dramatic Poetry,
1946—82*
Translated by Clayton Eshleman
and Annette Smith

René Depestre
*The Festival of the Greasy Pole*
Translated by Carrol F. Coates

Kateb Yacine
*Nedjma*
Translated by Richard Howard

Léopold Sédar Senghor
*The Collected Poetry*
Translated by Melvin Dixon

Maryse Condé
*I, Tituba, Black Witch of Salem*
Translated by Richard Philcox

Assia Djebar
*Women of Algiers in Their
Apartment*
Translated by Marjolijn de Jager

Dany Bébel-Gisler
*Leonora: The Buried Story of
Guadeloupe*
Translated by Andrea Leskes

Lilas Desquiron
*Reflections of Loko Miwa*
Translated by Robin Orr Bodkin

Jacques Stephen Alexis
*General Sun, My Brother*
Translated by Carrol F. Coates

Malika Mokeddem
*Of Dreams and Assassins*
Translated by K. Melissa Marcus

Werewere Liking
*It Shall Be of Jasper and Coral*
and *Love-across-a-Hundred-
Lives*
Translated by Marjolijn de Jager

Ahmadou Kourouma
*Waiting for the Vote of the Wild
Animals*
Translated by Carrol F. Coates

Mongo Beti
*The Story of the Madman*
Translated by Elizabeth Darnel

Jacques Stephen Alexis
*In the Flicker of an Eyelid*
Translated by Carrol F. Coates
and Edwidge Danticat